D0860314

THIS COFFIN
HAS NO HANDLES

THIS COFFIN HAS NO HANDLES

A NOVEL BY

Thomas McGrath

NEW YORK

Published in the United States by
THUNDER'S MOUTH PRESS,
93–99 Greene Street, New York, N.Y. 10012
Cover design by Loretta Li
Grateful acknowledgment is made to the
New York State Council on the Arts and
the National Endowment for the Arts
for financial assistance with
the publication of this work.
Library of Congress Cataloging-in-Publication Data
McGrath, Thomas, 1916–
This coffin has no handles :
a novel / by Thomas McGrath.—1st ed.
p. cm. — (Contemporary fiction series)
ISBN 0-938410-63-6 : $17.95.
ISBN 0-9348410-62-8 (pbk.) : $8.95
I. Title. II. Series.
PS3525.A24234T45 1988
813'.54—dc19 88-9752 CIP
FIRST EDITION
Manufactured in the United States of America
Distributed by Consortium Book Sales
213 E 4th Street
St. Paul, Minnesota 55101
612-221-9035

For the social revolutionaries, women, men, and children of all countries, from the great Mac Blair to my own son Tomasito

FOREWORD

In the opening chapter of this novel, Thomas McGrath pens one of the finest descriptions ever written of the huge metropolis, New York City, awakening to life in the morning. It is an astonishing work of prose, a barrage of images such that only a poet could write. But McGrath's intent is not to glorify the titanic enterprise New York City represents, but to convey to his readers what a staggering waste it is to channel the workaday energies of eight million people toward a goal as dismal as that of maximizing profits. *This Coffin Has No Handles* contains several other prose poems as finely wrought as this. Each describes an aspect of the cacophonous hubbub which New York City represented, in essence, to Tom McGrath, a Midwesterner at heart. Taken together, they added up to a soulless city, an assault on humanity, and left McGrath with little hope that things could change.

This, then, was the political reality McGrath began to confront when he first came to New York to lend a hand in the waterfront struggles. He found a community buffeted between gangsters, corrupt union officials, sellout priests, and cops-on-the-take. Like the West Side waterfront, it is a community that no longer exists. The working-class Irish, Italians, Yugoslavs, and Poles who used to live in the neighborhood when the docks were still working moved away.

Today, brownstones and brick tenements that used to house longshoremen's families and merchant seamen in furnished rooms have been gutted, renovated, and turned into condominiums. The waterfront neighborhoods have become fashionable, a "landmark district."

Like a time capsule, however, this novel, written in 1948, takes the reader back to a time, just after World War II, when the West Side docks were some of the busiest piers in the world. In numbers of passengers, tons of cargo, value of exports, and turnaround time of ships coming in and out of port, the West Side docks rivaled the biggest ports in Europe. There was a dark side, however. In numbers of accidents, longshoremen broken of health and spirit, pilferage, loan-sharking, dockside corruption, murder and mayhem, the West Side docks were in a class of their own.

Longshoremen were dying in industrial accidents and coughing up their lungs from job-related disease, as well as being gunned down by the gangsters. What is more, West Side longshoremen were still "shaping up" for work every morning—whereas on the West Coast, Harry Bridges' longshoremen's union had established a union hiring hall in 1935.

By all accounts the shape-up along West Street was one of the most disturbing sights in New York. A dock boss selected longshoremen at the pierhead each morning, pitting young men against middle-aged men, against each other, for a shot at a day's work. Those who were not chosen hung around the gin mills all day, waiting for the next shape-up in the early afternoon, or the evening shape-up if they still had not succeeded in getting a day's work. It was a profoundly demoralizing and demeaning spectacle and the practice was rife with kickbacks and favoritism.

Worse still, the natural ally against such abuses, the longshoremen's union, was thoroughly corrupt. Union leadership had sweetheart contracts with the shipowners' and stevedoring contractors—and a working relationship with the gangsters. Joseph Ryan, who had been president of the International Longshoremen's Association for over twenty years was a member of the New York State Parole Board. He regularly paroled ex-cons into his own custody, finding them jobs on the waterfront, and in his own union, as muscle.

A veteran of those struggles, Lou Amster, recalls union meetings of the ILA locals as singularly unnerving: "Half a dozen union officials sat at a table in the front of the hall. In the back of the hall were scattered, at the most, nine or ten working longshoremen, all trying to sit with their chairs close enough to the back wall so that no one could get behind them." Big, strapping ex-cons, who were on the union payroll for the night, walked up and down the aisles. If anyone spoke out against Joe Ryan's leadership of the union, these fellows wanted to know why.

What's more, waterfront gangsters held the West Side in a state of terror. If that sounds like an exaggeration, consider the career of Johnny "Cock-Eye" Dunn. McGrath made him a central character in this novel. Cock-Eye Dunn is reliably said to have murdered more than twenty men before he finally was sent to the electric chair in

1949. An accomplice who surpassed Dunn's death toll has escaped jail to this day and is living in retirement in Florida.

Some of the scariest passages in the book, ironically, are interior meditations in which McGrath, as novelist, gives readers a glimpse inside Cock-Eye Dunn's mind. He gives Johnny Dunn a past, an invented childhood, and imagines Dunn looking around him and seeing every kid on the West Side: shaping up as a longshoreman, meeting a girl, getting in debt to the loan shark, drinking too much, and dying young. Dunn opts instead to get into the rackets.

McGrath wrote a poem in 1949 about the road Johnny Dunn didn't take, the fate of his contemporaries: ". . . with eight kids and a mortgage, a wife and a rupture, and the years running out of his muscles like blood."* The tension in the novel, and that which makes it so unusual—and disturbing—is that novelist McGrath, as a radical, refuses to make simplistic moral judgments: "Johnny Dunn was wrong to become a gangster—he should have killed himself like everyone else doing an honest day's work for the thieves running the docks."

McGrath holds everyone on the waterfront accountable for the moral abyss to which the West Side had sunk: not just the gangsters and the stevedoring contractors abetting them, but working stiffs—"just doing their job"—and acquiescing in so doing to the shape-up and all the petty larcenies of their racketeer bosses. He even includes himself in moral responsibility for the enormities on the waterfront. He creates an interesting character in the book's narrator, an alter ego for himself, observing the horrors taking place on the front—but too cerebral and withdrawn and too unskilled at organizing to successfully catalyze a rank-and-file rebellion.

McGrath, the radical, carries his critique a step further and projects the West Side docks as a microcosm for all that is wrong with an economic system that would sell one man's labor for another's profit. He implicitly asks the reader, "What are Cock-Eye Dunn's crimes, compared with the crimes of the shipowners and industrialists who rob every working man and woman of eight hours a day of their lives?" Like Macheath in *The Threepenny Opera*, he asks, "What is murdering a man, compared with *hiring* a man?"

To stand up to this murderous machine on the waterfront was an act of heroism. Tom McGrath in this novel pays homage to the marvelous few who did: Harold Gates, Ray Condon, Johnny Miller,

---

*"He's a Real Gone Guy: A Short Elegy for Percival Angelman," from *Longshot O'Leary's Garland of Practical Poesy* (New York: International Press, 1949).

Sam Madell, Arthur "Mac" and Maggie Blair. They were grouped around New York's Waterfront Section of the Communist party. Nobody else at the time was willing to buck the gangsters, phony labor leaders, and other powers who ruled the West Side waterfront. In composite they (and their gangster antagonists) make up the characters in *This Coffin Has No Handles*.

Two of McGrath's closest colleagues in the Waterfront Section, Harold Gates and Ray Condon, seemed to show him, by their integrity and commitment, a way out of this moral quagmire. Gates and Condon were born and raised on the West Side of Manhattan, but rejected the fate of most of their contemporaries: wage slavery or a life in the rackets. They chose instead to become rebels. For McGrath, writing this novel at a time of profound personal disillusionment, Harold Gates and Ray Condon—and the handful of rank-and-filers who joined them in bucking the racketeers on the West Side—augured all the little hope he still held out for New York City, or humanity. They augured the possibility of a moral cleansing of society through revolution.

The narrator in *This Coffin Has No Handles* is an extremely pessimistic man, still reeling from the brutalities he has witnessed abroad in the Second World War. He seems to find hope in the handful of very human, very flawed individuals who make up the Waterfront Section of the Communist party. In real life, McGrath thought he had found, in Condon and Gates, two organizers who could carry the West Side away from the gangsters.

McGrath met them the first day he moved onto West Fourteenth Street, after a year teaching English at Colby College in Waterville, Maine. He even remembers the date, June 22, 1941, engraved in his memory because he opened up a newspaper and the headlines blared: HITLER INVADES RUSSIA. He and his wife Marian were barely settled in when a loud knocking at the door announced the arrival of skinny, high-strung Ray Condon, and his physical opposite, powerfully muscled, cool-thinking Harold Gates. They immediately wanted to know if he had any beer in the icebox, then sat down for a day-long recitation of the West Side's horrors that sent McGrath's head spinning.

Ray Condon had perfect West Side credentials: his father had been a police detective, his uncle a racketeer. His aunt Tillie worked at "the Biscuit" (the giant Nabisco biscuit factory on Fifteenth Street) and his brother was a longshoreman. Ray lived his whole life on Twenty-fourth Street. He was president of his class at St. Columba Parish School and captain of the settlement house football team. He crossed the Rubicon, however, in joining the Communist party. And he broke his heart trying his entire life to radicalize the working-class Irish on the West Side of Manhattan.

Ray Condon's lifelong friend, Harold Gates, was a little more successful than Ray. For a time in the 1930s, Gates was able to sway his waterfront teamster local away from the local racketeers and get a rank-and-file reform slate elected. A tremendous organizer, Gates was also tremendously articulate.

Tom McGrath used to listen to Gates talk for days on end. Gates had charisma, bona fide West Side working credentials (he had been working as a teamster from the time he was a young teenager, in the days when that still meant driving horses), and he had the intellectual verve to draw connections—from the waterfront right to "the Powerhouse," the chancery of St. Patrick's Cathedral.* Gates even had the distinction of having been taken for a ride by Cock-Eye Dunn, and living to tell the tale.

Imagine McGrath's horror then, and sense of imminent catastrophe for all plans to raise the West Side in rebellion, when amid threats on his life, in the middle of the 1945 wildcat longshoremen's strike, Harold Gates disappeared—into hiding as it turned out. The genesis of this novel was the harrowing two-week search McGrath made at that time, looking for Harold. As he combed the West Side, expecting to find Harold's body at the end of every alley and courtyard he searched, McGrath was both frenzied and emotionally sensitized to the living hell life had become for everyone connected to the waterfront. The agonizing search opened his eyes at the time to aspects of life on the West Side he had missed before: to the hell women were living every day in their tenements—babies howling, wet laundry hanging from every room, their railroad flats fetid and stifling. A dozen other painful vignettes that McGrath saw, as if for the first time, during that frantic search expedition, are etched into the pages of this book.

The strike which opens this novel, was the culmination of successive, smaller work stoppages. Joe Ryan sold out his rank and file at

*Cock-Eye Dunn and Joe Ryan were respected parishioners of a Roman Catholic Church on West Twenty-first Street, The Little Church of the Guardian Angel. The church had been designated "port chapel" for the seamen and longshoremen of New York. It proved to be a bulwark, however, against all efforts to clean up the waterfront—by radicals trying to build a rank-and-file movement in the 1930s and 1940s, and even by Xavier Labor Institute's waterfront priest, Father Corridan, in the 1950s. Veteran seaman, Robert McElroy, one of the founders of the National Maritime Union, considered Guardian Angel Church in the 1940s and 1950s to be something akin to "branch headquarters of Murder Incorporated."

every contract negotiation, so it was never hard to find cause for a wildcat strike. Each previous wildcat had required careful nurturing. The fear and isolation on the front were too great for spontaneous rebellions to take hold. Each wildcat rebellion required finding, and drawing out, individuals of character and courage. It took years to get such individuals to stick their necks out, and the wildcats usually lasted only a few days.

One of the real-life organizers, Sam Madell, whom McGrath puts into his novel, (like all his other protagonists here, pseudonymously,) devoted twenty-five years of his life to organizing a rank-and-file movement on the West Side waterfront. Another organizer, "Mac" Blair, a lifelong inspiration to McGrath, and the prototype for the section organizer in this novel, sacrificed his health to the battle on the front. Madell, Mac, and company, wrote leaflets, organized caucuses, and generally fanned the flames of discontent.

Seemingly, during every one of those twenty-five years, the entire rotten edifice of waterfront corruption was on the verge of crumbling. The West Side workers were perpetually just a hair away from overthrowing the do-nothing union leadership and rising up in open rebellion. East Coast seamen, in fact,had succeeded in 1936 in dumping their corrupt leaders and founding a new union, a model, militant organization of seamen, the National Maritime Union.

Each time, however, West Side longshore insurgents formed the nucleus of a rank-and-file organization, their efforts were thrown aside at the last moment. The combination of shipowners' bribes and union threats, police complicity and denunciations from the local parish priests strangled their efforts to build a fighting, democratic longshoremen's union.

So this is, in the end, a homage to a band of idealists who had nothing to show for their efforts day and night for twenty-five years, but the personal vindication that what they were doing was right. Quoting McGrath:

> It was a marvelous group of people and alas, it did not survive the pork chop policies and the red-baiting and the splitting that occurred after the Second World War. These people were special, it seemed to me, perhaps a breed that doesn't exist any more. They were both revolutionaries and intellectuals.

What marvelous vindication it is then (at least in the abstract sense of vindicating truth and justice) that the members of the Waterfront Section should be remembered in a book as fine as this, written by one of America's very best poets. McGrath's masterpiece, the epic *Letter to an Imaginary Friend*—thirty years in the making—will surely be remembered as one of the great books of poetry of the twentieth century.* With this novel, *This Coffin Has No Handles*, McGrath gives his waterfront comrades a shot at immortality.

JOE DOYLE
New York City
June 1988

---

*Readers of *Letter to an Imaginary Friend* should pause to consider the *Letter*'s curious opening line: "From here it is necessary to ship all bodies East."—after they read this novel.

THIS COFFIN
HAS NO HANDLES

PART I
Saturday

You are aware of the weather first of all, and the limits of the known world, the sign of the Army and Navy Store on the Avenue, or from the fifteenth story the line of mist out toward Staten Island. The light is clean and new, not yet soiled by the commerce of the day. Over the Bronx there is a small lost cloud, unable to go anywhere in the dead still air. In Jackson Heights, the last apple falls from the tree. On a street in Hoboken a tenement wall collapses and the dust is puffed up into the clean light. Up and down. The world is arranging its weights and measures.

A million workers charge down the dusty chutes of the cold-water apartment houses, are siphoned off and sucked away into the subways. The bottom has fallen out of the barometer of sleep. Adjustments are made: in the fur district the pressure of industry is rising; and through the fog of brick and stone, the steel bones of the skyscrapers downtown, you see the thin red line of humanity and profit rise in exact ratio to the falling line on sleep's soiled glass. Up and down.

When you go into the street, history begins. The headlines tie your hands and put you against the wall; or they arm you with little bottles of blue vitriol and tell you when to throw. Civil war in China. Starvation in Puerto Rico. Third day of the longshore strike. You are beyond the limits of the visible world now. You begin to move in other dimensions, but it is not too late to turn back, for you, the neutral man, the housewife on the Grand Concourse where the Bronx dreams on its seventeen hills, the man on the fifteenth floor looking at the line of haze toward Staten Island, or the caretaker of the C.Y.O. The strike, the civil war, do not involve the neutral man; they do not affect the weather or the qualities of the light which the headlines collect and flash black as the leaves on the tree in the little playground just down Seventeenth Street from Eighth Avenue flash green. You are aware, back safely within the visible world of objects, that it is a green day, although it is October, and the leaves are falling and are not really green at all. Nevertheless Central park is the green of an island in a calm morning sea. The underside of the leaves is paler, the green of barn paint mixed with milk. If you are sleeping on one of the park benches, this green is the color of the world when you wake. If you are a bartender, the green of the neon is that of a water gauge filled with fish blood. At Red Hook, a harbor policeman, you snatch a three-day-old corpse out of the water, and around his fingernails you see the dirty green of moss in an unused chimney.

But you see that the green is changing, and in the street the world of solid objects is taking on motion as the morning progresses. Nothing is constant. At fifteen stories up the quantity of cosmic rays per square inch per second striking your body differs from the rate at which they are bombarding the corpse at sea level. The streets are changing, taking on a new character, as people rush onto the metal runways and the subways race away to remote frontiers around Bath Beach and Pelham Bay. The city of sleep disintegrates, the crystal atom is smashed, and the components are tearing away at different velocities, outward and away. The tunnels clog with cars, a ship mourns, laboring toward Cape Hatteras, and three boys, none of them more than twelve years old, catch an empty on the New York Central on the first leg of their westward trip to Pueblo just as the third flight for Shannon Airport and Europe glints like a sliver of ice in the sun over Long Island.

Everything is dissolving, breaking up, racing away, trying to be free. You recognize the same desire in the people on the street. They have the light of hallucination in their eyes, and like maniacs driven by their own obscure compulsions they move in straight lines, bumping into each other, knocking each other down without ever looking at what they have hit. Like the light which touched the top of the Empire State Building early this morning, and which is now charging out toward the limits of space at a constant speed, they are propelled along invisible rails by a planless mechanics.

You do not have to think of them as human, because you are the neutral man. Even though they have this desire to be free, it is only an aspect of disintegration, movement away from the center, like the desire for liberty in the heart of a stick of dynamite. You see them pass on the street: blind, hurried, driven. In the Bronx you see the fanatical hitchhikers staring up the burning highway through the map of Maine. Off Red Hook the tides deposit the corpse on your grappling hook as surely as the sides of beef are hooked on the overhead trolleys along Fourteenth Street. And down toward the docks you see a small man with black hair and a bundle of leaflets under his arm, flung outward from the mass like a new moon not yet cooled or hardened, moving in a moving nimbus which is his unconsidered desire to be free.

7 A.M.

He came out of the subway entrance on Seventeenth Street, following two others. The roar of the departing train rose through the pavement and the lids on the garbage cans trembled cautiously for a moment until the sound died away in the depths of Fourteenth Street and the Village. Of the two who had come up from the subway with him, one was a cleaning woman who had just finished her job at the Empire State Building. She went directly across the street and up Eighth Avenue.

He stopped with the other man for a moment on the corner, feeling the faint warmth of the morning sun. Along Eighth Avenue and down Seventeenth Street, on the west and north sides, the slanting light gleamed on the stone, flashed from glass, from the heavy bars of ice on the sidewalk near a basement stairs. Ashes in uncovered cans caught it and softened it, taking the texture of cloth.

The other man, a seaman, put a hand under the denim jacket he wore instead of a shirt and scratched himself absentmindedly under his left armpit. Squinting in the light, he spat, pulled the fag end of a cigarette from his pocket, lit it and started unsteadily along the shadowed south side of Seventeenth Street, toward the headquarters of the seamen's union, his feet slapping the pavement in little irregular caressing pats: barefoot.

He watched the seaman idly for a moment, not seeing him, and then crossed to the sunny side of the street and started toward Ninth Avenue. A single heavy truck, coming up the street, caught the light and flashed it back at him, spotlighting him for a moment: black hair and dark Indian eyes in contrast to the long-jawed New England face with the frame of bone obvious under the skin. He had the faculty of small men of giving off a subdued crackle of nervous energy as if in his progress of the street he were becoming electrically charged. He was wearing a light field jacket with dark patches on the sleeves where the corporal stripes had been. Under his arm he had a bundle of leaflets.

He went past the cleaning and dyeing place at the corner, and past the newsstand, heavy now with the morning papers, their headlines black and screaming. On the other side of the street, the little black-mustached Armenian was washing the window of his cubbyhole store, his swarthy pockmarked wife was pelting him with cold scraps of language, and an iceman was just coming out of the store with his first three bottles of beer of the day. The iceman took the bottles across the street and put them carefully on one of the bars of ice and sat on the steps of 323. He had on a red undershirt, already stained with sweat. It was October but already, early in the morning, it was beginning to be hot. The iceman looked at the one with the leaflets with neither recognition nor curiosity, embalmed in a dream of Brooklyn which contained neither the sick wife there nor the fifteen-year-old son who refused to learn Italian. On the sidewalk in front of him the great bars of ice, wrapped in gunnysack, were sweating quietly through the cloth onto the pavement. It would be necessary to move them into the shade of the basement below, but for the moment the iceman looked at them dispassionately, almost without remorse, while they melted through the gunnysack, almost as slowly as he sweated through his shirt. For the moment he let the two processes of decomposition go on together, the melting and the sweating, the profit and the loss.

In front of the Anchorage bar and grill there was the smell of fresh coffee, and the thirty-five-year old virgin from Hollis, West Virginia, was standing at the counter, drumming her nails on the composition top, waiting for the seamen to begin drifting down to the hiring hall, to begin drifting into the restaurant for coffee-and, hotcakes, bacon and eggs, and beer and whiskey. She did not see the leaflets, but she saw the man, gave him a mechanical look and then drifted off into her morning reverie before he was out of sight. She was thinking of the dress manufacturer who had put his hand on her leg in the movies at the Gramercy Park theater some months before. The name of the movie was *Love in Ambush*, but she had made it up about his being a dress manufacturer—it had seemed like a good business, safe, dull, rich. She had slapped his face, and automatically he had got up and left. It was the second time she had seen the film. She went back again, twice while it was still on at that theater, but the man had never come back. Now, whenever the picture was showing at one of the small places that ran old films, she went to it every night, but the bourgeois had never turned up again.

At 3:45, in a tenement near the vacant lot in which the two Puerto Ricans had been stabbed by the neighborhood lads from the Catholic Youth Organization, in a second floor railroad flat which she shared with three other whores, a little Mexican girl, who had almost forgotten her name because no one ever called her anything but Dolores, was thinking of the sunlight, white buildings, and red beans, but the caretaker at the C.Y.O. a little farther down the street was thinking of nothing but the puke on the floor, the spoor of the broody, heavy, night-blooming animals who had passed through on the shadowy midnight. Neither of them saw the man with the leaflets, but they heard his steps, crisp and clear as the October light on the deserted sidewalk. Until they disappeared in the dark cushion of the tar-covered street.

When he crossed the street, almost at the corner, he neared Paddy the Pig's and saw a relaxed jointless form, as flat as a painted fish on a plate, taking its ease on the sidewalk. A sanitation department truck thundered past, waking the sleeper, shaking him in his cage of wine, so that he saw first the legs of the man with the leaflets and then the leaflets themselves, but did not lift his eyes any higher.

"Educate, organize, agitate," the drunk said, something stirring in an unused room in his head. "Yeh? That the ticket? Yeh?" But whatever it was was quiet again, because just at that time he saw a young steward, the brass buttons shining on his personally improvised uniform, crossing athwart his own outstretched legs.

"What role in the historical fuckin' drama are *you* prepared to play?" the drunk asked sourly.

But there was no reply, neither from the steward nor from the man with the leaflets, and the man on the sidewalk closed his eyes again, against the light and the strange creatures in it, and tried to go back to sleep. He would have five minutes, he thought, before the cop on the beat came by and told him that the night was over and he would have to move.

But he would have a longer time, on this particular morning. When the man with the leaflets rounded the corner he did not see the cop, who was at that moment mounting the stairs of the third house from the corner, having discovered there a young woman whose husband was in the army and who still had a preference for uniforms. The cop would have been interested in the man with the leaflets, but, hung from the first story of his erotic dream, he turned his eyes away.

On Fourteenth Street too, as the dark man followed it west toward the river, no one noticed him. Here they were involved in the fantasy of meat. The great red and white carcasses hung from the trolley in front of the warehouses, or moved on into the interior in stately procession, the glazed ribs in their gutted bellies flashing in the sun.

Toward the waterfront it was warmer and he unbuttoned his jacket. The street in the still slanting sun seemed paved with metal. Dazed by the light, deserted almost, it was like a black plain peaceful and empty, the few figures on it moving like somnambulists, dateless and incurious as the first buffalo. To the man with the leaflets, the street looked like a place that was going to have blood on it.

7 P.M.

I didn't want to have any part of it.

They had just given me my discharge three days later than the rest of the bunch I was with, because of some missing records. It was seven o'clock in the evening, in October, and it was hot. It was crazy weather, but that didn't excuse what I was doing. Dressed in my ruptured duck and a little brief mortality, I was heading down toward the waterfront, down to where the strike was beginning to spread its life in the streets, taking on a motion and a character of its own like a living thing. I didn't want to have any part of it, but I was going down there, just as if I had a date with a blonde, and I couldn't convince myself that it was only because the West Side had been my old stamping ground, the place I had lived.

Nothing seemed to have changed much since I had left in '41. The streets still had the smell of heat in them, of blood, sweat, and tears. The radios were blasting from upstairs windows, gangbusters for the kids, crooners, people selling chewing gum, frankincense and myrrh. Everywhere there was the stink of stale gasoline fumes. People talked on the steps of houses and kids pissed into the street. There were signs saying WELCOME HOME EDDIE; or GLAD TO HAVE YOU BACK FRANK; signed THE OLD GANG. No one had put out any flags for me. I didn't have anybody in the neighborhood who would miss me — I was a free man. But just the same I was heading down toward the front, where there was no good reason for me to be. I didn't want to have any part of the strike, but if the Organization found out that I was roaming around loose, they would give me a reason to go down there. I didn't want a reason.

I had learned about the strike three days earlier when I saw the old country in a drunken light. That is, I was a little drunk, not the light. The light was fine, the fine light of early morning on the Hudson, as clean and new as if it were the first time it was shining. It was just the way you would want it.

The gulls came out to meet us, mechanized dung heaps letting their liquid droppings fall on the green water, on the white, stinking, arrogant lines of the ship, and letting them go, bombs away, on the troops. We didn't mind at all. Even the gulls seemed right that morning. We had been a long time away, and it would have had to be bad for us not to like it.

After the gulls there was the Statue of Liberty, over the chained bay waters, Liberty, etc., holding her broken arm aloft. She was looking away from the country, out over the Atlantic, and she had a kind of glazed look in her eyes as if she had been expecting someone else. It didn't matter. She had stood that way a long time without anything happening, and here we were happening, even if we were as drunk as a monk at an Irish wake.

After the Statue, the Battery; and after the Battery, the skyscraper park around Wall and Pine — the magnificent white erections with more possibility of survival, maybe, than anything on the continent except the sequoias. And after the skyscrapers, the docks.

They struck out along the river like a piano keyboard with the black ones missing, like a set of teeth with the best ones knocked out. Like docks. Even like that, before we got in, even out on the bosom of the river, there seemed to be something wrong. Later, I saw that the something was that all the booms were down and that nothing was moving. All the fires were out, but I didn't know that then.

"Mjesus," whined the guy from Macon in a Scarlett O'Hara drawl complicated by a harelip and a vocabulary of seventeen words, two of them unprintable in seven languages: "Mjesus, Mrist, mney don't have no muckin' band."

But they had something else.

The dock was as quiet as a midnight graveyard. There were a couple of jobs on the other side, but no one was working on them. Little knots of men were sitting around as if the joints of their asses were locked to the dock timbers. Christ could have come walking down the North River and it wouldn't have stirred them an inch. That was when I knew what had happened.

One of the men there was a fellow I had known while I was around the docks four years before. He was an old ex-Wobbly, and he had a card in both the longshoremen's and seamen's unions but usually didn't work in either unless he needed the price of some liquor. His name was Conn and he was usually called Riverboat because he claimed to have been a Mississippi River pilot at one time. He had read Mark Twain anyway. More than Mark Twain too, I remembered. He was probably the best informed gashound on the front, that day or any other. I yelled at him over the side.

"What the devil do you think you're pulling off, Riverboat?"

He turned up the face of a prematurely-born child, squinting in the sun. He was a little drunk still, which would be natural at that time of the day or anytime.

"Hello, Joe," he said as casually as if he had just seen me ten minutes before. "We got a little reception going in your honor."

"What's coming off anyway?"

"The revolt of the goddamn masses, mate," he said, digging the tail of a cigarette out of his pocket. "Ain't you heard about it? This is the third day."

It was funny they hadn't sprung the news at us on the boat. Usually the army uses something like that. They had almost started a back-to-work movement among the troops in Africa when they got through building up the coal strike in the spring of '43. Maybe they thought this one would blow over. Or maybe, because the war was over, they hadn't worked out a new line.

"You mean you're not goin' to get us off this tub?" Blackie asked.

"You can walk off, can't you?"

"What about the equipment and crap?"

"Don't excite yourself," Conn said. "What they don't load on your backs we'll take off. We're still working military stuff. Everything for the front, yeh? Aren't you a bunch of goddamn heroes?"

"I just want off of here."

"We shall attend to that little detail with neatness and dispatch, if that's the way it's to be done," Riverboat Conn said. "Don't piss yourself."

"How did it start?" I asked him. A strike on the dock is always strange. With a union leadership that has specialized for years in keeping the men on the job whenever they had most to gain by striking, even a small stoppage, if it was the men who pulled it, was something important.

"It started," Conn said, "with a work stoppage."

I could see that he was going to be difficult and tossed him a pack of cigarettes.

"Only Luckies?" he said looking at the pack contemptuously. "What, no Fatimas? No Three Kings?" But he fished out a cigarette and stuck the rest in his pocket.

"It seems one man stopped work," he said. "There's a contract coming up and the companies don't want to pay anything and the union leadership, as they call it, is happy to get it. That might have made everyone happy but this one man. So he stops work. By resorting to moral suasion he manages to get a friend to stop work. If two men stop work, that's a strike, yeh?"

I had heard that particular maxim before so I knew what was coming next and said it for him: "So you were the third. Conn's blessed trinity."

"Brother," he said, "I've been on strike since before you were born."

"And the fourth man? Another friend?"

"Only God in his infinite wisdom knows," he said, and I could tell that he was serious about it. "I haven't seen anything like it. Not on the docks, that is. They just put their hooks in their pockets and walked home."

"And then?"

"That's all. They're still there, or in the beer joints."

"That should be the kind of strike you like," I said.

"You goddamn right. Individual initiative. Spontaneity."

"No organization?"

"A few guys come down to the docks, just to give the word if someone turns up and thinks he wants to work. Nobody does. Kelly is trying to rig a back-to-work movement but he hasn't had any luck."

"You think he can be dumped?"

"I don't know," he said, looking at the man next to him who was staring up at me. "Maybe they don't want to."

"It should be possible to do something with the strike."

"You damn Commies always want to do something. Goddamn it, you never learn that sometimes all a working stiff wants is a few days to be let alone."

"That's all I want right now myself."

"Well, I'll see you around, yeh? Leadership to the masses, yeh?" he said kissing off the palm of one hand against the other.

"Not if I can help it," I said. "It's somebody else's baby, not mine."

But when I went below to get my stuff ready, and while I was sweating and waiting for the order for us to disembark, I couldn't help being excited about it.

Along the street, people were beginning to come out to go to the movies or to the bars. Fellows came past with girls on their arms, talking low. On the corners and around the candy stores, the young guys were ganged up discussing what to do with their time and watching the girls come past in twos and threes, some of them with little white hats on their heads, switching their provocative behinds. It made me feel lonely watching them, which was silly, because I had a girl I could go round to see myself. I couldn't see any reason why I hadn't gone there, why I wasn't going there now, but I wasn't. I put the idea of Kay up on the rack where I could reach it easily and let myself drift in the tide, letting whatever part of me it was that could only be satisfied by going down those mean streets lead me along like a blind man behind a dog.

They had a charm of their own, those streets. In another country, uptown, along the Hudson, were the good houses. Or over there, across the river, in Jersey and beyond, in America, in a thousand little towns there were the white houses with the red shutters and the objective basis for life: the house, the one or two automobiles, the refrigerator with cold beer and chicken in it. In the bank, in a safety desposit box, there was Junior's college vacation and the deed to the old homestead and the map of Treasure Island. There was a pew in the local church, paid up for ten years, and there was a life subscription to *Country Homes and Gardens*, and the price and the patina of bourgeois living. Or here, in New York, there was the apartment fifteen stories up, where the growl and scream of the city was only the purr of a kitten smothered in five feet of whipped cream, with a view of the river and a view of the park and the thousand-year plan for staying on top.

That was in another country. And even there, behind each of those red shutters there was someone who was afraid. Christ knows why. They had the lid screwed on and they had stolen the pressure gauge, but they were afraid. They had the objective basis for the good life, but life wasn't good. They went racing away in the morning to their offices, and they spent the day in commerce and chicanery of one kind or another, getting a kick out of it at the time, the way you get a kick out of doing anything well, whether it is seducing an officer's wife or kicking a football. But in the evening when they came home (with the lid screwed on, and the pew rented for ten years, and the deed to the place in their sock) it all turned sour in their stomachs, and they were still afraid. The falling rate of profit went on working in the dark, the ulcer edged through another hundred-thousandth of an inch, there was a strike of some kind on the waterfront, war in China — the cankering worm worked in the night, and eighteen holes of golf didn't help things, nor the expensive psychiatrist with the European name.

You could see it everywhere. It had been like that since I was a kid. They had nothing to fear but fear itself, but it was everywhere. It was in *Time* where the mythical woman in the red dress was always saying such extraordinary and comforting things for the defeated guilt-racked novelist who wrote the news. It was in the newspapers which had never been thicker or more empty. You could say it was the guilt of a class that was no longer needed, that lived because of the sufferance and the ignorance of the rest of society. You could say it, but it was harder to believe it. Nothing the books said would ever put it into life. In the books you only felt it against your mind. But it was a real thing that you felt with every part of you if you had ever been near it or looked at it, and real things, even when they are the same things, have a different character from things in books.

But here, in these dirty, stinking, poverty-stricken streets, there was none of that fear. If there was fear at all it had nothing to do with guilt, and there were no deeds to the old homestead or maps of Treasure Island. This was the other country, the one that went three thousand miles west, along the railroad tracks, spreading out from there around the factories and the mines and into the farmlands, where sixty million workers, with the chisel and the hammer, sweated gold out of the rocks every day.

Down these streets the sweat never stopped running. Children were being born with the utmost agony into a trap from which they would never escape. Ninety thousand men and women were doing the two-backed beast this minute, shoring up fragments against their ruin. A thousand were plotting murder. Here an arsonist of ten was buying his first box of matches; there a twelve-year-old virgin was becoming a woman. A kid with his front teeth missing was taking his first look at the *Communist Manifesto*; an old man was dying in a doorway, and everyone was fighting, screaming, cursing, working and living, three-fourths of them in just the way that the movies last night taught them to.

That's the way the streets were, just then. The people were spilling off the steps, bulging from the windows. The houses weren't big enough to hold them; houses contracted in the heat, contrary to the laws of physics.

Somewhere in the Twenties, without noticing, I passed a stable. It is always a little odd to smell them, the one humanist edifice in the city. The ammoniac smell of urine and the smell of dung, converted, for a moment, the gasoline fumes in the air. Early morning on Eighth or Ninth Avenue you could smell it, too. The old-fashioned laundry wagons passed then, the horse-driven ones. The poor nags were chivvied along by drivers who were cursing their luck that they hadn't been put on the trucks. They kept the whip under the horses' tails, those guys. But after they passed, at the corner of Eighth and Seventeenth, say, the whole world and most of New York smelled of horse dung for a little while. It was the most civilized smell the town ever had.

There were no horses now. They were behind me, in the stable which was just as surprising where it was, next to a garage and a box factory, as the stables of Bethlehem would have been. Ninth Avenue was almost deserted. A drunken longshoreman was lying in the street, his hook in his belt. The girls with their challenging bottoms picked their way over the outstretched body and went on.

I didn't pay much attention to what was going on in the street. I was almost at Sixteenth when I got a shock. A little bit farther down, three guys were buddying up to a fourth as if the next time they saw him would be to identify him on a marble slab. From where I was at, they were all pretty indistinct and I thought at first that it was just a fight of the kind that starts in the bars a little later on. Then I saw that the fourth guy was wearing an army field jacket. In the light I could see that he was dark and small. The other three were all around him like old friends around a drunk that can't take care of himself.

They came rapidly up the street toward me and turned down the one beside the post office. It is a dark street, busy with trucks in the daytime, but almost deserted at night. When they turned the corner one of them took something out of his pocket. More by instinct than anything else I knew that it was a club. The dark guy spilled something from under his arm, papers that fluttered in the street like pigeons. Then I knew what was happening and the strike was on me. I started running as fast as I could, yelling.

They were going to dump him hard. If it had just been the routine kind of thing, they would have dropped him on Ninth Avenue and kicked him into the gutter and that would have been all. Taking him around the corner that way gave me a little time. The guy with the field jacket wasn't cooperating, either. He was hanging back like the bashful boy at a barn dance, and his leaflets were fluttering and dancing in the breeze.

It was louder than two skeletons jazzing on a tin roof. The dark guy was yelling bloody murder, which was only proper, and the guys with him were yelling too, maybe about who should have the first lick at him. I came charging up the avenue trying to call out the populace. It didn't faze the guys with the blackjacks. They had probably all heard too many cease-and-desists to pay any attention. Like good workmen they were going about their business.

I turned into the street, running hard, and I saw the hand with the sap in it go up in the air. I didn't hear the whistle of it, but I could damn near hear it coming down. It struck out like a snake and the dark man put up an arm, as much as he could with a man hanging on it, and tried to pull away. It didn't get him on the back of the head anyway. He was still standing when the arm went up again, but this time I was close enough to hear the meaty, leathery *thock* of the thing striking, and he was down on the sidewalk against the iron fence of a basement stair. He took two of them with him, one of them on his back beside him and the other on this knees. They tangled like a nest of snakes.

The man with the jack had his back to me, but he heard me coming and turned. I was on him before he had time to swing and before I had time to be scared. I was coming too fast to swing, but I hit him, half a chop and half a straight arm, while he was trying to get in position to clip me. He went back a little and I missed his jaw, getting him in the neck. I could feel his Adam's apple under my knuckles. Before he could get set, I swung again, with my feet under me this time, and caught him somewhere on the side of the face. He dropped his blackjack and started going back as if he had lost his balance. Three steps and he was on his can, half in the gutter and half out. I remember his sad, pinched, Irish face.

The dark man was tough. I had expected to see his hide hanging in strips from the fence, but when I turned he was actually getting up. He had one of the goons sewed tight to his pelt, and the other was in too close to do any damage. When he saw me he must have thought

I was another, because he attempted a slow waltz down the fence, trying to twist his partner enough to keep him between us. He got him turned, not with any elegance but enough so that I had a clear shot at him.

I must have been too excited. I had the back of the man's neck in my sights, with the full moon on it, and I missed. I got him somewhere against the back of his head and almost broke my knuckles, but he staggered and pulled away and that left only one of them.

One was too many for the two of us. We had him right between us and were trying our best, but we couldn't hit him. With the dark man it was maybe because one of his arms was almost falling off from the sapping he had got, but with me it was a case of buck fever. There were too many birds to shoot at. He was hung up in front of me like a punching bag, and I must have hit him twenty times, chop chop chop like a rabbit knocking down a celery bush, but I couldn't do any good.

The neighbors were in the thing by then and the whole street was erupting. The man broke away from us for a second, and I saw him stoop for the sap I had forgotten. If he had made it, it would have been the beginning of round one again, but the dark guy nailed his hand to the sidewalk with an army shoe. It seemed to me I could hear the bones go. When he stepped back for a swing, the man was gone down the street.

"Let's get the hell out of here," I said. I probably would have said it earlier if I hadn't been so scared.

Across the way a citizen was coming toward us, a little uncertainly, as if not sure he were going to help. But by that time we didn't need him. On Ninth for once there was a cab when you needed it.

"Where to, gents?" he asked as if we had all the choice in the world.

"Just get going and we'll tell you where," I said, looking toward the mouth of the street where the goons had been.

"Which way?"

"Forward, for Christ's sake!"

"Central Park is nice a night like this," he said as if he were selling a pair of lovers on the idea.

"Central Park, then!"

"Nice weather for this time of year," the driver said, as proud as if he were responsible for it.

Two men came out of the mouth of the street and stood under the light looking toward us. I couldn't be sure that they were two of the men we had had our go-round with. It didn't matter anyway. By that time the driver had got his mind in gear, and we went down the avenue with our flaps pulled in, all buttoned up and flying home through the thick darkness.

9 A.M.

Crip sat at a table near the window in the Automat. In front of him was Sixth Avenue, yellow with taxis at nine o'clock in the morning, and beyond was the park that led to the public library. The sun slanting in through the window was already warm, and the light blackened the leaves of the trees across the street until they looked like oiled leather. They wore the colors of the season, but now the sunlight, striking at just that angle, made them dark.

On the benches under the trees sat students with notebooks and old men. People were already moving off along the walks toward the library. A man with a large burlap bag at his side was spearing papers on a pointed stick and depositing the scraps carefully in his bag.

It was the time of day that he liked best, especially when the weather was fine. He could sit here and drink his coffee slowly and read the paper and then, if he wanted to, he could stroll through the trees toward the great ugly stone building at the other end. Not today. It would be impossible to go up there today, to the history reading room and the oily librarian. Perhaps tomorrow or perhaps not. He opened his paper, A *New York Times*, and began reading the editorials.

He read them as he did everything else, as he read the endless numbers of books, articles, documents, reports in the history room at the library—without any sign of expression. He felt toward the editorials as he did toward the history materials, a muffled and furious sense of outraged credulity. He reached the same conclusion as always: that he was being duped. He read through the editorials again to find out where the lie was concealed, but as always he failed. It was *there*, somewhere, off the edge of the page, hidden under the words. He was no better off than before he had opened the paper, than before he had started the ten-year research which no one had asked him to do but which some powerful current, short-circuited from the function which it was originally meant to power, was driving him.

Leaving his paper on the table he went over to the section where the coffee spout came out of the wall and got a new cup. He limped badly; one of his feet was club. Putting three heaping spoons of sugar into the coffee, limping back to the table, he was ready for the front page and, turning to it, read first the news of the strike. There had been a failure of a back-to-work movement, there was a statement by union officials. President-of-the-union Kelly denied that there was any strike in the real sense of the word. "The men will be back at work on Monday," he had promised. There was a story on a renewal of the Civil War in China, and he read this carefully, turning to the middle section where there was a map with arrows and studying it with a kind of angry unbelief, turning the names of the cities over in his mouth as if he could taste them. Then he closed the paper, finished his coffee and went out. At the corner of Sixth and Forty-first a bum approached him with the curious sidelong motion of a crab.

"'Scuse me, mister, could you—"

"Beat it," he said in a snarling weak voice, without looking up at the man, and limped on down the street, cursing under his breath in characteristic pointless anger.

He went across Seventh Avenue and across Eighth and turned into a rooming house in the Italian neighborhood. The door of the landlady's apartment was open. It was wild with the color of vases, porcelain figures of animals and birds, replicas of the Leaning Tower of Pisa, of the Empire State Building, of Niagara Falls, of Custer's Last Stand. On the walls were cheap lithographs and pictures from calendars, and everywhere there were paper flowers.

"'Allo, Crip," the landlady said, peering at him out of her jungle. Beside her she had a large pitcher of sour wine with ice cubes in it, and she was a little drunk.

He went on up the stairs still swearing under his breath, hearing the landlady laugh behind him. "Hah, old Crip mad already this morning," she told herself after a couple of minutes, a little pleased with herself for no reason at all.

But upstairs in his small room with the two chairs and the brass-bound single bed, Crip was no longer swearing. He had opened the top drawer of his dresser and removed a little box. With a key from his wallet he had unlocked it and taken out a heavy object in an oily cloth. He held it in his hands for a moment, as if listening for something, for something that might have been inside of him perhaps, as if in a moment he had subtly altered. There was no apparent change. He was just a nondescript unremarkable man of medium height with the kind of features that no one would ever remember. His only noticeable features were high eyes: the irises were too large, like the yolks of eggs that had broken and run, and they were an ugly phlegmy color. There was nothing remarkable about him now, not even his anger, as he unwrapped the oily rag and began to clean the snub-nosed gun.

9 P.M.

We didn't go to Central Park. At Twenty-third we had the taxi cut over and came down on Fifth to Sixteenth Street and got out. Then we walked down a few blocks and over to Sixth and got to this dark fellow's place. I couldn't see the sense in not taking the cab right to the door.

"You're being awfully careful, aren't you?" I asked him.

"I almost got a beating this morning," he said. "One of the same crowd that I ran into tonight. I don't know how interested they might be."

"It's hell to be popular."

We went into the place and up three flights of stairs and the dark fellow got out a key, having a hard time with the arm that was pretty sore now and due to be a lot worse.

"I'm just bunking in with the guy that rents this place," he said.

It was one of those places with the kitchen in the livingroom-sleepingroom and a little bathroom off to one side. The room was long and narrow and had two beds in it so close you could hardly walk between them. At the end near the windows there was one of those cheap desk-bookcases and a couple of easy chairs. Around the walls, about up to the level of the chairs there were more bookcases built out of new wood and not yet painted. On the desk there was a *Sunday Worker*, a copy of *The Education of Henry Adams*, and some army ribbons.

"E.T.O.," I said.

"Yeah. You?"

"Part of it."

He got out of the field jacket and his shirt and lay down on the bed. There was a welt on the arm where the sap had caught him. Not very big and not very bad looking, but when I put my hands on his shoulder the sweat started jumping out of him.

"If it's just the same to you," he said, "that's sore as hell."

It couldn't be anything else. I went into the bathroom. There was nothing in the medicine cabinet but used razor blades and a small bottle of Absorbine Junior. I took that out and rubbed it on the arm. He was grunting with the pain.

"You won't be able to get your pants on in the morning," I said.

"I'll sleep in them then. I'm due down on the front at six a.m."

"You better take a vacation from there for a while," I said. "If they tried to dump you this morning, and then again tonight, they'll sure as hell try to make a job of it tomorrow."

"I've got to take the chance."

"There are damn few things you really have to do."

"That is one of them."

"All right," I said. There wasn't anything I could do to stop him, and somebody had to go down there. It seemed to me then, though, that he had taken enough chances.

"Everybody gets dumped," he said. "I've been there three days now and I haven't had any trouble. All the other guys got it. I was beginning to look phony."

"I'm glad this makes you feel better then," I said and started rummaging in the kitchenette. It made me feel a little guilty, hearing him talk like that, because tomorrow I knew I should be down there myself, taking my chances with him and the others, and I didn't want that.

A kitchenette is a hell of an excuse for a place to cook. I lifted up a sort of venetian blind and the whole thing was at my fingertips, the icebox that would keep maybe three cans of beer cold, a couple of pans each large enough to boil an egg in, the pepper and the salt and the oil and the vinegar. There wasn't a kettle of any kind, not even a miniature one. The only good thing about it was a smell of dried beef. I filled the two little saucepans with water and put them on the two burners.

"I'm hungry," I said. The excitement was what had done it, I suppose. I felt like a kid at halftime in a hot basketball game, all hollow inside.

He nodded toward the larder rather hopelessly, and I started through it. There was the beer anyway, and I cracked two of the cans for us. The glasses, if there had been any, seemed to have been broken. I gave him his beer and sat down on the side of the bed. All the time I could feel his eyes tracking me around like a radar beam. His hair was black and he had eyes like a couple of black buttons. The eyes didn't go with the rest of the face for some reason, giving him a quality that made you look at him again.

"You look like a guy I know," I told him, thinking of Blackie Carmody who was small and dark and quick. He nodded indifferently.

"Here's luck," I said, lifting my can of beer. "May all their blackjacks be filled with marshmallows."

He lifted his can and drank. "What's your name?" he asked, putting down the can with his good hand. I had soaked a towel and put it on the arm. On top of the liniment it must have been hell-hot. It was all I could think of doing.

"Joe Hunter."

"O.K.," he said. "Mine's Bill Everson, and if I didn't get around to thanking you properly back there in the cab, I sure as hell want to now. You saved my bacon."

"I hope I never have to say the same thing."

"Funny, you turning up like that."

"I just came down for a look," I said. "I used to live down there. Seventeenth Street. I wondered what the front would be like, that's all."

"You knew about the strike?"

"I could feel the damn strike beyond the three-mile limit," I said.

"Yeah," he said. "It's a funny strike. I guess they all are on the waterfront. The whole damn thing is closed down. And just because one damn union pulled the pin."

"It's Kelly's union, don't forget. That cuts a lot of ice."

"I guess so. I'm from the West. I've seen a couple of strikes, but not one like this. What do you think of it?"

"I don't. It looks to me as if everybody got tired and went home for a rest. I don't figure it out and I'm not trying. I don't want any part of it."

"It was already on when I got in," he said. "I can't figure the damn thing out."

"They just got tired. Or maybe they want to dump Kelly. Or maybe it's because the war is over. I saw a guy named Riverboat Conn when I came in three days ago. He can't figure it out, so I know enough to give up."

I told Bill about my conversation with Conn.

"You used to work down there, then?" he asked.

"For a little while," I said. "Before the war."

"The C.P. sent me down." He looked at me as if I were supposed to say something.

"They'd send me down too, if they knew I was here," I said.

"Aren't you going around and check in? They need people down there. Not just the Party. Nobody knows his ass from his elbow, nobody knows what to make out of the strike, if anything can be made out of it. I'm lost in it. I feel like I'm the only man in the strike."

Somebody was certain to say that. Transport was the only thing that made New York important, and the unions covering it, with a few exceptions, were about the worst in the country. Kelly and his mob had been running the works ever since he got a start by breaking a strike after the First World War. He ran it like a racket, with every kind of tie-up, church, state, cops, and crooks. Nobody had been able to break it. Rank-and-file revolts had come and gone, a lot of hard work had gone into the field there, but nothing really had happened. One of our best boys had wound up in a tide flat in Jersey with his feet in a barrel of concrete, and there was no counting the ones who had been dumped and beaten or blackballed. If this was a complete tie-up, as Conn had said, it might mean that the men were finally tired of Kelly's kind of unionism. If they were all out, then it would be the best opportunity that had ever turned up. If you could organize it.

It would be a battle. There were a hell of a lot of men involved, and I knew our own forces were terribly small and scattered and weak. And, anyway, every big strike is a little bit like trying to drive a heavy truck down a mountain road at night with the brakes gone and the steering gear out of commission.

"I'm going out West," I said.
"You got an assignment out there?"
"I'm giving myself one."
"That's where you come from, is it? You were born out there?"
"I was born at the age of eighteen," I said. "Flat on my back on a street in Detroit."

10:30 A.M.

Patrick James Kelly was sitting at his desk blowing smoke rings. Outside, on Eighth Avenue, the traffic was roaring up toward Forty-second or down toward the bottleneck of the Holland Tunnel. It was noisy, but to P.J. Kelly, it seemed that an unnatural quiet had fallen over the city. With his mind's ear he was listening for the noises of the waterfront, and he knew that at ten-thirty of this fine October morning they were missing from the ugly music of the city.

Kelly was a big man, going a little to fat now, but not soft in any noticeable way. He had graying hair, neatly cut. The steel-rimmed glasses he wore made his eyes seem sad, an impression strengthened by the mouth which was wrenched down at one corner as if in response to some constant inward pain. He was perhaps fifty-five or sixty years old, but he looked forty-five.

He put out the cigarette in a cheap tin ashtray on the desk and looked at the calendar. CALL CAMINETTI was printed in block capitals. And under it in script, *Husk, ten forty-five.*

"That goddamn lousy wop," he said aloud and reached for another cigarette. He held it in his hand for a moment without lighting it and then pushed it back into the pack. He was feeling the disgust of a cigar smoker for cigarettes. He opened the right-hand drawer of the desk where the cigars were, looked at the box for a moment, rummaged at the back, brought out a pack of Lifesavers and popped one into his mouth. He had been told to stop smoking, and the cigarettes and the Lifesavers were a substitute. The box of cigars he kept in his desk as a challenge.

CALL CAMINETTI. It was something he would have to do sooner or later, but at the moment he was content to do nothing, sucking on the Lifesaver, leaning back in his chair, looking out on the avenue, thinking.

The office was a dingy place, only a floor of a loft building. The woodwork was thick with a hundred coats of paint, and the walls were yellowed. Beside the desk there was an old brass spittoon, the relic of an earlier time. *Almost of an earlier civilization.* Kelly was thinking of the avenue, seeing behind the buildings the ghosts of their predecessors and the phantom trail of the Ninth Avenue El.

The office hadn't been changed since he had taken over, just after the First World War. Now the union had expensive offices in the big new building next door. Kelly had an office there too, gleaming and rich, with a battery of phones and an expensive secretary, but at certain times he preferred to go to the old office, the first he had had, with the meeting room at the rear which was only a junk room now, where nothing was changed. Paint had been put on here and there, a new chair added. The spittoon was the same. *The smell is the same.* Kelly inhaled, sensing a rare perfume that might blow away in the wind. He felt lonely.

It was the strike that made him that way. It made him feel uncertain of everything, unsure of himself, and the smell of the office was a reassurance that there was permanency. The buildings had changed, and the El had gone, but the office was still the same. *I'm still the same.* Kelly told himself he could handle anything, but he was wishing for the cigar that he could not have.

Still, there was the strike, there was Caminetti.

The strike disturbed him. It should not have happened. The men were making good pay. All through the war there had been enough overtime so that a man could work as much as he wanted. There was probably more money along the West Side and in the working-class areas of Brooklyn and Jersey than there had ever been, and yet there was this strike which had broken without reason.

Like a safe dropping on your goddamn head. Those lousy bastards.

He kept thinking of the strikers. He thought of them with some resentment, but it was not strong enough to generate real anger and he began to grin. He was thinking that when he was young, working on the dock himself, he might have been one of them. He was thinking that it was the end of the war that had caused it, but he could not be quite sure. It left him uneasy.

I don't care how it started, how's it going to end? Sucking on the Lifesaver. *You can win all but the last.*

He heard the sound of feet on the worn wooden stairs and a man came into the outer room. He had a pinched consumptive face and was dressed in a dark suit. He wore a hat. Without noticing Kelly he went to a table and began gathering up some leaflets.

"What the hell are *you* doing, Monk?" Kelly asked him. He had watched the man, trying to remember his name, and then it had flashed up on the board for him.

"Oh, hello, P.J. I'm gettin' some leaflets. There's a lot of men floatin' around this morning. Thought we'd distribute some of them."

"Leaflets!" Kelly said. "I've got along without leaflets up to now.

We'll be running this union like a lot of damn Reds if we start handing out that stuff."

"The boys thought—" Monk Ryan started to say.

"Who's the boys?"

"Husk—"

"Husk? That'd be his idea all right. Modern methods!" But he was not angry.

"He wrote it up."

"Gimme one of them."

The man brought one of the leaflets and put it on the desk in front of Kelly. Automatically Kelly's hand dropped to the drawer at his right and brought out a cigar. He looked at it sourly a moment, thinking of the doctor, and held it out.

"Here. Take the damn thing. I can't smoke them anymore."

"Thanks, P.J.," Monk said. He held the cigar under his nose, sniffing it appreciatively like a connoisseur, thinking he hated the smell of them.

"Now get the hell out and peddle your papers."

"Sure." At the door he paused and called back. "The boys dumped a couple of them Commies this mornin'. They was thick down on the docks, waitin' to see if there'd be a shape up. They're running' all over the place."

"There aren't that many."

"Quite a few," Monk said uneasily, not wanting to be contradicted.

"Keep on dumping them."

"Yeah. It ain't easy. You can't be sure how the men are going to take it. They cut in on a couple of the boys and give them a bad time when they was trying' to dump one guy."

"You get paid to take your chances, don't you?"

"Yeah. Sure. It's tough though."

"Tough, hell! You don't know what it is to have it tough. You should have seen the days when Tony what's-his-name, the Red that got knocked off, had a real rank-and-file racket going over in Brooklyn. You should have seen Caminetti coming over here begging for help. You don't know what it's like to have it tough." It made Kelly feel good to remember Caminetti in those days. "You ought to have been around for the nineteen-twenty strike, then you'd have seen it tough."

"Yeah. I guess so. Caminetti ain't doin' so bad now though. He's got some of them workin' anyways."

"That's what he says. You been to Brooklyn?"

"I was there once and got lost," the man said grinning.

"Caminetti's got his troubles too. Now get the hell out with those damn things."

He heard the feet going down the stairs and the swinging clatter of the outer door, and tried to get back the thought on which he had been interrupted. He could not remember it, and it became very important, a key to the puzzle of the strike, but he could not remember. *All but the last.* That was it, but what did it mean? He had a sudden terrifying twinge of prescience. He had always told himself fatalistically, thinking of the struggles he had gone through, that you could win all battles but the last. Now it meant something else to him, something that had to do with his doctor telling him to stop smoking, and with the strike. It had something to do with death. *All but the last.*

He looked down at the leaflet on the desk but the print was loose on the page, floating, shifting and regrouping. He was beginning to realize that it was possible to die.

Coming out of the subway at Fourteenth Street and Eighth Avenue, Alton Husk stopped to watch the groupings of men at the end of Fourteenth near the river. From where he was standing there was no pattern about their movements; little knots of them merged like drops of mercury, moving aimlessly around, splitting again. He could see the scatter of leaflets and wondered if they were his own or those of the enemy.

Husk was a tall man, a couple of inches over six feet, and powerful. He had dark, crisp hair, short enough to suggest a crew cut, hazel eyes and rather thick lips. He looked a bit sullen, like a child pouting, but he was feeling almost happy watching the men at the end of the street. He liked to see established patterns broken, and the strike, although in a certain sense it was directed partially against himself, since he was Kelly's factotum, made him feel that he was more fully alive. He was continually having to look for these manifestations of vitality in the world, having to feed on them, drawing them into himself, as if there existed in him some kind of void. It was not a demand for physical danger or excitement, although at one time he had thought that was what it was.

"Hello, Al," a man said, and turning, Husk saw the dark suit, the hat, the thin figure and the leaflets. It was Monk Ryan.

Husk said, "I see you got the leaflets." His speech had the neutral quality of a westerner; it was easy but without a drawl, and precise without the midwestern twang.

"Yeak," Monk grinned crookedly. "P.J. damn near blew his stack when he saw them."

"Didn't like them, eh?"

"If he did he sure as hell hid it good."

"P.J.'s a little old fashioned," Alton Husk said smoothly. "He's been around so long he has the notion that nothing changes as long as he doesn't."

"I guess so," Monk said in a noncommittal voice. He was a delegate only because his father had known a Democratic assembly district leader named Merd who was in a position to ask favors of Kelly. Monk resented it when one of the big shots tried to put him in the middle. Goddamn it, he thought, I'm only tryin' to do my job; I'm just a guy with a job to do. He felt virtuous and angry.

"Still, things change," Husk said, looking at the procession of cars on the avenue. Suddenly he smiled and the change from the almost sullen cast of his face was dramatic and startling. He felt happy. "We'll beat the bastards, Mac," he said, slapping Ryan on the shoulder.

"Yeah," Monk said. "Sure." He wasn't quite sure whom Husk meant. "Look," he said, pointing across the street to a black-haired man in an army field jacket. "See that Commie bastard? He makes more trips down to the front than a crosstown bus." He was full of bitterness again. The goddamn Red, he thought; that's the one we tried to dump last night, the lousy atheist bastard. He was thinking of his wife, caged in a rear apartment of a Twenty-seventh Street walk-up, puking out her guts three times a day from no known disease, of the two kids, one of them only six months old.

"Dump him then."

Husk was looking across the street where a man was just turning the corner, a thin man with a high, bald forehead.

"Oh, sure," Monk said, not even thinking of the man any longer. "Mr. Husk, those guys down on my dock ain't workin' with me the way they ought." He meant that they were not giving him his share of racket money but didn't know how to say it.

"Of course not," Husk said. He hadn't heard what Ryan was saying. He was looking at the man on the other side of the street. Well, Barney, he thought. We meet again.

As if in answer to his thoughts the thin half-bald man turned his head and looked at him for a long minute. Alton Husk felt a brisk wind of fear, like the wake of a bullet, touch him in his most secret place. The last time he had seen Barney Last had been in Spain. He was up before a court-martial for desertion, and Barney had been elected to defend him. Had got him off too. The next time, though, Husk had made a thorough job of the desertion.

Last looked at him now as if Husk were a spectral image, as if Last could see directly through Husk to the walls of the bank just behind. Then, without every showing that he had seen anyone, Last went on down toward the waterfront.

"It ain't right," Monk Ryan was saying. "I'm supposed to get a better cut. Maybe you could talk to P.J."

"You know P.J. has nothing to do with any deals that you fellows have worked out."

It was a lie and both of them knew it. Nothin' to do with them, Monk thought, but he sure as hell could put me in; even if he don't make a rake-off right there, he could put me in; now I got to see that son of a bitch Merd and ask him to fix it and he'll want a piece-off.

"P.J. could pass the word. I stand good with the A.C. and U.," he added as an afterthought.

"No," Husk said abstractedly. He was looking across the avenue, to the newsstand on the downtown corner of Fourteenth where he saw Landers, wondering whether or not he should speak to him. "I'll take it up with him, Mac; see what I can do," he said with false heartiness. "You better get down to the front."

"Sure," Monk said. He settled his hat over his pinched face and started west on Fourteenth. Son of a bitch don't even know my name, he thought; at least P.J. knows who I am; goddamn college boy.

Husk watched him going down the street, recognizing Ryan's anger in the set of his shoulders, his stride. He was thinking that he didn't like the man, that he didn't like any of them. He had always had a kind of guilty uneasiness about defeated people. Once in Detroit when he had had a fight with a Negro. Afterward he had felt dirty. He had no intellectual prejudice against Negroes, Jews, anybody, yet there was this unclassifiable feeling, like a fear of being touched by a sick man, which he had never been able to get rid of. Momentarily he felt a positive hatred for Ryan, for the black-haired man, for Last, for all the strikers, the whole working class. He waved to Landers.

The latter came across the street carefully, looking left and right. He had a copy of the *World Telegram* and last night's *Post*. The *Post* was folded back around the labor news column.

"Hello, Trotsky," Husk said, "what do those fink labor writers have to say about it?" He nodded at the papers.

"They think that Kelly is a bum, but on the other hand they think the strike is a Moscow plot. So they think Kelly should be supported." He turned toward Husk the face of an intelligent laboratory assistant, removed his glasses and polished them expertly. "What's on your mind, Al?" he asked.

"Nothing much," Husk said. "I was just wondering how you felt about this." He waved his hand toward the end of Fourteenth Street.

Landers shrugged and put his glasses back on. "You can read it in our press."

"I don't give a damn what the *Militant* says, or *Labor* what-ever-it-is or any other rag that one of the splinters puts out. I want to know what *you* think of it and what you're going to do." He was suddenly angry with Landers's caginess.

"It's dangerous," Landers said carefully, folding his paper. "Kelly might get pushed out. It's just possible."

"How would you feel about that?"

"It depends," the other man said cautiously. "It could go too far. There's power just lying around in the street now. The wrong people could pick it up."

"Just like the paper says, eh?"

"You know my motives are different, Husk," Landers said, coloring.

"I know if you go getting out of line you'll be finished in that local, you and your Catholic friends down there. Tell that to the A.C.T.U. next time the fraction meets."

"I can't be ordered," Landers said evenly.

"No?" Husk smiled his sudden startling smile. "No use in fighting among ourselves," Husk said. "We've got a big enough battle on our hands."

But he knew that Landers, as he turned away and went down the street toward the waterfront, would remember what he had said.

There were so many things to balance. First of all there were the men, and while it was possible to guess how any one of them might behave, taken in the bulk they were beyond prediction. There was Kelly himself and his amazing capacity for doing nothing at all. There was the Association of Catholic Trade Unionists, which had never put on the pressure in the union, being willing to let Kelly have it so long as he was competent to keep the Communists out. Now, with the war over, the careerists in the A.C.T.U. would be pushing hard and the strike would give them ammunition against the Jesuits who ran the organization and who wanted to go slow, to maintain Kelly. The careerists could argue that Kelly was no longer to be trusted, that they would have to begin taking over locals. Already, along with Landers and the one or two other Trotskyites on the front, they controlled a small local. It had come as the result of a horse trade with Kelly: it was necessary to displace a handful of gangsters who had been running the local but who were getting out of line. It was Kelly's idea. Husk himself had felt that the new group would be as hard to manage as the old.

Too many things to control, he felt, starting across the street. There was Caminetti, who had the notion that Kelly was old enough to retire. Last of all he thought of the Communists, not as an organization, but in terms of a man, Barney Last, and felt again the little wind of fear.

He shook it off impatiently. There weren't many of them and only a few were effective.

"Always at the head of the fuckin' parade, yeh?" a voice said. "Mr. Alton Husk, Esquire, racin' down to the office to open up before the boss gets there. Give the workin' man his money's worth, yeh? Fair day's work for a fair day's pay, yeh?"

Husk recognized Conn with disgust. "Hello, Riverboat," he said, looking at the ruddy prune-shriveled face of the other man. "You still trying to be the number-one character on the waterfront?"

"I *am* the number-one character," Riverboat Conn said. He was a little drunk. "What we smokin' this morning?"

Husk took out his cigarettes and passed them over.

"Chesterfield," Conn said disgustedly. "Where's the Virginia Rounds? Where's the Gold Flake?" He tipped up the pack, shook out half a dozen cigarettes and handed the pack to Husk. "Burn the end off of this thing for me," he said. Husk lit the cigarette for him.

"What's your friend think about the fuckin' relationship of forces?" Conn asked, jerking his chin toward Fourteenth Street.

"Who?"

"Good buddy Landers. The Judas Christ of the Revolution."

"He's no friend of mine."

"Gettin' to be too many anti-Communist experts around here, yeh? Men can't spit without hittin' one," Conn said, looking at him shrewdly through the cigarette smoke. "You'll be needin' another job, Al."

"If this one folds up I'll become a Ninth Avenue character like you."

"You couldn't," Conn said, spitting. "There's only one character like me and that's me. Besides, I'm like Caesar's wife."

"What do you mean?"

"I'm above ambition."

"And I'm not?"

"I figure you want to take over the whole works."

"Take Kelly's job, you mean?" Husk grinned suddenly at Conn. "How about joining my conspiracy, Riverboat?" He put his hand on the other's shoulder.

"Puttin' you in the saddle would be just like turnin' Kelly in on a new model." Conn moved away so that Husk's hand dropped from his shoulder. "What price the managerial fuckin' revolution?" Conn said. Then: "You got the makin's of a cup of coffee on you? Contribution to Conn's Strike Fund?"

"Sure. Come on. I want some myself."

"I was figurin' on spendin' mine on a glass of beer," Conn said.

"You're a privileged character," Husk said, taking some change out of his pocket.

"Oh, I'm the fuckin' court jester all right."

He took the money and turned away. Husk went into the nearest restaurant and ordered a cup of coffee.

Conn had been both right and wrong. He did want to move in on Kelly. He wanted to displace him in more ways than one, but Conn had been wrong about the matter of his ambition. He had no ambition whatever. His ambition, if he had ever had any, had been lost on a hunting trip in the Coeur d'Alene district in Idaho when he was sixteen years old.

Alton Husk was of the third generation of a line of West Coast timber barons. The name had originally been Husik, but the grandfather had changed it on the day that he had acquired his second thousand acres of Douglas fir on the Cascade range; by the time that Alton Husk had reached the maturity of ten years of age the original name, and the fact that the grandfather had once worked with his hands, had been forgotten by the family. They were living in Seattle then, in a big house over the sound.

He was the only child in the family and had grown up a little bit lonely. His father, a bear of a man with a brusqueness which might have come to him from the immigrant Husik, never had much time to give to the boy. Nevertheless, Husk had a normal childhood, was good in school without achieving distinction, wanted in turn to be a timber feller, a locomotive engineer, a forest ranger, a flier; he had had all the normal ambitions and one he never thought of: to be loved by his father.

The hunting trip came when he was sixteen, in the late October of his junior year in high school. It was an annual excursion for his father, but it was the first time Alton Husk was allowed to go along.

On the third day in the woods he heard the smashing of brush and the great buck jumped out of the forest and raced smoothly along the lake shore. Alton Husk did not quite forget the gun in his hands, but there was nothing he could do with it. When the buck disappeared, cutting across a neck of land that stretched into the lake, he had not even managed to bring it to his shoulder and his father was beside him, cursing hoarsely.

"Give me that gun!"

He felt his father tear the weapon out of his hands, and then, as if in a dream, saw the hand raised and, without feeling any blow at all or even being conscious that he had been struck, found himself on the ground and tasted the blood in his mouth. He had wanted to rise, to strike back, but it had seemed preposterous. The blow had been as stark and sudden as if he had been struck by lightning.

He did not forgive his father. From that time, until somewhere in his twenties, he sometimes managed not to think about him, but he never forgave him and he hated him almost to the point of murder. After that it was not important any longer and he could think of him with no special feeling at all. He did not even resent the blow. Sometimes, thinking about it, he would feel that it would have been better if he had fought back; and, curiously, the thing about it that he resented most, although not at the time, had been that his rifle had been taken from him.

That was when he had lost his ambition, which, in all its disguises was only the ambition to be like his father. After that for a long time it was just a question of getting by. There was no need for an ambition anyway. Sooner or later he would have the timber and the mills.

The year following the hunting trip his mother, a comfortable-looking blonde woman, gentle and absentminded and, he realized later, unhappy, died of what he thought must have been ennui. The father had been too busy to have any need of her, and the servants had run the house. Her death hit him very hard: he had loved her in an immediate, puppylike way, having no one else to love.

A month after the death of his mother he lost his virginity to one of the housemaids. He was proud of the deed and ashamed that it had been performed with a servant. He had been a slow boy, and this new thing showed him the world on another level, but as the years of college went by, rowing during the term but not in the first boat, sailing the sound in the summer, it became too easy. He went through a period that was a kind of delayed adolescence, discovering that he could be excited about books and ideas; he dreamed of becoming a great scientist.

It was a blind alley. After a while he was no longer interested, stopped attending the lectures and doing any work and was finally advised to leave at the end of his junior year. He could not have said why he was resentful.

He had gone to Idaho then, back to the lake where he had had buck fever, where he had lost his rifle, and this time he got his deer, three of them, out of season, and did not even go down to see them after they had fallen. He spent three months in the cabin his father had built twenty years earlier, without a book or a radio, wrestling with himself, trying to find what it was that he wanted to do, and came out of the woods with the vague idea that he would become a Catholic. If he had met the right kind of priest his life might have been entirely different, or, if essentially the same, it would have been lived in other categories, but the priest was a salesman, intelligent but not intellectual, with no sense of sin whatsover. It was the sense of sin that Alton Husk needed. He was never going to be able to value life without some kind of absolute weight or measure to work from, and even this false weight the priest was not able to provide.

It was after this, that last failure, that he tried to break the pattern and in doing so established another. He forged his father's name to a check, feeling for the first time the pleasure of smashing a conception of himself—both to himself, his father, and his friends—and after a leisurely trip across country went to live in New York. Some years later, just as abruptly, he had gone to Spain. He went without conviction, as he had forged the check from no real need, but he still hoped for something from the excitement of war.

All it had brought him was fear. He hadn't believed it could exist for him, but it was there, and he might have made a weight and a measure out of it, as some of the others were doing, but he had failed there too, and it had ended with Barney Last being elected by the Brigade to defend him against the charge of desertion. A month later he had made the desertion effective; he ran away with a hatred for Barney and for the whole business of Spain as strong as his earlier hatred for his father.

In New York he did some articles on his Spanish experiences. He called the series "They Took Away My Rifle," and it brought him a certain amount of fame or notoriety—he wouldn't have been able to say which he thought it, and wouldn't have cared—and a couple of thousand dollars. His father wired from the West Coast, forgiving him, and he joined one of the groups of Trotskyites, acting again from no conviction except the hatred he still felt for Barney Last. He was sent to Detroit, to one of the big Communist-led auto locals, and in three months was a "personal engineer." It had rocked the groups he was with.

There were only four of them—Manzie, old Briggs, the Negro kid, and him. Briggs hadn't been able to believe it.

"You aren't selling out to the class enemy?" he asked. Briggs, as Husk remembered him, always lovingly used the old cliches. He was a fine honest old man, a revolutionary purist who boasted that he had been in and out of every political party of the past fifty years.

"Selling out? I can fight the Reds better inside, can't I?" It had amused him to put up the argument.

"We don't Red-bait," old Briggs was saying. He was almost apoplectic. "We don't Red-bait. We—" He started talking like an editorial. Husk looked at the others. Manzie had a speculative half-smile on his face. The Negro kid looked as if he might begin to cry; then he came at Husk and there was a fight, a small one.

It finished them. Briggs was too old to get over it and gave up politics. A few months later Husk had a list of new Communist recruits in the local and the Negro kid's name on it. A year later he discovered that Manzie had been on the company payroll all the time.

There was no future in being an anti-Communist expert for an auto firm. The profession was becoming too crowded, and the industry was top-heavy with power. The only way into the court circles of the leadership was to buy into it. It was a dull game anyway, Husk had decided. He had met Kelly on a trip to the East and had taken the job with him at once, not even going back to Detroit.

The new job paid less, but things had looked different from the other side of the board, at least for a while. There was power there; it was a question of how to use it. Kelly did not want to use it, but it had become a habit with him, the having of it. He wanted the twenty-five thousand a year, and to be let alone; he had been the boss for twenty years and he wanted to keep things that way until he died. Now Husk was impatient. Exactly what he wanted, he would not have been able to say—it was not money, or power even. At its simplest it was just that he wanted something to happen. Things as they were had become once more a sick ugly gray, and even the senseless strike pleased him.

He finished his second cup of coffee. It was time to go up to the office; he had an appointment with Kelly. "I figure you want to take over the whole works," Riverboat Conn had said. That drunken fool, Husk thought; and then: Is that what I want to do?

Even thinking about it excited him a little. It was something like the time when he had decided to desert. He began to think of how the strike was going, to see the wheels going around, to think of all the things he would have to think about. It doesn't matter a damn how it works out, he thought. It's all perfectly senseless anyway, everything.

It was his deepest judgment on life, his own and that of the world, and it made him feel happy again as he went up the worn stairs, into the smell of the past, calling:

"Hello, Joe. Sorry I'm late but this damn strike is taking up a lot of my time."

10 P.M.

When I got out on the street from Bill's place, I was still a little sore. There was no reason for it, except the way I felt about myself. He hadn't told me what I was supposed to do, but I knew what I was supposed to do without his telling me. I did want to go West. I wanted to see how I stood.

I was going to have to look myself in the face, a four-year-old face with the muddy footprints of the years all over it. New York and the things that I had been when I went into the fog of the army seemed a long way off. I had thought it was going to be a little like meeting an old friend whom you haven't seen for a long time and don't quite know how to greet, but the face I had to meet, the old friend, was only myself four years gone with patriotism and my country. It wasn't going to be so easy because the man behind the face had become something else.

Just what he had become I wasn't altogether sure. In the army, you are apt to be thinking so much of the past, of the man you were, that you don't see how you are changing—what you are becoming. Later, you think, there will have to be time to sort out what was from what had been. So I figured anyway. Now it didn't look as if it would be easy.

The years in the army were a long weekend away from my life and I was able to see that life a little more clearly now, and I saw that it had no more pattern than a crazy quilt. I had been born without a family, so to speak, my parents dying before I was old enough to remember them. After that I grew up in the home of an uncle. In Michigan, in a little town in the kind of country that should have been left to the forest. It was bad land but good country, and I never quite got it out of my head after I left, the sound of the pines like air escaping from a tire, the sound of the lake behind the house, continually washing itself on the shore.

That was mostly a shadow of childhood, because I went away pretty young, first to school, including a little while in college, and then up to Detroit for a job at Ford's. The sound of Michigan turned up sometimes, like a familiar symbol in a dream, like the face of someone whose name you cannot recall, but it wasn't something very strong. It wasn't really my home because I had never been properly born there.

I was born at the age of eighteen. It happened in a little fracas in Detroit which never even became a strike. I got a wallop with a policeman's billy, and I sprang, miraculous, fully formed, from my own head, like Athena being born from the brow of Jove. An immaculate conception, gestation, parturition, and all done in the twinkle of a nightstick.

It is proper to suspect such transformations. I went down as one man—not even as a man but as a lot of material that might have been a man, an infinitely reticulated web of manflesh, but with the interstices full of fog and moonshine and unformed desires of all kinds; some of them hanging new and screaming in the web, their eyes not yet opened; others securely embalmed in the mummy tape and bitumen of forgetfulness.

Between the blow and the fall, the miracle. I went down as soft and indecisive as a fishnet, but down there on the cold sea floor of Cadillac Square, the calcification set in, and when I got up with everything turned to coral, hard and sharp and shiny, the little mummies and the soft things that had hung screaming in the web of my youth had broken loose and scuttled away into the dark subaqueous caves of Detroit.

A lot of people were being born that way then, and later, in the war, a hell of a lot more. It is probably not the best way. It is not a very human process, in a way, except in the unhappy way that wars of all kinds, your own or somebody else's, are a part of the unhappy human process. When you are born that way, you are born for yourself alone, and that is never any good.

Anyway, that is the way I was born. After the event I moved around and there were a lot more strikes. I became a professional of a sort. It was satisfying enough, I guess, moving along like that. I had been born perfect, which is to say without history. I had neither past nor future to worry about, and one place or one day was just about like the next. I was born with function but no character, and that made it easier. Anyone can live better that way, as a neutral body, with no real self-consciousness, if by better you mean with less pain.

Of course, another way to put what had happened was that I got a rap on the skull while being an innocent bystander and woke up with a power of hate for the cop and the system of cops and started out to square things. Then, once my blood pressure went down, I would be back to normal, or nearabout, and I would change again. I did change, too, but not just that way.

They were still hammering the gold out of the rocks when I left Bill and got into the street. A few late Sanitation Department trucks were rolling past, clearing up the last wreckage of the day. Toward Sixth Avenue and Eighth Street everything looked bright and gay. The drugstores and the Nedick's places were doing land-office business and the newsstand on the corner was handing out the red-hot Sunday newspapers that had been printed, for the most part, a couple of days before.

Over to the west, the women's prison looked elegant and reserved, and down Greenwich Street it was quiet and cool. The few trees there, after the dirty hot streets I had come through, looked fine, but out of place. At Julius's bar it was noisy with seamen who seemed to have taken it over during the war. Barney Last was coming past the door, a tall thin man, partly bald.

"Hello, Joe," he said, putting his hand out. "I didn't know you were back. Discharged?" He pointed to the patch sewed on my shirt.

"Just got out this evening."

"That's good. We can use you around here right now. You know about the strike?"

"Christ, yes."

The way I said it must not have sounded very enthusiastic. He gave me a funny look.

"Maybe you think you should have a rest before going back to work?"

That didn't sound very good either, at first, and I was about to say yes, and a damn long one, when I saw that he was serious.

"I may not stick around here, Barney," I said at last.

"Well, Joe, nobody can tell you what to do. You got the dope on how things are going?"

"I saw Riverboat Conn."

"That wino? Still, I guess he knows as much about it as the rest of us."

"And I just saw a guy named Everson. One of our boys. He was just getting out of his second dumping of the day but he was still hopped up about how things were going."

"He's a good lad," Barney sighed. "But he's kind of young yet. Christ, I don't know how the damn thing will turn out."

"It just started."

"Sure, and the way it is, it could end tomorrow with the net result that the guys who are out would have lost four or five days' pay and got nothing more. No organization yet. A real anarchist's dream, this strike is."

"Our guys down there are a lot of weak sisters. Some of them couldn't find their ass with both hands. I can't see them organizing much."

"Is that what's eating on you? That why you want to pull out for some other place?"

It was part of the reason, I suppose. I shrugged my shoulders and didn't say anything.

"I'm in charge of this particular fling anyway," Barney said as if he weren't really talking to me at all.

"You mean you're head of the Section down there now?"

He shook his head. "Just this business of the strike."

"Why not the whole works?"

"Not enough people thought I should be," he said. "Look, Joe, I know we've got weak sisters, and some phonies, too. Bound to have. Things won't be any easier wherever you go, and this thing is important."

"What do you think you can make out of it?"

"Hell," he said, running his hand across his high forehead. "I don't have any idea. Maybe the whole thing will come down, Kelly and all. But I think if we can just get enough of a movement to force the locals to meet regularly, enough of a movement to protect the militants, keep them from getting beaten or blacklisted, we've got a chance to have elections held and get an honest leadership in a few of the locals anyway. Not Party guys, of course, except maybe in a few cases, but honest men. After that, it's just time and plugging. I don't think anything is going to change very fast in the whole industry. But it may be that they'll just say the hell with the strike, accept the lousy contract, and go back to work."

He pulled out a pack of cigarettes and we lit them and smoked for a while.

"Well," I said finally, "I don't know. Maybe I'll try to give you a hand. One man doesn't make much difference one way or the other—"

"It does now. We're strapped. Look, there'll be a meeting of some of our people. On Monday if the strike is still on."

"Where?"

"At the Section." He gave me the address. "You might come along down."

"I'll see."

Talking with him, I could feel the hatch coming down. Locked in.

He went on down the street and left me with nothing to do but go and see Kay. It was funny—I wanted to see her but I'd been putting it off just the way I wanted to put off going around to see the Party about what they might want me to do. I couldn't postpone things forever. Sweating a little in my uniform as I walked down Greenwich Street, I knew the long vacation of the war was over. I couldn't get used to the idea that I was about to live in the area of choice again. I wasn't even altogether sure I liked it.

1:30 P.M.

The sun was bright and hot on the windless Brooklyn dock. Beyond, in the river, the water was very blue, with a metallic sheen in the minute chop. The gulls wheeled over, crying incessantly their thin petulant screams. On the other side of the river, in downtown Manhattan, the sun on the yellowing pier, on the shabby Fall River Line boats, made these things seem dirtier than they were, but the skyscrapers around Wall and Pine streets gathered the sunlight to them with the arrogance of clean stone, of glass, of metal, of power. The corpse on the dock, the water still sparkling on him, gathered the sunlight also.

"I wish to Christ they'd get here with the meat wagon," the older cop said, spitting out into the river. "I got better things to do with my time than sit around here keepin' company wit' a stiff."

He turned away from the river and sat down on the twelve by twelve that ran along the edge of the dock. It was too low for him and he pulled his legs up toward his body, grunting, stretching the shiny blue-black of his uniform over his fat knees. His belly sagged against his thighs and he shifted again, straightening one leg and half turning. "He'll be stinkin' like a mackerel if he's left long in this sun. Them bastards on the wagon got the world by the tail. Jeez, what a racket!"

The other cop who was younger, a rookie, was thinking about the corpse. It was the first one he had seen except for the two or three times he had gone to a funeral. The papier-mâché features of the dead on those occasions had seemed natural enough, but there was something indecent about this thing lying on the planks.

"That must be a hell of a way to die," he said. "Out in the river like that."

The older cop grunted. "Nobody has figured out a good way to die yet," he said. "Anyway drowndin's the easiest way."

"Oh sure, drowndin's the easiest way," the other said. "Everybody knows that. What I mean, it's tough to kick off all alone like that, maybe at night, out in the middle of the river, an' then get pulled out by the Harbor cops and just tossed up on a dock like nobody ever give a damn. It's tough," he finished lamely, unable to say any of the things he was really feeling. It was as if he had something cold touching him in the warmth of his sex. "Nobody gives a damn," he said bitterly.

"I sure as hell don't," the fat cop said. He shifted again on the hard seat. "Mother of God, wouldn't I like a cup of coffee!"

"How'd it be if it was you?" the rookie asked. He was unaccountably furious with the other. "Suppose you's the one lyin' on the dock there? Suppose nobody give a damn about you? Suppose I was here and all I could think about was gettin' a cupa coffee? God damn it, it could be you too. Or me. You think the lieutenant would cry?"

"If you're dead it don't matter," the other cop said. "You're just cold meat. What the hell do you care what happens?" He shifted his gun and tried to find a comfortable position. "It's the soul that counts anyway," he said as an afterthought.

"Oh the soul!" the rookie said impatiently. He lit a cigarette and tossed the match into the water. He watched it float about, riding a slight smear of oil, until it disappeared in the dark under the pier. He tried to think of what horse he should be on. "You think they fished his soul out of the water too?" he asked almost involuntarily.

The older cop looked at him. He didn't like jokes like that. "The kind of monkey that gets dumped in the river don't have no soul," he said. After a moment: "Them harbor cops got it made. Nothin' to do but ride around in a launch."

"And fish stiffs out of the river."

"It's cool anyway," the fat cop grumbled. The sun was hot on the uniform. He loosened his collar and squirmed on his seat again.

"Who do you suppose he is?"

"How the hell would I know? You want to go through his pockets?"

"I guess so. And if they didn't I don't give a damn. I'm just sittin' here waitin' for the wagon so somebody doesn't come down and lug him off as a souvenir. What you got your bowels in an uproar about?"

"Oh... Nothin'." The younger man sat down near the other.

"Ugly lookin' bastard, ain't he?" asked the fat cop. He squinted at the corpse. "You look at his hands?"

"What about his hands?"

"Oh ... everything about a man tells a story," the fat cop said vaguely.

"What about his hands then?"

"Well, if he's got callouses that means he's a workin' man."

The young cop got up and went over to the corpse. He squatted on his heels and looked carefully at one of the hands. He didn't touch it.

"He's got green stuff around his fingernails, it looks like."

"I guess he's beginnin' to rot."

"There's some spots on his hands that look raw."

"That's the fish," the fat cop said. "They been eatin' on him. They like callouses."

"Is that a fact?"

"Believe it or not, I don't give a damn," the fat cop said sourly. He lost interest in the examination. After a while the rookie came back and sat down.

"I'm thirsty," he said. "I could use a glass of beer right now."

"If those bastards on the meat wagon ever show up we can get out of here. I don't see why they wanted both of us here anyway."

"You seen a lot of stiffs like this, I guess."

"Like him? Sure. Boy, the Depression, that was the time. Course there could be a few now too, the next week or so."

"Yeah? Why?"

"Strike," the fat cop said, spitting. "Bound to be trouble."

"They don't throw each other in the river."

"Some of 'em do. Look at this guy. Somebody put him in; he didn't jump."

"How do you know?"

"He's got a crack on the head, ain't he?" He pointed at a livid mark along the side of the corpse's head.

"He could of hit something when he jumped. Or in the water."

The fat cop spat. "Oh sure," he said. "He could of." He shifted the subject. "They last longer if they're O.K. when they go in," he said. "If they get shot or knifed first, that's bad. They don't last no time then. The water gets in, an' it rots 'em."

"They don't last very long anyway."

"On, no, they don't last long. They all rot after a while, give 'em a little time," the fat cop said, spitting, listening for the sound of the police ambulance.

10:30 P.M.

Kay's apartment was on Sixteenth Street, on the East Side. It was a quiet street even in the daytime, and there was no one at all on it now. The door was open down below and I climbed the first flight of stairs and went down the hall to her door. That was open too, because of the warm weather, I guess, and I went right on in. I could hear someone at the back, in the big studio room with the window over the garden. In the living room all the pictures were ones I hadn't seen before. The surrealist stuff was gone and there were lots of abstractions, big squares and rectangles of bright paint. This was the year for abstract art.

She was working in the studio. I just stood in the doorway and watched her.

She was a big girl with red hair and a square face that was a little like one of her abstractions. Under the light it was a collection of planes and angles, very cleanly designed. The cheekbones were high and left a little shadow in the hollows of her face. She had a perfect nose, the kind you don't see except on statues, and it was the nose that made her face exciting rather than plain. She was wearing shorts and her long legs were a deep tan. Moving among the canvases and the clutter of her work she looked a little clumsy, but it was just a brusqueness of movement that came from being sure of what she was going to do and doing it in a hurry.

I stood there for perhaps two minutes looking at her, feeling stupid, listening to my heart banging away under my shirt, feeling surer and surer that I shouldn't have come. Then I turned away. Standing in the dim hall and hearing the radios, the whisper of steps on the stairs above, the sound of people who had a home and lived in it and didn't think of anything else, I had a terrible lost feeling. I thought about us going West, and for a moment it seemed that it would be all right, I almost felt that it would, but I couldn't quite bring it off.

I remembered the kid I had seen in Paris, after we got in there. He had been in the cross-Channel jump and he had got hurt pretty bad, not shot up, but cracked up. He was staying with a French family I knew. All he would do was sit on the sofa and look straight in front of him.

A couple of his buddies got into town on leave one day and looked him up. I saw them in a little cafe in the afternoon. They had put maybe twelve glasses of Calvados on the table in front of the kid, and he was just staring straight ahead as if he had a window looking in on the bright and constant fires of hell itself. The others were a little drunk and trying to have a good time. Now and then a big staff sergeant would lean over and pat the kid on the shoulder.

"O.K., Junior," he would say. "Time to drink up."

The kid would reach out and drink one of the Calvados and go back to looking.

"Drink up, Junior." Again the mechanical reaching and drinking. It went on all afternoon, but it didn't faze the kid, and after his pals left he went back to sitting on the sofa again. When the time came for him to be sent to camp and then to the States, he got up and went to the door and turned and looked at the oldest daughter.

"Gee, Josie, I love you," the kid said, just as mechanically as drinking the Calvados. There wasn't anything he could do about it or her or anybody, and he went out of there still staring into his little window.

I was a lot better off than Junior. But standing there in the hall, I knew that really all I could say to Kay was: I love you. It had seemed like something to say, during the long years when, if you think of home, you think of the time you will get there, as if life were going to stand still for you after that, with no trouble with the landlord, the butcher, the baker, or the candlestick maker. It had seemed something important to say, but it didn't seem like anything now. I went back down the hall without speaking. It was nothing to say. And yet it is the big thing, the big thing to say, and maybe that was why I felt so cowardly, as if I were running away.

5:30 P.M.

The men have several large bottles of beer and are sitting on a dock below Fourteenth Street. It is a barge dock with no warehouse behind it. It is the afternoon and the sun is far to the west of the Jersey shore. The clumsy, humped-up barges are moored around with smoke coming out of the cabins. A few young boys are lying on the roof of one of them, now and again diving over the side into the oily river. It is dead calm. Behind them they can hear the occasional sound of a truck, and over and around it the hum of the city like a dynamo; but they have been drinking slowly and happily since noon and they are aware only of the warmth of the planks under them.

" 'S good to have a little vacation."

"When I's wukkin' in Mobile we tuk it easy like. Round noon that old sun is about to burn hole right through yuh. We tuk it easy then, lyin' in the shade some'eres. Man don't have to break his balls down there. You-all up heah go to wuk like it was fun."

"Why don't you stay there, then? Eff she'sa good, you damn fool come up here."

"Ah don't know. Mobile—'f you's to have plenty of that long green, 'f you's a white man with a plantation up the river and a gang of men to wuk it for yuh. 'F yawl had one of them places out along the bay, one them big house."

"Ah, balls," disgustedly: "if you shit rock candy, you'd make a fortune. If you had all that jack you wouldn't be in Mobile. That's for the crackers. If you had all that jack, know where you'd be? Right here, by Christ. You'd have one of them apartments up in London Terrace, and a nice little pussy to keep you warm in the winter if you didn't go down to Miami Beach or somewhere."

"I never been west of Joisey. I wouldn't mine see'n' Mobile or any other goddamn place."

"You don't know what you're talkin' about, brother. I was down there in the army. Not in Mobile, but I've been all over that goddamn South. I've seen Missouri. Three goddamn months. And Texas. I was stationed near San Antone once. They ought to give that goddamn state back to the Indians or the Mexes or whoever they got it from. Give it to the goddamn Texicans. I had a goddamn sergeant once, that son of a bitch, he was from Dallas. I should have shot that bastard. I wouldn't piss on the South if it was on fire."

"Sure, you can talk. But what the hell? A man likes to get around, don't he? When I was a kid I t'ought I'd make it. I t'ought I'd go all duh way out west. Montana, see? I t'ought I'd go to Butte and woik in duh mines. I got an uncle de'. Used to have. He got killed comin' east, fell off a boxcar in North Dakota som'eres. I never got out de'. Once I got up in duh country. Connecticut. I took my old lady up de' once, jees it must 'a' been nineteen-twenny-t'ree. We just been married. Dat's duh country, lemme tell you."

"Man, yawl never saw that country. Yawl nevah got out that bed."

"Ain't it duh trut'? And I never went back de'."

"Connecticut, she good state. Gooda for the farm'. Tabacci, pomodori—tomat'—alla kinds vegetables—"

"That goddamn Connecticut is full of goddamn long-nose Yankees that would steal the gold outa your teeth. When a smart Jew knows everything they send him up to that goddamn Connecticut to get a postgraduate course."

"New York's the town for a man."

"Ain't nothin' like the big town, man. Hand over that jug."

The jug goes around, the bottles are tilted, the sun catches a small cloud over Weehauken turning it to an improbable color. A small man with a wire-haired terrier at his heels and a bamboo pole in his hands comes along the dock and begins to fuss with his bait. After a few minutes he gets the hook baited and drops the line over the side. He wedges the end of the pole into a crack and sits back against a post and lights his pipe.

" 'F this heah's a strike, man, ah say let's have one evah damn month."

"Dat's what you say. Youse oughta hear my old lady when I says I ain't woikin'."

"It'sa gooda ting, take a break."

"Take a break, my ass. What's this goddamn strike gettin' us? No fuckin' where. It's a goddamn put-up job, that's what it is."

"Ah ain't nevah been in no strike until this'n."

"This is a goddamn circus. Strike? My fuckin' back."

"Strike or no strike, I don't woik when the boys is out."

"It'sa too early a see what come."

"Come? Nothin's gonna come. It's a goddamn joke, I tell you. Who called the goddamn strike? Nobody. Who's organizin' it? Everybody. Everybody takes off. O.K. What for? Who the hell knows? Look at this," he pulls a leaflet out of his pocket. *BROTHERS! DON'T ACCEPT THE PHONY CONTRACT.* "Brothers, don't accept the goddamn phony contract. You know who that is talkin'? That's the goddamn Reds, you fuckin' aye it is."

"Yawl think we should go back to work like that delegate say?"

"Fuck that delegate."

"I ain't scabbin' fuh duh old lady, I ain't scabbin' fuh no delegate."

"Thisa manifest' say don't accept contract?" He is looking at the paper upside down. "It'sa no gooda contract. That'sa right, no?"

"Sure that's right. But it don't take the goddamn Reds to tell me that. Now they want committees formed in the locals and on the jobs. Who's gonna do that? You stick your neck out, you'll get hit with a bucket of shit."

"In the old country sometimes, thesa anarchist—"

"Dis ain't duh old country."

"Somebody she's got to trya make the organization."

"What yawl think gonna come outa this here strike?"

"Whatever'sa happen, we take a break."

"Jeez, I don' know what'll happen. I don't like to go back to woik until some'pins settled."

"Nothin's gonna come outa the goddamn strike. Nobody knows what the hell's goin' on. Kelly's sittin' around with his finger up his ass. The Reds can't organize nothin'. Nobody else is doin' a goddamn thing but fuckin' in bars and beatin' up the old woman. Nothin's gonna come of it. It's a goddam fuck-up, that's what it is. It's a—it's a goddamn *farce*. Stop talkin' like men with paper assholes, goddamn it, and gimme the goddamn bottle for Christ's sake."

11 P.M.

"On a Saddy night," Blackie had said. "That's the time to get back to the old neighborhood."

So. It was Saddy night and I was back. Blackie had got back three days ahead of me because of the snafu with my papers at the separation center, but there I was with a couple of months' pay in my pocket and not enough guts to go to see my own true love. I had been in a fight and been offered a job. I was a civilian all right.

I should have stayed with Kay. What was it that was eating at me? I didn't know. I just knew I couldn't see her then. Tomorrow I would see her. But what would be different about tomorrow? Tomorrow always comes around, the fateful letter is placed in the box, the axe falls, the pinions howl in the gearbox of the social process and the arm drags you up and into the hopper. Expect nothing but evil from time; time comes around with his trusty skinning-knife and the next morning your scalp hangs in somebody's wigwam. There was no reason to suppose things would be different for me tomorrow.

Blundering along Fourteenth Street as if I were a blind man, I kept on going over it like a man who wakes up at night and rubs an arm that has got cramped and fallen asleep. What was wrong? I had thought that I would come back and that Kay and I would go West. It had seemed simple enough; it was all I thought about during the last months in the army. Now, and for no reason, that long wish seemed as crazy as any dream on waking. The Kay of the dream was different from the real Kay. That shouldn't have been surprising. Still, after a wish as long as the war, it is hard to relearn the lesson of the world—that it is stronger than your wish and obeys laws of its own. But why run away? Why not work it out?

It seemed then that it was my problem alone, to be worked out in isolation. The body, which does not care about permanent solutions, tried to give me its own wisdom: it is solution enough to be in bed with her. Genital logic, midnight vision, valuable and valid for the horizontal plane, it was not answer enough, not when what you had taken for reality was suddenly shifting along fault lines that had never been suspected.

There is no good in thinking about problems which have, for the moment anyway, no solution. I found myself at Fourteenth and Sixth, Avenue of the Americas, and thought of going down to Bill's place. I could sleep there. But it was early and I was restless and I thought I would maybe try to see Blackie.

I didn't really know why I wanted to see him. We had been friends in the army, which is a way of saying not really friends at all, because in the army you are only half a man. Now I felt like the other half of the man, and I wasn't sure I liked it, but there was no reason for Blackie to be interested in my problems.

I remembered the last night on the ship. I came up on deck just after lights out. It was about eleven o'clock and there was almost a full moon. From the forbidden area forward I could look over the side and see the water curling away from the prow like lace. The side lights were silver on the dark water, and now and again there would be a tiny nest of phosphorescent stuff, off to the side, glowing underwater as if a handful of cigarette butts was sinking slowly, still lighted.

"Gimme a light, Mac," somebody said, and I put my cigarette over my shoulder without looking.

"Oh, it's you," he said, sucking on my live cigarette. It was Blackie. He got the end burning on it and gave mine back to me and stood and looked at the water, standing beside me.

"You wouldn't think that's all it was that was in the way of us," he said, looking down at the lace-making job that the prow was doing. I knew what he meant, the water.

"When I was a kid," he said, "I used to swim in the river. The Hudson. There's a dock just down from Fourteenth Street that's usually open and we used to go there. Sunday afternoons especially, in summer. Used to be guys down there paintin', sometimes dames. I used to go off that dock and down maybe fifteen feet. Easy that much. You could see the piles down there all green, darker the farther down you went, with barnacles on them. I was all over the area around that dock," he said, "and sometimes off one in the Village where the scows and barges tie up. I swam damn near over to Jersey sometimes. I figured I knew what it was like."

He spat over the side.

"It's funny when you think that that's all that was between us and the States," he said. "Just the stuff I swam in when I was a kid, only more of it."

"Quantity changes into quality," I said. I knew what he meant, but it was so simple-minded and so damn true that that was all I could think of saying, a phrase from a text on dialectics. I didn't even know the meaning of it, except for the usual textbook examples, but like a fool, I said it. He had heard me before and knew as much about it as I did.

"You aren't shittin', brother," he said fervently. And probably went on noodling away at the differences between the Hudson and the ocean of Columbus. One difference was the years, but he knew that without my having to tell it to him. We had been together most of the time, in the army. He was a good guy, from an Irish neighborhood on the West Side, always biting his nails to get back.

"You think they'll spring us the first day?" he asked. He always talked like someone on a special pass from Elmira Reform School.

"Probably not," I said. I had got over hoping that the army would ever move fast.

"Maybe we can get a pass." His voice sounded as if it were stroking someone.

"Take it easy," I said. "They'll let us go in a few days. You don't want to fuck up in your last week."

"A few days ain't soon enough," he said. "I got a hell of a lot of business to do once I get out."

I knew what he meant there too. Everybody had that kind of business.

"I got to make up for lost time," he said. "The rackets all ran away without me. I'm in debt because of this damn war. I got to work fast."

"Who the hell hasn't?" I asked. I didn't even listen to what he went on talking about. Maybe I had heard it before, and I was certainly to hear it again, but I didn't bother to listen. All he was doing was laying himself out and putting himself on the morgue slab. I was too busy to listen, too sure my own problems were more important.

"What you want, Joe?" he asked after a while.

"I want to be free," I said all in one breath. It's a mouth-filling thing to say and it requires a fool even to think it. I said it. It didn't sound like much, caught in the gears of progress, the noise of the ship, the whisper of the prow making lace out of the Atlantic water a thousand miles south of the Grand Banks, at midnight, in the first autumn after the war.

"On a Saddy night. That's the time I want to get back to the old neighborhood. You know MacNamara's on Fourteenth and Seventh?" he asked. "Biggest dime glass of beer in New York. If they keep us out there at the camp more than today, I like to get sprung Saddy night."

"Saturday night or any night is O.K. with me," I said.

"Saddy night's the best, though. Everybody takes off and unbuttons himself that night. Nothing to do Sunday except go to church and you can make the bum's mass at noon so you don't have to get up in the morning. Evenings when the weather's good everybody's on the street or sittin' on the steps beatin' their gums or rushin' the growler from the bar down at the corner. The babes is hangin' around the candy stores just waitin' to get picked up. All the windows is open and the old man's got his feet stuck up on the sill and a can of beer in his hand readin' the Sunday paper already. If you got an old man," he said.

"Yeah, it's a good time." I knew what Saturday nights were like on the West Side. "And the kids are knocking off stuff from apartments where people have gone away, the younger ones are having a gang party with some little bag down in the basement, and over on Ninth Avenue a couple of drunks are trying to cut each others' heads off with longshoremen's hooks. A hell of a fine time."

"What the hell, that's the way it is. You don't have to get hit with no hook if you're smart. Just about now," he sighed—it was about midnight then—"the guys are coming out of the Legion club or the VFW on Twenty-third Street. That's where they meet now till they get some rooms of their own. They got a keg of beer up there and they just about got it finished now. You goin' to join one of them vets organizations, Joe?"

"I hadn't thought about it."

"I think I'll join both of them. Might as well. They can be a big help if you got something you want to get straightened out."

"What are you going to do? When you're not drinking beer at the Legion or VFW?"

"I got a dock coming to me," he said. "I got to get that worked out right away."

I knew what he meant, but I wasn't sure he was serious. I had worked on the docks myself a little while, trying to help put together a rank-and-file outfit that would dump out the phony leadership of the union. If you have a dock it means that you have a hand in all the rackets that go on in connection with it, the loading racket, which amounts to a tax on all goods trucked from the dock, the plain thievery of goods, a cut from the gambling, a cut from the shylocks as they call the money-lenders, maybe a piece of change from kickbacks if you are running a dock where the longshoremen have to pay a tithe in order to work steady.

"Somebody willed it to you?" I still wasn't sure that he was serious. He had talked about the rackets before, but in the army half of the guys from New York or Chicago got their kicks out of shooting the breeze about the tough bunch they were with before they got in.

"My old man," he said, and I knew he was serious.

I took a look at him again. It was maybe the only time since I had known him that I really did look at him. We had been together a lot, and were good friends as friends go in the army. Such friendships are always formed by chance, and since you are as likely to roll craps as a seven, about the most you can hope for is that the guy doesn't have lice. You may get close to somebody in the army, but it is always only half of him and half of you, the half that is in the army, that makes friends. Maybe you think you know someone down to the ground, and then one day he says something and you see that all you have been looking at is a cardboard outline and that there is something with some depth behind it after all. It is easy to make a kind of friendship out of common experience, especially if the experience is acquired under pressure. But then, when you have moved on, you remember the guy, or you have a letter, or you see him, and you wonder what has happened. Somebody is not around and you think it is the other fellow, a shape has gone away now and you are left with a stranger. But sometimes it is you that have gone away.

So I took a second look at Blackie. He wasn't big; his eyebrows were a fierce John L. Lewis black and they overhung his eyes like ferns on a cliff. The eyes themselves, although I couldn't see them that night, I knew to be as blue and guileless as a couple of unshot marbles. He didn't look tough at all. He had plenty of nerve, but he didn't seem tough.

"Your father left you a dock?" I asked.

"Sort of."

"I don't know that they had got around to legalizing it that way."

"My old man sort of helped run a dock," he said. "He didn't make nothin' 'cause he just got in on it when I went into the army and then he died right away."

"In bed?"

"Sure in bed, for Christ sake."

"So you think you got something coming. How are the boys on the dock going to feel about it?"

"I don't care fuck-all about that." He stuck his pack of cigarettes toward me and I lit them for us.

"I figure it's mine by right," he said. "My old man worked on that dock a long time. First just as a longshoreman. He never made a dime for years, he was too honest. Then just when he got smart he kicked off."

He stopped talking and waited for me to say something but I wasn't going to say it. He knew how I felt about the whole business of the docks, and I wasn't going to give him my personal absolution just because we had been buddies. The prow went on with its lace-making operation and the wind strummed through the rigging behind us.

"I got a right, goddamn it, Joe," he said a little fiercely. "Look, I got one brother older than me. He's a bum. He never would have been more than a wino except he got scared the army would get him, so he went down to the docks but he was just a damn chenango. Now that the war's over he's a gypsy trucker, but he'll be gassed up and flat on his back most of the time. I got the old lady at home and a kid sister and an older sister that lives in Philly whose husband is no damn good either. I got to make a break, goddamn it."

I didn't say anything to that either and after a while he said: "I wasn't askin' you to come in with me, for Christ sake. We don't have to fight about this. Even if you go back to them Reds on the docks they ain't going to change anything. They tried now since Christ knows when. They might do good if they ever dumped Kelly and they might not, but they'll never get a chance. We don't have to fight about it even if we don't see it the same way."

So I knew we were still friends, maybe even better friends than I had thought.

"Anyway," I said, "I hope you don't get knocked off. A lot of money went over those docks during the war. There must be a pretty rough mob milking down the dock you want. You don't want to wind up diving off that dock you used to swim from when you were a kid. With your feet stuck in a barrel of concrete maybe."

"You're the one that needs to worry about that," he said.

"Not me. I'm not sticking around."

"No? Where you going?"

"West."

"You got something on out there?"

"I just want to sit in the sun."

"I never travelled around much. Except down south after I went in the army."

"Come along out. Now that you've seen Europe, what there is left of it, you ought to take a look at the old country."

"I'd like to," he said. "But then what about my old lady and the kid?"

"O.K."

"You going back to them Reds?" he asked after a moment.

"I don't have to go back to them," I said. "I am one."

"Here in New York, I mean."

"I don't like New York. It's just another foreign country." But I couldn't have said precisely what I intended going West for. Thinking about being out of the army made me restless.

"Maybe it is a foreign country," he said. "I always figured Hoboken was the West Coast, myself. But if we get out on a Saddy night, boy, I'll show you how to get around."

Now it was Saturday night and Fourteenth Street. MacNamara's ("Biggest dime glass of beer in New York") reached out and took my hand. It was a little like the pubs we saw in Ireland where the only important thing about them were the bottles of Guinness and Jameson's or Paddy's or Bushmill's stacked up behind the bar. It was dark and ugly and the tables were dirty and there was an air about it that was as gloomy as the great Slavic soul. It was the kind of place where you would get drunk on the run unless you were an old timer or a West Sider who had been weaned in a bar like that. It was the kind of place into which you might figure you could throw a dozen hand grenades without hitting anyone who was worth saving. Right in the middle of it was Blackie.

He was talking to one of the bartenders, a guy who had an Italian accent. I put my dime on the bar and waited for the biggest glass of beer in New York. It came and it was.

Blackie was a little guy, and aside from the jet hair and the eyebrows like black brambles in a basement window box, the only thing remarkable about him was the feeling of energy he generated. He couldn't even sit down without making it seem a powerfully important act. When he was sitting you got the feeling you were looking at some potent machine that had just had a momentary power failure. It gave you a funny feeling to watch him that way. He had rounded cheekbones with whiskers on them, like black moss on doorknobs. They made him sore, but he never shaved them off.

He was busy in conversation now, and he gave off a little purr of unused energy, like a dynamo that is running at low speed. I hoisted the biggest glass of beer in New York and decided that it was also probably the worst. The radio was playing something: *Da-da-da, dah, love me forever* and then faltering in the mumble of MacNamara's guests. *Love me forever, love me forever* the radio pleaded as a big longshoreman with the hook still in his belt, and half of MacNamara's current supply of bug-juice under it, bumbled over to Blackie, walking as carefully as if he were wearing snowshoes, and said something.

Blackie broke off his talk with the Italian bartender and turned to look at the man. That was all. He just looked. The snow began to melt from under the longshoreman and he took a big breath and went on to one of the tables at the back of the bar. The big guy had just seen something in Blackie that I had never noticed. I looked at Blackie again, and he looked bigger. Maybe that was it. He had a way of looking bigger than he was. It was a convenient trick to have.

"Blackie," I called, right in the middle of *love me forever*, "the beer is lousy."

"It sure as hell is, chum," he said, turning to me as if he knew I had been there all the time. "What you want to do about it?"

"We could get out of here."

"That's the simplest thing." So we got out of there.

We stood on the corner of Fourteenth Street and Seventh Avenue and watched the subway entrance tossing them out on the night like an automatic kicking out used cartridge cases.

"Now I want a drink," Blackie said. We stood on the corner and looked around. South, at the entrance to Stewarts' cafeteria, some of the Greenwich Village Bohemians, like the last remnants of the G.A.R., were having a hot discussion. The little Negro was on the corner selling the *Daily Worker* just as he had been the last time I had been on that corner over three years before.

"There's a bar across there," I said. "The Spanish one. It used to be pretty good."

We crossed over and I bought a paper and we went in. It wasn't the same place. It had been a little dark corner, cool, quieter than any neighborhood bar, where the Spanish people in the neighborhood used to come in the evenings and drink vermouth with soda and ice. They were drinking blended whiskey now and the place wasn't dark and quiet anymore. Someone had talked the owner into a decorating job and hung the walls with fluorescent lamps. They gave off a queer green light that made you feel that the place was drowned in green sea. Then your eyes got used to it, and the light hardened, and looking at the faces around you, you saw that each wore a corpse-like pallor and the place didn't remind you of the sea floor any longer but of a morgue.

"Scotch?" Blackie asked.

"Better make it beer," I told him. "We're unemployed now."

"It's on me. I ain't unemployed."

"But I am." So he ordered Scotch for himself and beer for me.

The *Worker* was full of the strike, or what had happened at one dock or another, rumors of back-to-work attempts, the calls of nebulous rank-and-file committees of this local or that. There was an editorial on why the strike should be supported, on why the strikers should not accept the phony contract that Kelly wanted to sign—had, in fact, signed already. It was the only thing that made sense. From reading the stories it was plain that the writers were as balled up about what was happening as Riverboat Conn had been.

"You're go'n' to give me a bad reputation flashin' that Commie newspaper around," Blackie said, laughing.

"We're even, then. If you're going to be king of the rackets on the West Side, it won't do me much good to be seen going around with you."

"Crap, Joe. There's plenty of respectable people got their hands in there. I can name you two politicians right on my own street."

"Sure you can. They're respectable enough. But they're still sons of bitches."

"A guy don't have to be a son of a bitch."

"It grows on you when you get into that kind of business. If you aren't a dead son of a bitch first."

"We'll all be dead sometime," he said, shrugging, turning his glass around in his hand.

"You don't have to offer a bounty for your own scalp though."

He put his glass out and rapped it on the bar.

"You want another drink?" His voice was cold and careful. "You missed your calling, Joe. You ought to of been a chaplain."

"Have it your way, then," I said, and went back to reading the paper. I was a little sore myself.

He finished the drink and put the glass down in front of him.

"Look," he said. I looked. He was drumming with his fingers on the bar and his eyes, under the overhang of black hair, were as sick and unhappy as those of a whipped dog. Something touched me like a cold wind, and it wasn't just amazement that he should have been hurt at what I had said. On the barstool he looked even smaller than he was.

"Look," he said again, "I'm not goin' into this for fun, see? I'm goin' after something that's comin' to me, sure. I got a right to something. But goddamn it you don't have to figure I'm just a damn crook. I ain't a goddamn shylock. I ain't puttin' the squeeze on some poor old bastard with a candy store—"

"Hell, Blackie, I didn't say that."

"I ain't a prick," he said as if he hadn't heard me. "You think I'm just a punk out to hustle a fast buck. Maybe I am. I don't know. Look, suppose I go down on the dock or get a job pushin' a truck—what's it get me? The money's good now, sure, but how long's it last? There's always too many men for the jobs and then they start the kick-back so that you have to pay to work, or the bottom falls out of everything so you only get one or two days a week. I know what that's like. My old man had it for forty years. Where the hell do you come out? You can work fifty years and you're still in one of them fleabag flats down there, with four or five kids growin' up like little hoods on the street and your wife gettin' to be more of a bitch every day and you spendin' what you can afford and maybe a little more down at

Duane's bar or down at the Hudson Tavern or some other gin mill, keepin' loaded up 'cause you don't have the guts to turn on the gas and do a job on your whole family. I'm in a goddamn trap, Joe," he said in a tight voice. "I'm in a trap that's forty, fifty years long and there's nothin' in it but work and misery and never havin' a goddamn thing you want either for yourself or your old lady or the dame you get married to or your kids. It's a goddamn trap, I'm tellin' you, and the only way out is like breakin' out of the pen. Jesus Christ, I shouldn't have to tell you how it is."

"Look, Blackie," I said as gently as I could, "I know what it's like; a little bit anyway. I don't have a family, the way you have, so it's easier for me. I can change around when I want to—go somewhere else, take another job. I know what it's like, but I don't think you've got the right answer—"

"All right, what is the answer, then? Workers of the world unite? Where does that get me? Look, I'm not the kind of guy that reads *Time* or the *Journal-American* and feels like an old woman readin' a goddamn parish letter. Your racket makes sense—if you could swing it. Sure, if you guys could make something out of this strike, ever, it might help. If you could knock off all the rich guys and give everybody a square shake of the dice it'd be O.K. But how fuckin' long is it goin' to take you? How long are you goin' to be bangin' your head against a wall before you find a soft spot? Sure, you got an idea. But that's for the world, that's for everybody, but what about me? I'm just one guy, Black Carmody, and I got only one life to live, and I'm twenty-three years old now. I give four and a half years to the government. Now they give me fifty years' work on the dock and if I keep up the insurance I got enough to bury me. I want to live *now*. I don't give a damn about the next generation. They got to fight their own battles, see? All I want is a decent life. I only got one. There's only one way to get the money that I can see. You got any better ideas?"

"I don't know, Blackie. You'd be a good man to have on my side. You could do a lot in this strike, since you know the waterfront."

"And then? Suppose Kelly was dumped. Suppose I got in on something, head of a local, maybe? Then there's just two things. If I become a piecard, that's worse than being a crook, isn't it? Robbin' your own people? So then you have to fight *me*, don't you? Or suppose I stay honest? There's nothin' in that. Then I'm damn near as poor as if I was just sweatin' on the dock, and I work my balls off and take my chances. Right?"

"For Christ's sake, there's a little pleasure in doing what you think is right, what you want to do."

"I got no time to think of what I want to do. All I can think about is what I'm able to do. No, it just won't work, Joe. That's why I got to try the other way. Now have another drink and we'll go up and see my old lady and my kid sister. And stop tryin' to show me the way to God, you damn atheist bastard."

So we had another shot of the blessed sacrament, the stuff that keeps the world turning so smoothly, giving off light which it would be possible to see if one lived on another star.

9 P.M.

"The trouble with the labor unions today is that they don't have any leaders," Alton Husk said.

They had just finished having dinner and were smoking and drinking coffee. Kelly turned his cigarette over in his fingers, looking at it. It was wet an inch from the end, and fibers of tobacco were stringing out from it. He put it in the ashtray with disgust but did not answer. Husk was looking at him keenly through the smoke, wondering if he had provoked him. They had both drunk a lot.

"You're right," Kelly said. "There haven't been any labor leaders since Gompers. And he was no damn good either," he added, pleased with the epigram.

"Gompers started the whole thing," Husk said. "Without Gompers—"

"No, you're wrong, Al. I'm wrong. Gompers was all right. In those days a labor leader was somebody. He got more respect from the men. It was different then, Al—hell, I remember how it was myself. The men were different in those days somehow—" His voice had got soft and sentimental; the twist at the corner of the mouth was more pronounced.

"Working men never change," Husk said. "A belly and a pair of balls, that's all any of them are."

"I wouldn't say that too loud," Kelly said, chuckling. "It might get around."

"Do you think it'd matter? Working men have allowed themselves to be shit on for so long they've got to like it."

"In my day it was a little different, Al. Sure I know you get a little sore at the boys you got to work with now. Especially the young ones, by God. None of 'em want to work, all they can think about is more wages. Christ, it'd piss a saint to hear them. No, tell you what, it was different when I was working down there. You did a decent day's work and you got your pay for it and that was that. None of this crying all the time, no phony rank-and-file movements, none of these damn Reds."

He stopped talking and drifted into a reverie of the time of his youth.

When he was just a boy, when he had taken his old man's lunch down to him, if he were on a dock a long way off. Then perhaps he would cut school, and go fishing, or swimming off that dock in the upper village. *With Owney and Big-Eye Minola, the guy that got killed in the first war.*

"They're all bastard sons of Gompers," Husk was saying. "All of them right in the middle, between the boss and the workers, and all they really want is their jobs, their expense accounts, their cars, and their women. They don't even want the power they have. They're afraid of it. But, by God, they've got it and if they don't use it somebody certainly will."

Big-Eye Minola was the one that broke him in, and with Minola's own sister at that. *Sure, go ahead, take a crack at it, she don't care.* And after that they went over to Owney's place and his old man was lit like a firecracker and they had swiped his whiskey.

"The real power is with the workers," Husk said. "It's a fact. The Commies are right about it. The thing is how to use it?"

"You know were the greenest grass was in those days?" Kelly asked as if talking to himself. "It was right down by the Gowanus canal. What do you think of that? Right down at that stinking crick." He began to talk of his youth in a gentle marvelling voice as if he were speaking of the deeds of a young son.

Husk looked out the window. There was almost no traffic now. People were going by on their way to the movies or down to the bars. The street looked gray and ugly to him, a coffin with the ends knocked out, and he had a sudden vision of the people in it: swarms of lepers holding out their rotting hands for money; epileptics caught in their fierce unhealthy trances; jakelegs and paralytics twitching their way along, their heads screwed to one side, tongues hanging out, eyes rolling crazily; corpses with their throats cut from ear to ear, still bleeding, crawling in the gutters; packs of ravenous wild dogs with ribs punching out through the hair; over them all in the sulfurous air were great dung-dropping harpies, shapeless as dreams, and down the street, drowning them all, kneading them up into its slime, was a vast river of corruption and filth.

"I guess you don't see it like that," Kelly was saying a little apologetically. "But that's the way I see the street. The way it used to be in the old days on a Saturday night, days when there wasn't any movies and people sat out on the front and talked. Oh, they still do, but it's not so friendly. It's always fuck-your-buddy-week out there now. But, Jesus, it used to be O.K."

"Look," Husk said. "I'm trying to tell you something for your own good. Things won't go on this way forever. The war's over. We've got the biggest damned industrial plant that a country ever had and that's going to mean a problem, next year or ten years from now. First they'll snatch up the markets, but that won't last forever either. Sooner or later the thing will backfire on them. There'll be a smash-up, a depression, and then it's going to be a case of who's quick on the draw."

"I don't quite get you, Al."

"We've got about fifteen million organized workers in this country and God knows how many more that can be organized. And we've got a bunch of leaders that are still trying to play things the Gompers way, playing it from the middle, between the workers and the boss, getting the contracts."

"Hell, there's nothing wrong with our contract."

"I'm not saying there is, but the guys on strike think there is. Look, the business of getting a contract means this: that the labor leader has got to placate the workers without irritating the boss. Somebody has got to get screwed. Now the labor leader doesn't want any trouble. He wants to get a good enough contract to take care of the workers, yes. But he doesn't want to fight the boss too hard. He's willing to have a strike now and then—not a very big one if he can help it. He doesn't want a big strike because every time there is one, it riles things up down below, and where he only had a dozen soreheads in his local, now he's got a hundred. No, he doesn't like strikes any more than the boss does. The only real supporters of capitalism today are the little businessmen and the big labor leaders."

"I guess I don't follow you," Kelly said uneasily. "That kind of talk—" He was tempted to say that it sounded Communist but he hesitated, unhappily feeling his breast pocket where he had kept his cigars.

"I mean this: the big boys are just about through with this kind of system. Maybe this year, or next, or ten years from now when it breaks down, they'll have a fight on their hands to save their factories. When that time comes—look out. The working men may be sheep, but they can turn nasty overnight—the way they did with this strike. Then your simpleminded labor leader of today is either going to have to become a revolutionary or—out."

"I don't think so," Kelly said definitely. "I can't see that happening at all, Al. There's no reason why a depression should come again anyway."

"I'm just telling you what the big shots think."

"Well. Hell—I don't know."

"Now when this comes what'll be the most important thing of all? Not a big army or navy. Not owning a whole Washington-full of crooked politicians. No. The important thing will be who has the working man. If the Reds get him, that finishes it."

"So?"

"So the thing is to have him yourself."

"Well, we've got the union."

"I don't mean just one union, I mean all of them, or a lot of them anyway. And I don't mean the way we have them now, when they'd all drop out tomorrow if they could get work without their book. I mean have them in the hollow of your hand, so when you say jump they jump. There's only one way to get them that way."

"How?"

"Put on a battle for them. Throw the contract back. Haul them out on strike and get a decent raise for them. Now, hold on. I know we've got certain agreements of our own with the companies. All right. We can work that out with them. Maybe we have to squeeze them a little—"

"Then you're doing just what you said happens in a strike. You start out with ten Reds and wind up with a hundred."

"Not if you have the right leadership. If you leave it so that they *force* you to fight, that breeds it. But if you take them in hand, gently and paternally, you'll be able to turn it on and off as you like. And then, when the big crack-up comes, you have an instrument. Then you'll just about be Jesus Christ."

"But then they'll make you do just the things you don't want to. Socialism—" Kelly said, gesturing vaguely.

"No. The working man is the one who has the power—if he's organized right. Otherwise he's just a zero. All he wants is some food in his guts and a lay on Saturday night. Hell, we'll give him that. But we'll keep his hand off the switches. Damn it anyway, all I'm saying is that it'll be one kind of man who leads them or the other. But those who are in the middle, the labor leaders we have today, they'll be gone."

"And you want to start with my union?"

"You have to start someplace."

"I don't know that I want to start at all," Kelly said, laughing. "Anyway, I'm too old." When he said the words, he felt his heart jump like an animal inside him.

It was a month earlier. He was in bed in the apartment he had rented for Eve. Eve was a little drunk. It always upset him when she was like that, hurt him, as if she were his daughter rather than his mistress. He had got undressed quickly and into bed and had been dozing a little when she came in to him and turned out the light.

He heard her get into bed with a little sigh, felt her beside him, and was just about to say goodnight when he felt her hand seeking him.

He had tried to pretend to be asleep, but she kept clutching him, whispering at first, then panting and sobbing. *Pat! Pat! Please, Pat! I must! Please! I've got to*, fighting and clawing him and crying, and there was nothing he could do, nothing at all except try to soothe her with the clumsy tenderness of a man who is worn out, old and bitter. That was the last time he had seen Eve.

"It's the kind of set-up the industrialists will want later on," Husk said. "In fact—"

"I'm too old," Kelly said.

There was an extraordinary sadness in his voice that made Husk look at him as if he were a stranger. It was the face of a college professor, he thought, except for the twist at the mouth. The eyes looked weak behind the steel-rimmed glasses.

"It's just an idea," Husk said.

"It sounds a little bit nuts, but you're a brainy lad."

"Sure," Husk said. He suddenly felt for Kelly a boundless contempt and hatred. He gave him a quick surreptitious glance. Yes; why had he never noticed before the weakness of Kelly's eyes? All that talk about the good old days, Husk thought, all those lies; I should have known what that meant. Husk himself felt momentarily lightheaded, powerful.

Kelly began to talk about his youth again.

"You know," he said. "There was a drink they used to have then, the rich did. It was called black velvet. Ever drink it? You can't get it now, I suppose. Champagne and stout. Should have Guinness by right, I guess. The swells used to drink it. Jesus, the cutaway coats, the women—"

They sat drinking while Kelly talked about the good days of his youth.

11:30 P.M.

We were on Eighth Avenue, heading uptown.

"You might as well come by and see my old lady," Blackie said. "I told her about you. *And* my sister. She's a cute little kid."

"It's pretty late."

"It's Saddy night, for Christ sake. Nobody hits the sack before midnight."

"It's O.K. with me. I'm not going anyplace."

"You see your babe?"

"Yes."

"Everything jake?"

"I was restless, that's all," I lied. I didn't want to talk about it.

"Jesus, yes. The women don't let you alone," he said.

I passed that.

It had rained a little while we were in the bar, just a little whisk of water over the streets, but they smelled clean. At the corner of Fifteenth, a queer was arguing with a gob. We went past them, and in a minute two navy guys came running past us looking scared. Behind us on the pavement was the queer. He had blood on his mouth now, and the same undecided look on his fat face.

"Jesus," Blackie said, looking after the running sailors, "they get younger all the time. I feel like an old man when I see the kids they reached out for the last year."

I didn't answer him. He looked after the running sailors, the men of the future, going away from us as fast as they could.

In a few blocks we turned off and a few numbers down we came to his house. It was like most of the others on his block, six stories high and about twice as wide as you could reach. The landlady, or what I took to be the landlady, was leaning out of the first-floor window with her arms on a pillow, talking to somebody on the street. She gave us the kind of look that stripped the clothes off us, and then the flesh, and after she had classified our skeletons and saw who we were, nodded to Blackie and turned back to the woman with whom she was talking.

The first floor was paved with cheap linoleum meant to suggest marble. It smelled of bacon, cabbage, incense, and camel dung. On the second floor the odor changed to owls' eyes steeped in cauliflower sperm. It was just like the house I lived in. We went on climbing the olfactory ladder until we got to Blackie's floor and the smell of a bankruptcy in the seventh month. Blackie had a key to a door and we went in.

We were in the kitchen. You could tell by the scurrying of the cockroaches, even if you had been in the dark. There was a coal stove that had been fitted up with gas jets, an icebox and a cupboard. Under the worktable was the bathtub. It stood up high, as if it were on stilts. Taking a bath in it would be like swimming in a small-town watertower. That was like the apartment I had had too.

From the kitchen, the rooms were strung out in a straight line, a railroad apartment, the kind you could look through from one end to the other. We went on back through two bedrooms to the living room on the front of the house. There was only one light on and the room was dim. There was a woman there and a man and a young girl.

The woman was big and dark-haired. She looked as if at one time she might have been fat, but she was thin and weak-looking now. She was stretched out on the davenport against one wall. In the big chair behind the kerosene stove was the man. He was of medium height, I would have guessed. He had perfectly white hair and a thin long nose. Scandinavian, probably—he looked like a man who had retired from life at the age of twenty-five and had never regretted it. He looked as if he might not get up out of the chair. He was the kind of man whose deliberation suggested that each move was his last. All I caught was the complete neuter quality of him.

The girl would have to be the sister. She was maybe twelve, thirteen, possibly fourteen, and she was in the regulation uniform: sweater, short skirt and bobby sox. She had the same black hair as her brother, but it was managed better. It lay along the side of her head like a crow's wing. The eyebrows were arranged like an expensive hedge, but they were very black, and under them the eyes were like a couple of inkwells. She was just a kid yet, but she was going to be a beauty.

"Hello, Francis," the woman breathed from the davenport. "And I'm glad to see your friend." She didn't make a move to raise her head. I got the feeling that she was not very strong.

The man didn't say anything. He gave us a slow impersonal look, as if there were nothing about us that would surprise or please him. It surprised me. It was the look of a man who didn't need anything or anybody, and there are not very many like that.

The girl was more interested. "Hubba-hubba," she said. "The army is back."

She was looking at Blackie, but she was speaking to me. When she looked at me, I began to feel old, naked and alone. She looked at me with the eyebrows hoisted like signal flags and a hooker's smile on her face. All the kids were doing it that way now. Under the sweater her breasts were like a couple of brand-new baseballs.

"Hello, soldier," she said, putting her hand out to me. It was a hot little hand. I was glad to have to shake hands with Mrs. Carmody.

"Blackie wrote me about you," she said. "Are you really a Red?" She looked at me with wonder in her eyes, as if I should have two heads. It was a funny way to begin a conversation.

"Lay off Joe, now, Ma," Blackie said. "I didn't bring him up here for a sermon." He turned to me. "I'm puttin' Ma in a convent next week," he said affectionately. "She's gettin' too good for this world."

It seemed to be a standard joke and it pleased Mrs. Carmody immensely. She uttered a ripe fruity laugh that had just a shade of bawdy in it.

"I guess I could teach the Sisters a thing or two," she said vigorously. And then: "What a thing to say." She lay back with a sigh. It was as if there were something in her that was very alive and which she was trying to discipline, and as if the outcome of it all were only a form of fatigue.

"I'm an old woman," she said, with a certain amount of satisfaction. "And there's just a few things I want anymore."

"If beer is one of them," Blackie said, "I'll see if I can do something about it." He went over and put his head out of the window. "Store's still open."

"One of them is *not* a can of beer," his mother said. "One of them is you, Francis. Once I see you settled down, with a good job and a wife, I'll be satisfied." There was no tiredness about her when she said that. Whatever the other things were that she wanted, she wanted this one about as hard as anyone could want anything.

"I'll settle for the beer right now," Blackie said. "And when I make my first hundred gees I'll marry a chorus girl and make you a grandmother. That fair enough?"

"I'm not joking, Francis."

"Neither am I, Ma," Blackie said.

There was a brief strained silence. Then Mrs. Carmody sighed and waved her hand. "You'd better get your beer, if you want it. Harounian will be closing the store."

Blackie went out of the apartment, and after a moment the girl said: "I'm going down to see Hope, Ma. O.K.?"

"All right, Mary."

"Her mother's out. Do you think I could stay with her? Overnight, I mean."

"What for?"

"Oh, just for fun. She don't want to be alone."

"I suppose you can."

"Good night then. Good night, Mr. Manta," she said to the silent man. And to me: "I'll see you around, big boy."

"Sure," I said, and she gave me the regulation over-all look which she had learned from the movies and went out.

Mrs. Carmody laughed. "Mary is anxious to grow up," she said. "She's practicing." Then she sighed. "It's Francis I'm worried about. You know what crazy ideas he has, Joe?"

I nodded.

"His father was just like that," she said tiredly, "but I kept him in line. Pretty well, anyway. You try to talk some sense into him, Joe."

"I've been trying, but it doesn't seem to help."

"All I want is to have him settled," she said fiercely. "That's not too much is it?" There was an undercurrent of agony, almost of hysteria, in her voice, that shocked me.

"I guess not," I mumbled. What the hell could I say?

"Nobody can run somebody else's life," Manta said. It was the first time he had spoken. Sitting back beyond the oil stove in the shadow he looked gray and insubstantial. His hands, lying in his lap, were perfectly still, as if they didn't belong to him at all. "You can't do anything for anyone," he said in the flat, serene voice of a man who is defeated and no longer cares.

I suddenly got the feeling that it was this complete passivity in him that Mrs. Carmody valued. Valued is the wrong word though. It was as if she had a hunger for it but couldn't reach it, couldn't put her hand on it.

She gave a curious baffled little laugh. "I don't want to run his life, John," she said. "I just want to see that he's got a life to run for himself." Then the other thing in her, whatever it was, the part that was alive, that was responsible, maybe, for the surprising touch of bawdry in her laughter at Blackie's joke about the convent, this thing that wouldn't lie down and which seemed to be disciplined only into fatigue, refused to allow the compromise.

"I'm going to get him a job," she said a little grimly. "If it's the last thing I do, I'll do that. I've asked Father Burke about it. You wouldn't have me let him run wild, would you now, John?"

But John just sat there with his hands folded like a second-hand Buddha. He gave the impression that it would all come to the same thing anyway, whether she did anything or not. She gave him that long hungering baffled look again and turned abruptly to me.

"You shouldn't be giving up your religion," she said, chiding me gently, and in that jump from her contemplation of Manta to the importance of the church, I knew what she saw in him. He had what she wanted and what she probably thought she could get through religion, that same kind of peace that came from giving up. But she couldn't give up, not yet. Blackie was the cross she had to carry for a while, and inside her somewhere was that blind vitality you could hear sometimes in her laugh. That was the source of her feeling for Blackie. It was something that was there before religion, and it was stronger. I didn't wonder that she was tired. She was a battlefield.

"I knew a man once," John Manta said in his quiet dead voice. "He got shot pretty bad. His friends had to take him a couple of hundred miles to a doctor. They drove all night. In those days they didn't have the kind of cars they have now. Part of the time he was out of his head. When he was like that, he just talked of two things, a man he wanted to kill who was one of the men in the car, and the women he had had. That was all right, except for the man he wanted to kill. They were suppoed to be good friends. But that was all right."

He paused as if he were thinking about it and then went on: "When he was conscious all he could talk about was the priest. He kept wanting them to stop and find a priest. Then he would go out of his mind again and he would want to kill this other man or he would think he was with some woman. Then he would come to again and pray. They couldn't stop for a priest. They had to get him to a doctor. After a while he knew he wasn't going to have a priest and that he wouldn't get to the doctor in time. He stopped talking then, but he gave his watch to the man he had wanted to kill when he was out of his mind."

He stopped and sat there, quiet and expressionless, in the shadow of the stove, as if he had not spoken at all. Mrs. Carmody didn't say anything. She was looking at the ceiling as if she hadn't heard. Christ, what a pretty story, I thought. You don't just "get shot." And if you have to go two hundred miles to a doctor, it must be because you don't dare stop along the way. And who was the man in the car, the one the wounded man gave his watch to? What was it suppoed to prove?

Like an echo of my thought, Manta said, "It proves that the things you don't know about are the things you want most."

Did it? But the wounded man had given the other his watch at the last. It wasn't the conclusion that I had expected Manta to draw. There was another possible moral in the story: that it is only after giving up all thought of being saved that you can achieve an act of goodness. That would have fitted Manta's book, I thought; it belonged with the attitude of serene defeat that emanated from him.

"When I was a girl, now," Mrs. Carmody was saying, as if she had not heard Manta at all, "I didn't think any more of going to church than you do. It was a habit entirely. When you're young you don't know anything, and when you're old you can't do anything. Ah, I was a hellion when I was young, I tell you." Again I heard that rich laughter with the touch of the bawdy in it bubbling inside her. "It used to take two priests to hear my confessions in those days. That's the way young people are though." She sighed again. "I'm an old woman now," she said, as if to convince herself that she wouldn't have to go through the agony of the flesh again. And then, almost irrelevantly: "I used to think maybe Francis would be a priest."

That was part of it, then. Once they have had the idea of a son, no matter how ridiculous it may have been in the light of the years, there is something special about him.

"If he goes on like this he'll get into trouble," she said. "If I can get him a decent job he'll be all right. Make him take it, Joe, you're his friend."

"Sure," I said. "I'll do all I can." It was all I could say.

"Do you believe God exists, John?" she asked, turning her face to Manta.

"Yes," he said. "But he doesn't care about any of us."

"What's all this about a job?" Blackie asked, coming in with the beer.

"I'm trying to get one fixed up for you," Mrs. Carmody said. She sounded as if she were sorry to have to talk about it.

"It's out," Blackie said. He handed me a bottle of beer and reached one across to Manta. "I'll get my own job," he said, lifting his bottle and drinking.

"If I get this one for you you'll take it."

He looked at her and I could see that he was angry. He was a little drunk too, and I waited for him to say what he was thinking, but he didn't.

"Hell," he said. "Anything to oblige. Just so it pays about three hundred a week. No use startin' at the bottom of the ladder."

"Of course not," she said, and let it go as a joke. They put it aside then. Neither of them wanted to fight it out to a decision.

"Where's Mary?" Blackie asked after a while.

"Down with Hope Cary."

"Goddamn it, Ma, you shouldn't let her run around with that little bitch. Her name ought to be Charity, not Hope, and her mother's just a drunken old bag. Hope's too old for Mary anyway. She must be damn near sixteen."

"Mary will be all right. Girls her age are in a rush to grow up, that's all. They get crushes on older girls."

"Goddamn it, she's beginning to act like a little chippy."

"You're not setting her a very good example."

That finished that. We drank our beer, talking of nothing in particular.

"You want to take a stroll up the avenue with me, Joe?" Blackie asked after a while.

"I don't have anything to do."

"It's getting late," Mrs. Carmody said.

"It ain't late for a Saddy night."

Manta and I said good night to her and went on out through the apartment and down the stairs. On the street Manta said so long and started walking toward Ninth. A few minutes later Blackie came down and joined me.

"Who's the yogi?" I asked him.

"You mean Manta? Oh, just a neighborhood guy. I knew him since I was a kid. He's a kind of janitor at the C.Y.O."

"He's a funny kind of a guy."

"Yeah. He's a character, all right. He's just give up, that's all."

"Your mother know him a long time?

"Yeah, I guess so. He's been comin' up a lot lately. I guess she likes to talk to him."

That was it, then. Without knowing it, maybe, she was coveting the attitude that John Manta had. She was trying to learn a discipline, but she couldn't cut Blackie out of her.

"What about that job, Blackie? Your mother wants you to take it pretty bad."

"Yeah. The good old forty a week. I need real money, see? Know something? My old lady has got cancer."

That made everything fine. "Jesus," I said. "That's pretty rough."

"She don't know it yet, see? She went around to the doc a little while before we got back. He don't tell her what it is—just writes and tells me. He's not a good doc, just an old quack that Ma and the old man used to go to, the doc Ma had when she had me and Mary. So he tells me, and says I can break the news if I want to. It's not too bad yet, see? If I can send her to one of those bigshot specialists maybe something can be done. The old quack ain't sure. That's how it is. I ain't told anybody yet. Hell, if it wasn't for that, I don't know, I might take that job she wants to get for me, but I figure I got to have some dough and quick."

"Yeah." I could see how he would feel that way. "Look," I said. "It isn't as tough as you make it. You could send her to a clinic. Hell, there are ways to get this done without robbing a bank."

"A charity ward, maybe?"

"Charity, hell. What does it matter what you call it, so long as she's taken care of?"

"I wouldn't send a dog to one of them places. No, I got to have the jack, and I got to have it fast."

"It won't help your mother an awful lot if you get knocked off or pulled in."

"I'm not goin' to be, either."

We walked along for a moment without speaking.

"Look, Joe, I ain't gonna crap you up. Even if my old lady was all right I'd still go for the big money. It's just like I told you back in that bar, you're just nowhere if you're poor. I'd still go after it, no matter what. Only if my old lady was O.K., I'd do it different that's all. Hell, I'd take that job or any job just to keep her happy—I like my old lady, see? I don't like to go against her like this. Sure, I'd take the job, but I'd do a little work for myself on the side. The way it is, I've got to work a lot faster, that's all. I don't have time to be careful."

"You're trying to take over that dock?"

"Nah. I don't have the time. That's a long job and there's a million angles to it. You got to have a real organization for something like that, and you got to have an in with somebody big enough to square you if you have to get tough. Nah, I just took over a corner, that's all.

Maybe I'll take over a couple more pretty soon. That won't be so bad. It's a lousy racket but it's a lousy world."

"Remember what you said about not putting the squeeze on some poor bastard owner of a candy store?"

"Bars aren't candy stores."

"It'll come to that."

"It's a lousy world, Joe. I got to do what I got to do. Don't give me a bad time."

"O.K.," I said. I could see him with a number on his back or a hole in his head right then.

Over toward Ninth we ran into Mary and another girl.

"Hi," Mary said. And then to her girlfriend: "You take the ugly one."

"I'm goin' to have to spank hell out of you," Blackie said, grinning at his sister. "You got no respect for your elders."

"*I* have, Blackie," the other girl said. "You try me some time." She was a blonde of medium height, maybe sixteen years old. She was going to be awfully fat before she was forty, but just then she was as round and ripe as a peach. He turned to his sister again. "You get your can up to the house. You got no damn reason to be out on the streets at this time of night. Beat it."

They went along the street, the older girl giving us the mechanical whore's smile that was so popular that year, her bottom working in a way that was calculated to give you an edge.

"Mother of Jesus," Blackie said sighing. "I don't know what's got into kids like that. They all act like chippies now. When I went into the army, that goddamn Hope was still wetting her drawers, and now I suppose she's bangin' half the kids on the block. Jesus, what a place. I got to see that Mary doesn't tie up with her. I don't want her to turn out to be a little tramp."

It sounded funny, coming from him. But then I looked at him in the dirty light coming from the window of a bar, a serious little man with the weight of the vast and unregenerate world on his shoulders, and it didn't sound funny at all.

"You might tell me where we're going," I said.

"I got to see a couple of my boys up at the club."

It was a Democratic party club. We went up to the second floor of a loft building and there it was, a couple of big rooms with folding chairs and a big American flag on the wall. Six men were playing poker at a small table. Beyond them, in the other room, three nondescript politicians—the fat, the thin, and the stupid type—were holding a conference on political strategy. The place stank like a broken promise.

Blackie went up to the table and watched the game for a few

minutes. Two of the men chucked in their hands and the betting went around. A guy with a face like Gooch in the funnypapers took the pot with three deuces. There were probably ten dollars in the pot. The guy began congratulating himself, and saliva sprayed out through his buck teeth like rain through a picket fence. Another of the players, a big guy of twenty or so with simonized hair on his head and a face as sharp as a meat-axe, cashed in his chips. He came around to Blackie and we went out. The politicians hadn't even looked up.

"What's on, Blackie?" the guy said.

"Nothin' on," Blackie said. "I just got restless. Joe, meet Kenny."

I met Kenny and we went on up the avenue together.

"We'll try Duane's," Blackie said. "I want to get hold of Mella. I thought he might be up at the club with you."

"He went out," said the fellow called Kenny. "I think he went hunting for some tail."

Duane's place in the lower twenties was just about like MacNamara's. The glasses were smaller and there was more neon. It wasn't a neighborhood bar. There were some seamen and some unidentifiable floaters and there were a few girls. We got seats at the end of the bar and ordered our drinks.

"My turn this time, Blackie," I said.

The guy Kenny looked at me as if I were crazy. Blackie shook his head. "Save it," he said. "I'll square it." They had their whiskey and I had a beer.

It was getting toward midnight and the place was rocking, the jukebox was blasting, people were crying, cursing, being sick, trying to make love, trying to fight. Everyone was having a hell of a fine time. It was like having a free pass to the madhouse on the keepers' night off.

"How do you like my headquarters?" Blackie grinned.

"It's cozy anyway. If they get any more customers they'll have to put tables in the street."

One of the girls came over and started bending Kenny's ear while Blackie and I went on talking. After a while Kenny leaned over.

"We got a beef here," he said.

"What's eatin' on her?" Blackie asked.

"That guy Porky Farran."

"What about him, for Christ's sake?"

Kenny looked at me and then back at Blackie and shrugged his shoulders. "Porky's knockin' down on her. He put the bite on her for twenty-five bucks tonight and when she didn't come across he give her a clout on the teeth. Jesus Christ, Blackie," he said in an aggrieved voice, "ain't that a hell of a way for Porky to act? This little bitch don't make that kind of jack, do you, honey?" He put a hand out and felt the girl's bottom. "These little Puerto Rican hoors!" he said to me. "They're gettin' so thick around here they're just cutting each other's throats."

"I don't have so much money, twenny dollar," the girl said. She was eighteen years old, maybe younger, and pretty in a kind of bewildered, unformed sort of way. She was obviously scared of what she had done in telling Kenny.

"He say he fix me if I tell," she said.

"Porky's a son of a bitch," Blackie said. "I always knew it. What I didn't know was that he was a dumb son of a bitch."

"What the hell's all the business about?" I asked him.

"Porky's a pimp, see?" Blackie said. "This girl used to be part of his stable. We told him to get lost and now he turns up and tries to put the arm on the kid. That's a hell of a lot of money to ask," he said to Kenny. "Maybe Porky is gettin' ready to blow town?"

"He's dronk," the girl said.

"Jesus," Kenny said. "That's bad. Porky is scared, asleep or awake, but when he's drunk he's a mean bastard, and he's got a knife on him. We better get Mella, huh, Blackie?"

"If we knew where he was at."

"Maybe I better go look for him."

"Maybe you better."

"I don't think Kenny wants anything to do with this guy Porky," I said, after Kenny had gone.

"Ah, Kenny's O.K."

"That green around his mouth wasn't his whiskers."

He laughed. "You're always bitching, Joe."

I shrugged. "I wouldn't go up a dark alley with that guy covering my tail." I let it go. "What the hell is this about the girls?" I asked. "You putting the muscle on this pimp?"

He looked at me and I could see that he was mad all the way through. "You sure got me pegged for a motherfuckin' son of a bitch, haven't you? All right. I don make a nickel off them. Duane doesn't like to have the guy around, that's all. I told him to move it along. The numbers guys and bookies, that's something else." He spat on the floor and shoved his glass out for another drink.

"All right," I said. "Forget it."

But he wasn't going to forget it and neither was I. "I ain't a goddamn shylock," he said. And "I don't make a nickel off them," meaning the girls. Probably he didn't. But then Duane did, otherwise Duane wouldn't have minded this guy Farran taking his cut. Oh, Duane was taking it from them all right; Blackie wasn't taking a nickel, but Duane was paying him off, either for value received or as part of a straight shakedown. It came to the same thing, and Blackie knew it as well as I did. He didn't like it either. He kept slugging the whiskey, but it didn't make him any happier. "It's a lousy world," he had said. Well, it was; it was rotting away, and Blackie, the tough good little guy sitting beside me was rotting right along with it.

11:30 P.M.

Crip put down the book he had been reading and turned off the lamp beside the bed. The clock on the dresser said eleven-thirty. It was time for him to go.

He got the gun from the top of the dresser, putting the oiled rags carefully away so that they would soil nothing. The gun he put inside the waistband of his trousers. It was a nuisance to carry it there, but it was heavy enough that it would be noticeable in his coat pocket, and it was clumsy to carry it on his hip. With his loose double-breasted suit buttoned, it did not show at all. He looked at himself in the mirror, from where the buttons began on his coat almost to the knees. He pulled the coat down at the sides, using both hands, and then, satisfied, turned out the light and went out onto the dark stairs. As he went through the lower hallway he could hear the landlady's radio: comics. He heard the joke tossed crisply out onto the night air, and then the wild mechanical laughter from the radio speaker and the characteristic and pointless anger flooded back into him. It seemed like a personal affront. He had no sense of humor at all.

It was warm on the street, almost like midsummer. As he walked south, the garment district was deserted. Thirty-fourth Street was a gash of light. He stood on the corner gazing at the neon over the bars, wondering where he should start to look first, and decided that he would go on farther down. He was hunting for a man whom he had been hired to kill.

He had absolutely no curiosity about the man. He did not even know his name—it was just a face that he was hunting, and hardly even a face, just an abstract man. He didn't know, either, for whom he was to kill this man whom he had never met. It had been arranged; someone whom he had known in the past had come to see him, a price had been set, and the man who was to be killed had been pointed out to him. It had been a business deal, and if Crip thought of himself at all it was as a kind of businessman. Now he was going about his business hardly thinking about it all, not as if it were routine, but as if he were driven by some powerful instinct that told him where to go, what he was to do next, and he turned the corner, going south again, in a trance of concentration of which he was not even aware, held to his course as surely as an engine on its rails.

It was not a new job with him. He had been in prison at the age of twenty-two for a holdup which had netted him three and a half dollars. He had accomplished it with an old revolver of his father's, a cracked, useless piece of machinery for which he had not even had bullets. The act had been committed almost without thought, in a complete fury of despair, so that he was never able to say for sure what his motive had been. There was his dumb hate for the street in which he lived, the fierce hot midsummer night which had driven him from the reeking apartment, the clubfoot, the poverty, the bitterness of being a nobody. Then he was standing with the useless gun forgotten in his hand, and the frightened delicatessen owner was handing over the three-fifty, and before he was around the corner, almost, he was captured. He got three years.

By the time his first sentence was over, he had learned something. In place of the dumb, blind fury which had driven him, he had a sense of order and method; he was no longer a kid with a gun in his fist, but a professional. The years in prison had annealed the bitterness inside him.

After that there were other jobs—some successful, some not. He spent half his life in prison. It was on his last sentence that he became a student of history, partly out of his contempt for the other prisoners to whom he had nothing to say since he had never had anything to say in his life except what he had acted out in dumb show that hot night when he was twenty-two years old, holding the useless gun, taking the money which was not really what he wanted at all, following like an engine the undeviating rails of his blind dubious progress, dumb to all but a bitter sense of outrage. Partly, also, it was this feeling of outrage that drove him on, the feeling that he had been cheated somewhere, by someone he had never known, by events and powers whose existence he had not even suspected. And now, as he had first taken the gun, like a talisman, a magical object, he began to read, gutting the books in a cold frenzy as if they had to be forced, manhandled, into giving up the secret. He was not looking for knowledge. He was looking for the trick, the thing that had been hidden from him, and he might as well have been reading Chinese as American history; it was just a matter of what books the prison library had.

In the times when he had been out of prison he had had some success. Now, for five years he had been living on the proceeds of one robbery in the Middle West. He lived frugally, eating in cafeterias—he hardly knew that there were better places to eat—renting a room in a cheap rooming house. Mornings, sometimes whole days, were spent in the library, in the same intense and irritated concentration with which he now was hunting the man he was to kill, feeling a dumb malevolence, a continuous shock at what he was reading: thinking: *Jesus Christ, is that all there is to it?*

He had killed four men in the last five years. It was easier than robbery, and safer. Now, even with the bitterness and the outrage that never left him, he could think of himself almost as a businessman. He was moderately successful. He had accomplished difficult jobs. He had looked into the Mohawk translation of the Gospels which the Reverend Wheelock and Joseph Brant, the Indian, had made. He could speculate on the number of peacocks that Sir William Johnson had kept.

When he got to Twenty-eighth Street he began to investigate the bars. He was sure he would find his man in one of them. It could have been done another way, but he had done it this way before and he preferred to work the way he understood best.

At midnight the bars were booming and he passed unnoticed, coming in for a brief moment, usually not even bothering to buy a drink. He was an ordinary-looking man in ordinary clothing, and except for the slight limp, there was no reason for anyone to notice him. At about one-thirty he turned into a bar on Eighth Avenue in the lower Twenties.

As he entered, he could sense that something was wrong. The bartender was trying not to be curious about him. There were two other men at the end of the bar—one small, black-haired, not much over twenty, the other taller, almost six feet, with straight blond hair, dark eyebrows and brown eyes. After the first glance Crip did not look at them.

He ordered gin and put his money on the bar, feeling their eyes on him, thinking bitterly, *The bastards are saying to themselves that gin is a nigger drink*, and went out to the toilet without touching the liquor, looking at the three men in the back booth without seeming to look at them.

The toilet was small, dark, stinking. *It will be all right*, he thought. There was only one small window. He took his knife and scraped some of the gray paint from it and went back to the bar.

He felt satisfied now. He lifted his gin and drank it and ordered another. Standing against the bar his gun hurt his belly a little. He moved away, tossed down the second drink and limped out. He got around to the rear of the bar by going through the lower hall of a tenement, into the basement, and then on into the backyard. It was dark out there, and warm, and he didn't have much trouble getting over a low fence. Then he was standing near the window of the bar toilet, waiting. He got his gun out and held it under the right-hand flap of his coat. Very faintly he could hear the sound of the radio in the bar. He wanted a smoke, but he could be patient. *Tonight*, he thought, *or maybe another night. It's all the same.*

Midnight to Morning

As time went by the bar got louder and emptier. People still drifted in for a drink and a look around. After midnight the loneliness sets in and the neon of the bars draws them like moths to a flame. They come in and have a beer and look around, expecting, hoping that somehow life itself, whatever they are looking for—a woman, or companionship, or the biggest glass of beer in town—will be in the new place. Then they go on and try somewhere else. But sometime after midnight the bars contain only the floaters, or those who have taken root to the barstools, and a few groups who are still middling sober but trapped in a net of conversation.

Finally Blackie got up from the bar. "It doesn't look like the guy is comin' back," he said. He was more than a little drunk now, but it was only noticeable in his voice. "I'm sick of this dump. You want to push on?"

"I'm about ready to wrap it up for this night."

"You got a place to stay?"

"Oh sure," I said. There wasn't any place unless I went back to Bill's place and slept on the floor. Except for Kay. I decided I wouldn't go to either. "I'm fixed up all right," I said.

"You can bunk with me."

"Thanks, Blackie. I'm O.K. for the night."

"Hell, anytime," he said a little thickly, and he went out onto the street.

"That was an expensive night for Duane," I said, thinking of the drinks we had had.

"Part of my wages," he said grinning. "You want to take a little walk?"

We went along the avenue and turned over toward Eighth. Just beyond the corner there was a drunk sleeping in the doorway of a candy store. For a moment it looked like Riverboat Conn, but it wasn't. It was a nice night and he would be comfortable enough, whoever he was, except for the early morning when he would wake up chilled and stiff. At that time of the day, before the human machinery gets running properly, no one feels it's worthwhile to be alive anyway. He would be all right. But it wouldn't be long before it would be too cold for that kind of thing.

"I kind of envy a guy like that," Blackie said. "He may not be very comfortable, but he's got nothing on his mind."

"He's just dead but he won't lie down."

"Yeah. Who isn't?" He was beginning to feel sorry for himself. I guess he had enough trouble without looking for it hard.

"It's too late in the game for you to become a philosopher, Blackie. And too late at night for me to listen."

"Yeah. It's always too late for some fuckin' thing." I saw he was going to be profound. "Hell," he said, shaking off the dog on his back, "it ain't too late for a beer."

We cut across the street and went into another bar. It was almost empty. There were three guys in a booth at the back and there was the bartender.

"Porky Farran been in?" Blackie asked, while the bartender was giving us the drinks.

"Nah," the bartender said.

"Leave the bottle," Blackie said. The bartender shrugged, capped the bottle, and pushed it toward us. He walked back on his flat feet to the end of the bar and put his ear against the radio. He was chewing on a toothpick and looked as innocent as a hound dog, but he didn't take his eyes off Blackie for a minute. He was a square-built man, short and powerful-looking. He had the rectangular face and the blond hair of a Swede or a German. One of his ears was cauliflowered. He looked like bad medicine.

"Look, Blackie," I said. "I'm not here to help you put the muscle on this pimp."

"Nobody's holdin' you, Mac." He was sore again.

Nobody was holding me. I couldn't leave though. Blackie was drunk enough now to have a try at anything. I couldn't leave him there alone. Hoping that the man Porky and a couple of his guild brothers with baseball bats and knives up their sleeves wouldn't come around, I sat and drank my beer. It didn't taste good. The bartender kept his tin ear against the lips of the radio.

After a while the door opened and a man came in. We were all looking at him, Blackie and the bartender and myself, all of us, I guess, expecting Porky and trouble. He must have felt as if he were walking into the beam of a searchlight. He didn't turn a hair but came straight across toward the bar.

He was limping a little. There was something wrong with his left leg. Then I saw it. He had a clubfoot.

"Gin," he said, and put a dollar bill on the bar, and without waiting for the drink limped on back to the john. When he came back he put down the shot, straight, and got another. The bartender looked disgusted. In that kind of bar nobody drinks gin. It made me a little curious. There was something odd about the man. Perhaps it was his clothing—there was something a little old-fashioned about the dark suit he was wearing, but it was nothing you could put your finger on. There was nothing remarkable about him: medium height, middle-aged, a completely characterless face like a composite photo. Then he lifted his drink and turned a little toward me and I saw his eyes. They were colorless too, as if part of the iris had worn away. They looked soft, pulpy. They were quite inhuman. It was like looking through a couple of holes into nothing at all.

He drank the gin in one long pull and put down the glass and limped out. As if on cue the door at the side opened and a big moon-faced man with a black mustache came in. I felt Blackie stiffen and the bartender came over and stood carefully in front of us, against the bar, drying his hands on his towel.

'I won't have any trouble, Carmody,'' he said quietly. He had acted before as if he didn't know Blackie from Adam.

''Good,'' Blackie said. ''Let's keep it that way.'' He had his eyes on the mirror in front of him, watching the man who had come in. The big man came on toward the bar. He didn't look drunk to me. Then he saw Blackie's face reflected in the bar mirror and stopped dead.

''Come here, Porky,'' Blackie said. He got swiftly off the stool and crowded the big man along the bar into the corner, shoving him savagely with the nervous strength of a man who is angry and afraid. The bartender leaned over and put one hand under the bar and started to say something. I grabbed the whiskey bottle on the bar and stepped down.

''Get away from that and keep your trap shut,'' I said. He moved back a little way. Still holding the bottle in my right hand I reached down under the bar. He had a two-foot length of billiard cue there.

''Now turn up the radio a little.''

I followed him down the bar, keeping the club against my leg. I could feel my arm jerking as if it belonged to someone else, the way it is when you are a kid and you are first man up against a hot pitcher. He turned up the radio. The guys in the rear booth hadn't noticed anything. Blackie stepped back and hit Porky on the side of the jaw.

The big guy didn't try to defend himself. He just stood there and took it, holding his hands out away from himself.

''Don't, Blackie,'' he said. ''Don't, Blackie.'' He was deadly afraid. Again I got the feeling that I had had when the big longshoreman had come up to Blackie at MacNamara's. Blackie was beginning to be a man to be afraid of. I began to wonder if maybe he was carrying a gun. He hit Porky again.

''Don't, Blackie.'' This time I was saying it.

''I told you Ninth Avenue was off limits for you,'' Blackie was saying, talking very fast. ''Now you're out, Porky. Out. Get it? Don't come around here no more." He hit him again and I moved around the bar to stop him.

Porky must have thought I was coming after him with the baseball bat. He screamed once, high and shrill, like a woman. The bartender started to drop to the floor, and, not knowing what he might have down there, I took a cut at him with the club and he went down and stayed down.

Porky was fighting now. I could hear them, the grunts and the curses, but I couldn't look at them. When Porky yelled, the men in the rear booth had come boiling out and started toward us. Two of them stopped but the third one kept coming. He swept a beer bottle from one of the tables and smashed it and came after me. The light glinted on the dog-toothed edges of the bottle and I could feel my stomach jump as if I were going down an express elevator. Without thinking at all I kicked one of the high stools at his legs and threw the billiard cue as hard as I could. He went down, but whether from the stool or the club I didn't know.

The big guy had Blackie in the corner against the bar, and he was trying to break him in two. I put my hand over his head and got it under his nose and pulled him back and automatically, when he let go, Blackie clipped him and he fell against my legs.

"Let's get out of here, for Christ's sake," I said.

"Plenty of time." He was panting hard. He picked up the half-full whiskey bottle on the bar and went toward the man I had thrown the club at. The guy had a welt on the side of his head where the pool cue had got him. He was just getting to his knees, a little shaky.

"You still want a hand in this?" Blackie asked.

The man stopped trying to get up and looked at us.

"All right," Blackie said. He reached down and got the billy I had thrown. The barman was standing now, leaning on the bar as if he had a bad headache.

"Here," Blackie said, tossing the cue toward him. "Thanks for the cooperation, Jack. I'll be around tomorrow and have a little talk with you. I'll just keep this bottle to pay for our trouble."

Porky was trying to get up, staggering a little. While he was still bent over with his hands touching the floor, Blackie put his foot against the guy's tail and shot him out into the middle of the floor on his face. We went out into the street.

We sat down in the little park on one of the benches in front of the Ninth Avenue Health Center. It was dark and quiet under the trees there. A few bums were sleeping on the benches and a man and a woman were trying to make love.

"You goin' to change to whiskey?" Blackie asked, holding the bottle out to me. He spoke softly, panting a little. We had hurried after we got out of the bar.

I tipped it up and drank, still feeling rocky and hopped up from the fight.

"You didn't like that very much, huh?" Blackie asked.

"No," I said. "I'll fight if I have to, but I don't like it."

"I don't give a damn," Blackie said, lifting the bottle to his lips.

"I don't like getting pulled in on something like that," I said.

"You didn't have to stick around."

"Yes I did. You know damn well I did. I don't like to be used."

He lifted the bottle again and I could hear it gurgle for a long time. When he finished he was gasping a little from the liquor.

"Take off, then," he said quickly. "You ain't tied."

"The hell I'm not."

He took another pull at the bottle and emptied it. Then, taking it by the neck, he threw it across the street. It broke in a splash of glass, waking one of the bums, disturbing the lovers.

"You still want to be free?" he asked. "Fuck it all," he said after a while. He was crying a little. There was nothing I could do about that.

"Come on, kid," I said. "Time to go home."

He was silent all the way down to his house. When we got there he said: "Sure you don't want to stay here, Joe?"

"No," I said. "I got a place to stay tonight." I was thinking of trying Penn Station.

"No trouble," he said.

"Thanks, kid, no. So long."

"Good-bye then, Joey." I heard the door click shut behind him. My footsteps echoed in the empty street as if someone were following me.

2 A.M. Sunday

Penn Station was still humming like a dynamo. People were sleeping in the waiting room, or sleeping on their feet waiting for trains. As soon as the war started, it seemed, people had begun to travel like mad. Now perhaps they were going back home again, but for the moment they were just D.P.s washed up on the shores of the station.

I went down into the rat-run of the lower levels and found the flophouse they were running for G.I.s. There was a woman, Red Cross or a Sally or something, at a desk. The rest of the room was dark and you could see them sleeping on chairs and benches. She looked at me rather doubtfully and then decided to pass me.

"There aren't any benches," she said. "But there will be a few going out in an hour or so if you want to wait."

I couldn't have slept anyway. I sat down in one of the long folding chairs and lit a cigarette.

"You still want to be free?" Blackie had asked.

That was what I had said to Blackie on the boat coming in. Well, it wasn't the silliest thing I could have said, and it is the thing that everyone, more or less, wants in his own way. That was what Blackie really wanted, I suppose, but he thought he had a more practical way of getting it than I had. Coming back like that after three years or so on the other side, and maybe four or five in the army, you feel the lost years riding your shoulders like crows on a hanged man, and you remember the times you woke up in the night, sweating, feeling time running out of you like blood, drop by drop, the good years that you wouldn't even have noticed passing if it hadn't been that they turned a different color in the shadow of your uniform, becoming a visible part of the whole spectrum of loss.

Blackie was trying a shortcut, and he really didn't have any idea where it would take him. That fellow Porky. He might have been a pimp, but he was more than that. He had had his "corner" also, and the bar where we had had the fight had undoubtedly been part of it. Blackie could run him out. It was a cinch. He was a hard little man, and the boys over there, who have reasons to know just how hard a man is, knew what he was. I remembered the fear on Farran's face.

Still, it couldn't last, the bulge that Blackie had at the moment. Maybe Farran wasn't hooked up with someone very big, but sooner or later Blackie would run across someone who was. Then it would begin to be bad. Or maybe he himself would hook up to some powerhouse. It came to the same thing. In the first case, he would wind up out in the cold or else on a slab. In the second, he would get caught up into the machinery and whatever there was about him that was any good would be ground out. "I don't take a nickel . . . no old guy in a candy store . . ." It was no use, he was caught up in a contradiction. He wanted to have a handful of money, to be free. Maybe he would get it. But by the time he had it, he would be turned inside out and he would be just the kind of son of a bitch he didn't want to be.

He was in a bad spot. I thought of his mother, with her own desire to be free, to have him settled and off her mind so that she could really go about cultivating that passivity that John Manta had. With the cancer in her, to make it nice. She was going to cut her heart out over Blackie, trying to get the good life for him. And Blackie, poor bastard, with the knowledge in him like a cancer of his own, was going to have to help her do it in order to do what he thought he had to do to save her.

Oh, everything balances up one time or another, but the categories are all changed and the profit equals the loss. It would never do in business.

I thought of Kay then, all of her long-legged, redheaded lovely self, and, sitting there in the damn beach chair with G.I.s sleeping all around me, I thought what a fool I was. I could be with her now, I thought, and saw her as I had seen her so many times in memory when I was overseas. Here I was, back with the army. In a railroad station, waiting for orders, waiting for shipment.

In the years while I was away, I had thought I was all straight about her, but of course I had been thinking only of myself, of my part of it. Now I was all mixed up again, in spite of being born, fully formed and complete, at the age of eighteen in Cadillac Square.

That was because of the big switch, the change that had come.

It happened on a trip West, but I didn't fully recognize what had happened until later, when I was in the army. I was hitchhiking and got dropped off in a little town in Colorado. There wasn't anything special about the town, perhaps. There are lots of them like it in Colorado, New Mexico, Arizona, California, and probably in a lot of other places where I haven't been. But it was the first time in a couple of years that I had time to sit down and listen to what had probably been going on inside me all the time.

It was a small town, and the buildings were square and white in the sun. You would follow one of the little streets, twisting down the slope of a hill like an arroyo. At the bottom there would be a little square, and, in the middle of it, the sound of water from a well or a fountain, a whisper in the sunlight like the pines in Michigan, and the whole place would be dozing in the sun, the drowsy sound of bees worrying the silence at the edges and even the birds sounding sleepy and querulous. There were Mexicans there, and Indians with a smell both stale and wild at the same time. It was an exceptional town, perhaps. Living seemed easy and sensible. The Indians sat around and smoked and sometimes got drunk. The Mexicans never even seemed to get drunk. Out on the hills there were a few sheep and goats and a cow or two, and there was a little irrigated farming. It seemed a good way of living, but that may be the thing that memory does, wearing off the rough spots with the emory paper of time and leaving you with an impression of the earthly paradise.

Perhaps it was only a trick of memory. Perhaps the town does not exist at all—or at least not at all in the way that I remembered it later. Yet it must exist; it must be real, because in the two weeks that I stayed there, the town, or some quality in it or the light or the life there, forced me through a long process of dying and being reborn. I didn't know what was happening to me. I sat around in the sun and went through my boyhood, adolescence, and young manhood there. When I was done I was no longer the perfect being, fully formed as I had been born. I didn't get back the mummies and the trapped flies of my prenatal time in Detroit, but I got something else.

At the time I didn't know that I had got anything, didn't know that anything had happened to me. Even later I wasn't sure what it was that I had got, and perhaps it was something that I would never be able to say in two or three words and be sure that they really meant anything. It was something that had to do with order and dignity. Perhaps that was the sunlight.

Anyway I went on growing up almost as fast as Paul Bunyan. I didn't notice. The Indians didn't notice. They went right on smoking and getting drunk. If the Mexicans noticed, they were too polite to say anything, dozing in the square to the sound of the water, or driving their goats, or carving the ugly little statues of agonized Christs, the only real evidence that their life wasn't as fine and complete as it sometimes seemed to me later on.

The end of the process was that I became a different thing. I began to see that—in the army. I could see it now. The town had initiated me, drawn me back into humanity again so that I couldn't be the complete, finally formed, single and separate and isolated man that I had been. The town presented me with history, with responsibility, and I couldn't any longer be the simple, perfect, cop-hating kid I had been. I became undone, in process again. I didn't like it, but I couldn't help it.

The last months in the army, the time in the hospital, the period when I was learning that I was really in love with Kay—that was when I began to see what the town meant. I began to long for it, as if it were a physical projection of all my desires. I felt driven to go there, as if it were a solution, or a beginning.

So—thinking about that little town, wanting to go back there again to get myself oriented, to cross over the X-marked spot but at a new altitude, a new level, and still, for all that, wrapped in my cloudy ignorance—when Blackie asked me what I wanted after we got out, I said the thing that really the town had made me want, although I would never, before that moment, have been able to say what it was: to be free.

To be free. Yes, I had thought of going there with Kay. Peace, freedom, happiness, that was the meaning. But if that were the meaning, and if Kay were a part of my feeling about the town, why had I walked away without speaking to her?

Well—reasons of reasons. I didn't know whether she loved me. We had been lovers once, but that didn't mean anything. She was tied to her own craft, to her friends, to New York, to security. There were lots of reasons. Lots of reasons, but none of them strong enough to make me simply walk away, unless I was a coward.

Perhaps that was it, I thought, tiredly shifting around to find a soft spot in the chair; perhaps I'm a coward. I had walked away along the night streets feeling sorry for myself. I was still feeling sorry for myself when I ran into Barney Last.

There was the answer. It was the strike that made everything impossible. Even before meeting Barney I must have known that I was going to stay, that I was not going out to my sunlit town after all. My instincts knew it before my mind knew it; that was why I couldn't go in to Kay.

I was making myself responsible to the strike. But Christ, I thought, what about my responsibility to Kay, to my feeling about my town—my responsibility to myself? I didn't want anything to do with the strike. Was I going to have to go through it like a zombie, just on nerve and practice? I felt as if I were two men. The thing I wanted and the thing I knew I was going to do, had to do, were pulling me apart.

It was hard even to believe there was a strike on. I had been all over the waterfront and all I had seen of it was Bill Everson getting dumped. It was as if the strike came down to him alone. Then I thought of myself going down there before the shape-up of the longshoremen, in the early morning, while the rest of the city is asleep, before the teamsters go to the barns for their trucks. I began to feel that Bill and I were the only ones who knew the strike was going on. Maybe Kelly hadn't heard about it yet, or Caminetti over in Brooklyn, or the mobs, big and little, that swarmed on the docks like lice. I felt as if I were alone on the moon.

I closed my eyes and tried to go to sleep. I could hear the sound of people everywhere, coming and going through the station, and now and then I heard the subway, a muffled roar. Right under me trains were pulling out for everywhere, for Kay's country, the Maine deep, for the piney woods of the deep South, for the flat land around Chicago, for the white, arid, spiky, sun-drenched Southwest, and for the wild lost valleys and the cold lakes of the North; for Mobile, Kennebunkport, Medicine Hat, Mandan, Kalamazoo, and Pueblo. The lines ran out into the body of America like veins, whistles screamed, the ten-foot-high drivers thundered on the road, shaking the hills.

Tomorrow I would go on down to the waterfront. If the weather held, it would be hot; the sun would flash on the streets, on the heavy trucks roaring up and down the avenues. The bars would be full and the drunks would be sleeping in the doorways. Kids would be screaming past on kids' business. Over the whole of it, there would be the muted roaring, like a great river plunging over a cliff, the sound of the city. You would feel the earth shaking under you; the people would rush along the streets, caught in a frenzy of worry and speed, hurrying as from some terrible natural cataclysm, as if the earth were about to open at any moment just behind their heels, and I would be there somewhere, and Bill, and Kelly, and Blackie, all of us borne on the perilous tide. There wouldn't be a tree anywhere or a bird, or a blade of grass, and even the sun would seem as artificial as an acetylene torch. It would seem what it was: a wilderness of stone and iron, and at any moment you might expect to see great clanking mechanical furies wheeling over the heads of the stragglers and above the wounded and dying who lay on the sidewalks.

That was the way it would be. It was a hell of a long way from my little town, from the drowsy sound of water in a square, the sleepy bird cries at noon, from the lost country of the heart.

PART II
Monday-Wednesday

You hear the bells of daylight scatter their iron commandments over the city and a ragged cloud of pigeons circles from the fountain near the park. Blue-white, stone-color, glove-soft pinions, they break up like spray on a rock and explode in every direction across the high clear sky. There appears to be no pattern there, nor along the sidewalks where, like ant streams following a corridor of scent, people turn off into the sweet pockets of the banks or the dime stores. The river breaks up before the pool is made; the winner comes home before the betting machines are installed; unbalanced equations. You observe the rivers running crazily in circles around the island, the bridges turn to all compass points, and the bus comes down the street with no driver at the wheel. Nevertheless, patterns are taking form.

You note the pattern in the golden dust where the pigeon tracks end in air and sunlight. The iron hours fall from the bells onto the bedunged, shining roofs of the city, different and alike. The pigeons scatter, coalesce, circle and return to the fountain as weightless as pollen. You begin to be aware of the patterns of the day.

The first is the pattern of disintegration when the sunrise gun shatters the fortress of sleep. Crazed with breakfast coffee and the pangs of necessity, the people begin their vast migrations. They charge through the early streets as mad as elephants in the season of *must*. The doors of offices reach out for them; they fall into the great pitfalls of the factories; in the enormous wells of the elevator shafts, imprisoned prophets mourn in vain. A hundred suicides wearily climb the great cliffs of the highest buildings and fall, timing themselves, perfectly evenly spaced and shining like meteors, onto the iron plateaus of the avenues. Statisticians in frock coats rush out to determine the amount of scatter, checking against curves.

Under the glass dome of noon you see everything become fixed, static again. In the doze of midday, life is coming back again into the fur and garment districts, into the lofts of the chemical and radio industries. Workers sleep or sit in the sun at the entrances to garages and shipping departments. This is the happiest hour of the day, an hour in which there is no work, an hour too short to start the climb to Golgotha in search of amusement. The denim jackets and the work shirts gather the warmth and the sunlight of a perfectly free hour, the time when no one works or worries about being happy. You know, of course, that it cannot last. Sunlight spills from the blue jackets as the one o'clock whistle whirls them into activity; the curse of progress falls like a meteorite on a glass roof and the workers climb the burning stairs to the cave mouth, shot up in the stalactite-hung elevator shaft, jet-propelled, to the seven-thousand-story entrance to the hornacle mine where the mad scientist is waiting with his tiresome plan for minting ten-dollar bills out of their blood.

That is the end of the pattern of repose, and it is the only one of the day.

At six o'clock another pattern emerges. It is at that time, when the air is blue with exhaustion and the whole city barely manages to stand on its steel and stone foundations, the girders almost eaten through with fatigue and hatred, the bridges swaying drunkenly, their foundations sapped by malaise and industrial insanity; then, in the blue hour, when the bosses know enough not to come around, because since four o'clock every worker has been sharpening his knife; then, in the hour when the pressure has swung the hand past the danger marker and the red alert is about to sound, when the price of love has fallen so low that the market is closed for the day and there are only a few ancient sweepers, so tired they cannot stand, in the usually busy pits—then the quitting whistle sounds.

For a moment no one moves or breathes. It is a miracle—that it happens every day does nothing to change it. Since seven or eight or nine in the morning they have been waiting for it; at eleven they dared not think; at two-thirty they despaired; since four they have been working in mechanical fury, dreaming of hand grenades and heads on poles, and suddenly it is there, there, all over the shop, all over the city, hanging from the corners of the buildings like a flag, the only flag they have. It waves in the blue air of evening. This is the third pattern, which is of release.

Strength comes back into the arms of the Empire State Building. The knife is put back into the toolbox to wait for the day that cannot be borne, and suddenly the city is like a great mother, calling her children home. Sealed in the roaring tubes like current in a wire, they flow under the iron floor of the city. The tunnels, like mouths of great fish, spew out the wandering Jonahs; the doors of banks like mausoleums, the hole-in-the-wall shops like installment-plan graveyards, give up their corpses, and all over the city the crippled sheriffs with glass keys at their belts open the stocks in which thousands have been locked.

It is the hour and the pattern of renewal and release.

And after the last cup of coffee, after the baseball scores and the news report, when honor itself is lost, before it is necessary to think of sleep and of waking and of the new day which will be just like the one that had died, there is the pattern of search, when it only seems necessary to say the right word, to find the right bar, the right girl, the right memory, when it seems not only necessary but easy: to find the street where the way was lost, when the hand was shaken that can never be shaken again and you went away and left yourself there, the only part that could be of use to you now.

This is the pattern of search.

It always ends in a bar or a fight, or sorrow, or sex. It always ends in sleep and never quite there, for there are always the long dead empty streets in the moonlight, corners to be turned; you are a piece on an enormous chessboard and it is up to you to move.

But you do not have to move, because you are the neutral man. You can wait. The streets run up and down and cross each other. The squares are red or black. Nevertheless there are only so many pieces on the board. There are only so many moves that are open to each one. There are limits to possibilities and no matter how hard one thinks, there are certain things which cannot be done. This is the comfort of the neutral man in the pattern of search.

Monday 7 A.M.

When I got up Monday morning, after a second night in that Penn Station flophouse, I felt like a stiff getting down off the slab and trying to walk. It is a mistake to try to think before your digestive apparatus is working properly. I had had no luck with my thinking on Sunday, only a repeat of my sorry Saturday-night thoughts. It is a mistake to think on Sunday, and that is all I had done with the day. I had seen no one and gone nowhere. It seemed to me then that I had been a fool all the way down the line with Barney Last, with Blackie, and especially with Kay. I thought of her place, with the sun just coming in through the windows now and the smell, maybe, of coffee cooking, because she was an early riser. I could have been smothered in silk and scented down, and instead I was waking up with a burnt-valve taste in my mouth and a crick in my back like an aged weightlifter.

It was about seven o'clock in the morning and they were burying the remains of the night. Sweepers were advancing on the soiled acres of the station; in the waiting rooms women were spitting on their fingers and putting their eyebrows back in commission. I went down below and looked for a place to eat and wandered into the milk bar. After the coffee I didn't feel much better, and I knew that what was wrong with me was not just retarded digestion. It was too early to do anything at all. The world wasn't on its feet yet. You can't ask questions before eight-thirty or nine.

I went out of the station at the east end and walked uptown. At Forty-second there was nothing but the newspapers, smelling of black ink and murder. I bought a *Times*, a *Trib*, the *News*, and the *Worker* and went right on north. They were washing down the windows just the way I had done when I was in college and had a job as swamper in a cheap restaurant. Farther up, they promised new cars as soon as they could get their factories retooled. Then I got into Central Park with the pigeons and the squirrels and remembered that I hadn't got anything to feed them. I had never got used to the habit of feeding wild animals anyway, thinking that if they can't take care of themselves none of God's creatures can, but Kay had taught me that you never intrude on them in the park unless you have something to offer. They had to shift for themselves that day. I sat down on a bench and examined the unhappy state of the world. There was nothing in it for a guy like me.

At a little before nine I left the park and walked down to a bus stop. By that time everything was all right. They had got the mask clamped on, the particular mask of the day, and they were prepared to go through with it. There was hardly any evidence of shock, only the usual controlled hysteria.

I got the bus and rode down to Union Square. There they were perturbed about the problems of tomorrow. I walked west and then cut down deeper into the Village. At nine I was at the headquarters of Barney's section. I went on up. A guy with a cigar was sweeping the place out and offered to let me help him. I shuffled the chairs around while he made passes underneath. At nine-five somebody came in and opened up the bookshop cubbyhole.

"If you're here for the meeting," he said, "you're going to have to wait a while. Barney got tied up in something. He'll be along in about ten minutes. You want something to read, you help yourself." So I waited.

Monday 7:30 A.M.

At seven-thirty when Joe Hunter was leaving the Pennsylvania Station milk bar, Mary Carmody came out of the apartment where she had stayed overnight with Hope and picked up the milk bottle at the front steps. She climbed the stairs to her mother's flat and listened at the kitchen door. There was no sound. Because she had no key to the door, and because she did not want to wake her mother or Blackie, she put the bottle of milk on the floor in the hallway and went back downstairs to see what time it was by the clock in the window of Harounian's store just as P.J. Kelly woke from his haunted sleep, sweating and constricted by too many covers and read seven-forty on the handsome timepiece on the night table and tried to sleep again and Alton Husk called out, his voice muffled by sleep and a dream of his boyhood.

Mary was dreaming of what she would do when she grew up. She sat on the front steps and watched the approach of an ice truck, thinking of what it would be like to be older. Not as old as her mother, of course, nor as old as Hope's mother because they were of an incredible age to which she felt they must have been born, just as she herself seemed to have been born, and perhaps be fated to remain, at that age between the girlhood which she did not want and the young womanhood which she did not seem able to achieve. To be as old as Hope, who was in her second year of high school, who could have dates, not the silly kind where a bunch of them would go to the movies, but real dates, with Lonnie or Bert or one of the others, and who if she smoked a cigarette did not cough the way others did, and who knew all the things you did when you were grown up and made no secret about it. Mary was planning to grow up as quickly as possible. She thought of the things Hope said and how she acted, but not without a certain dissatisfaction, as if to be as old as Hope were not enough in itself, because there was something too cheap and easy about being Hope, just as Blackie said. It would be better to do something else when she became grown up, and her thoughts drifted off into a wish for fine clothing and riches and indefinable things which she could not put a name to until she saw the image of the grand lady which she had become, a Hollywood star perhaps, sitting in a green chair with a white woolly rug under her feet, in a long transparent gown, holding a cigarette in a foot-long holder, the smoke curling about her smiling, sphinx-like enchanting face.

The cigarette smoke woke Lucille and she opened her eyes into the tame gray cloud just over the bed and saw the hill of green silk that was Alton Husk's pajama-clad body.

"Good morning, darling," she said lazily with the complete happiness of someone who is not yet entirely awake.

"Good morning," Husk said without turning his head, looking through the smoke at Kelly's unhappy face, at the plans he was making like the layout of a city, everything precise and exact as it should be and yet with something missing because he could not be absolutely sure of Monk Ryan, Caminetti, Last, P.J. Kelly.

Who, turning in his burning bed for the tenth time, tried futilely once again to pull sleep over his head like the bedclothes, thinking of the green grass of Gowanus. *Go ahead, Big-Eye said, you got to be a man sometime* and of the days of fishing off the dock, cutting school, when there was time to burn. He tried to shrug the memory away, lying stiff and straight in the bed like a corpse in a coffin, waiting for the sleep that would not come.

Blackie rolled over, waking, tasting the night-before in his mouth, thinking, Christ I've got to get up I could sleep for a week. And closing his eyes drifted out on the dark water, while Joe Hunter, thinking moodily of sunlight on a white town watched the slow progress of a swan on the tiny lake and told himself that it would be necessary to go to see Kay in the evening and that everything would work itself out if you gave it enough time; and the bells rang eight o'clock, startling the pigeons, two minutes ahead of the clock in Harounian's window in front of which Mary Carmody plotted to hurry the slow hands, five minutes late with the fine clock on P.J. Kelly's night table which rang dismally in the rich room, summoning him forth into life, so that he rose groaning, thinking, God, if I were only young again.

"You look just like a little boy," Lucille said tenderly, seeing the face unprotected by glasses and the pouting full lips. She felt a spasm of desire go through her and put her hand out, touching him under the covers.

"Don't touch me," he said sharply, crushing the cigarette into an ashtray. Kelly can be brought around, he was thinking; he can be swung. And then put the idea away with his fine plans, feeling like laughing at them and at himself. It doesn't mean a damn thing, he told himself; not a damn thing one way or the other; nothing you do makes any sense. And leaning over saw Lucille's hurt face, the big mouth naked of lipstick and looking, he thought, a little obscene, like an unfamiliar organ on a totally strange animal. Did I kiss that? he wondered; how disgusting. A little bubble of laughter formed in him, the pressure of it mounting as he saw the hurt on her face changing toward bewilderment and then anger. And as she tried to rise from the bed he put one hand on her shoulders, holding her back, and with the other he pushed her legs apart, watching, with complete detachment, while her face clouded and changed like litmus paper touched with acid. He pushed the pajamas down from her wide soft hips, still holding her shoulder with one hand, and felt her kick out of them, mounding the covers around their feet. As he moved over to her he heard the alarm clock on the table at the other side of the bed, shrill and insistent, and he brought his face down toward her, watching with satisfaction as her face went out of focus, the muddy wells of her eyes, the great cool ridge of the nose, the mouth like an open wound, and the whole of it enormous, misshapen, a vast pulpy mass of pitted gray.

P.J. Kelly silenced the alarm clock and picked up his gold brocaded dressing gown, shouting for the Negro man-of-all-work who took care of his apartment. When the man did not come immediately he pulled off the nightshirt which he wore and, still holding it as if it were something which did not belong to him, walked over to the bathroom and turned on the hot water. He looked at himself in the mirror, seeing the tousled hair and the scowling face, and pulled his lower lip down with one finger to look at his teeth. It was part of a ritual which he still performed long after he had stopped caring whether the teeth decayed or not. Without his glasses there was no softness or melancholy about his face, and the little droop at the corner of his mouth suggested anger rather than pain. He sat down on the edge of the tub, waiting for it to fill, and felt his belly spread out on his upper legs. He touched it with his hand, feeling disgust at its looseness, and then, looking down, saw it as a moon-shaped expanse, neutral as dough but heavy as a burden. It was like an object that had been fastened to him and which he could not get rid of. Somewhere inside it, in the dark somewhere, a process was going on which he knew with amazement and fear was the process of his death. For a moment he regarded his stomach with something like awe, and then, grunting, he turned off the tap and climbed into the tub.

After a few minutes in the warm water he felt better. There was no use in worrying, he told himself. *Might live to be a hundred.* The doctor had told him to give up cigars and excitement, that was all. *A lot of people have high blood pressure.* P.J. Kelly, feeling the warmth of the water breaking over his chest, began to have a kind of confidence in his own offhand statistics.

Still, it wasn't the blood pressure that was worrying him. It wasn't even the strike. It was just that recently he had begun to feel that really, one day, there would be an end to Patrick James Kelly, high blood pressure or not. He began to feel it now, his death, as a process which had got started somehow and which there was no way to stop. He tried to think when it might have begun and succeeded in dredging up again the soiled and used images of his boyhood. It was not back there, anyway. Perhaps it was the strike after all that made him feel this way, unsettling the steady round of his life, the poker games with the boys, a little drinking now and then, a visit to Eve, the trip south in the winter. When things are going smoothly, P.J. Kelly thought, you don't notice anything and you don't worry about anything. *What you don't know don't hurt you.* He soaped himself thoroughly, hanging to his little raft of words, thinking that no one was going to edge him into taking any action about the strike that he did not want to take, not even Husk, whose ability he trusted. *I'll just sit it out.* All that was really necessary was to wait, not to get excited, and they would come around to him just the way they always had now for twenty years. He would have the strike ended just the way he wanted it, with no trouble, on his own terms, without any change at all. Without any change at all, that was the way he wanted it, and then he could go back to the poker games at the Kelly Demo Association for a few weeks, and then it would be time to begin thinking about the annual trip to Miami. I'll get things back to normal, and on my own terms, he told himself, thinking of the doctor and of the cigars, thinking of his death. *Holy Mary, Mother of God.* The words jerked into his mind and he yanked the stopper out of the tub and shouted again for the Negro. *What you don't know won't hurt you.*

Mary Carmody was thinking that there were a hundred things that she did not know yet, remembering the words she had heard from Hope, turning them over in her mind as if they were material things which she had in her hand. That was the words they said when they were swearing. That was the words they said when they thought they would make you blush. She felt a certain curiosity about the words because so much importance seemed to be attached to the syllables, but they were not new to her, really; she seemed to remember them from the time she was a little girl. Then she began thinking back from them to the boys she knew and the words seemed ridiculous until she thought of Lonnie, who was even older than Hope, and of his mean challenging look. She remembered what Lonnie looked like, and it made her feel uncomfortable; then she thought of something about him and giggled and said, "Hello, Sister," as the nun went past on the sidewalk in front of her. Nuns were strange, in their way. Of course they were holy, but the clothes they wore were strange. She tried to imagine herself in one of the floppy hats with the white cloth bound around her cheeks. People said they were bald-headed. She looked down the street at the long full pious rusty-black unhappy dress of the Sister and thought of herself inside it. A wind that had never blown rustled her heavy skirts, and she giggled again to herself, looking down at her short dress; then, as Harounian's fourteen-year-old son came out of the store and regarded her critically, she smoothed the skirt over her knees and put her legs down, giving him the practiced look of boredom which said that he was just a child and had better be on about his business. But young Mr. Harounian, pretending to have seen more than he had, crossed the street and stood in front of her with his thumbs stuck in his belt and made an improper suggestion.

"Run along, Junior," she said in her most mature voice. "I hear your mother callin' ya."

"You ain't so hot," he said in a rather hoarse voice. "You think you're smart, but you ain't so hot. Lonnie says you don't know what it's all about yet."

"Your ma's callin' ya," Mary said imperturbably. "Run along, apron strings."

"Ah, screw you, Mary," he said uncertainly. "I'm older'n you are."

"It ain't how old you are that counts," Mary said wisely. "It's how good you do."

Victor Harounian took this piece of wisdom with him as he went along the street toward the apartment house where he lived. He had his mouth puckered up to whistle but no sound would come except a breathy wheeze, and he took it as a personal insult that, although he had tried for years, he could neither whistle properly nor force the world to take him seriously. Mary, looking after him, thought about Lonnie and about what Victor had said. It's not fair, she told herself rebelliously; I can't help how old I am. And just then young Harounian whistled one note clean and bright and stopped in astonishment, almost running into Barney Last who was coming down the street with his head full of half-completed plans about the strike, and who was too busy to see the young man being born in front of him on the sidewalk or the skirmish which Mary Carmody was fighting with herself on the front steps of the house across the way. He turned the corner onto Eighth Avenue just as Joe Hunter finished with the papers, folding them neatly, and Blackie sitting on the toilet seat in the little cubbyhole in the hall read with interest the news of a bank robbery in a four-day-old paper that was lying on the floor.

He was trying not to think about the night before and especially about his friend Joe Hunter, for now, with early morning remorse, he felt he had treated his friend badly. Jesus, I got no right to drag the guy in like that, he told himself; I guess he's pretty sore. After his bowels had responded he felt better, as if he had lost part of the black and nameless grief he had felt in his belly on rising, but the roar of the water flushing the toilet set his head throbbing again. He went softly back into the kitchen and sat down in a chair, lowering his head into his hands.

Kelly's breakfast table was covered with a bright cloth, and the breakfast dishes flashed white in the sun that fell through the windows at the east and south. The apartment was high enough up so that he had a good view of the island, of the white buildings plunging through a couple of small clouds downtown and of the checkerboard pattern of Manhattan between Fourteenth and Forty-second. The Negro put the grapefruit in front of him, but he pushed it away and waited for the bacon and eggs. When they came he ate rapidly, as if famished, and wiped his mouth on the back of his hand.

"Bring me some coffee, for Christ's sake," P.J. Kelly roared.

"Yes, sir," the Negro said and brought it to him. He put it in front of the big man and disappeared into the hallway. When he came back he had the papers and a half-dozen letters. These he placed in front of Kelly and disappeared again, going this time into the hum of the refrigerator and the sizzle of more frying bacon in the little companionway kitchen. Kelly could hear him moving about as he opened the mail and glanced up now and again in annoyance. Damn place, he thought; built for a woman. He looked with distaste at the decorative crockery on the rail that circled the room and thought of his wife. It was too cute for him; he had never got used to the rich apartment. He snorted aloud and thumped on the table, looking at the first letter he had opened. Mr. Kelly got a bad mood this morning, the Negro thought, and picked up the Silex half-full of coffee as a peace offering. He put it on the table in front of Kelly.

When he was finished drinking coffee, Blackie's stomach felt a little better. He heard the worn slippers whispering around the kitchen, but he didn't look at his mother. She hadn't said anything this morning. There was going to be a row; he could feel it in the air. All right then, he told himself, peering at the cracked cup and trying to think of nothing at all; a row. Images of the night before kept coming back. Again he saw Porky's scared face just before he hit him. Unconsciously he wiped his right hand along his trousers leg as if it might be dirty, and leaned back in his chair, lighting a cigarette. Even in respose there was an urgency about him, and the simplest move was quick and almost fierce with unused energy. He had had a quarrel with Joe. Already it seemed a long time ago, as if Joe were a friend out of the distant past, as if the quarrel were something that had happened when Blackie was a boy. He's got no right to get sore, he told himself, resentfully. He remembered other troubles they had had between them, and that they had always got over them, and for a moment was comforted. Still, he couldn't help thinking that there was something final about this. I saved his bacon once, he thought, taking some comfort from remembering that as from remembering a charm.The sound of burning echoed in his head, the fierce smells, the nightmare struggle to escape, and again he saw Joe Hunter's body, half in and half out of the hatch, and felt the solid weight of it as he dragged it out of the circle of fire where the weeds were already beginning to blaze. He could smell Joe Hunter, burning. "Ahhh," he said, his shoulders twitching convulsively.

"What's the matter, Francis?" his mother asked, turning away from the sink.

"Just thinking," he said in a noncommital voice. "I pulled Joe out of a tank once. We got another guy out and then Joe almost didn't make it himself. I went up and he shoved this guy out till I could get holt of him. Joe got burned pretty bad on one leg. He used to dream about it all the time. Hard guy to sleep with after that. He was a good buddy though," he said in a voice almost tender, looking through the cigarette smoke and the wall into a smoky reek of oil and hot metal.

"You don't have to think about those things now," Mrs. Carmody said. She came over to the table and sat down, a big thinning woman with the shadow of a handsome past still on her. She looked very tired.

"No," Blackie said harshly. "I don't have to worry about him. We had a fight last night."

"Fight?" Mrs. Carmody was startled.

"Not a real fight. A jawing match. He got sore."

"What was it about?"

"Oh—I don't know." At the moment he felt that it would be impossible, even if he had been willing to talk about it to his mother, to explain all the things that were behind the quarrel. "We're different," he said finally. "We want different things, I guess. I don't know."

"It's a shame. You were such good friends all through the war."

He knew suddenly that it was true, that they had really been good friends, although he had never before questioned or weighed his feeling for Joe Hunter.

"Yes," he said heavily. "He was a good buddy. I guess I liked him better—" He was going to say that he had liked Joe Hunter better than he had ever thought. "I guess I liked him better than he did me," he said smiling wryly, but he felt the self-pity in his words. "Ahhh, Judas Priest."

"He's a nice boy," Mrs. Carmody drummed her fingers on the table. "It's too bad his mother died when he was so young," she said as if talking to herself.

"His old man too."

"Yes, that's what you wrote. Well, I don't suppose the quarrel you had was such a bad one," she smiled. "You'll both get over it. After all you were friends in the war."

"Yeah," Blackie said. He was thinking that the war seemed years away, as distant and unreal as the wars in history books. It made him feel old and alone.

"I suppose he'll get a job here in New York and you'll see him a lot. He used to work on the docks, didn't he? I expect he'll settle down now—" Her voice trailed off.

Blackie got up abruptly. He felt he knew exactly what she was getting at and he didn't want to fight with her about the job she wanted him to take. Not at this hour of the morning for Christ's sake, he told himself.

"I'm goin' out after the paper," he said and went down the stairs leaving his mother thinking, not of the job she wanted her son to take, but of the first year of her marriage when she and her husband had been planning to have a house in Queens within five years. It hadn't worked out. After a while they had both forgotten about it, or stopped speaking about it anyway. She hadn't thought about it, nor about her dead husband for a long time, and now she found that she could think of these things without any real sorrow, with only a kind of gentle melancholy that was soothing and almost pleasant.

The pain moved in her belly and she held herself perfectly still, like a person listening for some sound just beyond the point of hearing, or like an animal frozen into immobility waiting for the hunter to pass. She held her breath, waiting, her body rigid, but there was nothing except the dull burning sensation which she had learned to live with. She got up resolutely, hoping that it had passed, and started to work clearing away the cups and plates. It caught her again and left her bent over the table, gasping a little. Then she forced herself to go on clearing away the dishes and after a moment the pain went away again leaving only the burning inside her. Each time it came back it was new and paralyzing, something that could not be prepared for. It was like the first time she had felt Francis kick inside her, a profound shock that nothing had prepared her for, tearing her life into two halves, into the time when she had been only herself, whether sad or happy, and the time when she was to become an appendage to the thing inside her that kicked her and chained her to itself. When he came it had been a painful birth. She remembered that through the pain and the fog of partial consciousness she had been able to think only of one thing—that when she had had him she would be able to sleep, and she had gathered her ravelled will and borne it.

She gathered her will now and went methodically about the morning chores. There was only the usual pain, but she bore herself carefully, as if carrying something which must not be shaken or disturbed. I never got through bearing him, she thought in sudden despair; he's kicking inside me now; oh God, Holy Mary, let me have peace.

"All right, young lady," she said briskly as her daughter came in from the hall, "it's about time you came back. Let's see you do those dishes. Francis has gone out for a paper."

"Francis Carmody," Kelly read. "The son of one of your old friends—" Old friends, hell, he thought. He vaguely remembered Carmody, but it disturbed him that the man was dead. "—everything possible for a young veteran," the letter said. "In these times, and considering the present situation—" Kelly saw the face of Father Aloysius Burke, the veined too-red cheeks and the air of wooden dignity. That bastard is always bumming me, he thought petulantly, tossing the letter with the others on the table in front of him. Then he remembered that he was thinking disrespectfully of a priest and checked himself. *Still, he is a bastard.* Burke reminded him that he had promised to give to the fund for the parish paper. Father Burke praised his brandy. *But he's not a bad old skate.* Kelly got up and went into the other room where the telephone was.

"Hello, Father," he said when he had the connection made. "What's this about Francis Carmody?"

Blackie was thinking that it would be impossible to avoid the encounter with his mother over the job, and he was wondering how he would manage it. He didn't want to hurt her. It was no use arguing that he was doing better by himself. As far as his mother was concerned he was doing nothing, and if she knew or guessed about the taking over of a couple of bars, it would only make it worse. I won't do it, he thought. No matter what she says. And felt himself weakening, thinking of the tiredness in his mother's big body and the thing he could not tell her. I can't, he told himself, trying to whip up his determination, no matter how much she begs; maybe in a week or two, maybe in a month or so when I get things running better.

It cost so much for Kenny and for Mella, and yet he had to have them, would have to enlist others. Maybe in a month, he thought, I'll have enough, and I can send her to the hospital and then I can even take the job.

Walking in the sunlit street, nodding to Harounian the grocer, saying hello to Monk Ryan who went past sidling along crabwise to hide the fine black eye he was wearing, Blackie felt as if he were full of rusty nails and pieces of broken glass, discovering a searing love for his mother which he had never experienced before, a terrible flash of revelation that made the whole street look different, the feeling growing inside him, choking him like a fist at his throat. My God, he thought in wonder and horror, the goddamn war never ended. He turned into the smell and the shadow of his apartment house.

Joe Hunter climbed the smelly worn stairs, feeling the pull of the muscles in his bad leg as Barney Last turned the corner at Seventh Avenue and Fourteenth Street and P.J. Kelly put down the phone, thinking and not wanting to think about a scheme that was going through his head, and Lucille, the sun highlighting her handsome bottom, padded to the bathroom, while Alton Husk reset his alarm clock and the gulls wheeled over the Hudson crying their meaningless lost cries.

Monday 9 A.M.

They began to filter into the meeting in dribs and drabs and twos and threes. When Bill Everson showed up I waved to him and he came over and sat down. I thought again how much like Blackie he looked, not so dark, and without the handlebar eyebrows, but with that same air of extravagant energy. I could have used some of it myself.

"How're your lumps?" I asked.

"Pretty good. Those hot towels and that liniment did the trick for me. When Harris—that's the guy I'm staying with—got home I had him heat up some more water. Took it easy Sunday. I feel damn near human this morning."

"You make another trip down to the front?"

"Yeah," he said. "It's pretty quiet down there this morning. Hardly anybody around."

"It's too early."

"Maybe. There've always been guys down there though, figuring, I guess, that the strike might be over any day. There weren't even any pickets out this morning."

"That's good," I said. "Not about the pickets, but about no one showing up to work."

"It doesn't have to be so good."

"No." I knew what he was thinking—that the men had simply adjusted themselves to the strike and were staying in the sack a little longer. That meant that they weren't going to take a hand in it but were willing to let Kelly's goons and the progressive opposition in the union slug it out between themselves. I couldn't kid myself about who was going to win a battle like that.

The place was filling up and there were still others milling around the literature cubbyhole when Barney came in. He had some sheets of notepaper in his hand and stopped to talk with a chubby dark-mustached man whom I did not know. Then he saw us and came over.

"Hear you had some trouble, kid," he said to Bill, putting one foot on a chair and smiling down at him.

"It's all right now."

"Glad to see you turned up, Joe."

"Hell," I said, "I had to find out what kind of a circus you were running, didn't I?"

"Well, there's lots of time to go West," he said carefully, looking down at his notepaper. "What do you want out there anyway?"

"A man can just want to go somewhere, can't he?" I asked defensively. It seemed to me that the sun didn't shine so bright on my little town when he started wanting to know my motives. "New York is no damn good anyway," I said. "It sets the whole country on its head and it does the same thing for the Party. Chicago would be better, or Detroit—hell, even Kansas City or St. Louis or the West Coast."

"You're not figuring on going to Chicago or Detroit are you?"

"No," I said and suddenly I was furiously angry. "Goddamn it, if we did half as much work in Detroit or Chicago as we do in New York, we might have the kind of labor movement that wasn't the bosses' dream. But this stinking town where everyone is chained to an overstuffed desk-chair—"

"I'm not chained to a desk-chair," Barney said. "Call your shots."

"You know damn well what I mean."

"Yes," he said quietly, sitting down and taking out a cigarette. "I know what you mean, but I wonder if you do. What you say about concentrating on those towns is correct, and I won't argue that there aren't some of our people who have dug in here pretty solid. We learn awfully damn slow, Joe. But what about this business? Can we move it out West somewhere, so you'll feel more happy about working on it?"

"Let that go," I said. "I'm working with you."

"You're not very happy about it."

"I don't have to be happy, for Christ's sake."

"Don't you?"

"What did you mean when you said I didn't know what I meant?"

"I don't know what you have in mind when you talk about going West, Joe, but it sounds to me like it was just a way of saying that you were tired, that you want to take a rest, a long vacation."

"Throw in my book, you mean?"

"Maybe."

"Joe doesn't mean that," Bill said in a shocked voice. "That's a hell of a thing to say, Barney."

"Isn't it?" Barney said without looking at him. "How about it, Joe?"

"No," I said slowly. I wasn't angry with him anymore. "I don't think so Barney. I never thought of it that way."

"Good," he said smiling and clapped me on the shoulder. "Now let's put this show on the road. As soon as this fracas is over, by God you *will* get a vacation. I probably shouldn't have dealt you in on it your first day out." He went to the front of the room, put his foot on a chair, and rapped on the wall for silence.

"O.K., boys," he said. "We're late already so everybody should be here. Let's get a chairman elected and an agenda worked out. The longer we have to spend here the less time we'll have to be down on the front where it's important."

Barney started the meeting off with a general report on what had happened, the question of the contract, the situation in various locals, probable lines of action that the leadership might take. It was a brief report and only for the purpose of giving us the whole picture. A lot of the guys in the room were from Brooklyn or stuck in the little locals where there had been almost nothing doing and where they couldn't see the forest for the trees. When he had got finished a little Italian got up to speak.

"In Brooklyn," he said, "last Friday and Saddy there was men goin' back to work. Some places were almost workin' normal. Others they had maybe twenty, thirty percent of the men back. Then Saddy afternoon they begin to get the word lay off; Caminetti, he would just as soon they hung up the hooks again. Now this mornin' nobody's at work, and the word is that Caminetti ain't tryin' to put anybody back on the job. What I want to know is when did Mario Caminetti become a rank-and-file leader?"

That set off a discussion of Caminetti's possible motives with opinions ranging all the way from the conjecture that Caminetti was afraid to push the men too hard to go back to work, to the guess that he had convinced himself that Kelly was finished and was therefore waiting to see which way to jump.

"I don't think Caminetti, he believes Kelly is washed up," the Italian said. "If he did, he'd be in there with a knife tryin' to finish him off. This Caminetti isn't like Kelly. Kelly's a crook, sure, but Caminetti's a gangster. Didn't they find out he was tied up with that Murder Incorporated outfit? Kelly, he's been around so long he don't have to rely on any one mob, but Caminetti, he's got his own, and he's got a hand in every dirty business in Brooklyn."

"Tony's right about Caminetti," Barney said. "The main interest he has in the Brooklyn union is that he needs it for his rackets. That's just the reason why I don't think he'd try any funny business with Kelly. Kelly wants the men back to work. I don't see why Caminetti would cross him up, because Caminetti isn't interested in getting himself elected for life to some top union job, no matter how high it pays. Caminetti has got the Brooklyn waterfront and that's all he needs."

"Caminetti is a hog," Tony said. "He'd steal the corset off his grandmother."

"Kelly isn't his grandmother. No, Tony, if Caminetti has taken off the pressure to go back to work—if he really has and it's not just that he can't hold them—then somebody must have been putting ideas in his head and don't ask me who. Maybe Strack from that big Jersey local. He likes to talk like a militant sometimes."

They discussed that possibility and a few others. I was beginning to feel like a foreigner. Things had changed so much in the time I had been away that I no longer recognized some of the names of important Kelly stooges. They kept talking about a guy named Husk who was brand-new to me. Then we closed the discussion and there were short reports on the work in several locals. We weren't represented in a lot of them. Finally a general line was worked out for work on a local level, and by then it was noon and we knocked off for lunch.

Bill and I, along with Barney and a friend of his named Fred Abbott, sat in a White Rose bar and ate pastrami sandwiches. Barney was worrying.

"I wish Kelly would make a move," he said. "I can't figure out what the hell he's up to this way."

"What's the matter?" Fred asked. He was a chunky man with a head as square and hard-looking as an ornamental doorstop. He had on a blue shirt that was too small for him so that three buttons were open. The hair on his chest was as thick as a bath mat. "Isn't P.J. scab-herding the way he did in the old days?"

"Oh, there've been a few back-to-work moves, sure," Barney said. He speared half a dill pickle, chewed it and took a deep swallow of beer. "They were all organized sort of off the cuff by somebody in this local or that. Nothing big, so it wasn't hard to stop them. Scabs? Hell, there hasn't been any real scabbing in America since sometime before the war. Remember what it was like in the thirties?"

"Christ, yes," Fred said. "They run them in in truckloads. It does look as if scabbing were dyin' out, all right."

"You had about fifteen million unemployed at one time," Bill said. "When you have a big labor surplus like that, a lot of people on relief or maybe not even on relief, you've got the makings. You don't have that now."

"I know," Barney said, "but I don't think it would be so easy to get them anyway, even if you had fifteen million unemployed."

"What about the vets?" I asked him.

"What about them?"

"Kelly might try that."

"I don't think so," Barney said. "I don't know. A lot of the guys I knew in the army were sore enough at one time or another to break a strike just for the hell of it. You know how it was when they heard about strikes at home. They've had time to cool off a little now. No, what really worries me—I don't know what the devil it is. Kelly just isn't trying. You can feel that in the strike, just the same as when you pick up a rope you know whether the other end is tied or not. He's not hanging on to his end at all. Why, for Christ's sake?"

"Look," I said, "you know the thing most likely to happen in this thing—that the men get tired and go back to work without gaining anything and are just a little bit more certain than before that there isn't damn-all they can do about the union even when they want to. That's happened often enough before on a small scale in the locals. Probably Kelly is just waiting for the whole thing to fold up."

"He's taking a chance," Fred said.

"He's not taking a hell of a lot of chance unless we do better than we have done," I said. "He can afford to sit on his ass and call up the papers every day and tell them that there has been an important meeting and that most of the men have agreed to go back to work."

"You're right," Barney said. "What do we do about it? You got a rabbit to pull out of your hat?"

I didn't even have a hat. We finished our sandwiches and went back up to the section which was as hot as hell on a Sunday morning.

Monday 11 A.M.

The dock is bright in eleven o'clock sunshine. There is a mist of smoke over Jersey but the river is clean and bright. Over it the gulls hang on their curving wings and a barge loaded with flashing scrap drifts on the water, nudged by a tiny tugboat. The men lie in the sun, smoking, and Plato Moreno, the stubby old Italian, has put a fishing line out but does not bother to look at it. He has leathery dark skin and a slight scar on one cheek. His eyes are a smudgy brown, and there is a strong smell of garlic about him. He is speaking to the long wiry Negro.

"Trouble with thisa strike," he says, "no organizaish, no organizaish at all. Thisa strike, itsa needa the plan. No organizaish," he says, spitting disgustedly.

"Yawl make a plan foh to get some beer," the Negro says. "I'm gettin' pow'ful thirsty settin' here. How 'bout you pickin' up a few bottles foh us, Tiny?"

He is talking to a little man with bushy hair and red eyebrows who is cutting his initials into the wood of the dock.

"Fuck it," Tony says. "You ain't got nuttin' wrong wit' yer legs, Link."

"Ah cain't rise up right now," the Negro says. "I just found a sof' spot on this ol' plank."

"I t'ought you'd sprained yer ass or sump'n. Where duh hell's Dewey dis mornin?' Ain't it his toin?"

" 'S his turn, rightly."

"If youra wanna catch fish," Plato says. "Youra need the bait. If you wanna strike, you must have the organizaish. This kina thing make me laugh. No plan, no nothing. Justa buncha men run around like crazy. Don' get nothing done that way. You gotta have plan, Link."

"Ah hell, man, yawl always jawin' about it. Make up one then, Plato. See 'f hit does yawl any good. I don't see you catchin' any fish anyway, man. You need bait foh that."

"I hada uncle once," Tiny says. "He give me a bank when I was just a kid, see? Just a kid's bank, see? I kept sockin' my pennies and nickels in it. I t'ought I was gonna have a fuckin' fortune stashed away deh. I had a plan to buy me one of them airguns, see? Den I'm gonna hunt rats in duh cellars. In dem days duh landladies in the cold-water places would pay you fuh killin' rats. No real exterminator rackets in dose days. I figure I'll make a lot of jack. Just a dumb kid, see? So I goes right on savin' an' me old lady is encouragin' me and the uncle is flippin' me a shillin' sometimes an' me brudder's callin' me a heel 'cause I don't slip him a few pence on a Saddy night. So dat goes on fuh munce and I figure I got a couple pounds in duh bank easy, so one day I t'ink I'll crack it and see have I got enough fuh duh beebee gun so I can put my plan into operation. What yuh t'ink?" He pauses and flips his knife blade into the planks. "Me brudder had took duh damper," he says in an aggrieved voice. "He stuck up me private bank, like, when I ain't deh and he's blowin' me pounds on a goil I was figurin' on makin' myself. Don't tell me about no plans."

"Look like yoh brother got a better plan than yawl did, Tiny."

"Yeah."

"Trouble is," Link says, "there's too many plans. Ever' son of a bitch and his brother got plans till hit won't stop, and they all got plans fo' you. Take them newspapers, yawl think theys to tell news? Theys to tell yawl what to do, 'cause that there man writes the newspaper, he got notions in his head about what's good fo' yuh. Government men, they all got plans, preachers, insurance collector men. Yawl know sump'n? Tha's all crap. What good that do me? I'm just down here, tote dat barge, lif' dat bale, tha's ol' Link. I don't need them no how, but I got to hold still fo' them. They's livin' on me like lice on a dawg."

"Yeah, it's a fact. You gotta have some of that though, Link. De's smart men down de' in Washington. You gotta have somebody to run the country."

Moreno snorts and twitches his line out of the water. "Thatsa trouble," he says. "This America worka man he'sa like a bambino, always looka for his mama. Must hava governament. Must hava mister P.J. Kelly."

"You got any better ideas?"

"In Italia—"

"Dis ain't duh old country, fuh Chris' sake. You mean they got it better than we have?"

"Ina Italia, Mister P.J. Kelly—" He makes an expressive gesture. "Pop-pop," he says.

"You mean dey knock him off?"

"Pop-pop," Plato says again. "Justa like that."

"Jesus," Tiny says aggrievedly, "that ain't duh way we do here. You ain't naturalized yet, Plato. Knock him off, huh?" He scratches the thick mop of his hair thoughtfully. "Maybe dey got somp'n in dat," he says.

"Ain't nobody goin' to bump off mister P.J. Kelly," Link says. "I don't reckon so."

"I'm not say bump off," Moreno says. "I'm say get plan, get some organizaish, then you win strike, get contract, kick out thisa Kelly."

"It sounds easy duh way you say it."

"Yawl make up a bomb and Tiny here throws it."

"No bomb. Must get some men, make plan in your head," Moreno taps a finger on his skull. "Everything'sa happen up here first," he says. "Thisa the seat of reason."

"Dat's just somp'n to get hit on if you start organizin' too hard. Pop-pop."

"Thisa the important thing," Moreno says stubbornly. "Looka that sea gull. I closa my eyes, he ain't there."

"Like hell he ain't."

"That'sa because you look. Closa your eyes, he ain't there."

"You're nuts, Plato. Sure he's there."

"How you prove, eh? If you eyes close', if Link's eyes close'?"

"Den if everybody was blind there wouldn't be no sea gulls. Hell, there wouldn't be no sun even."

"Sure."

"Holy Mudder of God, Link, you hear dat? Some people got bats in de' belfry but Plato's got sea gulls."

"Everything up here first," Plato says complacently, tapping his head again. "That'sa where you make things work out."

"Yawl better pull in that fish line, then," Link says grinning. "Yawl fishin' in the wrong place."

Monday 12:30 P.M.

Mrs. Carmody cleared the dishes from the table and put them in the sink, letting the water run until it had covered them. She put the salt and pepper shakers carefully away in the cupboard and closed the door, thinking: it had better be now.

"Mary," she said, "don't you think you'd better be getting back to school?"

"Gosh, Ma, I got a half hour yet," Mary said. She was sitting at the table with one leg twisted under her, looking at a copy of a magazine.

"I want to speak to Francis," Mrs. Carmody said.

"I won't be in the way, will I?"

"I suppose not," Mrs. Carmody said, sighing. She had wanted to talk with Francis alone, but now she was almost glad that her daughter would be in the apartment.

She walked heavily on through the bedrooms into the living room at the front of the house. Blackie, who had been silently sitting at the table, got up and followed her. In the living room Mrs. Carmody adjusted the pillow on the couch and lay down with a little grunt of relief, putting an arm across her forehead as if by shutting out the light she could shut out her fear. Blackie sat down in the big chair between the stove and the window, fished out a cigarette and lit it. He sat sprawled out, with his legs over the arms of the chair, but he did not feel relaxed. He could see Harounian's sign through the window. On the opposite side of the street a woman was shaking a dustcloth. The motes hung golden in the noonday sun.

"I want to talk to you about the job, Francis," Mrs. Carmody said gently but inexorably.

"You know there's no use talkin' about that," Blackie said sullenly. "We talked about that. I don't want that kind of job."

"We've got to talk about it. I can't help it—it's all I've been able to think about since you've been back."

"I can't help it, Ma."

"Yes, you can help it, Francis, and you've got to. I've never asked much of you or of anybody else, but I'm asking this of you now."

"I can't help it. I got my own life to live."

"If you go on like this, you won't have any life at all."

"I can't help it. I got to do the way I want to," he said heavily. He got up and put his cigarette out in the ashtray, thinking he would leave, but he saw her lying on the worn couch, heavy and sick, with the arm over her face so that he would not see if she were crying, and he could not go. In the street the last of the golden motes were gone from the air. People passed along in the street. Foreshortened, because he was looking down at them, they seemed like deformed toys jerking along as if half run-down.

"You don't have to worry about me," he said with clumsy gentleness. "I ain't a fool. I'll take care of myself."

"It isn't even what people would call disgrace," Mrs. Carmody said. "I don't even think of that. Once, when I was young, that would have mattered a lot but it doesn't matter now. The older you get the more things you give up. It isn't that. But if you go on they'll break you, Francis. They'll kill you or break you. I've lived long enough to know how it goes, and I couldn't stand that. You're not even happy, the way you're going on. Do you think I can't see that?"

"I'll get along."

"No you won't. After a while you get so you don't need it anymore, the thing you think is happiness when you're young, but you've got too far to go yet, son."

He didn't answer, looking into the gut of the street at the queer mechanical men. A small boy was trying to bring a puppy out of the play-lot across the street, and even at that distance Blackie thought he could hear the scratching of nails as the dog braced his paws in resistance. From the rear of the apartment he heard the muffled movements of his sister. She'll begin to cry too in a minute, he thought in anquish and loathing.

"I asked Father Burke," his mother was saying, "and he said he would try to do something. He sent a note with Mary just before dinner. He wrote to Mr. Kelly and this morning he got a call from him and you can go down and see him anytime.

"I don't want to see him or anybody else."

"It might be a good job."

"I know what kind of a job it will be."

"It isn't much, Blackie," Mrs. Carmody said in a choked voice. "This is all I'll ever ask you to do for me."

"Well, I won't!" he said, shouting, feeling the terrible unconscious irony in her words. He jerked as if he had been struck with a whip. "Goddamn it, let me alone, can't you? All I've got since I been home is this nag, nag all the damn time. Christ, you're enough to drive me nuts!"

He fumbled and got out another cigarette, lighting it with shaking hands, looking into the street that was full of sunlight and emptiness. Behind him he heard his mother begin to cry, the long, gasping, dry sobs of a grown up, and, above that, the quick frightened sniffles of Mary. Submerged hysterical laughter moved in him. He felt perfectly numb.

"I've got my reasons," he said finally in a dull voice.

"What—reasons could you have—to go against me like this?" his mother asked, as if she were not speaking to him at all but were calling on the dumb walls for an answer. Through the haze of tears she saw the cracked and crazed plaster on the ceiling and tried to concentrate on looking at one line that was the heaviest and then lost it in among the others. Momentarily she thought that if she might just lie there until she died, looking at the cracks on the ceiling and not thinking at all, she would not want anything else, not even to have her son do what she was asking. But the pain kicked in her belly and the moment of total fatigue and peace went away with its coming.

"What reason?" she asked, trying to stop the sobs from shaking her.

"Plenty," he said in the same stricken tone. He knew it would not be any good to tell her it was because she was sick, that he was doing what he was doing because he loved her; he knew that she would not recognize the arguments. If she knew she were dying, he thought, it would only make this one desire stronger. He stood in front of the window, small and dark and glowering, like a tight knot of misery, watching the youngster on the pavement beating the puppy to try to get it to follow on the lead. Abruptly he began to talk about himself.

"I got to do things my own way, Ma. I been away a long time while everybody else's been makin' money. I don't have nothin' and I don't even have a trade of any kind. What can I do? All I could get would be longshorin' or workin' as a teamster or in a warehouse or a box factory or something like that. I don't know how to do anything and I'd never get anywhere. For a while when I was in the army I thought I'd got to school, maybe, learn to be a welder or a machinist or something like that, but those jobs are foldin' up now and anyway it would take too long. Once I even thought I might go to college maybe, but that would take four years. We might even have a depression then and I still wouldn't have any jack. Where would you and Mary be then? We wouldn't have nothin'—"

"I don't want anything, Francis," his mother said in a tired voice. "There's only one thing I want before I die."

The words whipped him again and he plunged on:

"What about me? How do you think I feel? When I went away I never thought nothin' of how we lived, I guess I was too young, but I want it to be decent just once, see? I want to have some money around the house, not like when the old man was working down the dock and we were broke half the time. I want you to have it decent for a while now I'm back; I don't want you to have to live in a joint like this all the time and have to be workin' every day—"

"No, Francis," his mother said sadly. "That's what everyone wants. When I was young, that was what I wanted for my own folks. That's what your father wanted too, and we both went to work early, before we were married, but it didn't do any good. I guess everyone wants that for their folks sometime or other, and then they want it for their children. After a while you see that it's the children that count. The old people go without for so long and then they're not young enough to enjoy the things even if you get them for them. That's the way it is, son. You don't have to worry about me. All I want is peace. And you don't have to worry about Mary. She's smart and she's pretty and in a few years she'll be married. It's easier for girls, in some ways. They don't take things so hard, I guess."

He saw the lumpy tear-wet hand over her eyes, the nails misshapen and ugly from work, and he turned back to the window to keep her from seeing his face. Images out of his life began jumping into his mind: the dead-tired figure of his mother after Mary had been born, in the days before he was old enough to know what tiredness meant; his father coming home at the end of the shift, clothing stinking with sweat and his shoulders still bent from the weight of a heavy load, sitting dull and ox-like waiting for supper; the sounds of fighting from the next apartment; the pool of vomit in the hallway and the constant smell of toilets and drains. The images came faster and faster, jerking into his mind without volition, memories of incidents, sounds, smells, all jumbled together running faster and faster, mixing with the tired gasping sobs of his mother and the stifled crying of Mary in the other room, all running together and racing through his mind faster and faster until they blurred into one single image of misery that he saw as a dark river and realized that he had been looking with blind eyes at the tarred pavement of the street where the little boy sat on the sidewalk, crying and cursing in despair, and the puppy's claws screeled on the concrete as he braced himself.

"You want me to give up everything," he said fiercely, thinking of himself now and what he wanted. "You don't give a damn what happens to me."

He heard Mary crying wildly in the kitchen as she felt the terror in the living room, hating them for it as if they were taking advantage of her youth.

"I've got my own life, for God's sake," he said desperately, while his mother tried to control her painful burdened breath, staring at the cracked lines on the ceiling running out and around from the center, getting lost again in crazy tangles or fading out into the flat gray or nothing at all, as patternless but as permanent as the fact of life.

"Please," she begged, "please, Francis."

"I can't! I can't!"

"Just this one thing."

"No! No! Oh Christ, let me alone!"

"You're killing me!" the mother said, trying to raise herself on the couch. "Oh, Francis, son, please! Please! You're killing me!"

He heard the words almost with a sense of release, as if he had been waiting for them all along, and at the same time they seemed to hang in the room, palpable, ringing like iron. He felt stunned and empty. A strange man came out of the store across the street. An image of the painting of The Last Supper flashed into Blackie's mind. He looks like Judas Iscariot, he thought automatically, and then recognized the man as Mr. Harounian the storekeeper. The black river of the street flashed in the sun and the puppy howled.

"All right, Ma," Blackie said. He turned from the window. His mother lay back against the pillow, and he saw the ruined handsome face, the eyes like raw sores, the eroded lines of pain and worry gullying the pale cheeks and forehead.

"Whatever you want," he said in a dead voice. And then, feeling that he had betrayed her, that he was killing her as surely as if he had held a knife, he knelt beside the couch and nuzzled her damp hand. "I only wanted to help you," he said, his voice wild with despair. "I only wanted to give you what you should have."

He felt a dumb sense of wonder that he could be capable of this betrayal. I never thought I'd turn her in, he told himself; I never thought that.

"Of course you did. Of course you did, son," his mother said, stroking his hair. "You're giving me all that I want, all that I want, Francis." She began to cry again, easily, the happy crying of relief.

"Don't do that," he begged. "Don't cry anymore, Ma."

"No," she said, trying to smile, patting her hair tiredly and mechanically. "I won't cry anymore."

"Try to rest."

"I will. I won't cry anymore."

But when he went out of the room it seemed to him that she had not stopped, that she would never stop, that the apartment shook with sobs, and not just the apartment, but the house, the street, the neighborhood. He remembered the sound from his childhood and it seemed that he had never escaped. It did not seem to him then that he could escape anything, his mother's death or his own life which he saw running away from him like a dark river of misery.

"Sorry, kid," he said gruffly when he saw Mary still sitting at the table. She had her teeth gripped on the corner of her handkerchief.

"It's all right," she answered coolly, hating both him and her mother in one quick flash of emotion. "I won't be a kid much longer," she said, feeling a resentment which she did not understand.

Poor dumb kid, he thought, going down the stairs and into the sunlight of the street where Mr. Harounian was trying to explain something to the little boy whose dog still howled and struggled on the sidewalk.

Monday 4 P.M.

We had a plan. We'd had two more hours in the foggy dew of the section headquarters, the sweat saturating the air that was thick as a blanket from cigarette smoke. A visiting dignitary from another section, a guy named Carl, had given a talk that sounded like a football coach reading a new rule book, but finally we got down to it.

It probably wasn't the best plan in the world, and there were chances that it might backfire, but you have to work from something. We knew we had to get some kind of overall organization to try to pull together all the scattered efforts being made more or less extemporaneously by local rank-and-file committees. We needed to work out a simple negative of the refusal to accept the contract. Then we could organize the picketing and cover the whole front where now there were only little knots of pickets here and there, each group going it alone and depending for its initiative on one or two militants who had some idea of what was needed. The strike was living all around us, but so far it lived as if it consisted of several blobs of protoplasm, primitive and undifferentiated, each little knot of substance trying to perform all the necessary functions of itself, almost completely autonomous. What we had to do was to speed up the evolutionary process. We had to group all that protoplasm into one body, insert a backbone and put a head on the end of it so that it wouldn't unravel. That was what our plan was supposed to do.

It had to be done quickly. Aside from Kelly and his mob, who sooner or later would have to take some kind of definite action, there was the strike itself which, the longer it existed like this, independent of anyone's will, began more and more to take on a shape of its own, to acquire its own characteristics and its own laws of motion. The longer it went on that way, the more difficult it would be to control, like a child that you start to train a little too late.

The strike had its parentage from the men's desire to be rid of Kelly of which the revolt against the contract was the Holy Ghost and the visible sign and their almost equally strong desire not to have to take any real action to make the desire a fact. Then there was the will of Kelly to have them back on the job with no changes made, and the will of the militants to push the strike to its limits and finish with Kelly. So that was how the strike was growing up. And probably because the blind contradictory wishes were the real parents, while the two contradictory and conscious wills were only the rival godfathers, the offspring, in the character it was creating for itself, a fifth element, bore more resemblance to a wish than to a will. It was like wish without an object. What we had to do was transform the wish. We had to show the men that their desire would have to be hardened into the will to achieve it. Then we would have to organize that will.

It was simple enough. You could make it sound simpler by saying that what we had to do was to provide leadership for the strike. We had to get as many involved in the thing as possible, and that was where the danger came in. If we were to try to call a big mass meeting it would probably flop, or Kelly would be certain to have his goon squads out and they would break it up.

Still, we had to have something, and we had decided that the thing to do was to work up an organizing committee of our own people and non-Party militants and then, with this as an authority, try to get together a few hundred people who were interested in doing something with the strike and let them elect their own leadership. A few hundred isn't a lot when there are thousands on strike, but once we had a genuinely elected leadership, even if it had been elected by only a small number, it would be able to work. After that it could be broadened out again. If we could get all the honest rank-and-file members of the various locals, it wouldn't be really unrepresentative either. The danger, of course, was that Kelly would still smell the thing out and either try to pack the meeting or smash it. It was a chance we had to take. We would just have to be careful to whom we issued the invitations.

It was a gamble, but I felt good about it anyway. I had been feeling that the whole business would be like trying to get your hands on a black cat in a dark room, as if we would be working under the compulsion of the strike, not as free agents. I had felt the hatch being screwed down over my head. Now it was like getting out into the sun again, even though there were a lot of things that we couldn't calculate. We were dealing with qualities, and there is no way to measure them. Still, if you use the proper chemicals, the precipitate is always the color you want. If you get a man cornered, even in the double end of the board, and if you have enough men, you can always get him. It wouldn't be as easy as shooting fish in a barrel, but there was no reason I could see why it shouldn't work.

I went out into the warm afternoon sunshine. I felt as if I had got out of a fog that was not the fog of the section meeting. That was where the release had come from. I felt extraordinarily light and carefree, as if it were just really now that I was getting out of the army, getting out of a long dark where you are always being pushed around by people you can't see, fighting in darkness. That the big fog of the army was necessity didn't change the way you felt. After a while you were just worn down, the skin was off the ends of your fingers and you were scrabbling on jagged rock with the naked nerve-ends.

The sunlight felt fine. In the late afternoon, on the few dwarf trees on the street, it was soft and pleasant, not like the blowtorch of mid-day. It was as if a part of the sunlight that fell on my little town had come into the street. I knew I could go around and see Kay that night. It's wonderful what just having a plan of some kind will do for you.

Monday 8:30 P.M.

Kay was working around in the studio just as she had been the night before. The door was open and I walked in. This time I didn't wait for all my private voices to begin telling me that it would never work out. I just walked in and I was only a little surprised when I found I could speak like a normal human being.

"Hello, Kay," I said.

She didn't say anything but came walking over to me as carefully as a sleepwalker, keeping her eyes on my face as if I might disappear when she blinked. She put her arms around me and hugged me hard. We kissed in a kind of desperation, the paintbrush she still held digging into my back. Her hair had a faint smell of turpentine in it, just as I remembered it.

"Baby," she said painfully and pulled away a little, her arms around my neck, looking up at me, her eyes fierce and questioning. I reached back and took the paintbrush out of her hand and she nuzzled her head against my chest.

"You surprised me," she said. "I didn't expect you for, I don't know, a couple of weeks, I guess."

"You glad to see me?"

"What do you think?" She looked up at me as if not quite certain. "It's been a long time, hasn't it?"

"Over three years," I said. "Are you shy?"

"I guess I am," she said with a little broken laugh. "Isn't it silly?"

"I am too."

We stood there hanging on to each other like a couple of strangers who are trying to dance, the three years between us like a wall that it didn't seem possible for us to get over. I was beginning to feel like a ghost haunting the wrong house.

"We'll get over it," she said.

"Sure."

I kissed her then but it didn't make me feel any better. She was getting used to the situation faster.

"Joe, you're a fool," she said, grinning at me.

"I guess I am."

"I *am* glad to see you," she said. Her fingers began worrying loose the buttons on my shirt, and I tossed the paintbrush on the floor and put my arms around her. I felt dumb, awkward, crippled. There seemed to be something I should say, a phrase, one word even, that would explain everything, that would make us equal, make things all right. I couldn't find it. Then, under her hands, everything changed. It wasn't necessary to say anything. All the tension went away, as if I were being released from intolerable pressures, and I felt a freedom that was like a physical change, as if my body were coming alive all over its surface.

"So glad, darling," she crooned softly. "Glad. So glad." Then she said thickly: "I can show you better than I can tell you."

I lifted her up and carried her toward the bedroom, hearing her voice, fierce and incantatory, whispering in my ear, and my own answering. "Now," she said, "now," and her legs opened and I felt her, harsh and honeyed and electric fur.

Later, lying in the darkness, I waited for it to come, the absolute loneliness of satiety, the feeling that you are all alone in the world and that everything has been tried and has failed. I was scared, waiting for it, and then I felt something else, the thing I remembered and was afraid might have been lost: something that must have been happiness but seemed more complete, a feeling of rightness and ease so perfect that at the moment it would have been easy to die.

Tuesday 9 A.M.

When I woke up in the morning it was about nine o'clock. The weather was holding, and the sun was almost as warm and bright as midsummer. In the back garden, just outside the windows, a couple of birds were already taking up their business of the day, hanging their songs on the solid morning, little tinsels of melody as clear and meaningless as jets of water.

Beside me Kay was still sleeping. She had one hand under her cheek and was curled up like a little kid. When she was sleeping she didn't look as bright and competent and chromium-plated as she would later on. Everyone looks a little helpless when they are asleep, and she looked very young and, in a way, weak, vulnerable. For some reason that became a part of the morning too, and made me feel good. I got out of bed quietly, so as not to disturb her, and went in to take a shower. When I got through I went back into the bedroom for my clothes.

"Good morning, darling," Kay said, smiling sleepily. Then: "You don't want to wear those things, do you?" She pointed at the uniform. "I've kept your other things around just in case."

She got up and went to a closet and came back carrying a couple of pairs of pants, a jacket, and some odds and ends of civilian clothing. I had forgotten all about them.

It gave me an odd feeling to dress in them now, after such a long time. When I was finished I went into the bathroom and looked at myself in the mirror on the door. A man with my face looked back at me and I went doubtfully into the bedroom again.

Kay looked at me critically. "I guess they'll do. Unless you want to be stylish."

"They'll do. I don't have so much money that I can afford to start buying new stuff—not at the prices they're getting for things now."

"What are you going to do about that?"

"About what?"

"About putting money in your purse?"

"I'm working on it," I said.

She went into the bathroom then and in a little while I heard the shower going. I walked out into the studio and looked at the pictures. The walls were covered with them. I looked at them all and then went around pulling the surplus canvases away from the wall where she had them stacked. Now and then I would stop and put my hands in the pockets of my jacket just to get the feeling that I was in civilian clothes.

I felt fine. I didn't have the feeling of strangeness anymore, from the way the rooms had been changed, and I didn't feel awkward about Kay or at odds with myself about whether I should stay in the city or go West. I kept walking through the apartment touching things, feeling like a colt that has been let out to grass after a long winter.

"Like it?" Kay asked, coming into the studio.

"Hell yes," I said, looking at her.

"The picture, you dope."

I turned back to the painting in front of me. It was another abstraction, just about like the others.

"Not very well."

"I don't either," she said. "I'm getting sick of doing abstract stuff. I'm just about done with it. Two or three more things and then I try to do something else." She sounded as if she knew exactly what the something else would be.

"It's coming along all right?" I asked.

"The painting? It's going to be O.K. I'm going to be a painter, Joe."

"Sure you are."

"No. I don't just mean an artist—somebody that paints. I mean a *painter*. A good one. I don't know how good yet, but good, just the same."

"I always thought you would."

"Did you, Joe? Why?"

"Not because of the painting. I don't know anything about that. It's just that you're a pretty competent sort of person. So, if you wanted to become an artist, I just expected that you would become one."

"It's nice to have faith," she said, laughing. "I'll show you what I'm working on now."

It was a self-portrait, not yet completed. It looked as if she were getting the nose wrong. Then I looked at it again and it all seemed to be coming apart, but I supposed that was because it was still in progress, or maybe she saw herself differently from the way I saw her. The red hair was all right, anyway.

"I'll give it to you when I'm finished," she said. "If you want it."

"Thanks. I'll have to find a place to hang it first. I'm supposed to get my old apartment back from the guy I let have it when I went into the army, but with places hard to find, I don't know how he'll feel about giving it up."

I said it as casually as I could, and she let it hang in the air for a moment while she fussed with the canvas.

"Don't you want to stay here?" she asked very quietly.

"Christ, yes." That was the thing I had wanted her to say.

"You'd better stay, then," she said decisively.

"I wanted to hear you say it." I must have sounded as serious as a husband ten years gone with matrimony.

"Anything for a pal," she said airily. "I'm tired of sleeping alone, anyway."

That wasn't what I wanted her to say, but nothing could damage the morning, which smelled already like my little town. I was beginning to feel that I had come home.

"What are you going to do, darling?" Kay asked. She poured herself some more coffee and leaned back in her chair. The day before, that question would have had me hung up by the thumbs.

"I'm not sure."

"Don't you think you'd better find out?" To a person who was always as sure of what she was going to do as Kay was, uncertainty must have had the character of an unpleasant disease.

"I'm not worrying," I said. "I know that I can work something out. If you'd asked me yesterday—hell, I don't know what I would have told you. I was hanging from the ropes. When I was coming back from overseas all I could think of was going West. There's a place out there that I know. I used to think of that place a hell of a lot when I was in the army, about as much as I thought about you."

"That's nice."

"I'm not kidding. I used to dream about that place. I always hated New York. I always felt I had a rock on my chest, that I was between the upper and nether millstones, that the pressure was going up and they were screwing the lid down on me."

"I get the idea."

"No, you don't. I can't really explain it. I never liked the place, but it got worse in the army. I got into a hot spot once. My tank got plastered and it burned—that's how I got that burn on my leg. That wasn't bad, the burn, but we were in there, and the thing was burning and there wasn't any light. It was getting thick with smoke and the smell of burning, and hot, and we were fighting in the dark, the hatch cover was down and it was stuck. We were tearing our fingers on it, and she was getting ready to flash like a piece of fireworks with us trapped in it and some of us screaming and fighting like a nest of snakes."

Just talking about it was bad enough. My leg twitched and I remembered the way I had felt. I had not even been afraid if what I had felt at other times was really fear. I had felt only a vast oppressive restriction, as if my skin had become suddenly too small for me, as if my lungs were about to burst out between my ribs. It was like being dropped into an air lock at minus ten thousand; my brain was exploding through the eyesockets and my heart was ripping open like a giant flower with razor-edged leaves. My chest was bursting with air and I couldn't exhale. It was the nightmare of smothering when you are just conscious enough to know that all you have to do is remove the pillow from your face, but you don't have the strength to move or a tongue to cry out. The hatch was the pillow, and just the other side of it was air and light—the world—and we had no way to get through it but to claw through the red-hot steel with our burning fingers.

"I came by here Sunday night," I said after a while. "I even came into the apartment. You were messing around back there, cleaning your brushes or something. I just looked at you a while and then went away."

"Why did you do that?"

"Go away? I guess I didn't think it would work out, Kay. That's funny, isn't it?"

"I don't think it's so very droll."

"No. About the tank business—it doesn't bother me anymore to amount to anything. I still dream about it sometimes, that's all. It used to be bad. Every night I'd have to fight my way out all over again, over and over, until I got so pooped out I couldn't do anything. Then I got so that when I thought about you and my town it'd go away. Coming in though, and those days out at camp before I got discharged, it started to repeat on me. I had it every night. I guess that's why I was hating the city so much when I first came in—I was feeling lousy and I hated damn near everything."

"But you said that if you thought of me or that crazy town you talk about it got better?"

"Yeah. It usually works."

"And yet you didn't even come up to see me? All you could think of was getting on a train and going West?"

"I guess so. I knew you'd never want to go out there. I guess I thought it would just be a beating I would have to take and I wasn't in condition to take it."

"Why did you come back, then?"

"I don't know. I saw some guys the first night in. They wanted me to stay and take a hand in the strike. I didn't want to, but just the same I had to. I couldn't go away. I thought I would stay and just go through the motions. Then, yesterday, after a strike meeting, I got a notion I could take you with me. Just a flash, like the night I first saw you and knew right then that I was going to make you."

"It was easier to make me than it will be to get me to start tagging you around the country."

"I know it."

We sat there and looked at each other like a couple of fighters sizing each other up. I knew just where we were then and that nothing was going to be easy, but there wasn't a thing that could shake me that morning.

"I guess I should tell you something," I said. "I guess I've told it to you before, and I wrote it to you when I was overseas; you've said it too and it didn't mean much—it was just something we said the way other people say it without thinking or meaning anything. I love you."

She reached out for the ashtray but missed and the ashes went on the rug. I couldn't tell from looking at her whether she liked what I had said or not, and right then it didn't matter.

"It just happened—bang like that—when I was in the hospital. One day I wasn't in love with you and the next day I was. I always felt good about you—a warmth and tenderness—and I was always crazy about having you in bed. This was something else. Everything was different, even the light on the fields had changed, and I was in love with you. I tried to tell you that in the letters, but there wasn't any way you could be sure it was different from the way I had said 'I love you' before. I know how it used to be. We liked each other; we were even crazy about each other in a kind of way, and it was fine, but it didn't mean a hell of a lot."

"Do you think I love you?" she asked almost in a whisper. We had begun to talk as if we were a couple of children lost in the woods on a dark and scary night.

"Yes," I said. "But I think you're afraid to admit it even to yourself. That's what I'm going to make you do."

"Can you?"

"I've got to, Kay. That's all there is to it. I've got to."

"I don't think I like having it sprung at me like this," Kay said after a minute.

"I can't help that."

"I don't think I want to fall in love with you."

"I can't help that either."

She stubbed out her cigarette and I thought she was going to cry. Then she got up and paced across the room.

"Joe," she said in a strained voice, "can't we just have it as it was? It was good, wasn't it? You liked it. I was happy the way it was. Can't we just leave it like that?"

I shook my head. "You know we can't," I said. "You don't want the responsibility of being in love. I'm not sore at you for not wanting it. I don't blame you. But that's the way it is, and I can't let you get away with it because I love you and I can't change it."

"I can't change it either. I love you all I can, Joe. Let's just leave it the way it is. It's always been fine here. We can be happy if we just let ourselves alone."

"No," I said. "I won't leave it at that. Besides, I won't be staying here. I'm going West, remember."

"You don't have to do that."

"I don't have to, but I'm going to."

"You're just running away."

"The hell I am!" Barney had said something like that and hearing it again made me angry. "I'm not running anyplace. I know just what I'm going to do. But even if I didn't want to go there, I'd leave New York because I've got to wean you away from this place and make you take on your share of responsibility for us if it's going to mean anything."

"What do you mean, wean me away?"

"You know damn well what I mean. You're like an agoraphobe—you're afraid if you move out of the magic circle where your mother and your friends are, the sky will fall on you. And until you get over that you won't be grown up and you won't be able to admit you love me. You'll be sacred to take a chance on anything."

"So I'm a coward as well as irresponsible?"

"Don't get mad, Kay. There isn't any use. I'm not trying to give you a bad time. I'm not trying to trick you. I've got to make you love me, that's all there is to it, so we might as well know how things stand right at the beginning."

"I think you're the one who wants to run away."

"No. There's no use in our quarreling about it."

"I think I'll just tell you to get out of here."

"No you won't," I said. "Will you? Do you want me to go?"

"No," she said, and now she really was crying. "Don't go. Let's not fight anymore."

"All right," I said. I put my arms around her and stroked her hair. I didn't want to fight. I didn't want her to cry either, but there wasn't anything I could do about it.

Later we were lying on the bed and Kay was saying, "When I was little I never had anything. My father was no good. He thought he was an artist, but he wasn't. He was just no good, and the artist business was just a convenient kind of justification and an excuse for treating us as if we were of no importance at all, as if he didn't have the slightest responsibility for us."

"I'm not an artist," I said. "You're not going to be marrying your father."

"He wasn't really mean." She went on as if she hadn't heard me. "He even tried to be nice to me—I think he liked me anyway—but it was always as if you couldn't be sure of him. He was just not there when you needed him for something. I suppose it was because, really, in himself, he knew he was a failure. He was always thinking that he could work better in some other place and we'd have to break camp and follow him around. Then, after a little while in the new place, it would be the same thing all over again, and we'd have to move once more. I never had a real friend all the time I was little, because I never was in any place long enough. Even if we had been, I don't suppose I would have had one. He was better at acting the artist than being one, and wherever we were, people were sure to think we were queer somehow."

She lighted a cigarette and watched the match burn down toward her fingers. "I'm just telling you this so you see my side of it," she said. "Anyway, that's the way it was. Sometimes he'd be drunk for a long time. That was better in some ways, because then whatever it was that was eating him would be still and he would just sit around and maybe make a swipe at a canvas every couple of days, feeling sure that this time he really had done something. Then he would sober up, and of course when he looked at it, it would be just the thing it really was—nothing—and we would be on the move again. He never really admitted that the pictures were junk of course, but they were. I've got a couple of them. I'll show them to you sometime . . .

"Anyway, that's the way it was. No money ever, and my mother going crazy trying to keep us fed and clothed some way. She wasn't a very good dressmaker but she made all my clothes for me. I don't suppose he ever thought of what it was like for a little girl to look different from the other kids. If you look different from the gang, you look like a freak. Maybe he even thought it was cute. He usually dressed as if he were going to play the part of the artist in that opera, whatever it is, but a little girl can't get away with it. Kids aren't bohemians."

"Your old man sounds like a bum without the convictions of one."

"I don't want to make him seem too bad. He just had a businessman's notion of artist as bohemian. I never disliked him—I just didn't like the kind of gypsy life he made us lead. After I got old enough to know anything, it got worse—never knowing where you were going next, never being able to put your roots down and be able to say 'this is home,' lots of times not even knowing how you were going to eat or pay the rent. Still, he wasn't really mean—just irresponsible.

"I guess I blame my mother just as much. Oh, she was long-suffering, and the loving wife, 'whither thou goest, I will go' and so on. Maybe in a way she was kind of a saint—that's what my aunt thinks anyway—but she just let him get away with it, when he probably wasn't even troubling to be good in bed, and became a nervous wreck from trying to keep clothes on me and a little food in the house. You think it's my mother that I'm tied to, but it isn't. She didn't have to let him treat us like that," she said bitterly. "I like her all right, but I don't need her anymore. When I did, she wasn't much help.

"That's the way I lived," she continued, "until I was fourteen. Then mother got a divorce and we came to New York to live with my aunt. Even then, it wasn't much better, because we had no money and had to depend on my aunt to keep us. But, anyway, I could go to school and begin to find out what it was like to have a friend. After a while I found out what I wanted to do and persuaded my aunt to send me to an art school. Maybe you think that was easy. And now, just the last few years, I've begun to have what I want. I've got my own place and *nobody* can take it away from me, and I've got my friends here, and I'm coming along all right with the painting. For the first time I'm free and independent. I'm *me*. Now do you see why I don't want to give this up?"

"You're still living your life for your mother."

"I've got a responsibility for her now."

"You've got a responsibility to you. To us."

When she didn't say anything, I said: "You wouldn't have to give up the painting when we go out there."

"I know I wouldn't. It's not that."

"Well," I said, "you had a bad time, and I don't blame you for being scared, but that just makes it harder for me."

"You're not thinking of me at all," she said with bitterness. "You've got an idea in your head and you're just treating me as if I were some kind of problem that you had to solve.''

"No, I'm not,'' I said, trying to think what I would have to do to break her down.

"Darling, if you would just stay here, everything would be fine.''

"No it wouldn't. If I ever gave in to you, I'd have to become a banker or a Methodist minister before you were convinced I was a safe bet.''

"I'll never go away with you.''

"Yes you will,'' I said confidently. "What are you really afraid of?''

"You, Joe. If you think you have to leave New York, you'll never stop running.''

"I'm not running.''

"Yes you are. You really want to stop doing the kind of work you're doing, but you won't admit it, and until you do admit it to yourself, you'll always be going somewhere else, just like my father did.''

"I'll never quit,'' I said angrily.

"Maybe you won't, I'm not saying you will. But you would like to, and that is going to keep driving you. If you could just *want* to do what you are doing it would be all right. You'd be a settled man then, the way you were before you went into the army and that would be all right. I might go with you then, but not the way things are now.''

"You're all mixed up about me,'' I said. "When we get out there where we're going, I'll be a settled man.''

"I'll never go.''

"I've got to make you go, honey.'' I pulled her against me and kissed her. "I'm going to get around you somehow,'' I said. "I'm going to take you like Grant took Richmond.''

She wrestled in my arms like a boxer trying to break out of a clinch. Then she relaxed and smiled up at me. "Your tactics are unfair.''

"Everything's fair, they say.''

"I won't change, darling.''

"I'm going to change you,'' I said, laughing.

I suppose she was too mixed up to do much painting that day, but I went out of there with my heart as happy as a month of Sundays, as captain of my soul as the grass was green. The birds were singing and the street was running with laughter. I had the world in a jug and the stopper in my hand.

Tuesday 3 P.M.

I had a lot of names on my list and it was about three o'clock when I got around to seeing Brian Munson, a fellow I had known pretty well on the job before I went into the army. I had never been at his home before, but there was something familiar about the address. It wasn't until I got down toward the end of the street, almost to Ninth Avenue and the post office, that I thought of the fight that had taken place there when I first met with Bill Everson. It was the same street. I crossed over, trying to read the numbers on the houses, but they didn't have any. Nobody gives a damn where you live in New York, and if you're anonymous, so much the better. Then I got located by finding a candy store with the number over the door and counted my way back. The names on the letter boxes in the house were peeling off, as if they had been afflicted with mange, and there was hysteria in the paint in the vestibule. Then I saw the name.

I went up through the layers of radio, the programs of news, the sound of crooners, the whinny of voices advertising something—the three total weathers of murder, love, and corruption, all piped in like the city water. The apartment was at the rear on the third floor, and it had the clam-quiet of a burnt-out undertaking parlor as the sound of my knock fell away into the dust in the corners. I tried again, and just as I was about to give it away, there was the sound inside like a couple of snakes sliding down a roof of feathers. The door slapped open and a head came out like a jack-in-the-box.

It looked at me with the suspicion of a veteran insurance adjuster. I didn't blame her a damn bit. Nothing but bad news ever seems to come into a house like that. She got a look at me and decided that it was no good. The door started to close slightly.

"Is Mr. Munson in?" I asked.

"Who wants him?"

"I do. Joe Hunter. I used to work with him before the war."

That helped things a little. She opened the door a bit more and looked at me almost as if she thought I were a human being. She was a medium-sized woman, skinny and blonde. She looked as if once she might have been pretty and maybe a little rattle-headed in the kind of way that a lot of men like, but just now she looked bleached out and indecisive. She was wearing a pair of sloppy old bedroom slippers that whispered when she moved.

"I'm a friend of his," I said. "Brian will remember me."

"Won't you come in?" she said then, with the real courtesy that so many working-class women have. "Brian will be glad to see you."

I wasn't sure of that myself, but I sat down on a chair at the kitchen table and waited. After a few minutes she came back with Munson behind her. He was carrying part of a loaf of bread. He put it on the table and we shook hands.

"Glad to see you back, Hunter," he said. "My kid Johnny, he's back too, but he didn't go back on the job as fast as you."

He gave me a quizzical shuttered look as if he might have guessed what I wanted. I wondered if he had remembered my name or if his wife had told him. We had worked in the same gang for a while, before I went into the army, and I had got to know him pretty well, but you can forget a lot in what was almost four years. His hair was whiter than I remembered it, but he still parted it in the middle and it still had the little curls at the ends. He looked, except that the hair was white and he had no mustache, like one of those young blades you see in the pictures from the old days, pictures of the beefsteak parties the political clubs used to have, or pictures of some sports club or baseball team. You could imagine him in a pair of striped tights with his hands up as if he didn't know what to do with them, a real John L. Sullivan pose, squaring off for a lesson in the manly art of self-defense. There was also a certain air of courtliness abut him, something old-fashioned and fine. He talked like a West Sider who has somehow cut away part of his accent.

"I'm glad to be back," I said.

"You came about the strike, didn't you? I been kind of expectin' somebody to drop around to see me," he said sardonically.

"You didn't have to wait," I said, smiling. "You know where we live."

"Yes," he said. "I guess I know that." But he didn't say why he hadn't tried to look us up and he got a wary look on his face as if he were afraid I was going to try to sell him something he didn't want to buy. His wife was standing behind him and I could see the milk of human kindness drying up in her. She didn't like that kind of talk at all.

"Bring us a couple cans of beer, Effie," Munson said, and she started rooting around in the icebox.

"You think anything can come of this strike?" He spoke as casually as if it were no concern of his at all.

"Sure," I said. "All we have to do is start working the right way."

"You know how that is?" It would have sounded better if he had smiled.

"I think so. At least we've got a plan that should work out all right."

Effie banged a couple of cans of beer on the table. I could feel the fear and resentment coming out in her actions. She was afraid of what I was going to say to Munson. She didn't want him involved.

"Spill it, then," he said, putting the can down on the table. "It's got to be good to work."

I told him about the scheme we had worked out for organizing a good-sized meeting and electing a committee, suggesting people whom I thought might be willing to work on it or at least help us get it going. Some of the names he vetoed, suggesting others in their places. He began to be a little interested and lost a bit of that clammy calculation.

"Well, what do you think of it?" I asked him.

He shook his head and swallowed a little more beer. "It might work," he said finally. "I guess you know that you open yourself up pretty wide, that way. If Kelly gets wind of it, he might pack it and then where would you be?"

"We'll just have to be exclusive about our invitations to this first meeting," I said. "After we get a committee representing a hundred men or so, each of whom have some kind of following on the job or in their locals, it will be able to call mass meetings in Manhattan and Brooklyn without having to worry too much about goons."

"What about Jersey?"

"We haven't a damn thing over there," I told him. "I don't know what's happening across the river. So far, about the only guys we've had to work with are our own Party people, and with the war a lot of our people went into the army or into other jobs. Our organization in the industry went all to hell. There may be quite a few of our guys scattered around where we don't know anything about them. It's kind of of like working in the dark. In Jersey we don't seem to have a damn thing."

"There's a guy named Keyes over there that's tryin' to do something. Jim Keyes. Used to know him pretty well. I thought he was a Red."

"I never heard of him." I put the name down in my notebook. "I'll try to get some dope on him. You know where he lives?"

He shook his head. "What do you want me to do?" he asked.

"You could do a lot to help us scare up the right people for this meeting."

"Yeah, I could," he said. He smoothed down his hair with the flat of his hand. There was a fight of some kind going on inside him; he was thinking now, and worried, and there wasn't any of that cool sardonic calculation left in him. Effie could see it too, and didn't like it. She started to speak and then checked herself, watching him.

"We'd like to have you on the provisional committee that calls the meeting," I said. "A lot of people know you as an honest man." I just put it out there and let him look at it. I didn't want to try to hop him up or twist his arm. I could see now that he wanted to work with us, but he was having a fight between what he wanted to do and his fear of possible consequences.

"You got no right to ask him," Effie said fiercely. "Who are you to come in here and tell him what he should do?"

"He can't make me do anything, Effie."

"Yes he can," she said bitterly. She turned to Munson: "He comes in here and talks about what should be done and the next thing you're thinking you should do it. He's not a—a priest!"

"I'm not trying to be anybody's conscience." I was beginning to be a little sore myself.

"I've seen it happen before," she went on faster and more angrily all the time. "I saw it happen with my dad before we was married, in the nineteen twenties when they had that big strike that Kelly broke. My dad held right out till the last and then what happened to him? He couldn't get his job back for two years and all that time we were nearly starvin' to death and all the neighbors lookin' at us funny because my dad was on the outs with Kelly and his bunch. What'll happen to you, Brian, once they see that you're workin' against Kelly?"

"Sure, I'd be marked lousy," Munson said. He didn't look at either of us. "I'm marked lousy now with some of the delegates."

"Where would you be, then?" Effie asked scornfully. "Out in the cold. What could you get out of it?"

"A lot of things," I told her. "A decent pension system for one thing. A hiring hall so that every worker got a fair shake without the star gangs and the favoritism you have now. Cut down the speed-up and get a little protection in the work—the way they're overloading and speeding up now, some of those jobs are dangerous as hell. You know what the accident rate is. Hell, the contract isn't the only thing."

"Those things would be fine, sure, if you could get them, but people have been fightin' for things like that for years and what come of it? Nothing. You got no right to ask Brian to take chances. What if something happened to him? Do you think anybody would care? Nobody would care. *Nobody.* Not the church or the government or you either. All we got is this place and Brian's job, and that's all we'll ever have, but it's ours. Nobody can take it. It isn't much, but it belongs to us. When you're young you can take chances, you want a lot of things and you'll take a chance to get them, but we're not young any more, and when you get older you know that this is the way things have always been and always will be, and if you're smart you just get used to it because nobody in the world cares what happens to you."

I didn't say anything, waiting for Brian to make up his mind. She was right about most of it. I looked around the room. It was very clean and neat. The little icebox had been painted recently and the stove, a coal stove converted to gas, was blacked. I could imagine what the other rooms were like, the funiture which was old and had been recovered several times, the arms neatly mended where they had been broken. I could see the worn carpet on the floor of the living room and the bare boards or linoleum on the others. Those windows that had sunlight part of the day, if there were any, would have a couple of window boxes or flowerpots. The place would be terribly hot in the summer and hard to heat with a kerosene stove in the winter. It would smell bad then, because these cold-water places had been built originally with fireplaces in them, and those had been bricked over later but no one had bothered to fix any chimneys to allow the oil fumes to escape. The plumbing would be falling apart, as it was in all the places like this one, and there would be a never-ending war with the cockroaches. And then, all it would need would be for Brian to have an accident on the job and they might lose even this. She was right, from her point of view anyway. It was my job to try to influence Munson's choice, but there are some men who have to choose for themselves.

"I guess Effie's right," he said reluctantly. He didn't want to look at me. "If it was ten years ago, maybe—" he let it die away. Effie gave me a look of triumph and went out of the room.

"You're the doctor," I said. "Your wife's wrong about one thing though—we'd try to take care of you as far as a job is concerned. We've got to figure that if it fails some of the leaders will be victimized, and we'd try to find them a job somewhere."

"I'm too old to learn a new job, I guess," Munson said, smiling sadly.

"You're not so old."

"Old enough." He got up and picked up the bread he had put on the table when he first came in. "I was up on the roof feedin' the pigeons," he said. "Want to come up a minute?" We went out and climbed three more flights of stairs to the roof.

When he opened the door I heard the throaty chuckle of the birds, a drowsy sound in the slanting sunlight that fell on the roof. They got more and more excited as he began to open the little trap doors of their cages and then they were fluttering around his shoulders, their wings slapping together like pieces of leather. He broke up the bread and scattered it around for them and they came down and landed on the roof, walking back and forth importantly the way pigeons do.

"They're pretty, eh?" he said. "Nothing special about them though. I never tried to breed any fancy kind, not even fantails. Look at this one."

He held out some bread in his hand and coaxed one of them out of the huddle. It flew up to get the morsel and rested on his wrist. "Look at this," he said, holding the bird out toward me. Its feet were all swollen and knobby with deformations. It looked as if it had leprosy. He stroked its head gently.

"I guess he landed on something hot," he said. "Hot tar someplace, maybe, or on a chimney that was too hot or something like that. I come up here one day and there he was, just sittin' on top of the dovecotes. I guess he couldn't go any farther. His feet were terrible then. I doctored him up a little and he's all right now."

When he started talking about the pigeons he became a different man. He talked rapidly as if he were excited and he even looked younger. When we were downstairs, he had seemed at first a little standoffish, and then somehow ashamed, but now he was as relaxed and easy as if we had been friends for years.

"You've had the pigeons a long time?"

"Oh, maybe ten years," he said, waving his arm and letting the pigeon flutter back down with the rest of them. "You'd be surprised how many people keep pigeons. I guess I must know fifty guys, here or in Brooklyn or up in the Bronx that keeps them. Some of them have great big flocks, but I never tried to build mine up much. The landlord here, he doesn't like havin' them, and if I was to have a whole lot, he'd probably get nasty. Some guys, all they do when they ain't workin' is sit up on the roof and fly their pigeons. They try to catch others they see goin' by. Like those."

He pointed to three that were circling about a half block away. Then he picked one of his birds out of the flock and launched it into the air. The bird made a halfhearted circle and started back to the dinner table, but the three strange ones followed him in to have a look at what was going on. Then they circled away again.

"I could have got those if I'd wanted them," he said. Then, as if he had been thinking of it all along: "I'll help you try to get that meeting organized."

"Not unless you really want to," I said. "We're not so shorthanded that you should stick your neck out if you think you can't risk it."

"I'll give you a hand. But about the committee—I don't think I better be on that."

"All right."

"I'd like to. I just can't afford to take the chance."

"Sure. I understand that."

"When I was younger, I always figured I wouldn't take nothin' off no man, no matter how big he was, so I had a lot of fights. Ninety-nine fights and never won a one of them," he said smiling crookedly at the old joke. "I figured if I didn't win, I could take a beatin', but I wasn't goin' to run." He crumbled a handful of bread and tossed it to the pigeons. He looked old and gray again.

"Effie's right, though," he said. "You can't beat it. This setup isn't a man that you can either lick or get a beatin' from."

"No, it's not." I wanted to give him the absolution he was asking for, but I couldn't.

"I'll help you get the guys to the meetin' anyway," he said. "You come and see us again."

"Sure," I said, and opened the door to go downstairs. He had picked up the pigeon with the sore feet and was examining it again. Then he launched it into the sky. He couldn't have been feeling very happy, having found out just now that there are times when you have to run away after all.

Tuesday 6 P.M.

By the end of the afternoon I had worked through all the names on my list and I was satisfied. Some of them had been like Brian Munson, a little leery of getting too close to the buzz saw. Others just looked at me and ran, but the majority met me halfway, the way Munson did, and enough of the others offered to work on the committee so that when I started back to Kay's place at about six in the evening I was happy.

At Fourteenth and Seventh I saw Riverboat Conn across the street. He gave me a hail and I walked over. His face yoked age and immaturity in violent contradiction, and he wore a look of amusement.

"Hello, Commissar," he said. "What's happenin' on your front of the class fuckin' struggle?"

"Knocking off the day, Riverboat. How's the weather in the country of alcohol?"

"Zero zero. You can buy me a beer, yeh? You ain't on duty." He underlined the word with a wise leer and clapped me on the shoulder.

"All right."

We went into a joint and sat down in a booth and got the drinks. "Cheers," Conn said and dropped his down the slot without—so far as I could see—swallowing at all. He stuck the glass out at the waiter before the guy could turn away.

"I guess you know you're apt to get your head knocked off," he said conversationally.

"I didn't know. How come?"

"When Kelly gets wind of this little party you got comin' off, he's going to take a lot more interest in you guys than he has to date."

I didn't like the sound of that. I wasn't thinking so much of what Kelly might or might not do as I was of Conn's knowing about the meeting. If he knew about it, it would probably be all over the front in the morning. Conn was a good enough man in a lot of ways. He was honest by his own lights and he was smart enough. The trouble was that he was rum-dum. He must have guessed what I was thinking.

"I don't drink with any of Kelly's goons," he said. "You can fuckin' well relax, if that's what you're thinkin', chum."

"Well, you know about it. Think it'll work?"

"Nobody pays me to think," he said. "How about a smoke, now

that we've had our aper'tif?"

I handed him my cigarettes and he went through the act: "What," he said. "No Sweet Caporals? No Players' Navy-Cut?" He took half the pack and gave the rest back to me. "Your trouble is," he said, "that you're always tryin' to organize somethin'. You got to learn to let things go to hell for a while. The only way the great American proletariat is going to learn anything is at the end of a baseball bat. Hell, they know all they have to know, they just won't get off their cans. They like bein' crapped on. They ain't goin' to move until their assholes are on fire. You're just wastin' your time."

"We've been over that a few hundred times," I said. "Let it lay."

"O.K. You asked me what I thought of your grand strategy. Did I ever tell you the story of Low-Life MacMahon?"

"You probably have."

"Well this Low-Life he had a plan too, see? He was one of those far-seein' jokers, always bustin' his brain how to make a quick buck. An angle man, yeh? Well, we had a strike once, a real strike, not one of these three-for-a-nickel affairs like this one, but a strike where we were out three or four months. A seaman's strike. We were damn near starvin' to death. The Wobs had a stewpot and the Commies had one, but it wouldn't begin to feed half of us. We were bein' converted by Sallies all over town, sleepin' in the subways—hell, it was tough. It began to wear down the spirit, see, and that was how Low-Life MacMahon forsook the cause of the embattled proletariat and decided to make himself a fortune. He had a plan all worked out for doin' it.

"It seems he read in a magazine somewhere about how easy it was to do a Houdini act, get out of handcuffs, locked trunks, all that kind of crap, so he got together a couple of nickels and wrote for the instructions. Once he got through the first page he was lost. He began to carry the banner all over town, workin' himself to the bone in order to get hold of the jack for the rest of the lessons and then after that to buy the equipment—the patent handcuffs that would open when you squeezed them in the right place and all the rest of it. He also bought a couple of yards of chain and some padlocks to go with it. Then he got a guy to stooge for him—to be the guy that would come up out of the crowd, after Low-Life had put the spiel to attract them, and who would volunteer to lock him up in his chains and handcuffs. Low-Life gave him instructions on how to do it in such a way that when Low-Life got ready to do the Houdini, the chains would fall off his arms and legs like breakin' a few pieces of spaghetti. They rehearsed it for about a week.

"Then, just as he got ready to make his debut, the strike ends—I don't know just how it ended, but it did—and this stooge that Low-

Life has trained shipped out the first thing. That almost run Low-Life crazy, because he was a nervous kind of type anyway and easy to upset. He's down at the union hall racin' round like a rabbit in the matin' season, tryin' to find another stooge. Finally he locates a guy and gives him a quick initiation and they get ready to put on the big act the next day.

"So the next day they go down to a vacant lot on Twenty-third Street—there was a vacant lot there then—and Low-Life goes into his spiel about how he is a second Houdini and in a few minutes they will see the greatest escape-artist in the world go into action. He keeps it up until he has a pretty good audience and then calls for a volunteer from the crowd to lace him into his chains and handcuffs. His stooge steps forward and clamps on the irons. Then Low-Life pretends to sweat and strain for dear life to get out of the iron, but he's just givin' them a run for their money. He ain't puttin' on the pressure yet.

"So about that time a cop comes along and sees the crowd and comes over to find out what's in the wind. Low-Life sees him comin' and begins to strain in good earnest at the chains, but he's havin' a hard time.

" 'All right,' the cop says, 'now move along all of yez and you, bosko, get them things offa ya and get movin'.'

"Low-Life struggles some more and nothin' happens. The crowd don't move because they are entranced at the act he's puttin' on.

" 'Come on now,' the cop says, giving Low-Life a light rap on the ear with his nightstick. 'I want this broke up and all of you outa here right now.'

"Low-Life gives a loud groan and the sweat begins to break out on him like on a cold beer bottle in the noonday sun. He looks around for his stooge to come and unlock him, but the stooge is by this time almost to Tenth Avenue and going fast. He has it in his mind to ship out right away.

" 'I told you to hurry it up, Jack,' the cop says, givin' Low-Life another sharp rap on the head. 'Let's see some action here.' All the time the crowd is gettin' thicker, and Low-Life is thinkin' that if his stooge hadn't fucked him up and if the cop hadn't come along he'd have taken five, six bucks out of them marks.

"Low-Life lets out a groan. 'I can't do it!' he says.

" 'Like hell you can't,' the cop says. 'I seen you guys before. Now shake those things off before I get sore and decide to run you in.' And he starts givin' Low-Life a real bad roust.

"By this time Low-Life is about to go fruit, and he begins to yell and curse at the stooge, and the cop naturally thinks he is the one who is in line for the bad time, and he starts in on Low-Life with the nightstick like a snare drummer goin' into the long roll. He is swearin' and Low-Life is yellin' and the crowd is havin' a hell of a fine time.

"That cop came near to beatin' Low-Life's brains out before he convinced himself that Low-Life is tellin' the truth and that he really can't get out of all that gear. So he sends the crowd on its way and manages to work Low-Life—who isn't feelin' much like takin' a walk at that time—by easy stages down to a blacksmith shop on Tenth Avenue. It took them three hours with hacksaws to get him out of all those chains. That night Low-Life, with five black eyes and about ten heads growin' on his head as a result of the nightstick massage, comes down to the hall with the ornaments of his trade in his hands.

" 'Here,' he says, dumpin' the load of scrap iron on the floor, 'take this. After the Revolution we'll have a museum of the instruments of torture of the bourgeoisie. Take them irons. Karl Marx said the workers had nothin' to lose but their chains, and by Christ, there's the chains!'

"Now," Riverboat Conn said. "There's what happened to the great plan that one man had. You got enough for another beer, yeh? O.K. Call the fuckin' waiter."

Tuesday 7:30 P.M.

Blackie Carmody came home through the dusky street. From outside he could see that there was no light in the living room of the apartment, and there was none in the kitchen when he entered. He hoped that his mother was sleeping, but when he closed the door he heard her calling him from the front of the apartment and he went on into the living room. She was lying on the couch in the deep shadow with her arm over her eyes as she had been the night before. He felt his guilt and his love cutting him like a knife and wished that there were something he might say to her, but it seemed to him that there was nothing that he could ever say again that would have any real meaning. He was afraid even to say anything affectionate to her for fear he would let his feelings run away with him so that she would begin to suspect that something was wrong.

"Did it go all right?"

"Sure," he said. "Why wouldn't it? I saw Kelly. I got the job."

He didn't want to think about the job then. He noticed John Manta sitting in his customary place behind the stove.

"Hello, John," he said. "I didn't see you at first."

Manta said hello in his dead voice without even looking at him. "Thank God," his mother said, giving a long sigh as if she were sitting down to rest for the first time in a long and tiring day. She said something to Manta and they went on with a conversation which he had interrupted, both of them speaking in low tones with frequent intervals of silence as if they were in a sickroom. Blackie went to the window and looked into the street.

It was dark, shadowy, patched with blurs of light like coils of faded yellow yarn. It was the way it had been on a thousand nights, but to Blackie it looked different from all the ways he had ever seen it. HAROUNIAN MEATS & GROCERIES. That was familiar enough. Up the street toward Eighth Avenue there was the newsstand and farther on there was a subway entrance. Across the way, just a few doors from Harounian's place, was the candy store which had been there when he was a child. Still, none of it looked the same. HAROUNIAN MEATS & GROCERIES. Where had the big switch come in? Westward the street cut through the tenements to the docks; eastward it ran to the other river. Nothing was changed, yet nothing was the same. HAROUNIAN MEATS & GROCERIES was just the same as it had always been. It must be because of me, he thought wonderingly; it must be because I've changed.

There was no way he could avoid thinking about it. The quarrel with his mother the day before, the meeting with Kelly in the afternoon, rose up again out of the dark pit of his mind asking to be relieved. The street suddenly became peopled with himselves—the boy going to school, the one lounging in the candy store, the one who had gone off to war and the other one who had come back, the man he had been yesterday before the quarrel, the man who had come back from the meeting with Kelly when he had got the job—the street was full of himselves, going and coming, crossing each others' paths, overtaking and passing one another— But where am *I* he thought in terror, where am *I* ?

"We named him Francis Xavier after my father," Mrs. Carmody was saying in a voice almost soft as a whisper. She went on in a low drowsy tone talking through the darkness at John Manta, telling some rambling anecdote out of the past, but Blackie did not hear her. He was wound into his sudden vision of a street that swarmed with his dead selves, and he saw it now as an appalling symbol of his treachery, his deception, as if he had willingly adopted all the disguises that seemed to be passing in the shadows under the window. He could not forgive himself for having yielded to his mother's wishes, was unable to justify himself on the grounds of love for her. All he could see was a hateful weakness in himself that had made him abandon her and that had allowed himself to sell out, at the same time, all his own hopes. Where does it end, he asked himself in pain and amazement; where will I stop; I sold out everything.

He saw Joe Hunter pass on the street. "I don't take a nickel . . . No old guy in a candy store—" The words echoed in his memory. When was that? It was something that Blackie Carmody had said.

Harounian came into the street and began to pull an iron screen across his windows. He moved with complete unselfconsciousness, as if he were alone in the street. Did it ever happen to him? Blackie asked himself, wondering if Harounian had ever seen the earth open at his feet, found himself becoming something he had never dreamed he was, looked into the street and found it crawling with multiple images of himself that were not really himself.

Francis Xavier Carmody. It was possible that there was no end to the transformations and the disguises, that he would go on changing again and again with the years, and he wondered once more, with loathing and amazement, if there were any limit, now that he had let go and was drifting. *Francis Xavier Carmody.* Well, you had to have a label to be recognized on the street which was a different street from the one that it was the day before when you had been someone else, someone that you thought you knew completely and who was labeled Blackie.

Manta was trying to say something to him and having a hard time getting his attention. "Blackie—" Manta said, "Blackie—"

"Call me my own name, for Christ's sake," Blackie answered. "You heard what she said. Francis Xavier Carmody." He went out without waiting for what Manta had to say. On the steps of the house he paused for a moment, looking at the street which swept past like an assembly-line littered with the debris of his previous transformations. They were fading out now, those images of himself, dissolving in the shadows as he stood on the steps, staring at them blindly, asking in mortal anguish: Where is Blackie Carmody?

Tuesday 8:30 P.M.

Crip dragged his dead foot up the stairs to the door of his rooming house and paused wearily on the step. Inside he could hear the maudlin singing of the landlady, just above a whisper, and it enraged him for no reason that he would have been able to formulate. He had been hunting without any success during the day, and he would have to go back to it again after he had had supper. His leg pained him and he was very tired. He wanted to be able to lie down for an hour before he went out to eat, and the sound of the landlady's voice grated on his nerves. The fatigue worked on him like a drug; he found himself thinking that he was getting old, and then wrenched the thought away angrily, swearing in his mind. So far as possible he had stopped thinking about himself years ago and now, sometimes for days, he would go on without ever once thinking that he was an individual with a name which he had almost forgotten.

He opened the door and shuffled across the worn carpet and climbed the stairs, swearing to himself at this leg as he always did. It was the only part of him with which he was not satisfied because it was the only part of him which he could never forget. At the top of the stairs, in front of his door, as he fumbled for his key, a little wind of warning blew around him, and he paused, holding the key in his hand, listening. He thought he heard a sound of movement from inside his room.

There was no light under the door, and Crip believed that if anyone had come to see him—no one had in the years in which he had been living in the house—and sat waiting for him in the dark, it could only be because the man wanted to kill him. He was perfectly sure in his own mind that there was a man in his room now, with a gun in his hand, waiting for him to open the door, but he did not question himself about who it might be, since in his world the relationship embodied in the act of killing had been thoroughly dehumanized, hypostatized in the coin which paid for it and which was the only nexus between the killer and the killed. Crip did not think of the man in his room as a man at all but only as a force, an instrument, a machine which was the reflection of a transaction which had taken place he did not know when between people of whom perhaps he had never heard, but who, somewhere in the dark of his ignorance, had willed that he be dead and had sent this machine on its way to his destruction. He began to swear to himself in a fury of despair, not because he was afraid, but because this thing in his room, whose name he did not know and who must have been sent by other men whose names Crip could not guess, was another proof of his own ignorance. He felt as if the night and the darkness had come with him into the dim-lighted hallway, and he stood before the door, shivering in a paroxysm of impotent hatred and inarticulate outrage, listening to the sound of the steady breathing from within. He put his head lightly against the door, listening, and felt it move slightly. It was not locked.

He got the gun out of his pocket without thinking at all and, launching himself from his good leg, whipped the door open and jumped into the room.

There was a man in the chair beside the table. He had been sleeping and he woke suddenly now, turning in terror and falling from the chair. Crip did not see his face. He hit at him with his revolver and felt only the heel of his hand connect and drew back for another blow before he heard the whining fear-strung voice begging him to quit.

"It's me, it's Jake," the man said, whimpering. He did not try to get up from where he was half sitting, half lying on the floor. Crip went to the wall and switched on the lights. He was cursing steadily in a low passionate voice.

"You son of a bitch," he said, "I thought it was somebody trying to stake me out. You're lucky I didn't give it to you when I came in."

"I just come to see you and I guess I fell asleep in the chair," Jake moaned. He got up from the floor now and sat on the edge of the bed. His nose was bleeding and he wiped it on his handkerchief, looking at the blood on the cloth with distaste and curiosity.

The landlady was calling from the foot of the stairs. "Are you all right up there? I thought I heard someone fall."

"Naw," Crip said from the door. "I'm all right. Go on back in there."

"Is your visitor still there or did he leave?"

"He's here all right."

"I didn't think you'd mind if I let him wait in your room."

You lousy, dirty bitch, he thought, you rotten, lying slut. "Naw," he said. "I don't mind."

He did not hear her door close, but he closed his own, still swearing at Jake in the same level passionate voice.

"I told you where you could see me if you wanted to," he said. "I don't like any damn monkey coming up here like a nosy hoople. How did you find out I lived here anyway?"

"One of the boys knew," Jake said. "I want to see you in a hurry and I ast around and one of them knew. So I came up here. I dint think you'd mind."

"All right, talk and then blow. What you want to see me about?"

"It's this guy I'm workin' for," Jake said. He was beginning to get his confidence back. His nose had stopped bleeding and after one more glance at his handkerchief he put it back in his pocket. "This guy wants some action. He wants this to come off quick. I tried to see you the other day, but you dint show up."

"How the hell long have I been on it?" Crip asked. "A lousy couple of days."

"Well, the big fellow, he wants some action right away. I—"

"Nobody's going to tell me. Who the hell is this big fellow anyway?"

"I don't know. I'm just a middleman. A guy tells me to get somebody to do a job and I get you. Then this fellow tells me the big fellow is sore because you ain't done it."

"I'll do it in my own good time."

"All right. I'm just supposed to tell you."

"You can haul ass out of here, then."

"All right, I'm goan."

"And next time you want to see me, you know where you can find me and I don't mean here."

"O.K., Crip, you don't have to be sore."

When the man was gone Crip sat for a long time at the table. It took time to work off the anger, the helpless objectless angry hate which was the only intense emotion he ever felt, the one he lived on, a feeling fed by that sense of being outraged and denied which had been with him since the time he had taken his father's useless gun and before.

He was thinking that he would have to move, and he hated it. It was not that he was in any way attached to the room he had lived in so long—it was simply that he had got used to it, so that he no longer even noticed what it was like, and that was as close as he came to any kind of feeling of comfort. Still, he would have to get another room. It would not do to keep this one, now that it was known where he lived. He preferred to look for people rather than having them look for him.

He thought again, with blind and impatient fury, of the "big fellow" whom he did not know. It was as if he were sitting in a circle of light and someone from out in the darkness were prodding him with a club. He drew the image from a memory of a time when the police had been grilling him, and when his mind connected the two images, as if a circuit had been completed, a little shock of uneasiness went through him. He put it aside abruptly, cutting it away from him as he had cut away all other feelings except the angry hatred on which he lived, got up and crossed over to the closet.

Inside was a battered suitcase made out of imitation leather. One of the straps had cracked almost in two, and he examined it, swearing to himself as he placed the suitcase, opened, on his bed. He opened the four drawers of the dresser, working quietly so that he would not arouse the landlady again, and took out the clothing. It took him two minutes to do the packing, to put in the four shirts, the socks, underwear, and shaving equipment. He did not have another suit of clothing or another pair of shoes. There was a worn overcoat in the closet, and he put this on. Although he read a great deal, there was not one book of his own to go with him. When he had finished, the suitcase was only half full, and he looked around the room to see if there was something he might be missing. There was only one other thing belonging to him in the room, and that was a calendar hanging on the wall. He thought for a moment of opening the suitcase and putting it in and then decided that he would leave it for the landlady or the next tenant. Opening his door, he went to the head of the stairs and listened. There was no one in the hall. He did not want the landlady to see him leaving because it would have meant explanations and he simply wanted to disappear. When he was sure that there was no one in the hall, he went back into his room for his suitcase. At the door he again thought of something and, setting the suitcase down, went back, took the calendar from the wall and tore it up. It was the only thing that he had done that evening that gave him any satisfaction.

Wednesday 11 A.M.

"I heard you wanted to see me, Al," Landers said, sitting down in the booth.

"Yes, that's right." Husk didn't look at Landers but crooked a finger at the bartender and called, "Two of the same" without asking the other man what he would drink. When the whiskey arrived, he drank half of the glass and sat moving it in absentminded circles on the table. Landers took off his glasses, polished them, and sipped at his drink distastefully.

"What's on our mind, Al," he asked.

"What would be on my mind, for Christ's sake?" Husk asked irritably. "The strike."

Landers took another sip of the whiskey and pushed it away from him.

"It doesn't look as if anything much would come of it," he said.

"That's your opinion," Husk told him with an edge of contempt in his voice. "Do you know about this meeting they're trying to pull off?"

"I heard a rumor about it, that's all."

"That's all, is it?" Husk said. "Damn it, you're at least supposed to know what's going on. Or are you too busy organizing on your own? What's the ACTU doing?"

"They don't seem to be doing anything much," Landers said. "Why?"

"They won't either. Some of the lawyers in that mob are itching to get their hands into the union jackpot, and some of the priests that run it with them want to move in on Kelly, but they aren't going to move. They get their orders from the Powerhouse, and Kelly is still in strong with the bishops, archbishops, and the rest of the Catholic brass. They won't do anything."

"Why are you telling me this?"

"I just don't want you to get any false notions of how much use that Catholic trade-union racket is going to be to you. I'm completing your education, that's all."

"Thanks," Landers said stiffly. "If that's all, I'll be on my way."

"Sit down, for Christ's sake. I've got something to say to you." Husk drank the last of his liquor and poured what remained in Landers's glass into his own.

"This meeting could be important," he said, speaking rapidly and incisively. "They'll get all the potential leaders in on it, the honest ones and the plain soreheads, and they can probably get a committee going. That could be bad, because it will be an elected committee, not a self-appointed one, and the men will feel some responsibility for it. They probably will have some important people on it also, with a few of their own. Last, maybe, or this guy Hunter who's been floating around the last few days, or that little wop from Brooklyn—just enough to give it energy, and an extra sense of direction, you understand. If they do, they'll embalm this strike and it will last until it gets dangerous, or they'll raise it up out of the grave, like Lazarus, and if they can do that, it will be hell among the yearlings. You won't be able to redbait a committee like that out of existence very fast. If you try it, you're apt to have it backfire because the men will know the guys on the committee and won't listen to you."

"Then you want the men back at work immediately?"

"I want you and some of your people to get to that meeting. They can't screen the delegates to it, so you'll be able to get in all right. I don't want it Red-baited—not as a meeting. But I don't want Last on that committee, and anybody else that has any ability that gets nominated, no matter whether he's a Commie or not, has got to be marked lousy."

"That could backfire too."

"Not if it's done right. You can't just say that a man is a Communist and therefore shouldn't be on the committee. The men in that meeting will know who's a Red and who isn't, and most of them have had some dealings with them. With the pressure on the way it is, a lot of them will be willing to work with the Commies if they don't think the committee is being loaded—and Last and his boys won't try that. No. It has just got to be insinuated, without any Red-baiting, that in order to have its hands clean the committee shouldn't have any Reds on it. Then you can challenge any rank-and-filer that might be dangerous on the committee as being too sympathetic to Last and his bunch."

"Then you want as weak a committee as you can get?"

"Yes. And I want you on it, if you can get on it, and as many people as you can count on. You understand?"

"What I don't see is what you figure on getting out of it."

"Maybe we're going to become real labor leaders," Husk said smiling. "Maybe then we'll go after a real contract."

"And then?"

"There are a lot of other unions." He began to tell Landers what he had told Kelly, his theory of what the present union chiefs were like and what they would have to become. He outlined the propositions in considerable detail.

"It's just another labor front," Landers said. "Like Mussolini's or Hitler's."

"Not quite."

"Essentially."

"There's no disputing of essences," Husk said grinning. "This is going to be a hundred-percent American. Maybe two or three hundred percent, if inflation keeps up." He signaled for another drink.

"Where does Kelly come in?" Landers asked.

"Don't worry about that."

"What keeps me from giving this scheme to Kelly—telling him what you're trying to do?"

"Nothing. Only he won't believe you, that's all. And where the hell would you be then, if I didn't want you around here and sicked some of P.J.'s goons on you—some of those special parolees he has hanging around? If he told them to murder their mothers, they would have to do it or he would just give them a bad report and they would go up the river again."

"I won't be intimidated," Landers said, trying to make his voice level.

"I'm not trying to intimidate you. There's no reason you should go to Kelly anyway—hell, we're in the same boat."

"We're not."

"That's what I've got to make you see. I don't think you're a half-baked Quixote like some of your friends. Look at it this way. There are really only two main power sources now—the worker and the capitalists, America and Russia, the Reds and the Republicrats or whatever they call them in the various countries. You and your six friends think you are going to stand in the middle and take on both sides—you say that's what you intend doing, but it never works out. You get pulled toward one pole or the other. You can go on being a damned fool or you can decide where you want to jump. That's what I did. I was one of your boys too, and then I saw that it didn't make any sense and I jumped. I'm not saying that it isn't useful sometimes to have a front to work behind, a kind of third position, but that's just a maneuver and has nothing to do with the actual relationship of forces. In reality there are only two armies, and all your third group can do is encourage a few desertions or set up a smoke screen here or there."

"I won't admit that," Landers said. He felt as if he were being pushed into a corner, and he wanted to get up and leave, but he couldn't bring himself to do it. He felt a sick lassitude settling inside him.

"No, you won't admit it, but it's your ego and not your brain that won't let you."

"It's not ego that drives you, I suppose?" Landers had wanted to say something cutting, but when the words were out he felt that they were inadequate, the speech of a defiant schoolboy.

"Not anymore," Husk said easily. "I'll tell you about that sometime. Look at it this way," he went on. "We both want to fight the Reds. It's not a hell of a big problem now. The American worker is anti-Communist just now because he's getting the propaganda from all sides—you, me, the press, radio, church, and so on. This anti-Communism is emotional, sentimental, you might say, not based on any facts except the kind the newspapers give. It's a completely unreasoned kind of feeling. That's all to the good because it can be used more readily, and it's easier to find a new lie each day than to try to build a reasoned case for yourself or for capitalism, if that could be done. But what about later on, when the American dream turns into the American nightmare again? In the thirties it was close to going all the way Left. In a time of crisis even the American worker has got to try to use what he has inside his head. What about next time there's a crisis? As long as Joe Worker has his belly full and a piece of tail when he wants it, the truth hasn't a chance against a good lie. But when he gets hungry, he's going to have to look and see if capitalism is really the great maternal bosom the newspaper editorialists say it is. That's why the big attack on the Communists is starting now, and it isn't anything to what it's going to be. And how are the so-called labor leaders acting? Sure, they're putting on the blast just as fast as the president of the Chamber of Commerce, including the heads of unions that the Commies built. They're lining up with the boss, with finks and gangsters, with the Church and the rest of them—like Kelly in this union. But goddamn it, when the heat goes on and we have thirty million out of jobs, the worker will *have* to think no matter how hard it hurts. Unless you have a safe militant-seeming leadership, he's certain to go to the Reds. God knows the Commies are clumsy enough. They haven't learned yet that the American worker is still new enough to be half-anarchist. So the Party boys over-organize him whenever they get the chance, and kill off all the spontaneity and initiative he has. But the Commies can't fumble forever, and the way the press propaganda puts it, no other alternative is left to the workingman except the Reds or the workers own sons of bitches—the present labor leaders."

"And you want to short-circuit the power—is that it?"

"Right. And so do you. Hell, it wouldn't even be fascism. I don't know what it would be—we haven't invented it yet. Anyway," he said gaily, "we may fail entirely."

"You don't sound as if you'd care much," Landers said in surprise.

"I don't give a tinker's damn," Husk said, as if he were enjoying a huge joke. "It's all crazy anyway. I don't care one way or the other how it comes out."

"Why are you doing it, then?" Landers asked wonderingly.

"Oh," Husk said, shrugging, "I guess I'm bored. I don't know. I'd like a little action."

"I think it's because you're still the son of a timber baron."

"Maybe," Husk said indifferently. "What difference does it make? No. I'll tell you what it is," he said smiling ironically. "It's because of my philosophy, Landers, the philosophy of—what'll I call it?—activism. I'm helping to create the new man, the one that doesn't know where he's going and doesn't give a damn because he knows that the world is essentially meaningless anyway."

"That's nihilism," Landers said uneasily. "I think you're crazy."

"I don't recognize the category," Husk laughed. "No, really, when you get down to it, a man's motives mean nothing. That is why history is judgment—it doesn't give a damn about motives. You figure what a man is, on the basis of his acts, not his reasons for them. But there aren't many men in the world—only vegetables with legs on them. They become one thing and stick to it. It's just a way of dying early. The only way you can really keep alive is to create yourself every day. When you break with what you were, you give yourself a shot of life. The more arbitrary the act, the better. If you could really think up an act to cut yourself off from the human race, you'd become immortal."

"You mean betray?" Landers asked softly. He found both repugnance and fascination in what Husk was saying.

"If you could really betray the human race, they'd make a god out of you," Husk said. "You can't betray the human race because it has no significance. Only Adam and Eve could betray it, and then only because God existed. If there were no God, how could anything have been betrayed? And isn't God dead now?"

Landers said nothing. He was thinking of what Husk had said, wondering how much of it was serious and how much a joke.

"I don't agree with all you've said, or what you want to do, but I'll make that meeting," he said at last.

"Sure you will," Husk said. "You don't have to agree with all I've said—yet. I'm going to make you my first apostle."

Landers smiled weakly, held out his hand, and then went out of the bar. Husk stayed for a while sitting at the table, thinking. He felt good to have his scheme begin working; already he felt alive and new, as if he were taking on new and unknown characteristics.

Wednesday 9 P.M.

By nine o'clock we were just so many shadows in a fog. We had escaped onto another plane, into the conditions of dream where the pressures were different and new to us; we were behind the mirror where everything meets and mates with its opposite, not as in life, but the way things do in the country of sleep where contradictions occur without any change, where the laws of motion are different or unknown and you move in slow motion, in a lazy undersea drift and blur, subject to the shift of enormous submarine currents whose direction you cannot guess.

There was no reason why it should have developed that way. The meeting began promptly at eight o'clock as we had planned it. For a half hour they had been coming in twos and threes and sixes and sevens, as bright and cheerful as a handful of new dimes. Everything was according to plan, and it didn't bother me when Barney leaned over and said: "You see who just came in?"

"Who?"

"That Trot, Landers, and a few of his ACTU buddies."

I turned to watch them. They split up and formed the diamond just the way their book of parliamentary procedure told them to do—some at the front, some at the rear, a couple on each side of the hall, half way down. When they started to speak, it would look like whatever they were pushing was getting support from all over the house.

"Pretty, eh?" Barney said.

It didn't worry me. We had done a good job of work, covering the front in Brooklyn and Manhattan. We had even got a couple of boys working over in Jersey, and we were supposed to have some delegatres over from there. We had done everything we had intended, and there was no reason why the meeting shouldn't do the things we hoped it would.

It wasn't a very pleasant hall. It was badly lighted and the cigarette smoke made it dismal and gloomy-looking. The place wasn't really big enough either, but there was nothing to do about that. The windows were open, but in spite of that it began to smell like a tea pad. My head began to ache dully, the way it used to do when I was in the hospital.

"Let's hook her up," I said. It was almost eight-thirty.

Barney smiled. "Take it easy, kid," he said. He nodded toward the side aisle. "Tony's on his way to the pitcher's box."

The little Italian whom I'd seen at the meeting in Barney's section went up on the platform. He had been elected head of the organizing committee, he explained, and he went on to tell why the committee had called the meeting and what we hoped from it. He read a proposed agenda and it was adopted immediately.

"Now let's get a chairman elected," he said, "and then dissolve the provisional committee and I can sit down. Nominations open."

Some one behind me immediately nominated Brian Munson. I hadn't even seen him come in, but I looked around and he was several rows behind me on the far side of the room. I turned to the fellow who had nominated him and tried to explain that Munson wouldn't want it. He immediately thought I was telling him that Munson was no good and started an argument. Half the people in that row of seats got into it, pro and con, and little Tony up on the platform wore himself out rapping for order. I broke off the conversation, damning myself for a fool, and Landers got up and made an effective speech in which he intimated that Munson was a fine man but that he was a bit too sympathetic to the Communists and that this committee should be free from such a taint. In the rear, and for no reason that I could be sure of, a fight started. Finally Tony got everything under control again. Munson surprised me by accepting the nomination; other names were tossed into the hopper, nominations were closed, and the vote was held. Munson won in a walk. As he went up to the platform to take over from Tony, he tossed me a wink. He didn't look like the same man who had been feeding the pigeons.

Tony came back and sat down beside me. He was sweating so that I could smell him.

"Jesus," he whispered. "Everybody is full of beans tonight. I wish they'd save their goddamn energy for a picket line. Every son of a bitch and his brother wants the floor and half of them don't know what they're gonna say until they're under the gun."

"This is the first meeting where they can say what they want without taking a chance of getting dumped by a goon if what they say is out of line," Barney said. "You've seen those rubber-stamp meetings some of the locals run."

"I've seen 'em," Tony whispered. "But goddamn it, if everybody runs off at the mouth like this it'll take a month to get a committee elected, let alone get a program worked out."

Munson was having a hard time holding them. Every man who got the floor wanted to talk of anything except the business at hand. We heard biographies, hard-luck stories, histories of the rank-and-file movements, analyses of the strike, predictions, prayers, incantations to bring seven years of bad luck on Kelly, dirty stories, gags, reports on the prices of commodities, alfresco theories of economic development, hints at who was going to be the next president, supposedly inside stuff on what was going on in Wall Street, reminiscences of the old days and the labor leaders of those times, including a rambling anecdote by a man who claimed to have known Gompers. We heard romances, short stories, and dream sequences complete down to the last transformation.

The way it seemed to me, we were passing over into the realm of fantasy. Even the room no longer seemed to be real. Under the fog of smoke, in the thick air, the faces blurred, and when men in the far corners got up to speak they seemed to move like underwater plants. Their faces, disembodied, floated up under the lights, unreal, transient, moving in a stream of incomplete images.

"What I want to know," Riverboat Conn was saying, "is who are these magicians?" He was involved in a history of labor fakers from Powderly onward, and he was speaking of them in terms of magic. Where he had come from I didn't know, I hadn't seen him come in. Then his face, like that of an old child, had materialized over the speaker's stand, and he had begun talking in the thick voice which he used for oratory and which was not very much different from the otherworldly sounds you hear from spiritualists' trumpets.

"Stop him, for Christ's sake, stop him," I was praying under my breath to Munson. The meeting was beginning to move under its own momentum. In a moment no one would have any more control over it than over a dream.

"The chair recognizes Jim Keyes," Munson droned and I relaxed a little, remembering that Munson had said something about Keyes being a good man. I hoped he was, because he had just been elected to the committee.

"I'd like to talk about the dead men in this room," Keyes said.

From where I was sitting I couldn't even get a good look at him. All I got was an impression of a slender, deadly serious individual with blazing eyes, and then, hearing his words my mind went off under its own power, tossing up the image of the man who had been found in the Jersey mud flats with his feet in a barrel of concrete. I could hear the wind screaming over and see the oily mud where the tide was out. The rain was falling as if it would never stop.

I heard the wind in the pines again and the sound of the lake behind the house, the idiotic repetition of the waves, doing over and over the same thing. What is he talking about? I asked myself. Keyes was off on another tangent, telling about someone's childhood, a mythical experience that repeated all the symbolic experiences; the wagon that the kid did not get, the girl when he was in high school, the sound of people growing old. I could hear a high screaming wind blowing just outside the windows, but it was dead calm in the room and it must have been my imagination. Under his words, and under the sound of the wind I could hear something else, like a giant weeping, and the sound of curses which no one had invented yet, spoken in no language known to man. The wind screamed across the Jersey flats where the dead man lay wrapped in his dream of concrete, a good man who had been a union organizer and had fought Kelly and wound up in the rain, in the oily mud.

I couldn't hear Keyes at all anymore, not the words he was saying, and all I could get was the way he felt, and the sound of his voice separate from whatever he was talking about. It beat in my ears like the sound of something heard far off or underwater, remote yet known, clear in spite of the screaming wind which I could hear in my mind while it was full of the image of that dead man. In the blur of smoke I could see the faces turning toward Keyes like drowned objects in a dead tide. I could see them drifting together, mating in little whispers of approval, falling apart in a sleepy hydropic dance while the voice of Keyes droned on like the sound track for a dream, the things he was saying, when I could pick an image out of the thick stream, becoming more and more incoherent, stretching out of shape in the new pressures of fantasy, alive in the air as a flight of bats but insubstantial, inconstant, impalpable, until the whole room seemed to whirl slowly under the dim lights, in the pool of smoke like autumn water, while outside the wind screamed as shrill as a gull on a mud bank, and far-off shouting voices were borne on the shadowy air.

I'm not sure what Keyes was saying, but it was some kind of collective biography, as disorganized and broken up as the life of a man, spoken in a hoarse tired voice and expressed in crude strange images. He never finished it. The shouting that I had seemed to hear, in the blur of sensation, under the strain of fear that the meeting would degenerate into nothing at all, became real. Men blocked the entrance at one side of the hall and then streamed in, running toward the front and the rear. I could see the smoky light gleam tiredly on the clubs that some of them carried. They were shouting.

It paralyzed everyone for a moment while the goons gained the platform and swept around at the back. A few others who had been planted in the meeting went into action, and reinforcements continued to stream in through the door. Then someone at the side of the hall bolted, and the next moment there was a file of pushing, fighting bodies trying to get down the stairs. I could hear whistles blowing, but it must have been a trick, because it was too early for the cops. Everything was mixed up and it was hard to tell who was who in the fighting.

I tried to get up to the front where Munson was having a hard time. Two men were on him, but he was backed against a wall and was holding out. I got up to the platform and pulled the legs out from under one of them. He came down, falling on the floor, and I hit him as he was trying to get up. I saw Barney Last go down, and Landers trying to make a run for it, and then somebody hit me on the back of the neck, stunning me, and I turned and tried to hold on. They rode me over to one side of the hall. I was trying to get my back to a wall so that they couldn't hit me again, but they got me over to a window. I felt it go out when we hit it, and then the warmth of blood. They had me halfway out, the bottom edge of the window cutting into my back until I thought it was going to break. I felt the pressure building up in me again, as it had that time in the tank. The lid was coming down and I yelled in agony, waiting for the flames to lick through, struggled crazily, half turning, spitted on the window, and saw the street sixty feet down in shadow, the spikes of the picket fence like a row of bayonets. I could feel the sweat running over me like cold fire and the aluminum taste of fear fouling my mouth. I was going over. I could already feel the nightmare suspense of the fall, the spikes on the fence tearing into my body. My insides knotted as if a blowtorch had been turned onto my balls. In a dream as long as a sixty-foot fall, I heard myself screaming, and then the pressure was less and I fought my way in, wondering what had happened, and saw, down on the floor, one of the men who had had me, and Blackie Carmody, his face ghost-white smashing at another one. The mob swung us apart and carried me—still with my last attacker whom I kept hitting again and again, mechanically, even after he was unconscious and would have fallen except that we were too tightly packed—out of the hall and down the thundering dust-hung stairs into the screaming cold wind of fall where the whistles of the police were sounding on the avenue.

PART III
Thursday-Friday

You prepare yourself for the pragmatical circus.

In the morning, despair; in the evening, hysteria; and in between the patterns of alienation. In the mechanics of morning they are fastened screaming to the endless belt of necessity; in the day, in the patterns of profit and loss, they are moved on the board in a plan they cannot foresee, but evening hangs on the wind a flight of grand pianos and the blue key of hope which is meant to fit all doors. These are the masks of the day: the hunted, the victim, the hunter. There are the desires of the day: to be free, to destroy, to escape. The domain of the alarm clock, the domain of indifferent bells, the domain of the neon. Morning, noon, and evening.

In the evening, when the first stars calm the disordered sea, and the lights, soft on the streets, run like a school of fish, when the bars like confessionals, when the theaters like magic rites, call to renewal, and the little winds of personal hope cook the prairies of wild flesh, then the avenue opens, the houses move apart, and there seems no limit on the private wish.

The domain of neon is the color of desire. The papers have all been read. History sleeps for the night. Behind the barred windows, in the tastefully decorated padded cells, the restless lunatic has stopped screaming, and the last suicide of the day, wearily climbing the stairs of the ninety-fourth floor, pauses at the landing in a moment of release and begins the long descent into another dream.

Begins the pragmatical circus, the carnival of pursuit. At Times Square they are unlocking the cages, but already the desperate early ones have crawled into the lions' den and the snake pit, spreading the elastic bars. The unlucky ones shake hands with the slot machines, and the loveless sit in the booths taking an endless picture of themselves. Some with champagne, some with a can of smoke, investigate the pressures on the floor of the alcohol sea, but all these are the Old China

Hands in the spreading Asia of a lost continent. They have been there before, and they will return again, because they have international passports fashioned of stainless steel and lettered in Esperanto. Their pockets are full of slugs to fit turnstiles not yet invented; they were born with the necessary maps outlined on the palms of their hands. But there are others.

On the Great Plains of Childhood, a couple are approaching the Great Divide at the speed of fumbling hands. Their only protection is ignorance, a .22 mounted on a .45 frame, and for provisions they have a half pint of cheap whiskey. They are coming down the old Chisholm Trail in a secondhand Ford. They lie under the black cliffs, clothed only with each other. Beyond them the last of the buffalo graze, humped, snorting and doomed to perish, but these two do not notice, lying in rapt marmorean ease. These are the pioneers. In these, perhaps, it is the necessary redemption, for they too are birds of the evening, passing a savage coast, and are not part of the circus. But to you, the neutral man, it appears only that they have not yet been captured, that the grand piano has not yet been mechanized. How long will the warmth last in the cold winter? When the windows were broken in the cyclonic vacuum of despair and the cold winds come into bed smelling of the dead buffalo and the vanished tribes, smelling of the timeclock and the morning whistle, how long shall that honey breath hold out? You do not consider these things, for it is the role of the neutral man to be an eye among the blind; you observe only that the circus moves into the streets.

On the atolls of parks are the hunted lovers, with all around the shark-toothed roaring waters of Manhattan. Their clothes are out of style and moonlight like acid falls through their torn hats. The coral cuts their feet, they have no guns or fishlines, the monsoon season is at hand, there is a blight on the coconut trees, and they are outside the shipping lanes in a latitude that has not yet been computed. These are the survivors.

The waters of hysteria move up the human markers. At eleven o'clock hope begins to be abandoned. Everything is tried to see if it will work. The opposite of the noonday plan is the midnight dream and the nexus is irony, but the opposite of the pragmatical hunt is accident and the nexus is chance, and though the beggar fall into the bed of the banker's wife, it is only when he has become impotent from hunger. The express starts for Buzzards Bay, jumps the rails and pulls into the station at Tallahassee; but the dispatcher had written Omaha, and the engineer had wanted to go to Duluth. Red into black, odd to even.

The mechanical piano gets stuck on the one tune that should be forgotten and neighs brass notes like a randy stallion. The bells have broken loose and float above the city ringing all the hours at once, and if the arsonist manages to burn down the fire station, it is only because that night there will be no other fires. In the police stations they are beating a murderer. He has confessed and is telling the truth but the police cannot believe him until they have beaten him into recanting. The fixed dice forget their cunning and the street signs their numbers.

Still, no one can surrender. There is still the last bar to be tried; there is the possibility of finding the whore who will satisfy, the drink that will quench, the hope that will survive the night and lift its sunflower face in the morning to color the world with a different light.

Nightmare city, where the lost tribes are hunting the hairy mammoth. Cracks open in the pavements. Walls collapse. Hell is around every corner and the devil under every bed, the usual hell, the familiar devil, there is nothing even terrifying about him, and there is just the chance that he may, at last, turn out to be the one friend who has always been needed, as long acquaintance sometimes changes to love. But there will always be morning, morning, and as the clock hand moves toward twelve, toward the hour of sleep and of transformations, the dark shadow of morning falls on the white night. They are slowly sheathed in that lead against the chance of X-rays of hope. That sunflower seed will never be planted.

And the streets slowly begin to empty as the vitality is dissipated. The liquor in the bottles undergoes a chemical change until alcohol is as weak as blood. Coming on each other suddenly, the old friends shake hands, but the hands come loose at the ends of the sleeves and they are forced to stuff them awkwardly into their pockets. One meets the necessary woman at the edge of the park, but she is sleepwalking, and he finds suddenly that he has forgotten his own tongue and can speak only a language which he cannot understand. Another finds a body dead in a gutter but when he calls the police it is himself that the wagon takes away to the morgue. Accidental death.

All the chances are taken, all the riders are down. The grand pianos are there, but they have been mechanized. The blue key works, but it opens the wrong doors.

Thursday 4 A.M.

I could feel that unbearable pressure building up inside me and over my head the weight of the hatch welded tight. There was a red edge of fire and oily smoke, and I knew there must be the smell of burning flesh but I could smell nothing at all. I could hear the screams, but they seemed far away, until I realized that I was the one who was screaming. Then they seemed to tear my lungs, but there was only the faint gasping, all thinned out by distance even when the lid began to come down on me, shutting me away in a dark place, airless, built of welded metal that was too hot to touch and which was shrinking until it would crush me. Then I was falling through space, and below, just where I would land, were the bayonet points of an iron fence.

I woke up trembling, wet with sweat, and found that there was only the cold room and the sound of Kay's breathing. A car went by on the avenue and a tree scratched against the window. A long way off there was a chime of bells dying away. I looked at my watch; like tiny embers the phosphorescent hands pointed to four o'clock. I knew I would not be able to get back to sleep.

In the brightness of the bathroom I felt better. After I had wiped off the sweat and washed, I went into the big room and sat down in a chair, but it was too cold there and I had to go into the bedroom for my clothes. I found them in the dark, not wanting to put on the light for fear of waking Kay. Her breathing was shallow and regular and comforting coming through the dark.

When I was dressed I hunted up the bottle of whiskey she kept, but the taste of it was no good and I put it away. I couldn't sleep and I couldn't drink and there was nothing to do but sit up with myself until morning, so I began to go over the pictures she had hung up everywhere, examining them as carefully as if there were something I expected to find. Nothing in that.

There was one picture which was painted on glass, on two levels, one back of the other and separated by a couple of inches of space. Both sheets of glass were fastened in a large box-like frame. It was an abstraction like all the others, geometrical shapes brightly colored and neatly arranged and no doubt very satisfying to the sense of design if you are lucky enough to have one. It had more than the others because of the extra depth. All it needed was some figures in it and some motion.

But of course that would have ruined it, because if you could have introduced motion, life, it wouldn't have been art any longer. One of the figures would have been certain to have walked off the glass, and in any case it would have been messy, not the nice, neat, brightly painted package of perception that it was. If you could give it motion it would explode in your hands, the way the meeting had, or the way a friendship did, and the figure, like Blackie Carmody maybe, would have got down out of the frame and opened up on you.

It was better to look at the pictures than to think about that, but I couldn't go on looking at the pictures forever. There was the fact of Blackie. I ain't a prick, he had said. I don't rob no little guy in a candy store. Well, that was the fiction of Blackie. Probably that could be painted into an arrangement of squares and triangles and last for all time. There was no reason why the sentiments shouldn't last for all time, now that they were dead and no longer any relationship to the living, moving Blackie who had helped break up the meeting, and who was now one of Kelly's plug-uglies, and who might one day control that dock he had once dreamed about, and who would one day do worse things than robbing old men in candy stores.

If it could have been left that way, even, it would have been all right, but there was also the other fact that he had probably saved my life. "I'll t'row yuh t'rough a winduh." I had heard that one before without ever expecting that I would be the one. Yes, there was that other fact about Blackie. It couldn't be avoided even though it would have simplified my feelings. The red and black squares were all mixed up.

That was what the meeting had done. We had had that nice idea in our heads and Kelly had knocked it out with a baseball bat. He had banged the lid shut and screwed it down tight. Everything was mixed up, crazy, in pieces in the dark: the plans we had made, the character of Blackie Carmody, my own feelings about everything.

I opened a window and looked out. It was dark and cold, almost like winter. The fine unseasonal weather we had been having was all gone. Under the streetlights, the pavement looked hard as black metal, cold, glittering, and perfectly inhuman. Over the city hung a low ceiling of thick cloud like a suspended weight. I felt chilled and miserable. Looking out on the world at that time of the morning it was impossible to believe that the sun would ever shine again, or that the white town, so warm and kindly in its endless summer, could exist at all. It didn't seem that there could be anything in the world but this stone ruin of a city with the black oppressive ceiling pressing down on it.

It was unlikely that morning would ever come, but the time got to be five o'clock, then six, finally six-thirty. After a while I knew that it wasn't just morning that I was waiting for, and that I didn't want to see Kay when she woke up. Since she had been sleeping when I came in the night before, I decided that I had better leave her a note, so I wrote one out and stuck it on a corner of the easel.

She was still working on the self-portrait. It didn't look right. It wasn't just a question of getting the nose wrong. All her features were there, but they looked a little out of focus. It was like seeing someone through a rain-wet windowpane or underwater. Of course the eyes were only the dead eyes of paint and canvas, with a shadow of character that might have been an accident of brushwork. They stared at me blank and hard, turning as I moved. Over them the brow arched up like a smooth rockfall into the thickets of hair, and the cheeks were hollowed with mystery. It was a stranger's face, I thought, or rather the face of someone once known, forgotten, encountered years later when just enough of the original features remained unaltered to tease the brain into memory without being strong enough to supply the face with a name.

Thursday 7 A.M.

Patrick Joseph Kelly awoke to an unaccustomed feeling of happiness. He lay in the bed a moment trying to trace it, a big man, his body beginning to fall apart now with age, with a little twitch of pain at his mouth, and eyes that looked weak without his glasses. It was impossible for him to tell the source of the feeling of ease and release, and it was infrequent enough now for him to try to account for it. It might have been a dream *I dreamed something maybe* but there were no dream traces in his memory and *I didn't dream that anyway* in recent months all his dreams had been unhappy ones. He had begun to realize, not as an abstract proposition but with his whole body, that he was mortal, and the fear of death, deepening the erosion of pain around his mouth, had expressed itself in certain repeated dreams of empty streets, of great white tenantless buildings that were not quite hospitals, dreams of dark ships, of soundless trains gliding from huge shadowy stations. He went over these images now, slowly, searching them for some other meaning, like a worshiper painfully making the Stations of the Cross. In the cold light of morning the images were without their power, as if they drew from some source of darkness and sleep, and they were able to heat the midnight circuits of his brain only into a slight generalized uneasiness which he pushed back out of consciousness chuckling suddenly *I fixed those bastards* with delight before the cause for the laughter, the breaking up of the meeting the night before, became alive in his mind.

He got energetically out of bed and went into the bathroom to shave. Even his appearance, from which for a long time he had got neither satisfaction nor even assurance, pleased him this morning. He thought that he looked younger. Through the window he could see the cold murky morning hanging over the backyards of the city, and this too was pleasant. He had hated the unseasonal autumnal summer of the past week, and the coming of the cold suggested winter and the long vacation in the South when it would not be necessary to think of the problems of the union. He would have to settle the strike first and *I've got them running* it seemed to him that the solution was already working itself out. He had broken up the meeting. *I've got to get the companies to kick in a little bit more.* He began to think of what minor concessions the employers would be willing to allow *Got to give a prize* to tempt the strikers back to work. Wiping the last of the lather from his face he went into the next room and picked up the telephone.

Hearing the sleepy voice on the other end he felt the superiority of the early riser and said:

"Damn it, Bert, if you lawyers ever had to work for a living you'd learn to get up earlier," and smiled, hearing the mumble on the wire, the cleft at the corner of his mouth deepening like stigmata.

"What do you want, P.J.?" the voice asked in his ear.

"Just a minute," said P.J. Kelly and went into his bedroom for his glasses.

"Listen," he said, picking up the phone, "I want you to take up this contract again. We've got to give the boys a prize. I don't care what it is, but work it out."

"Christ," Bert answered in a sleepy grieving voice. "The companies won't want to give a red cent."

"It doesn't have to be money. Maybe an extra man or so on a shift. Smaller loads, safety men—I don't give a damn."

"It won't be easy."

"What the hell are you paid for anyway?" Kelly said, the West Side accent growing in his speech. "You go down and see their shysters today, see? All we need is a little something and we'll have this damn thing off our hands."

"I thought you were just going to let it work itself out?"

"I changed my mind. It's a free-for-all now. We'll beat their brains out," Kelly said, feeling, for the first time since the strike started, that he knew exactly what he was going to do.

"All right," Bert said. "That's your department, P.J. You have some plans?"

"Plans!" Kelly answered contemptuously. "What the hell do I need plans for? You get working on this thing right away."

"Of course. Shall I call Husk? He helped negotiate the contract."

"No, don't call Husk. Don't call anybody. This is just between you and me, get it?"

"All right. I hope it will work out." Bert did not sound cheerful.

"It'll work out," Kelly said. His mouth drew into a sneer of pain. He hung up the receiver thinking with amusement and disdain of the lawyer, *He won't take a chance*, seeing in him what he had always seen: the natural inferiority of the man who thinks too much. His mind flicked to Alton Husk, but he put the name away from him.

Now that he had taken his second action in the strike, by setting the lawyer in motion, Kelly was not as pleased with the morning as he had been. His strongest wish had been that the strike would somehow blow over, that the men would go back to work, that nothing would have to be changed, and now he was already making a concession. It did not really matter *I'm cracking the whip* since he was making the concession to break the opposition, he told himself. He began to see it in terms of a fight, a backward step in order to bring an opponent off balance, and as he went into breakfast and the morning mail the uneasiness drifted away like a light fog lifting in the sun.

There was a letter from his wife. Kelly put it to one side and read through the rest of the mail, accepting the food the Negro put in front of him without looking at it. When he was finished he took out a cigarette, looked at it distastefully, put it down, and told the man to bring him a cigar. It was his first in weeks and the taste of it was strange but comforting. Then he picked up the letter, feeling its thinness and guessing at what it contained. He was tempted to put it aside until a later time but decided against it *Annie doesn't live here anymore* and slit the envelope open with his knife, thinking of a song long out of fashion which was about a girl with his wife's name.

The letter was what he had expected. She would need some more money. She had been visiting friends on the West Coast and now she was going to Mexico for a month. It was a brief letter *your wife, Annie* signed with weak indecisive but clearly written characters, and it recalled to him the thin almost bloodless face *she's getting old* and the high-held head that could not quite keep the wrinkles at the neck from showing. The skin was beginning to fall away from the flesh, to become too big for her. Kelly felt a little stab of pity as he held the image in his mind, but it was himself he was pitying, it was a reflex of his fear of dying, and he rubbed out the pity *she gets everything she asks for* and began, even while he asked the Negro to bring the checkbook, to substitute for it the more familiar feeling of resentment.

She was one of his failures. It seemed to P.J. Kelly that people were always failing him *CaminettiBertAnnieConnO'NeilCharlie* his mind tossed the faces up on the beach of consciousness like a tide dropping its debris at high-water mark, the flotsam running away in a little curve toward the past and out of consciousness again. Only his mother could he remember without some form of regret, and he did not think of her as a person, but almost as a kind of religious image. He did not even think of her as his mother; she had been enshrined too long ago. His father he could think of now with a kind of weary tolerance. His father had been good to him, but of course they had had to fight when P.J. Kelly became a man. He could not remember now what the specific issue had been—it was just that having to oppose his father was something which he took for granted as natural. That had been in the days when he was just a worker on the waterfront, desperate, hungry for something he could not name, trying to break out of the narrow corner and the mean streets.

Annie had come later, when he began to get established. She was not a neighborhood girl, and he had been proud of her, of the Boston family and the education. Just the same it had never worked out. He could never get close to her. Sleeping with her *she never got any fun out of it* had been like going to Mass. She had made him feel clumsy and unclean. The lights had always to be put out, and they had to be under the sheets as if the covers were the very rooftree of the house of matrimony under which alone the act of love could be domesticated and made decent. He had seen her naked only once in their married life *a damn good looker* and remembered being a little shocked at seeing the breasts, the somewhat heavy hips which he had used under the sheets in the darkness of release and submission. Naked in the light she had hardly seemed real. In the darkness she was only an extension of himself. He realized suddenly but with no surprise that she had never made him happy, not even when they were first married, when he had been very proud of her, very much in love.

There were no children. He had wanted a son, but she had never become pregnant. He had blamed her for it, perhaps because he was uneasy, worried that he might be sterile. After a while he got used to the idea that he would never have a son, and it caused him sometimes to attach young men to himself, to give them jobs and keep them around, even, sometimes, when he did not need them.

It had never worked out. Now, thinking of his wife with whom he had not lived for years, Kelly felt no resentment toward her at all, and again the pity, which was partly for himself, touched him. He thought of the sternly held head *she's getting old* with a faint colorless admiration while he put the letter aisde, knocked the ashes from the cigar which the doctor had forbidden, finished his coffee and prepared himself to face the problems of his day.

It was going to be a long hard day, but Kelly looked forward to it with pleasure. For days he had done nothing, waiting for the strike to die out, but now, after the action of the night before, he felt better. It was not that he had any elaborate plans, since he was no good at working them out, but he felt that now the strike had become a kind of free-for-all and in that kind of situation he felt sure of himself. He had no plans now, beyond a few actions which the new situation made necessary, but he was perfectly confident of working things out as he went along. If one thing did not work he would try another. He would have preferred to do nothing, but that was out of the question now.

He went into the other room and made a telephone call to Caminetti in Brooklyn.

"Listen, Caminetti," he said brusquely. "Get over here. I want to see you."

He heard the sputtering voice, the slight Italian accent over the faint buzz of distance lining the wire. "What you want, P.J.?" Caminetti asked.

"I'll tell you when I see you."

"I'm pretty busy over here today—"

"Goddamn it," Kelly exploded. "I said I wanted to see you. You get your ass over here and don't give me any shit about how busy you are." The West Side accent was thick now. "You'll be busy when I tell you to be and by Christ you'll come when I call."

"I don't like that talk—" Caminetti started to say.

"I'm not asking you to like it. I'm telling you to get over here." He heard the buzzing of the wire and silence.

"O.K.," the voice whined. "I'll make it. When?"

"Two o'clock. The office." Kelly hung up. The little scar of pain at the corner of his mouth looked sharp and wolfish now. He no longer looked like the Kelly who was afraid of death, the Kelly who dreamed of the days of his youth and who had seemed for days unable to act.

The eyes behind the steel-rimmed glasses still had a suggestion of melancholy, but he no longer looked like a tired old man as he flipped over a leaf of the calendar on the desk, read *Thursday*, reflected that it would be a long day, and padded into the kitchen to get his cold cigar.

Thursday 4 P.M.

The wind snarled like a wolf on the avenue. Grit cut at my face and eyes; dead leaves whirled in the gutter. It was still only afternoon, but people had lights on in their apartments. An ugly dung-yellow patch of sky showed toward the west, but the rest of the city was covered by a corpse-colored cloud that hung just over the tops of the buildings like a tent with the edges staked down. Everyone on the street seemed to be running, as if to escape the weather, the day, or the city. It was a day that had rotted right across the middle, mean as a bitch and cold as a whore's heart. I walked across Fourteenth Street and into a dust devil that was coming down Greenwich Avenue. Half blinded, my eyes streaming, the taste of sulfur and dead summer thick on my tongue, I got to the door of Barney's section and staggered up the stairs.

At first I thought no one was there. It was dark in the meeting room. It seemed big and empty with no one in it, like a railway waiting room in a small Middle Western station. There was a litter of cigarette butts on the floor from last night. Posters and banners along the walls brought me into the focus of exhortation. I put the lights on and heard someone call from the rear and went back to where Barney had a kind of office. He had an electric heater on, and it was warm. There was a field of light around the desk under the droplamp. He leaned back in his chair and smiled.

"Hello, Joe. Did you see Bill Everson?"

I nodded. Barney had asked Everson to have me run down some people for him and I had been out on it all morning and most of the afternoon.

"It's pretty dead," I told him. "The men got a shaking up last night when Kelly's goons broke up that meeting."

He shook his head in absent-minded agreement and started looking through a drawer. I got around in front of the heater and lit a cigarette, beginning to feel warm for the first time that day.

"We'll never get them moving again," I said. "They're all clamming up, crawling into the storm cellars."

"Oh, we'll get them moving again, Joe." He sounded tired but confident. "It's a setback, of course, but it won't necessarily break us."

"I don't know. It looks like the wind-up is pretty close."

"You feel that way?"

"I'm not sure how I feel. I feel lucky I'm not spitted on a picket fence."

"Tony said he saw that but couldn't get over to you. He didn't know how you got out of it."

"Reinforcement arrived," I said. I didn't say who it was.

"You think the strike's lost, Joe? No," he said as I started to speak, "I want your rock-bottom opinion on it."

"All right. It's lost."

"You want to call it quits?"

"Goddamn it, Barney, I don't like that kind of a question!" He had suggested something like that before and it made me mad. "If that's what you think of me, then say it."

"I didn't mean anything except that maybe we put you on an assignment too soon. And then last night—I've seen guys get occupational shell shock out of something like that and—"

"Don't try to snow me, for Christ's sake."

"O.K., Joe, put it on the line."

"I'm in this until it's over," I said. "Then I'm heading West. But I'm in it until it's finished. All right?"

"All right, if you mean it. We could release you now, you know."

"Skip it. I say the strike is lost. You say it isn't. You're the big wheel here. What's the next job?"

"Tell me why you think it's lost?"

"Hell," I said, "we started out with a plan of operation. Last night Kelly took the props out from under it. He put sand in the gears and stole the steering wheel. Where the hell are we?"

"Where, then?"

"In the cellar. In Kelly's backyard, blindfolded, with our arms cut off at the elbows. And Kelly is right there behind us with a baseball bat on his shoulder and the umpire is about to call batter up."

"Yes," he said as if I had said nothing at all.

"We're off the reservation. We're out of the area of the plan and that means we're Kelly's meat."

"Why?"

"Because we're too small yet to have the influence of number. All we can hope to do is get the right kind of a lever and the right place to rest it. If we have that, numbers aren't so important. Well, last night we lost the fulcrum and the lever too."

"Maybe not."

"Like hell we didn't. Here's Kelly, who has the strength of the already dead, the strength of inertia, and he has us right out in the open — all we can do now is improvise, and in that kind of a battle he's the old maestro."

"Unless we can pull it together again."

"We don't have the time. You know that a thing like this, unorganized, can't go on very long. We had our chance. Time's almost up."

"Maybe not. We have to figure it isn't."

"I agree that we have to figure it isn't. What's next in the book?"

"We get back to working on the committees again. Try to merge whatever local organizations there are into one overall committee for Manhattan, one for Brooklyn—even Jersey if we can get anyone working out there. Then make another try to broaden out the committee we elected last night."

"What committee? There were only a handful of men elected when the meeting was broken up and I suppose most of those guys are still running."

"Not all. You didn't see this?" He tossed a paper at me and then went on explaining it to me as if I couldn't read. "The committee is still alive and it has worked out a program. Not bad either." I glanced down the column and read it—the usual demands for a new contract, better working conditions and so on.

"The committee phoned the story in to the papers," Barney said. "Then Krouse—he was the second one elected, wasn't he?—got scared. He now claims that he was elected without giving his consent. But the rest of the committee is still holding, it looks like, so maybe we can make this damn strike stand up like a man yet."

"Maybe," I said. It was pretty tremendous news. I had never expected to hear any more about that committee that we had elected. "Mother of God, Barney, maybe we can get another meeting—"

"Not right away. It'll take a while to gather them up the next time. They'll be a little scared."

"But if the committee—"

"We don't know yet if anybody will listen to the committee. So far it's just an ad in the papers."

"Sure. But if the committee papers the waterfront with us doing the legwork, we *can* pull it together."

"There are a lot of angles to it, Joe," Barney said wearily. "Will the committee hold together? This guy Krouse is running. What about Homestead and Daniels and Keyes and the others—when the heat really goes on? I was out to try to see Homestead and Daniels this morning—nobody seems to know where Keyes lives."

"How did the other two sound?"

"That's just it, Joe. I didn't see them. I guess they're pretty worried that Kelly will send some of his boys around to their places. Anyway, neither Homestead or Daniels had been home." Barney gave me a sour smile. "The goddamn committee has gone underground," he said.

Once again we were out of contact. It was the old story. Still, I felt better knowing that the committee, wherever it was, was still functioning. The wind in the street, where evening dusk was sweeping down like a dust storm, seemed less bitter. I let it blow me up Greenwich, and at Fourteenth I saw a small dark-haired guy and thought it was Blackie.

"Hey, Joe," he called, and it was Bill Everson. "How they going?" he asked smiling. "I think it's going to snow. Want some coffee?"

We went into a bar and grill and sat in a booth. Everson didn't look as much like a kid as he had the first time I had seen him. He kept drumming nervously on the table.

"You think we'll win this thing?" he asked finally.

"I don't know," I said, thinking of Barney. I began to tell him about the committee. He didn't even look as if he were listening.

"I used to think we just couldn't lose," he said. "I figured we could just do it by the books. Now—I don't know—we've just got to work with what comes along."

I told him about what was happening with the committee. I didn't build it up. There was no use letting him hit the pipe. He was even more cautious in his opinion of it than Barney.

"Anyway," he said, sighing, "we've got to figure on losing all the battles but the last, haven't we?"

"What's riding you? You sound like a professional mourner."

"Nervous, I guess. Last night, after that fight, I went down to the section. I thought some of the guys might come down, but Barney and Tony and some others went up to Barney's apartment."

"So?"

"There wasn't anybody at the section. I thought somebody followed me home. I waited in front of the house and he went on past."

"He didn't have to be following you."

"No. I guess I'm just nervous. I didn't expect anything to happen last night."

I didn't answer. I hadn't expected anything either.

"I didn't even get into the fight," Bill said. "I just got swept out with the rest."

"You didn't miss any fun." I could still see that fence sixty feet down and feel the window going out at my back. "You want some whiskey to go with that coffee?" I asked, trying to put the eye on the waiter. Bill shook his head.

"You know, Joe, most of those guys were wearing field jackets, just like me. It's lousy when a bunch of GIs have to fight over something like that."

He didn't have to tell me how lousy it was. I thought of Blackie Carmody, who had been my friend and who had gone as phony as a nine-dollar bill but who had saved my life the night before. I didn't answer.

"What do you want, Joe?" Bill asked suddenly. I waited for the whiskey to come and tasted it and found that it tasted as bad as the liquor I had tried to drink at Kay's place that morning. I put it aside.

"To be free," I said, remembering that Blackie had asked me the same thing.

"That doesn't mean anything unless you define it."

"I can define it. What do you want?"

"To be honest and generous."

How did I define what I meant? I began to see a white street, twisting and narrow under a powerful shaft of clean sunlight, a sleepy sound of water—

"And to hate everything that is a sham, everything that cripples people."

The street followed a hillside contour, dropped away into the narrow toy valley, at the bottom lost itself in a small square, in the sound of water from a small fountain, in sunlight—

"And to like whatever is good in man."

The birdsong was hung across the moon like a spangle of small bells and overhead the sky went up forever and the hills pitched up into the clouds and there was no feeling of pressure, of tearing haste or of being trapped in a dark place—

"I think that's what I want. To be a good Communist. It's not my definition."

"Look," I said, thinking of something else. "Can I bunk with you tonight?" I suddenly knew that one of the things that had been eating me all day was that I didn't want to go back to see Kay that night. I remembered how cocky I had been, telling her how I was going to make up her mind for her. It seemed silly now, on a cold night, with the wind in the streets like a mad dog, and with a job to do that was like putting together a jigsaw puzzle when you are wearing mittens and working in the dark.

"Sure," Everson said, and didn't ask me why. "You better take my key," he said. "I got to see a couple of guys and I may be late." He held out the key.

"Where are you meeting them?" I asked. "I could drop around there and pick you up."

He named a bar on Eighth Avenue. I remembered that I might meet Blackie if I went into his bailiwick.

"I guess I won't," I said and took the key.

Outside the wind snarled and bit at us. I had to go up to Harlem. We said so long, and Bill went away along the street. He walked cockily, like Blackie, but he hadn't got very excited about my information that the committee was still functioning. There in the cold night I wasn't very excited about it either anymore. I tried to imagine P.J. Kelly and what he was doing, but I drew a blank. Maybe he was doing nothing again. All I could be sure of was that I was in a cold street with a wind like an animal tearing at me, and that all of us, Bill and I and Barney and the rest, were hunting in the lawless darkness for a species of man that might not even have been born.

Thursday 9 A.M.

At nine o'clock in the morning P.J. Kelly came out of the subway, bought a paper and crossed the street to the building that housed the old offices of his union. It was a cold windy day with a low sky of broken clouds, but just as Kelly crossed the street a thin finger of sunlight broke through the scud, followed him to the door, and was waiting for him when he got to his desk in the office above.

Standing at the desk, he scanned the paper, folded it, and hung his coat on a hook behind his chair. He sat down at the desk and turned a page on the calendar. THURSDAY. Kelly wrote just below the date the name Caminetti and after that Husk. Pausing for a moment he wrote *police* in smaller script and then, under that, very faintly, he traced an indecisive wavy line which was to help him remember something else. From the right-hand drawer of his desk he got out a cigar, rolled it in his fingers, breathed of it as if it were a delicate flower, and then placed it reluctantly on his desk. Monk Ryan came up the steps and into the office, bringing the cold, stale smell of the street, and the sun, which had been coining money on Kelly's desk, suddenly went out. Ryan glanced at Kelly, who was staring at his calendar, and went into the other room for some leaflets. He put the lights on and shuffled around a table.

"What the hell are you doing, man?" asked P.J. Kelly.

Ryan came into his office uncertainly. He looked sick. The cold in the streets had pinched his face, and the skin had the color of skim-milk and water. His hat, pushed up on his head slightly, showed a slanted forehead, wrinkled like a monkey's. One eye was very black and swollen. He was ill at ease.

"Jesus, you're a beauty this morning," Kelly grunted. "What happened to you?"

"Last night at that meeting. Somebody clouted me."

"You look like somebody gave you a black eye on top of a black eye."

"Yeah. I got the first one a couple of days ago."

"You won't win any fuckin' contests."

"Yeah." For Christ's sake, Ryan was thinking, you don't have to tell me, you old son of a bitch. Aloud he said: "You want me for somethin', P.J.? I just come up after some leaflets—"

"Fuck the leaflets."

"Husk said—"

"Fuck Husk," Kelly roared. "Who the hell is running this place?" Ryan's glance told him quite plainly that, as far as Ryan was concerned, it was P.J. Kelly who ran it. Kelly began to feel rather foolish for shouting at the little man. "Change of tactics, son," he said, looking at Ryan's marginal face, the watery intelligent eyes. "Have a cigar." He held it out to the other man like an assistant handing a doctor an important instrument and Ryan took it, thanked him mechanically, inhaled it as if he were an addict and the cigar pure cocaine, and put it into his pocket thinking, why doesn't he give me a cigarette, he knows I don't smoke these damn things.

"Well," Kelly said, feeling that after the kindness he could again say what he thought, "buzz the hell off, will you? Caminetti's coming over here and I want some privacy for a change."

"What about the leaflets?" Ryan asked. He could see Husk and Kelly, one on each side of him, each with a different command, and ground his teeth in silent hatred for the both of them. I just want to get along, he assured himself. I don't give a fuck for anything else if the bastards will let me alone and just let me get along.

"Leave them," Kelly said. He was looking through the dirty window into the cold and dusty street, not thinking of Ryan, who turned away, crossed the room, descended the worn stairs and went out into the wind, hunching his shoulders under his coat for warmth, thinking of Kelly: the old bastard has got a hard-on for somebody, he's all hopped up and he don't look so old and pooped out. I'm glad it ain't me. Ryan's face twisted with hate and then relaxed. He put his head down against the wind and thought tenderly of his sick wife.

When Ryan left, Kelly got another cigar out of his desk and this time lighted it, inhaling deeply, sitting back in his chair, squaring his shoulders. He was feeling very good. A memory of the time he had first moved into the office flashed through his mind and he chuckled, thinking that in those days he had been too much of a man *I can still beat those bastards* for the opposition and that he had not lost his grip. The words on the calendar pad caught his attention and he briskly dialed a number.

"Captain Daniger," he said, and waited. When he heard the voice of Daniger he began to talk rapidly but without haste, in a crisp, clear voice, as if he were a broker sending his orders down to the curb.

It took five minutes to complete the call and he dialed again, this time Father Burke.

"Hello, Father," Kelly said heartily. "Did you get the check for the boys' club? Good. I put that young fellow—what was his name?—Carmody—I gave him a job, just as you asked. Now look, Father, I've got something to ask you. You know Dumont of the Catholic union group. Yeah, Dumont. D-U-M-O-N-T. Father Dumont. He's giving me some trouble. I want him called off. Now look, here's what I want—" He went on carefully like a housewife ordering groceries. When he was finished he said: "Thanks, Father. I hope you don't have to go all the way to the Powerhouse to square this. How about coming over some night for some cards? I've got some good brandy," and waited for the meaty voice on the other end of the wire to finish a labored joke, laughed heartily, and said good-bye. When he was hung up Caminetti was just coming into the room.

Caminetti, next to Kelly in power in the union, was a square man of middle height, perhaps forty-five years old. He was very dark.

Although he was freshly shaven, his jowls shone almost blue under the light. He crossed the room stolidly on legs like posts, his small sloe eyes not looking at Kelly. Built like a brick shithouse, Kelly thought, looking with distaste at the heavy face.

"You wanted to see me, P.J.?" Caminetti asked. He had a surprisingly high weak voice. Now he looked at Kelly and the eyes, protected by little ambushes of fat, were as beady and expressionless as those of a lobster.

"Yeah," Kelly said and then, knowing his man: "You got somebody out in the hall?"

"Just one of my boys," Caminetti said apologetically in his high womanish voice.

"You don't need a bodyguard here," Kelly said. He shouted for the benefit of the man outside: "Hey, you out there. Get the fuck out. You ain't needed." And turned to Caminetti.

"Now," he said. "What the hell do you think you're trying to pull off in Brooklyn?"

"I don't get you, P.J."

"Don't give me that shit, Caminetti. What's coming off there?"

Caminetti shrugged. "Some of the boys go back, then they come out again, that's all."

"Your ass, that's all. You were pretty happy about getting them back to work when nobody would go back along the front over here. Then your men go on strike again and you're still happy?"

"I can't tell them what to do."

"No? You been trying pretty hard for about ten years now. If anybody talked back, nobody was listening."

"What's the beef, P.J.?" The dark beads of eyes fastened on Kelly's cigar. "What you beating my brains out for?"

"This. Somebody gave you the idea that you could do yourself some good by taking the men off the job again. You're getting anxious, Caminetti. You interested in taking over my job, maybe?"

"Hell, P.J.—" Caminetti waved a deprecating hand, his eyes watchful behind their half-shutters of fat.

"Caminetti, the rank-and-file leader," Kelly sneered. "Caminetti, the friend of the workingman." He got up and walked around the desk. "You're a fool, Caminetti. You think I'm getting old, maybe?" He tapped Caminetti on the shoulder with the hand that held the cigar. "Listen," he said. "I was battling down here when you were just a punk doing your first bit up at Elmira. I was around this front when it was a battlefield, and you think I'm going to take any shit off you? It wasn't your idea having those men knock off work the second time. You don't have that kind of ideas. You think I don't know what goes on around here? You're getting rocks in your head, Caminetti. Now give it to me. Who put you on this angle? Some of Father Dumont's boys?"

Caminetti shook his head. He was sweating slightly. He rubbed a hand against the side of his face.

"The first time you sent one of your boys around to hint that maybe it would be all right to walk off the job again, I heard about it," Kelly said pityingly. "You goddamn fool, Caminetti, somebody's got you on their sucker list." He went back and sat down in his chair, leaning forward confidentially. "All right," he said quietly. "Let's have it. Right off the arm. I'm not going to play around. Give it to me or it's your ass. Who was it? Dumont?"

Caminetti shook his head and wiped the sweat off his forehead. "You ain't going to like it, P.J."

"I'll love it," Kelly said, his voice ugly with confidence. "I'll give him his goddamn head to carry under his arm. Dumont?"

"No," Caminetti said. For the first time he looked really frightened. "You won't like it," he said again, shifting his eyes to the desk, to the floor.

"Shoot it."

"Husk."

There was a moment of full silence in which a bus roared on the avenue and the windowpanes shook, a moment when the cigar smoke turned bitter in Kelly's lungs while he thought *I knew it I knew it all the time* before he stood up shouting.

"You lying ginzo bastard!" Kelly stood over Caminetti holding the cigar like a knife while Caminetti sat very still, sweating, his eyes turning frantically like sea animals looking for hiding places under rocks. He began to speak rapidly without looking up.

"I never even thought of it," he said. "You know me, P.J. Did I ever try to pull any stuff like that? He talked me into it, the son of a bitch; he give me the idea that you were agreeing to it—"

"You dirty lying bastard," Kelly said flatly. He suddenly felt very tired and let himself down into his chair again. "He talked you into it, did he? Like talking a whore into a fifty-dollar lay, about that hard, wasn't it?" He put his cigar into the ashtray, feeling his heart as cold as a toad in a hole. *I can't even break this son of a bitch*, he thought, frustrated rage turning toward self-pity.

"I thought it was something phony," Caminetti was saying in the same high rapid voice. "I was going to ask you how you stood on it—"

"Oh bullshit," Kelly said tiredly. "Get out of here, Caminetti."

Caminetti got up out of the chair. He was still trying to explain.

"Cut it," Kelly said.

"We ain't going to have trouble about this, P.J.? We worked together too long—"

"Oh hell yes, we're buddies, only this is fuck-your-buddy week, that's all."

"We don't want to have no trouble, P.J." The eyes came to rest on Kelly's middle coat button.

"You get those men back to work or we'll have some trouble."

"That ain't easy." The high voice was becoming a whine. "You see this?"He fumbled a newspaper out of his pocket. "That committee they elected. You read it."

"That shouldn't give you any trouble. You've persuaded guys before. So they stayed persuaded."

Caminetti met his eyes for the first time. "It won't be easy," he said.

"Get out." Caminetti put the newspaper back in his pocket and turned away.

After Caminetti had gone, Kelly sat looking at his cold cigar, trying not to think of Husk. He smoothed his own newspaper out and looked at the story. *They've all got their knives out for me.* Feeling sick with self-pity he got up and walked to the window *but I can fix their wagon* creating a phantasy of an abstract man, a member of the committee whom he was smashing with a club. The street looked bruised and empty under the heavy sky, and Kelly had a sudden frightening feeling that it had changed since the time when he had fought his way up out of the cold and the battle into the quiet and warmth of the office. *What the hell is happening to people?* He was unable to reconcile himself to Time, which he felt was working on the street like a chemical. Then he saw the solid pillars of the bank that had been there for forty years, the blind newsdealer in his little shack, and the feeling of strangeness went away. *They'll never drag me back there.* The crosstown bus moved away from the curb. A tall man bought a paper. *And I treated him like a son like he was my own kid.* The newsdealer blew on his hands; wind whipped at the papers in front of him, and Kelly walked back to his desk. He underlined the name of Husk. He was thinking that it was going to be a very long day and that he was very tired. He ran a pencil through Caminetti's name. *I'm still P.J. Kelly,* he thought. Just the same, it was going to be a long day.

Thursday 9 P.M.

I came down the rattletrap stairs in the rat-infested tenement and stood on the street for a moment, trying to light a cigarette. The wind blowing through Harlem was full of dust and cinders and scraps of old newspaper. I walked west past pawnshops with steel grills on the windows, past the dark lure and neon of bars where jukeboxes mechanically ground out the sentiment of the day, where the rich smell of meat intruded itself on the wind in the streets. Where the park went up vertically toward the big barn-like apartment houses that grew on the higher plain above, I climbed the stairs, seeing the forlorn huddles of lovers on the black cold ground.

Above the park the wind was stronger, colder but cleaner with a tang in it from the Hudson. It thrust people along the street, whipping their clothes around them. I let it carry me along to the subway.

It was warmer there, almost pleasant, and I got a paper to read while I waited for the train, not wanting to think. But that was no use either. I kept seeing the faces of the longshoremen whom I had been sent to contact. They had given up. I could talk to them, and they would even agree that the strike could still be won if they held out, but they weren't kidding either themselves or me. They wouldn't go back right away, but that was the end of their efforts. The breaking up of the meeting the night before was a sign to them. I knew that it would be impossible to hold them much longer against the pressure that was being put on. Kelly's delegates and the gangsters that controlled this or that dock had been visiting them, too, threatening them with being blackballed if they didn't go back. The only thing that would put life into them would be some kind of activity from the committee. It would have to be more than a program phoned in to the newspapers; more than that same program turned into a leaflet and distributed along the front; more than the thin picket lines we were still able to maintain in some places. There was too much slack to be taken up. Everything was loose and raveling out.

A local came into the station and I got into the first car, standing and watching the rails disappear into the tunnel ahead while the uprights between the tracks flashed by like a solid fence. The rails curved into the shadow and another track crossed ours, overhead, a line of rails going away from us almost at right angles into the darkness of the solid rock. A string of lights, fictive and poignant, flashed over, a train bound for the frontiers, Pelham Bay, or New Lots Avenue, bearing its mysterious cargo toward the boundaries of the night. Trains were running everywhere, above, below, around, toward the peripheral limits of the city, as if the stony heart of it had disintegrated, exiling all its anonymous millions. A terrible loneliness gripped me. It seemed that all these voyaging thousands must be alone. You could look at them in the car with you, their faces set like those of zombies, and think that there wasn't one that really had a place to go. And if you were a zombie yourself—that didn't change anything. It was not like looking at the Indians in my little town, whose faces might be blank too, but you knew it was because they were looking at something inside them more interesting than the world. If the Indians had no other home, it was there inside them; they were not a product of disintegration like the voyagers in the subway.

The train slowed and nosed easily into a long station. It was a local stop. Platforms ran along the sides, long empty stony plains. In the middle there were the double tracks of the express; to the left, on the platform on the uptown side, there were two men. One of them seemed to have fallen, and his friend, a great raw-boned man with a square, brutal face, was helping him up. I thought that the fallen man, who was shorter by a head and almost fat, might be a little drunk. He got shakily to his hands and knees. His friend put out a long arm in the immemorial gesture of assistance, helping him, lifting him gently, bringing him into a delicate balance, still bent over a little and seemingly muzzy with drink, so that the short man came finally into a graceful and precarious compromise with gravity and weakness, leaning against the strong left arm of his friend. For a long cataleptic moment, as if time had stopped on this tableau of friendship while the station rocked in thunder of the train, they stood in this trance of weakness and aid. Then the tall man pulled back his right arm and in one terrific whipping motion brought it up, smashing the shorter man on the jaw. The short man straightened up and went over backward like a lead soldier. I could almost hear his head smash on the concrete. Then, the big man, still with the same graceful unhurried gestures as when he had appeared to help the other man up, dipped into the unconscious man's pocket and brought out his wallet.

I saw all this in one long roaring second when time seemed frozen as the train shook the station into thunder. It was over while my throat was still thick with the yell which I had not voiced. I looked quickly at the others in the car. Some of them had seen it happen. Now they looked down at the floor, embarrassed, unwilling to admit that they had seen it. An express roared through the station on the center track, not stopping. It cut off the view of the other platform like a falling curtain, then vanished into the dark tunnel.

It was like a quick change of scene. The tall robber was gone now. The little man had been pulled back into the shadow near the stairs so that he was hardly visible. I could just see his legs.

I got out of the train and ran back along the platform. People were coming down the stairs and onto the platform on the other side of the station. They were passing along beside the body of the fallen man. I shouted to them and pointed. A few of them looked at me across the black river of the tracks. I could see they thought I must be drunk or crazy. One of them shouted something unintelligible at me. They must have seen the body there, but they didn't give it a second glance.

There was no way to the other side of the station except to go out, cross the street above, and come down the other side. When I got down there, another train was in and people were getting on and off. I shouldered through and went over to where he was.

He was coming back to consciousness now. There was blood all over his face from a smashed lip. One of his teeth was broken off and hanging by a thread. I helped him to sit up and the train began to pull out of the station, the faces at the window looking at us with the same vacant brutalized stare with which they looked at subway posters. Feet clicked and scuffled past. Nobody stopped. He began to groan.

"Take it easy," I said. "You're all right now."

He tried to say something, choked and spat. He swore a little bit, poking at the broken tooth with his tongue. Then he spat again and I saw the dirty white clot of substance which had been his tooth, islanded in the red blob.

"Can you walk?"

"Guess. Maybe."

He got up and then remembered something. "It's no use," I said. "He rolled you."

He swore weakly. "You see it?"

"I was coming in on the train. I thought you were drunk and that he was helping you up."

"I come down here alone," he muttered. "Nobody in the station but him. He come up and asked me for a cigarette. I put my hand in my pocket and he slugged me."

"You got subway fare?"

He fished in his pocket and came out with a bill and some silver. "About two bucks," he said, spitting again. "Out of about sixty."

"You can get where you're going, then. I've got to be on my way."

"Yeah. Thanks, Mac. How come you stopped anyway? Hell, I could have been dead and nobody would have stopped."

"Sure, somebody would have stopped."

"Thanks anyway."

"You'll be O.K.? You could go up and report it to the cops."

He spat again. "What for?"

"Yeah. Take care of yourself."

It seemed even colder when I crossed the street to the downtown entrance. I thought of all those absolutely neutral eyes that had seen the man slugged and seen him lying unconscious, and that had not warmed with anything more human than alarm or embarrassment. You could die there on that street in the screaming wind, and they would walk right over your corpse without even looking down to see what was underfoot. My going over to help was the act of a madman. That was what the zombies knew in their wisdom: put out a hand, just a finger, and you are snatched away; time and the city pull you in and smash you and tear you like a great machine.

The street ran away from me in both directions, as wasted and empty as the moon. No, you could not expect birdsong or ease, sunlight or the sound of water here. I knew I was going to have to see Kay.

Kay's place was full of people. Conversation rattled through the room like dice in a cup. All the combinations turned up, all the points were made. She gave me one quick glance and nodded, but did not speak or come over to me, so I knew that she was sore. I went around to one end of the table and got a drink for myself and found a place to sit down where I could look at her, the sweep of red hair, the little hollows in her cheeks, the wide generous mouth. The drink tasted flat.

I listened to them discussing the plight of the artist. It seemed that he was in a perilous situation, which I took to be normal. After a while one of them, a fellow I had known slightly before the war, came over, shook hands, sat down beside me, and wanted to know what I knew about the strike. I told him not very much, and he then proceeded to tell me about it, and after a while they began discussing that. There was a girl with dark hair and bangs on her forehead, with dark slant eyes and a small mouth. She had on a dress almost as big as a pyramidal tent but was almost totally incapable of keeping her legs underneath it. I watched the legs from time to time as she reset the tent in a new position. A man with what looked like false eyebrows came over and sat down on the floor.

"One could have a lot more sympathy with them," he said, meaning the strikers, "if they weren't such dull sods. If they were really after something, it might be worthwhile. But actually all they want is a few more grubby dollars so that they can get a bit drunker on Saturday night and go home and beat their wives with a bit more fervor. If they were really challenging the system, then of course one could applaud. But—" He shrugged the rest of the sentence into the middle of the room, lifting the eyebrows. He had a grainy, drawling voice with what I suppose he thought was a cultured accent.

"Yes, of course," I said. "To a true revolutionary, I suppose the strikers seem like a bunch of clowns, don't they? Still, it's easier to paint a strike than to make one—or don't you think so?"

"Of course no—it's much more difficult to paint it."

"He loves to say things like that," the girl with the bangs told me. "He's the Oscar Wilde of the painting set."

"Tell me, Hunter," the man said. "Do you really believe that this strike will in any way further your revolution?"

The way he used the word put it into capital letters formed out of filth. Under the possibly merely plucked eyebrows he had little raisiny eyes like a gingerbread man.

"It it's handled right. If anything is learned from it."

"You think that is possible?"

"Yes."

"It seems to me," he said. "that you would do better to put your trust in the intellectuals. Movements, after all, are made by an elite, you know."

"I guess I just didn't know."

I went back to looking at the dark girl rearranging her legs. Kay and several others had gone over to the other side of the room and were discussing one of her pictures. It was the self-portrait which she was doing. It still didn't look like her.

The man with the eyebrows went on expounding the doctrine of the elite. He sounded like a latter-day Cotton Mather explaining who were the Elect of God.

"The man who invents a new emotion," he said, looking at me, "is the greatest revolutionary of all."

"Hear, hear," the dark girl said in a bored voice.

"Whereas the American workingman, when he goes on strike is a vulgar materialist who—"

"Only wants his bottle and his pussy. We've heard all that," the dark girl said.

"Exactly."

"Look," I said. "I'm not trying to suggest that the men who are out on the docks now are finished revolutionaries. Just the same, they're fighting the Church, the cops, the politicians, gangsters, the crooks who run the union, and Christ knows what else. And they're doing it blind. They don't know what they're up against, and they wouldn't believe you if you told them. But even if they don't know it, they're still doing something, learning, shaping themselves."

"What nonsense!" the man said. "D' you know, those ideas are very old-fashioned?" He yawned, either at the ideas or because he was sleepy, and got up to go. "Are you coming along, darling?" he asked the dark girl.

"No," she said. "You're getting so you talk all the time, Peter. You're becoming a pain in the ass."

Then Kay and the group that had been looking at her picture came over and people started saying good-bye, and in a few minutes they had all gone.

"Still converting the heathen, darling?" Kay asked. She came over and sat down beside me and put her head sleepily against my shoulder.

"I guess."

"You're wasting your time on Peter."

"I provoke easily."

"Could I provoke you?"

She let her hand crawl under my jacket, along my ribs. I could feel all the coldness of the day and the street melting out of me. "I was mad at you for leaving the way you did this morning. I'm not mad now, though."

I could feel the warmth of her breath on my neck. Across the room her portrait stared at me, eyes of paint, not interested in us. Like the eyes in the subway, I thought suddenly, and the room was instantly alive with the images of loss.

"You'd better give me a drink," I said. "There's something we've got to talk about."

Without saying anything she crossed the room, poured me a drink, brought it back and set it beside me.

"It's the old trouble, isn't it, Joe? You don't know what to do about us. About yourself, really."

"I'm going West as soon as the strike is over."

She didn't look at me. "Without me?"

"If I have to. I don't want it that way, but I'm going."

"And your great plan to wean me? To make me a responsible citizen and worthy of your great love?" Her voice was both sad and mocking at the same time.

"Plans fall apart. Or get knocked out of your head."

"That wasn't the way you talked before," she said accusingly.

"This is now."

"You *want* to let me go!"

"No. It isn't what I want. But what I want, what has that to do with anything? You didn't want to love me anyway."

"Oh, darling, you didn't have to believe me! You didn't!"

For a while neither of us said anything. Then Kay got up, crossed the room, got a cigarette and came back and sat down. The portrait seemed to be looking at me accusingly, but the eyes were still blank and neutral.

"What is it, Joe?" Kay asked. "What has happened?"

"Nothing has happened."

"Is it because of that meeting that got smashed up?"

"No."

"You would expect things like that might go wrong, wouldn't you? Is it because of the strike? Do you think it's lost?"

"I guess it's lost. It hasn't anything to do with that."

"Yes it has. What is it, then?"

"I just don't want to hang around here. I've got a place I want to go, so why don't I go there? If I hang around here I'll just get caught in the machinery. I—"

"You mean me? You mean I'm the machinery you'll get caught in?"

"No. I mean—"

"Yes. That's it, isn't it? You're afraid I'll unmake you. You're just hanging on in this strike on your nerve—you didn't want to get into it, even. And now you're afraid that if you stay around, instead of making me into the responsible person you want, I'll soften you up and wean you away. Isn't that it?"

"It isn't like that at all. I just don't fit in here anymore, with you or with my work. I just want to go out there for a while and get on my feet and get straightened out—"

"And you think a month or a year in some town with a bunch of sleepy Indians and Mexicans and sunlight and a village square with a fountain in it—you think that will do the trick? You're just running away."

"Goddamn it, I'm not!"

"Oh, not because you're afraid of anything real, like getting knifed or shot or beaten. You could go along for years this way, living on your nerves, taking your beatings, getting ulcers or whatever the occupational disease is. It's me you're afraid of, and the soft part inside you. And all you're asking of that town you're going to is that it help you to be reborn again, all hard and shiny, so that you won't care about me or yourself anymore."

"No, Kay. I think maybe it is because I'm afraid. Plain scared. Listen, I'll tell you something."

I told her about the meeting and about Blackie turning up as one of the goons and then about the robbery in the subway. "I don't know what it is," I said. "It's just as if the world had turned into a bunch of wild animals eating each other. Or like that time I was in the tank—everyone fighting and screaming and clawing at each other. That's the way my world is. Maybe I'm scared."

"But that's not new to you. And just because you were once in the war, that doesn't mean that now all your enemies will be on one side and that they will all be wearing the same uniforms. So you shouldn't be surprised about Blackie, should you?"

"No. I shouldn't be surprised about anything. Let's not talk about it."

"We've got to talk about it."

"All right, then. Here it is. We want different things. You want to stay here. You've got your mother—you're tied to her—and you've got your painting which you are going to be good at and you don't want to get tied too tightly to me. I've got my own work, and I'm going West and after that I don't know where. Nothing can be worked out."

"Darling, it was fine before. Before the war, and even now, after you came back. Can't we just let it go at that?"

"No, damn it. You're throwing yourself away for your old lady. And hell, I've got to know where I stand. With myself and everybody, whether it's you or Blackie Carmody."

"With time, maybe—"

"Time wouldn't change anything."

There wasn't any use to talk about it because everything had been said. I got up and went toward the door.

"You're leaving?"

"I'm staying with a guy. I've got to get an early start in the morning."

"Don't go, darling." She came over and put her arms around my neck. "Stay here, darling. I want you so hard. Please. It'll look different in the morning."

"No. Christ—" I thought of the darkness, the cold murderous streets. I wanted to stay more than I had ever wanted anything. Wherever she touched me, my body was alive and furious. "Goddamn it, no!" I said.

"You *are* afraid of me."

"All right. I'm afraid, if that's the way you want it."

"Will you come by before you go West?"

"If you want me to."

"We're both afraid."

"All right, we're both afraid." I was sick of hearing the word. Then I put my arms around her and kissed her. It was as if something sharp-edged and powerful was moving inside me. I felt all cut to hell as I went out, leaving the litter of cigarette butts and dirty glasses, like a tourists' picnic, and my own drink untasted on the floor.

The wind was still tearing at the street. My leg was hurting. A few blocks away I thought that someone was following me and I stopped in the shadows. No one came along the street, and I couldn't have heard footsteps anyway, with the wind. I thought of what Everson had said and thought that all of us were getting jumpy. Afraid. That was Kay's word. It seemed as if nothing would be easy or simple or good ever again. I shuffled along in the cold wind. I wanted to get to Everson's place and get into the warm bed and sleep for a long, long time.

Thursday 10 P.M.

At about ten o'clock Blackie Carmody was preparing to go out. During the day he had not left the the apartment, had sat in the big chair which Manta had been used to occupy on his occasional visits, smoking cigarettes, not speaking. He sat there now and watched the light go dead in the store across the street—the Harounians were making a rare midweek visit to the neighborhood movie—and kicked the litter of the daily paper away from his feet. He had not read the paper, but all day long he had been going over the events of the night before, the break-up of the rank-and-file meeting.

He had told himself that it had only been a job, that since he had been hired to do it and paid—or would be paid—that it was all right. The fact that it was something that he would be paid for was important. It meant that he had no special responsibility for it, or rather that his responsibility was to the job. The laborer is worthy of his hire—the phrase ran through his mind. He could not remember where he had heard it or what the context was, but he felt that it meant a kind of responsibility toward an undertaking. *To do a job.* Yes, that was all right. That was right. It meant that you were capable and responsible. Nevertheless, Blackie Carmody felt a vast guilt, a midnight quicksand, sucking at his feet.

To pull a job. That was something else again. That was what he had done that night with Joe Hunter when they had taken the bar, when they had beat up on Porky. To pull a job left you feeling good, like a time when you were a kid and you put something over on the old man or on one of the Sisters, or on a priest, or, later, an officer. But there was no good feeling about the night before, about the meeting. When you pulled a job, you knew it was wrong by the standards of other people, but they were always people whom you hated or distrusted or despised. It was wrong, but it was someone else's wrong, that was why you felt good, because their wrong was your right. Then what was wrong about the night before?

It was not right that he should feel bad about it, he thought. If you felt bad about doing a job, about doing something which you had been hired to do, paid to do—or would be paid for—in hard money, what did that mean? There was something wrong. Hard money should make it right, because it was pay, not something you had swiped when you were a kid. Then he began to think of Joe Hunter.

It was the second time that he had saved Hunter's bacon, counting the time in the tank which he had never counted before. There was no reason for him to feel wrong about Hunter, but nevertheless he did feel wrong, as if the second action had not reinforced but had actually canceled out the first. He began to go back over the first time, when the tank had burned. Images of fire crowded his mind. But the images had a dead quality about them now, like the memory of scenes from a film: nothing would burn in that fire: they belonged to another world.

"I better get goin'," he told himself, crushing out his cigarette, putting the images and thoughts away in his mind, carefully, as if they were brittle or sharp.

His mother was sitting at the kitchen table with a heap of stockings in front of her. She took one of them, drawing it over her hand, and ran a quick filament of thread across the hole.

"I think I'll go down the street."

"Yes, Francis," she said tranquilly. He thought with an instant rush of anger and remorse that she wouldn't have said it like that two days ago. He looked at her, thinking that she was dying and that he had condemned her, and tried to speak, watching the thread growing like a bush in the hole of the stocking.

"Where's Mary?" he asked.

"She went down to see Hope. She'll be coming up soon," she said, glancing at the clock.

He went into the hall and down the flight of stairs to the first floor. His sister was standing at a doorway talking with Hope who, seeing him, lifted her breasts against the robe she was wearing and gave him a glance hard with challenge and invitation.

"Mom wants you," he told his sister, and went on down the hallway to the street door, thinking of her and her friend with weary irritation and a little spurt of desire for Hope.

The street was like a dark tunnel with only a little light at the far end where the avenue crossed. A few women, cushions under their arms, leaned out of dark windows talking softly to one another. On tenement steps groups of children whispered and giggled. Near the end of the street he passed the Catholic Youth building, and Manta gave him a silent greeting. He turned up the avenue toward the clubhouse.

A game was in progress. Blackie nodded to Kenny and to Mella and sat down to wait. The smell of the place was strong and distasteful to him, and he looked with disgust at the litter of cigarette butts on the floor, at the pictures of politicians on the wall, their eyes hooded and predatory or blank and empty as stone.

Of the men playing, Kenny was young and good-looking, with a weak and wary face, eyes that were brown and warm, and slick, oiled hair combed to painful perfection. Mella was short, swarthy-faced, with heavy lips and eyebrows and coarse curly hair. The strong light dissolved the unity of their faces into a collection of distinct and separate features until the faces became fantastic and meaningless, as a word becomes meaningless and strange when it is repeated over and over again. Blackie shook the feeling of alienation away from him and the faces once more composed themselves into the look of men whom he knew. He threw his cigarette to the floor and spat with disgust.

The cards went around for the last time and the betting finished. Kenny won the pot, carefully pocketed the money, and got up from the table. He walked with a slight swagger. He's hopped up because he won, Blackie thought sourly, wishing that Kenny had lost.

"What's up, sport?" Kenny asked. He went through a little ritual of getting out a cigarette and tapping it on a shiny case. Blackie said nothing, waiting while Mella came over and sat down heavily beside him.

"Something on?" Mella asked.

"I wanted to talk to you."

"Lay it out," Kenny said.

"Not in here."

"What's the matter with here?" Kenny asked. "Our dues are paid. You're too jumpy, Blackie."

"I wasn't the only one who was jumpy the night we went to hunt for Porky."

"I couldn't find Mella," Kenny said. The slight patronizing edge went out of his voice and it became a defensive whine.

"He doesn't wanna talk here," Mella said. "Let's go."

"If I'da found Mella—" Kenny began.

"I don't care about that now. Forget it."

They went down the stairs of the loft and into the street. At the corner there was a drugstore, now closed. Blackie stopped in front of it, digging in his pocket for a cigarette. Now that it was time to say it, he felt a powerful backwash of the feeling he had had when his mother had forced him to agree to take the job with Kelly. He offered the pack of cigarettes to Kenny who shook his head and produced his own shiny case.

"Take one, for Christ's sake!"

Kenny took the cigarette. "What the hell is it, Blackie?" he asked complainingly. Mella took the pack from him, shook out a cigarette and handed the cigarettes back to Blackie.

"I'm finished," Blackie said abruptly. "I'm gettin' out."

"You mean you're quitting?" Kenny asked in outraged astonishment.

"That's what I said."

"Jesus, but Blackie—"

"What's the deal, Blackie?" Mella asked.

"What difference does it make? I'm finished. Through."

"With the corner? Hell, we could take over a couple more bars—"

"You take 'em, Kenny. I don't want them."

"Yeah? Well—hey, you didn't hear anything, did you? Somebody hasn't got sore? Somebody isn't getting ready to lay for us?"

"Nah. We weren't big enough for anybody to get sore at."

"I don't know," Kenny said dubiously. He gave Blackie a quick glance. "You're sure you haven't heard nothing?"

"What is it, Blackie?" Mella asked patiently.

"I went to work," Blackie said. "My old lady, she wanted me to. She fixed it up. I got a job through Kelly."

Kenny whistled softly. "You made the connection," he said in a marveling voice. "You're in like Flynn. How'd you do it, Blackie? You taking over that dock you always wanted? Don't forget you got pals."

"Christ, you make it sound good," Blackie said bitterly. "That's not the way it is. When I said work, I meant work. I got a union book, that's what I mean. That's all I got."

"But there ain't nothing in that. Hell, you mean you're going to *work* down on the docks?"

"Yeah."

"Well—" Kenny said. He looked at Mella uncertainly. Mella was staring across the empty street, looking at neither of the other two. "Well, I guess you don't want to say anything about it," Kenny said in tones of flat disbelief.

"That's all there is."

"Sure. You're doing it because of the old lady." There was an edge of derision in his voice.

"If you're going to work on the dock," Mella said, "that's no reason why we still can't take those bars. You don't work down at the dock all day and all night."

"That was part of taking the job," Blackie said wearily. "She was worried. I can't do it on the side, or she'd find out. She's—" He stopped, thinking of his mother until it was like a pain. "Listen," he said, "the bar is out. But if you know of a fast one, anything that will pay off big, I'm in."

"A stickup maybe," Mella said quietly.

"Yeah."

"No, for Christ's sake!" Kenny protested.

"Could be," Mella mused.

"It's got to be worthwhile," Blackie said. "It's got to be fast and big."

"Yes," Mella said. "Maybe I'll hear of something." He looked directly at Blackie for the first time.

"So long," Blackie said and turned away, down the avenue.

"I don't want any of that kind of stuff," Kenny said. Mella was silent. "He must be scared," Kenny said. "He's running out. His old lady! What the hell did his old lady ever do for him?"

The two began to walk back toward the Democratic clubrooms. "Look," Kenny said quickly, "it's still on, isn't it? You and me can handle it without Blackie."

"Blackie was a good boy," Mella said. "He was smart, and he was tough when he had to be."

"We don't need him."

"You ain't so smart, Kenny," Mella said heavily. "And you sure as hell ain't tough."

Kenny followed him up the stairs of the clubrooms. He felt a sudden emptiness followed by blind anger, first with Mella, then with himself, then at nothing at all; at last he knew a terrible sense of frustration and restriction, as if he were having a cruel joke played on him by forces whose nature he was unable to guess. He was experiencing the same kind of feeling of muffled outrage that a little businessman feels when he realizes that the next day or the next week will bring bankruptcy.

Walking down the avenue, Blackie was feeling almost happy again. He was involved in a dream of success, a fast job and then—out. On the dark avenue it seemed plausible, although he had always believed that the man with a gun was a fool. He had come to see that only the methods of business were successful, and the man with the gun was only on the fringe of business, someone who sold his labor and skill at a low price. Still, there was the possibility of a coup, of one fast one and out, of getting the longshot just one time. A voice that was smaller and drier than his own told him that the outsider never won; he pushed the voice into the darkness of the avenue. He was no longer in the area where choice was allowed.

He turned the corner, walking now on his own street, almost at the CYO building.

"It's him," a voice said.

Wrapped in the integuments of the dream, Blackie did not at first see the flicker of movement in the shadows. There was the sound of rapid steps, the harsh hurried breathing of men in a hurry or excited or afraid.

"Get the Commie son of a bitch!"

The first man got him by the shoulder, clumsily, gripping and pulling, too excited perhaps to get his arms. Blackie hit him cleanly, a quick, hard, rounding punch with his right hand, and the grip loosed on his shoulder as the man went back. Another had his right arm then, turning him, and he clubbed with his left at the third and fourth men, feeling the crunch of bone as he hit a nose and then the quick electric snap of muscle as he missed. The first man came back in and got him by the hips and he bulled them along for a couple of yards, trying to free his right hand, stabbing and hammering with his left, butting with his head, trying to free one of his legs so that he could kick. The man who had his legs worked around to his right in the clumsy dance up the street, pulled back for an instant and Blackie felt the instant cutting pain, then the heavy eating misery as he was hit in the testicles. He let out one long, high involuntary scream, bending over, and the man who had his right arm moved in swiftly, hitting him fast and repeatedly on the back of the head and neck, like a butcher cutting through a tough bone, and he went down.

He was still not unconscious and he turned onto his belly, putting his hands up around his head and over the back of his neck. A foot smashed at his ribs and he arched in agony, half turning to shield his side.

"Kill the Red bastard!" he heard the panting voice and started to say, no, you're wrong, it's me, Blackie Carmody, but his voice was lost in a sense of mortal outrage as he thought, this is me, Blackie, and it's my own street, it's my own street where they're ganging me. Then the shoe smashed him behind the ear and he was still and unconscious.

He came out of a chaos of darkness and shouting and into a condition of absolute pain. He could no longer localize it. There was a long ache in the middle of him, making him want to vomit. Then he recognized something else. It was his right leg.

He was lying half on and half off the sidewalk. His legs were stretched across the gutter. Two of the men were kneeling or sitting across his body so that his arms were useless, a third was sitting on his right foot, and the last of them, the man whom he had hit with his first blow was standing beside him.

"Hold it!" the man said. He went into a little dance of impatience, standing on the edge of the gutter while the other twisted the foot. Blackie tried to move his right leg, to kick, but the leg would not move. Then he knew what had happened. They had broken it at the knee, across the edge of the gutter. After that he began to scream.

The man in the street pulled his leg, twisting the foot, and the one on the edge of the gutter danced in impatience. Then he brought his right foot into the air, like a man stamping a snake, and smashed it downward. It seemed to Blackie that he could hear the grinding and splintering of the bones in his kneecap, and he screamed again, trying to faint, while the man in the street pulled and twisted the leg, turning it again, and the other one danced his crazy dance once more before bringing his right foot into the air and smashing the already broken knee.

Footsteps sounded on the pavement, running. They seemed a long way off and he began to shout, loudly he thought, but he was only moaning. The pain in his knees made him forget the rest of the body, but he could not faint. He heard the footsteps again, more clearly, and the sound of far off shouting. Then there was another flurry of movement on the pavement, behind his head, muffled cursing, a groan. Out of the fog of pain he saw a face—Manta. The man's nose was bloody, his face was twisted in anger or hurt, and his right arm swung uselessly in the sleeve of his coat.

"Blackie!" he said. "They got you." And began to tug at him with his left hand, transposing the pain to a new level.

"What the hell," a voice said. "Who's the dead soldier?"

Blackie recognized the wrinkled face of Riverboat Conn peering at him.

"Help me," Manta said.

"Who is it?" Conn asked. He peered, blinking, and Blackie smelled the murky reek of alcohol on his breath.

"Him," Conn grunted, straightening himself with effort. "I wouldn't piss on him if he was afire. Finky son of a bitch," he said, spitting, and stepped carefully off the curb, as if it were very high, and crossed the street.

"Easy, Blackie," Manta said. "I'll get some help."

"My legs."

"Sure, we'll get you to a hospital."

Manta gave up trying to move him and walked away, calling to someone farther down the street.

I'm beating Mom to the hospital, Blackie thought irrelevantly. It struck him as funny and he began to laugh weakly and hysterically. Jesus, I wanted to send her, and now it's me that's going. He thought of Manta with the bloody nose, the face which had lost for once the attitude of complete indifference and passivity which it always wore. By God, he thought, he made a move; he thought that he didn't have to stick his neck out, but he stuck it out before he thought; he got caught in the strike anyway.

Then the irony of being beaten by Kelly's goons came to him. He could not understand how it happened, but it seemed to him supremely funny. Crying and laughing, groaning and half hysterical with pain, he waited until in his partial delirium he heard the long blue wail of the ambulance on the windy night.

Thursday 11 P.M.

It was impossible for Crip to see in through the windows of the bar.

Moisture had collected and was running in dirty rivulets down the panes; even the door was fogged over, and Crip was forced to open it, bringing the night and the cold into the warm, lighted place. He stopped just inside the door, saw his man in the gloomy warmth inside, and went out again. It would have been better not to enter at all. The warmth weakened him. It was cold outside and he had not taken his coat with him.

In the tenement house through which he went in order to take up his watch beside the window of the bar's toilet there was a smell of cooking and winter, of bacon grease and kerosene stoves, the smell of his home, and he was glad to be outside again even though it was colder. The window of the toilet was also steamed over. He wiped it, but the moisture was all on the inside. Standing in the fury of the wind that whipped through the alley like a beaked bird, he swore in mechanical senseless fury at the coated glass. He got the gun out of his pocket and held it in his right hand, under the left-hand flap of his jacket, his collar turned up against the cold, a little man, shivering, cursing for reasons that he could not define, but in his own way satisfied because he was doing a job that he knew how to do.

It would have been better to do the work some other way. He had no guarantee that the man he was hunting would come back to the toilet. Other nights he had waited with no luck at all. Still, he was patient. He would curse the waiting and the weather, in a continual fury of outrage and impatience, but he could wait, as he had waited other nights. If not now, another time, he thought, swearing with the cold, and saw the door open and a shadow on the glass.

It was not the man he wanted. He put the gun back under his coat to keep his hand warm, and with his face just outside the light that came through the dirty pane he watched the man, hating him for being someone else. The man inside was comfortably built, almost fat. He opened his fly hurriedly, almost with anxiety, glancing down at the urinal. As he began to make water he broke wind loudly, sighed, and, putting one hand for support on the wall in front of him, leaned forward, relaxing with his head against his forearm. Then, lifting his eyes, he began a minute, almost leisurely survey of the literature on the walls, pursing his lips and squinting slightly in the faulty light, as he read the hurried anonymous scrawls, puckering his lips in distaste or inclining his head briefly in interest or corroboration, once taking out a pencil and running a line through one of the verses. Finally he stepped back, shook thoughtfully, buttoned his fly with his left hand, placed the pencil in his pocket, and, with a last gesture of smoothing his clothes, his hand going into his pocket to shift his underwear, he pulled the door open and went out.

Crip leaned forward, thinking that the man had written something, but through the dirty pane of glass he could make out nothing. He stepped back into the darkness, swearing to himself again, not so much at the man as at the world in general, the constant frustration, whether it was the inability to read a thing written over a urinal or the lack of one sound leg. It was an old vendetta.

It was after eleven when the hunt ended. Crip heard the sound of the hand on the knob, the door opened and a man entered: dark head, cocky bearing. Crip brought his hand, warm from his body under the jacket, up to the level of his eye and fired twice as fast as he could pull the trigger. The man reached out, like someone falling, and pulled the chain of the toilet. The man fell out of the square of light bounded by the window, and for perhaps a second Crip heard his spasmodic kicking, like the jerking of the legs of a poleaxed animal or of a chicken whose neck has been wrung, a fleshly thumping of the walls of the toilet. He had a moment of almost clairvoyant realization, turning to a feeling of being physically outraged, as he realized that he had shot the wrong man. Then the tardy action of the toilet began and drowned everything else in the muted tearing sound of rushing water.

Thursday Midnight

I got to Bill's place about eleven-thirty and there was nobody home. Seeing it for the second time, the room looked bigger, more comfortable, but hardly like home.

There was a coffee pot and some dirty cups on the table. I washed the pot and got some coffee going and went in and took a shower. There was plenty of hot water and I began to be really warm for the first time in the day. When I had finished, I found an old bathrobe that might have belonged to Bill or to the other guy. Then I discovered an electric heater in the cupboard—probably the landlord didn't allow them to be used—and plugged it in. The filament glowed red and golden, and in a few minutes the air in the room began to have that sandy quality that lets you know it's toasted like the famous product used to be.

The other fellow's bed was a mess, but Bill's was neatly made with military corners. Breaking into it was like opening a safe. When I was there, with the heater going and the hot coffee inside me, I began to feel good. Outside I could hear the wind like a couple of cats fighting on a fence, and it was fine to be out of it in a warm place.

I didn't think about Kay. Maybe, somehow, it would all straighten out. I knew it wouldn't, but I couldn't make the final admission. It seemed that all I had been doing since I got back was trying to straighten things out, to make smooth the path, unwalk the crooked mile.

I went on straightening things out and came out of a doze with a shock, like a clumsy hogger pulling into the last railroad station at the end of a bad run.

The lights were on. The little heater was busy translating the several components of air into a sandy substance that hurt when you breathed it. The wind was biting at the walls. Nobody had come home.

I listened, sure I had heard someone knocking, waiting for it to come again, too lazy and sleepy to get up. It was just a little after one, so I couldn't have been dozing for more than a few minutes.

I thought for a moment I heard footsteps, the springy cocky footsteps of Blackie Carmody or Bill, but I realized that they were far away in another part of the house.

I pulled the plug out of the wall and switched off the lights. The heater glowed like an eye in the dark and outside the wind howled. I thought of Bill and the other guys out there in the cellar of the world, fumbling around for a lost key. Everyone gets his turn. I hoped they were in warm places. Then I began to push out on the big river of sleep, and somewhere far away I heard the last of those authoritative footsteps dying away in the darkness of another part of the forest.

Friday 7:30 A.M.

Brian Munson stood on the cold street, folding the papers neatly so that the wind wouldn't whip them away. He read the weather report: Cold; overcast; high winds; and the date Friday, October.

The wind was high on the avenue and it chilled him through his jacket. Across toward the waterfront he heard the thrumming of a ship's horn and the cracking rattle of a hard-rubber-tired truck. Cramming the newspapers into his pocket he turned back to the house he lived in and climbed the flights of stairs to his apartment. It was almost warm in the kitchen and there was the morning smell of coffee. The lights were on because the day was dark and overcast and the kitchen had a window opening only on the wall of the next house. Brian Munson heard the shuffling of his wife's footsteps in the next room and flipped the paper open on the table, waiting for his coffee.

Effie Munson came in wearing an old quilted bathrobe. Her feet in great soft shapeless bedroom slippers padded as softly as if they had been wrapped in sacking. She took the coffee from the stove and poured it for her husband, waiting for him to speak, her back to the stove from which there came a little warmth. She was shivering slightly, not yet used to being out of the warmth of bed, and her fading blonde hair was as mussed and untidy as a dust mop. She was still sleepy. It was early yet and there was no need for them to be up, but a lifetime of early rising could not be canceled out by a week of strike in which there was no need to get up. Yawning, she kept her eyes on Munson as he read carefully through the paper. As precisely as an engineer reading a dial, she watched the news reflected in his face. She would have preferred to go back to bed just for a quarter of an hour on this cold October morning, but she waited in front of the almost heatless stove, shivering a little, nervous. She had to speak to her husband and she was afraid.

Munson read slowly, moving his lips slightly as if the only way he could get the reality out of the printed columns was to form the words to himself. In the bad light of the kitchen his face looked washed out, covered with dirty lines, like a piece of handwritten paper that has been wet so that most of the ink has washed off. He read first the news of a murder that had occurred in a bar on Eighth Avenue and then the news of an announcement by the Rank-and-File Committee. Following that he went on to a quick survey of the national and foreign news, put the *Daily Worker* on the table in front of him, opened the other paper and turned to the funnies. With the same seriousness he read "Li'l Abner," glanced at the sports, folded the paper and finished his coffee. He looked up at his wife standing beside the stove and drew a deep breath.

"He come home yet?" he asked.

Effie shook her head.

"I suppose he's got plenty of friends now," Brian Munson said painfully.

"Don't be hard on him, Brian," Effie said. "He's just a young boy."

"I guess somebody'd give him a place to stay, anyway," Munson went on, as if he hadn't heard his wife. "He's moving in important circles these days. You can't expect him to be home all the time, now that he's got important business on his mind." There was still more wonderment than bitterness in his voice.

"Johnny's all right, Brian." Her voice had a soothing quality in it as if she were talking to a child. She came over and began to brush her hand over his hair as much perhaps to quiet herself as her husband. "He's a boy. He don't know any better yet. We've got to be easy with him, Brian. He's our boy."

"That only makes it worse," Munson said with weary bitterness. "If he was somebody else's kid, I guess I could understand it better. If he was the son of some wharf rat that never taught him any better you couldn't blame him for it—"

"Don't be too hard with him. He's all we got left now, with the others gone away."

"But he's my own kid. I never laid a hand on him when he was little. I never told him nothing that wasn't right. If he wanted to do something I let him do it. If he wanted a thing I tried to get it for him. Jesus, woman, you want me to shake his hand and congratulate him for doing a thing like that?"

"He didn't know any better, Brian."

"If he didn't know any better, then he's no good."

"The boy's just come out of the army," Effie said, smoothing her husband's white hair. "He's restless yet. You talk to him, but don't be mad. After he's been gone all that time, we ought to have it nice for awhile."

"If that's what he learned in the army then goddamn the army, that's all I've got to say," Munson said fiercely. After a moment he said: "I'll talk to him in my own way, that's all there is to it. You're always too easy with him, Effie."

"I can't help it, Brian—I keep thinking of when he was little—"

"He ain't little anymore," Munson said heavily. "You think I'm just sore at him? hell, I'm his father, ain't I? Now you go on with your work, Effie, I'll talk to him if he comes in. He isn't a little kid anymore." He picked up the papers again but he did not read. Effie shuffled into another room of the apartment in her clumsy slippers. After a while Brian Munson poured himself another cup of coffee. It was cold, but he drank it anyway, looking through the kitchen window at the blank, black-crusted bricks of the wall of the house next door.

Johnny Munson stood for a moment in front of the kitchen door of his parents' apartment. Light came through the curtain and through the clouded glass of the upper half of the door, etching the chicken wire that was embedded in the glass, interlocking octagons of black lines. Above him somewhere a radio was playing; then the music was washed out in the roar of a toilet. He pushed the door open and went in. Seeing his father sitting at the table with the papers and the coffee cup in front of him, the white, distinguished-looking head, he had a moment of panic, but he stood with his back to the door, a slender boy of twenty or so, tired and cold and dirty, a two-day blond beard softening the lines of his face.

"So you came back," Brian Munson said without surprise, and waited. When his son did not speak he pushed the papers forward on the table, a meaningless, irritated gesture. "Why did you do it, Johnny?" he said in a low voice. "Why?"

"How did you know?"

"I was there."

"Yeah," Johnny Munson said bitterly. "I might have known you would be." He went over and stood against the stove, lighting a cigarette.

"Why, Johnny?" Munson said again. "*I* know it's hard after you come back out of the army. I try to see how it is, I guess you're mixed up a little but I never thought—" He stopped speaking and shook his head.

"You never thought I'd scab, is that it? Say it then."

"I never thought you'd turn up as one of Kelly's goons. I never thought you'd turn up at a strike meeting with a bunch of dirty, scabbing—"

"Don't, Brian," Effie Munson said, coming quietly into the room. She gave her son a warning glance and put her hand on her husband's shoulder.

"Let him say it," Johnny said savagely.

"Now listen to me, both of you," Effie said. "You know I didn't want you to get tied up in this strike. When that man Hunter came around I tried to keep your father from going to that meeting. It just causes trouble when you do a thing like that. But you, Johnny, you shouldn't have done what you did. A boy like you ought to know better than to do a thing like that. You're going against your own people, if you do. Now let's not talk about it anymore."

"That's all right with me," Johnny said angrily. "But he won't let it go at that."

"You're right and I won't," Brian Munson said. "You think it's that easy, Effie? You think you can take back a thing like that so fast?"

"I'm not trying to take back a thing."

"You know where your friends are, then."

"Stop it," Effie said desperately. "Stop it, both of you stop it. Johnny just got home. He's just a boy and he didn't know any better—"

"I'm not a kid any longer," the boy said sullenly. "He treats me like I was ten years old."

"Maybe you better go back to the people who understand you better," Munson said. He looked down at the table and fiddled with his coffee cup. Effie gave one despairing glance at her son, begging him not to speak. "Brian—" she started to say placatingly.

"All right, then!" Johnny said. He spoke loudly, afraid that his voice would break. "I'm going!"

"Go on, then," his father answered tiredly. "I don't want a scab around here."

Effie put a shocked hand over his voice, her own mouth open in speechless protest, watching the face of her son go white, then red, then white again, and feeling under her hand the hard set of her husband's jaw. The boy tried to say something, failed to find words, and turned away, pausing for a moment with the door half open and his hand on the knob, looking down at it in deep and outraged amazement as if the door had opened of itself, taking his hand to lead him out of the apartment. Then he was gone.

"I knew you would do it," Effie said, turning her stricken face away from her husband, not even crying. "Right away when you told me what he had done, I knew you would do it, I knew it before you even made up your mind."

Brian Munson reached out to her, touching her hand clumsily, but she drew away. "A man's got to stop somewhere," he said finally, in a spent voice. "I give in on everything, before. Sometime you got to stop, Effie, or you ain't a man no more."

"Do you think I haven't given up things?" she asked passionately. "All the time to raise him, all the scrimping and saving, all the worry during the war. Do you think it was ever easy with me?"

"No," he said humbly. "Harder maybe, you a woman. But it ain't the same thing, Effie."

"No. You're a *man*," she said, hurling the word at him like a curse.

"No," he said, putting his hand out in the same futile gesture. "It's nothing I begrudge him, all the things we gave up, raising him and the others, things we denied ourselves, times I worked till I about dropped to get a few extra dollars. Times when you was sick after having them, getting old too fast with having to look after them and the house and everything else—not even that."

"What is it, then?" she asked. Her anger was ebbing away, leaving her with a wasted, resentful feeling. "What else is there?"

"Well," he began, fumbling for the words uncertainly. "There's—other things. Things—"

"Oh, Brian," she said sadly, "you're always fooling yourself. What else is there? All we can do is take what we can get. We're all alone. Nobody cares about us, you know that, whether we live or die. All we have is the family, not the one we're born into, but the one we get. What else do we have but that? And now—" She began to cry for the first time, heavily, like an old woman.

"No, Effie," Munson said miserably. "Don't do that. There's still us, Effie."

"What are we? What are we now? Oh, Brian, why did you do it? Why?"

"You got to stop somewhere, Effie. When I was young I used to think I'd take nothing off nobody, I wouldn't let anyone walk over me. That's what I told that young fellow Hunter. But it hasn't been like that. When we got married and we started getting the kids, I couldn't be like that. I give in on a lot of things, being careful on the job, not talking back. I let the world walk on me, Effie. I thought, well, I don't have to agree with them, I can just keep my mouth shut and say nothing. But if you say nothing, that's a kind of agreement, and that's the way it was, kicking back on the job, letting the priests and the newspapers educate the kids, not agreeing, but not fighting back. But a man's got to stop giving in sometime."

"But why now? Why on something like this?"

"I don't know, except I had to. Maybe it's because if you give in on the little things, one at a time, you get to giving in on the bigger ones without knowing it. Then something comes along and you can't give in no more, and you have to stop on the hardest thing of all. That's how you pay for giving in on the first things, the little things. Sending Johnny away, that was the hardest thing I ever had to do."

"Then why did you?"

Munson hunted for words again. Then he said: "If you let somebody scab and don't do nothing about it, it makes it harder for next time there's a strike, harder for yourself and for everybody." He knew that he was not saying what he really felt, but he could not find the words.

When his wife said nothing, he put out his hand in a blind, ineffective gesture. This time she did not draw away. She had stopped crying and felt dumb and heavy, sitting on the uncomfortable kitchen chair at the table. Finally Munson said, "I had to do it if I wanted to think of myself as a man. Maybe it's different with other people. For decency, Effie, honor, maybe you'd call it. I don't know."

"None of those things are real at all," the woman said. "Not real like Johnny, being a family, or money is real."

"They come out of real things like those, though," Munson said doggedly.

His wife did not reply but got up and began working mechanically about the kitchen. Munson folded his paper carefully, taking a long time about it. Then when he had finished he got up and put on his jacket. At the door his wife spoke without turning: "You could bring him back." Munson went out of the apartment without making reply.

It was cold in the streets. A raw wind was blowing. Although it was morning, the street was heavy with a cloudy twilight in which the buildings seemed gloomy and oppressive. Munson turned into Eighth Avenue, crossed Fourteenth and passed the library at Jackson Square, not even thinking of where he was going. He thought of his son and then of Joe Hunter, letting his legs carry him along. Automatically he began to hurry a little.

Thursday 2 P.M.

Sitting in the cold gloom of Thursday midafternoon, Kelly saw the door open, and the tall figure of Alton Husk came into the office. Kelly stirred, sighing a little, and stuffed a dead cigar into the litter of the ashtray.

"I'd have been in earlier," Husk said, "but I got tied up with something. This is keeping me pretty busy."

"How's that?" Kelly asked. "Busy with what?"

"The strike."

"Oh," Kelly said. "That." And rising suddenly to his feet he pulled the drop cord, flooding the area around the desk with light.

Husk stood easily beside the desk. Wearing a loose topcoat and a dark hat, he appeared bigger and taller than he was. Looking at him, Kelly noticed for the first time the overthick lips. The face was handsome, plausible, and there were little fictive lights in the hazel eyes. The eyes themselves seemed hard and flat and strange, devices only for picking up and turning back the light from the lamps, and for a moment Kelly merely felt distaste; then the anger.

"Sit down," he said.

Husk turned away and removed his coat. A part of the office was still gloomy with the chill and lifeless light of the out-of-doors. When he had taken his coat off he felt cold, but there seemed to be warmth in the chair under the circle of light.

"I saw Caminetti," Kelly said abruptly.

"Did you?" Husk said readily. "What did he want? Caminetti always wants something."

"Nothing. I told him to do something about that committee."

"Oh, that. You handled it pretty fast, P.J. I didn't hear about it until just about the time it was going to be run off. All I could do was send a few boys around to see if maybe they couldn't organize it a little differently. When did you find out about it?"

"I always knew about it," Kelly said heavily. "I guess I was born knowing about it, or about things like it."

"You acted fast."

"You must think I'm getting old, Al. Sure I acted fast."

"What's on your mind now?"

"You were going to organize the meeting the right way—that it? You do a lot of thinking, don't you, Al? You want to make the world fit a pattern that's in your head. Now me, I just make the heads fit into the world the way it is."

The words had a clever ring which his mind recognized, but they had a bitter taste in Kelly's mouth, *It's not true* while he watched a smile move across Husk's face, changing his eyes as the shadow of a cloud changes the color of water, making them less flat and hard and shallow.

"Good enough," Husk said easily. He was thinking of the plans he had had for the meeting and of how Kelly had upset them. Kelly's action had come like winter lightning. It had been thoroughly unforeseen and it had shaken Husk into an awareness of elements in Kelly which he had not expected. It had given him a momentary feeling of his own insignificance, but the feeling had passed, partly into a kind of masochistic amusement at his own ignorance and misjudgment, partly into the confidence that he would still succeed with his own plan.

"I learned that when I was a kid," Kelly was saying. "That's one thing my old man taught me. Your old man ever beat you, Al?"

"No," Husk said. The question stirred an area of uneasiness in his mind. What was Kelly getting at? "Maybe he would have," he said, with more bitterness than he expected, "if he had known I was around."

"My old man always knew I was around," Kelly said. "He always figured I was up to something. Sometimes I was." He was not thinking about the green grass of Gowanus now. "He figured sometimes I let him down," he said.

Husk looked at him. At the moment he could not imagine Kelly when he was young, Kelly as someone's son.

"Your old man ever feel like that, Al?"

"No," Husk said. He thought of the hunt in the mountains and did not look at Kelly, surprised that he had lied about something which was no longer important to him.

"I never let him down," Kelly said almost prayerfully. "I never really let my old man down."

"Sure," Husk said uneasily. He did not want to talk about the improbable childhood of P.J. Kelly. He remembered things Kelly had said in other times, talking about the good old days. They had seemed true enough then, but now he could no longer associate them with the big graying man with the severe glasses and the bitterness at the corner of his mouth.

"I'm talking about Caminetti," Kelly said wearily.

"I don't get it." Alarm went through Husk like an electric shock.

"I'm talking about the deal you made with Caminetti."

"I never made any deal. What do you mean, P.J.?" He looked at the corner of the desk and kept his voice steady.

"I know all about it. I made Caminetti tell." Kelly plodded on as if each sentence were a heavy load which he was forced to bear. "He was here today. I forced the bastard."

"It's a lie," Husk said.

"Don't talk like a kid with his hand in the cookie jar," Kelly told him.

"It's a lie," Husk said thickly, unable to think. "A lie."

Kelly was suddenly fiercely angry. He got out of his chair and came around the desk. "Don't tell me that, you son of a bitch! Stand up!"

Husk came quickly to his feet. He was still trying to protest, to say it was a lie, even as his mind recognized that it was no use to deny it, that Kelly already knew. The childish denial ran through his mind and he had a moment of blind panic, wondering if Kelly were going to strike him, a feeling that had in it no fear at all of Kelly as a man. He stepped forward one pace and put his hands on the desk like a prisoner at the bar, looking straight ahead at the wall of the room beyond the desk.

"Why did you do it to me, Al?" Kelly asked. There was genuine pain in his voice. "Why did you do it to me?" He sat down in his chair again and slumped forward, pushing the ashtray away from him. "You were like my own kid," he said, self-pity creeping into his tone. "You could have been my own son. Why did you, Al?"

"I'm not your son, goddamn you," Husk said passionately. "Leave that the hell out of it." He brought his eyes from the wall and looked at Kelly, seeing a big body partly gone to seed, the finger of pain on the mouth.

Then the fury went out of him and was replaced with something else which he could not name as he heard Kelly say again in a tone of wonder and self-pity, "Why, Al?" He stepped back and sat down in the chair again.

"An idea," he said flippantly. "A passing notion."

"Why?" Kelly insisted.

"I tried to explain it to you once. You didn't listen."

"I listened. It didn't make sense then and it doesn't now."

"To you."

"All right, to me. But how could you do it, Al? I could have helped you to a lot of things. I liked you. I wanted to be like a father."

Again Husk felt the anger in himself. "A lot of things!" he jeered. "The things you wanted me to do. Sure, you liked me when I did the things I was told to do."

Kelly looked at him for a long moment. "You're a fool," he said at last with tired bitterness. "Did you think it would be so easy to push out the old man? I've been here a long time. I fought to get here. You're just a damned fool."

"Have it that way, then. I'm going."

"Oh, you're going all right. Go on."

Husk picked up his coat and hat, and turned to the door.

"Go a long way," Kelly said. "You sold me out. Get the hell off the front altogether."

Husk went out without making a reply. A current of air came in through the door. To Kelly it smelled of the street, the cold, winter and death. It hung in the office for a long time while Kelly sat with his hands on his desk, doggedly trying to keep his mind blank; then he fumbled in the drawer of his desk for a fresh cigar.

Friday 9:30 A.M.

The bar is on Ninth Avenue. From the outside it looks like a rundown butcher shop or a small stable that has not moved with the times to become a garage, a warehouse, a chain store, or a cheap delicatessen. Inside, in the cavernous echoing acres of dirty tables, booths with checkered oilcloth, great ornamental lights that no longer work, there is a continual twilight, the Victorian sleep, spittoons, mementos, pictures of clipper ships, drunks, and jakelegs. The jukebox, a rainbow that has been smelted into an ugly lump, has little liquid rivulets of running light, but it keeps the light to itself and does not disturb the womblike crepuscular haze.

The jukebox contains twenty-four records including a Ladnier-Bechet disk of "Wild Man Blues." The disk is in good condition. No one plays it except the young energetic barman, at the hour of closing, around three o'clock in the morning, when he is counting up the take and the streets are full of their own night music, the solitary old autumnal whore, or, in summer, the winos and gas-hounds, recumbent and somnolent in scratch-house doorways. There are three tangos which no one plays either, and there are the songs, the loved unhappy ballads of Eighth and Ninth avenues: "Mother Machree," "Kathleen Mavourneen." The latest lachrymo-mechanical heartthrobs come and go, but there is a record of "That Old Gang of Mine" which is sadly worn.

There are perhaps a dozen men in the bar. At the back, in one of the larger booths, are three strikers: Plato, gloomy and preoccupied, turning the stem of his glass—he is drinking wine; Link, the Negro, drumming on the table with his fingers and feeling uncomfortable and contained because it is a strange bar and he is not sure of its tolerance for Negroes; the little man from Brooklyn, staring into the glass with bright interest as if every day were his birthday.

The young bartender leans on the walnut picking his teeth, and the old proprietor, feeling his hernia, rests himself against one of the enormous useless standing lamps, waiting for the time, at eleven o'clock, when he can turn his post over to his fat wife, go into their apartment at the back and turn on the police shortwave. As an old policeman he likes to know when things are happening in the city, a murder or a fight, a burning tenement or a simple case of a stolen car.

"Whata yuh t'ink of duh plan now, Plato?" the man from Brooklyn is asking. He feels a certain amount of satisfaction that things have gone wrong. "Duh Reds had a plan, huh? What happened to dat?"

"Thisa plan, shesa no good," Plato says patiently. He wants to explain what was wrong with it, but before he can say any more, Link raps his knuckles on the table and says impatiently: "Whe' Dewey? Dewey say he gonna be here this mornin'."

"Yuh fuckin' right it wasn't no good." Then: "Dewey's gonna get here when he wants to."

"A plan—" Plato begins to say.

"Thass all finish' now. We screwed, anyway yawl look at it. Jus' a question of time when we go back to work."

"I ain't goin' to be foist. I told my old lady I t'ought I'd get a paycheck next week, but I ain't goin' to be foist."

"Yawl talk like a virgin."

"I figure to stay a virgin when it comes to bein' a scab."

"Trouble with thisa plan—"

"Duh trouble was Kelly and his goons. You can't take them into no plan."

"Wh' Dewey?" Link asks fretfully. "He say he be here. I ruther we's down on the dock."

"Yuh can't go down the dock this weather. It'd freeze the balls off a brass monkey."

"Good weather sho' gone. Yawl think the strike's lost?"

"Shit!" Plato says.

The little man shrugs his shoulders. "We lost ever damn one so far," he says. "This's your first strike, Link. Relax. Wait till you been screwed for fifteen years like me before you talk."

The door opens and a man comes in. He stands just at the entrance of the bar, squinting in the diseased light. He is a man of medium height with a large head. It turns on his scrawny neck like a jack-o'-lantern on a pole, like the head of a turkey buzzard. He is blond, and his face looks as if it had been recently boiled. His blond hair makes him appear to have no eyebrows, but they are there, half-moons of newly minted coin, the milled edges sharp and clear when you look. The nose is famished. His cheeks, bluish and pallid, are marked by a little map of veins of no possible country. When he sees the strikers sitting at the rear, he lifts his head like a horse smelling water at the end of a hot day and goes back toward them, walking carefully like a man on stilts.

"How's the fucking war?" he asks in a jeering voice. "How's the high command this fine shitty morning?"

"Hey, Dewey! Yawl sound full of piss and vinegar!"

Plato turns his glass on its stem. The other man looks up with a half smile. "It your toin to buy some beer." Dewey lifts his hand and the bartender spits out his toothpick.

When they have their beer Dewey turns his colorless eyes on Plato.

"Well, Plato," he says, "you go around to that meetin' the other night?"

"I go."

"And you got your brains beat out, huh? Old man Kelly is too many for you. The trouble with you and all those other jokers is that you think this strike is like a fuckin' problem in arithmetic, but the truth of the motherfucker is that it's just like rollin' the dice—sometimes you make the point, sometime you seven out."

"You got to try," Plato says.

"Ah, balls. Let all them bastards piss up a rope. What's it get you?"

"Yawl don't want to lose this strike no more'n the rest of us, Dewey."

"We ain't got no fuckin' chance, man. They're just sittin' down somewhere, some of the goddamn big shots, and they're decidin' what the hell is goin' to come off. You think you got anything to say about it? You ain't got a goddamn thing to say, you got fuckin'-aye nothin'!"

"What you do, then?" Plato asks.

"Dewey ain't t'ought of that yet."

"You don't do nothin'," Dewey says. "You just sit and wait for something to happen. If it's a break, you jump right in. Sure, you can try this and try that. Maybe you find somethin' good. With this goddamn strike—well, if the men want to strike that's fine, then you're a striker. If they want to go back to work, back you go. You think you got a chance to decide something? You ain't got a goddamn thing to say. You think you know whose fault it is? It ain't mister phony fuckin' Kelly. It ain't the governor. It ain't the fuckin' president of the country—none of them motherfuckers. It's the whole goddamn stinkin' shootin' match, that's what it is."

"Who you mean?"

"Every fuckin' body," Dewey says cheerfully, taking a strong pull on his beer. "You think anybody's honest? Everybody's a crook in this fuckin' country, only some are crookeder than others, and some is too damn dumb to make it pay. That's one thing I learned in the army anyway."

"That's a crock of shit, friend. You ain't duh foist that's said it, but it's a crock just the same."

"O.K., pal. I'm just tryin' to put you wise."

"You think everybody no good, eh?"

"That's right, Plato, every goddamn one, only some is lucky and some ain't. I don't give a fuck. I get along, see? Only I ain't bein' fooled by all this crap, whether it's Kelly that's shootin' the shit, or the Reds, or the president of the U.S.A., or the pope of Rome. I don't believe my old lady when I know she's tellin' the truth. Fuck the whole works, that's my motto."

"Thatsa not good to say."

"The hell it ain't."

"They's some honest people in this world."

"Yeah? You show me one, Link, and I'll show you a guy with rocks in his head. Crooks and dopes, that's the way it is."

"What you t'ink about duh strike?"

"Look, when it first started, it just went along under its own steam, didn't it? Then the Reds came along with their fancy ideas and Kelly breaks up the meetin'. Now," he shrugs, "hell it's just like pullin' a number out of a hat, it's every man for himself. Well, maybe some guys might try something that'd work. I don't think so."

"You think we's screwed, Dewey?"

"We're always screwed, goddamn it. We was born that way. Nobody gives a fuck about what happens to you. You just roll for the point and hope the seven don't come up. Take your chance, pull a number out of the goddamn hat, and ride your fuckin' luck when you get a break, that's all, and fuck the pope and the president and Mister P.J. Kelly. I just wish the whole world was made out of gunpowder, that's all, and me with a box of matches in my hand—"

Friday 10 A.M.

I woke late, hearing the sound of rain at the window behind my head. It was a dirty morning and the rain was weak and thin, a kind of secondhand rain. The other bed was mussed and empty. Everson's roommate had gone out. Everson was not there either. I wondered if he could have come in and gone out again without my hearing him.

It would be necessary to get up, but for the moment all I wanted to do was to lie there listening to the steady seethe of the rain at the window. It was a little like the sound of the lake and the pines in Michigan. For a few minutes I went away into the country of childhood where everything was easy—easier, of course, than it had ever been when I was living in it—but the sound at the window became the sound of rain again and I was once more back in the kingdom of confusion.

There was someone I was supposed to see at ten-thirty. I wondered if he would be there, or, if he were, whether or not I would get the brush-off. The day before we had managed to get out a leaflet on the demands of the committee and had distributed it. Then we had gone back to the job of contacting the delegates to the meeting which Kelly had smashed.

It was uphill work because they were all scared and discouraged. Most of them figured when the meeting failed that the strike went with it. Now, when a member of the small solid core of rank-and-filers who were with us went around to see a man, he was apt to be received like a ghost at a wake. They were suspicious of us, or afraid, or too disheartened to do anything. Here and there we ran into one who was red hot for us, but these were few.

It was like trying to get the slack out of a long rope. You would keep pulling it in until it looked as if it would never end. Then, just when the tension built up until you were sure that you were really pulling something attached to the other end, the half-knot or snarl or whatever it was would come free and it would be all loose and easy in your hands once more. We were out of contact, not physical contact, although that was hard enough to reestablish, but out of the living contact between ourselves and the men. The slack in the middle was what the strike had become. We could reach out and touch other hands, but the hands were all those of the dead or sleeping. No one would take hold.

I went into a place for coffee, opened the morning paper, and there it was. It wasn't a big story. A man had been shot in a West Side bar. His name had been William D. Everson. He was an ex-soldier, recently discharged. That was all they found to say of Bill.

I sat there going over the story again and again, feeling a little numb. I remembered what he had said the day before, about what he had wanted. "To be honest and generous—" What else was it he had said? I had hardly listened. Now it seemed terribly important that I remember everything about him, every word he had spoken, and I couldn't remember anything, hardly even the way he looked. I had thought I had heard his footsteps the night before. That was as close as I could get to him—a memory of the sound of another man's footsteps. It seemed that, in forgetting, I was killing him again, acquiescing in the process of making his death acceptable, like the horrible capsule of news in the paper. After a while I started for the section. My leg was hurting. It was cold in the streets. I felt very lonely. There was nothing to do but go on.

At the C.P. section headquarters, there was a little knot of men at the head of the stairs talking in low tones. Someone was working on some picket signs. At the rear an old-timer was cranking out a leaflet on the mimeograph. I went back to the cubbyhole office and found Barney at his desk writing something. The heater was on and the room was warm.

"You hear about it?" Barney said. He looked shot, beat out.

"I read it in the paper just now."

"Yeah. One of the boys heard of it last night and called me. I went around." He looked away from me and gave me a tired shrug of his shoulders.

"He was dead then?"

"Yeah. Died instantly." He pushed the papers away from him. "What a hell of a place for it," he said.

"What difference does the place make?"

"None, I suppose. Just the same—"

"He was a good comrade."

"Yeah. A good man."

"That's what I mean."

"What I don't understand," Barney said, "is why it was him. Why not Keyes? Or Daniels, or somebody else? Bill had only been around since the first of the strike. He was good, but he wasn't dangerous enough that they should kill him. Why not somebody more important?" he asked in a strained voice.

"Give them a little more time."

"There's a story going around that it could have been a mistake."

"Mistake?"

"That the hood mistook him for somebody else. Shooting from outside, through a dirty john window—"

I had a sudden vision of how it might have been, seeing another man in place of Bill Everson—Blackie Carmody—the same dark crisp hair, the same short, stocky, cocky body. "No. No. Christ no." I felt like vomiting.

"What?" Barney gave me a look of astonishment. "For God's sake, Joe—"

"No, Jesus, it wasn't that way."

"What's the matter, Joe?"

"If it's that way, damn it, then it's nothing but—nothing but a lousy accident."

"Well," he said slowly, "there are accidents. It doesn't change it. It—"

"No. To get beat by Kelly, the way we were Wednesday night, that makes some sense. It's a reversal. There's a connection, even if it is an ironic one. But this—hell, it wouldn't mean anything, not anything."

"That's not good talk, kid," he said quietly. "It's not how he died. It's what he did when he was alive."

He got out a pack of cigarettes, took one and passed them over. "This damn weather," he said irrelevantly. Then: "Winter makes me feel bad, or it does this year anyway." I looked at the windows streaming with rain, thinking that it wasn't the weather that was depressing him.

"Well," he said. "We've got to keep pushing. He wouldn't have wanted us to go into a week of mourning for him. We've got things to do. Assignments. Things—" He broke off with a long unhappy sigh. "I sure liked that kid," he said.

After a moment he said: "I telephoned his folks. We're going to send the body on to them. I was wondering—" He hesitated a moment. "You were a friend of his. It's silly, but I'd rather have a friend than a stranger take care of it."

"All right."

"He's down here."

He gave me a card with DONOVAN FUNERAL PARLOR on it and an address. "All you'll have to do is stand by. They'll be getting the casket ready or whatever they do. Then they'll send him out tonight."

"I'll go over this evening," I said.

"Do you think it's stupid?"

"No. I think it's right."

"O.K. Fred should be here now. He'll have some assignments for you."

I got up and went to the door.

"Hey," he called. "I almost forgot. Keyes got in touch with us early this morning. He says he's got a couple of others, and he's going to come around and talk with us tonight."

"That's good." It was the most positive thing since the meeting.

"So it's not all bad, Joe. We still got a chance to make it. A long shot, but a chance."

"Yes," I said, but was not convinced. I was thinking of Bill Everson and I suppose he was too, because he touched the papers on his desk with disgust.

"Christ," he said. "Reports. Everything in black and white."

I suppose he was thinking of Bill Everson, whose report would be a little too long ever to be read completely.

Thursday 5 P.M.

When Lannigan came in, Kelly had a sudden crazy notion that Husk had come back, an irrational quirk of happiness and renewal before the cold air of the street, coming through the opened door, brought him around once more.

Lannigan closed the door behind him and came over to the desk. He was not as tall as Husk, and he was older. He had the almost colorless eyebrows of some redheaded men and a nose that had been broken and set badly if at all. His mouth was thin and straight, a swift slash across his face.

He stood in front of the desk, pulling his hat from his head now and showing himself to be a little bald, and said "Hello, Mr. Kelly" in a voice that held something of both truculence and ingratiation.

"Sit down," Kelly said sourly, discovering a dislike for Lannigan as intense and irrational as the momentary gladness he had felt when the man came in. Lannigan sat down in the chair without removing his overcoat, not looking at Kelly, his thin mouth compressed while Kelly, thinking with distaste of what he was going to say to him, groped for a cigar and lit it without offering one to the other man.

"I'm having some trouble," he said abruptly.

"Yeah?" Lannigan said in a tone of surprise.

"I've got work for you," Kelly went on in an even voice. "This committee they elected the other night is making some trouble. I thought you might be able to do something about it."

"Yeah?" Lannigan said again, giving Kelly a stare, guarded, calculating or innocent, and touched with what Kelly felt as faint amusement or derision.

"Get over to see Caminetti," Kelly said. "He'll know what to do."

"Caminetti?" Lannigan said. "I thought—" He shrugged his shoulders. "Caminetti plays awful rough," he said, pinching his hat and looking through the window at the lighted offices across the street.

"Moro sent you over from his dock. Isn't that supposed to mean something?"

"Yeah, but—I guess I didn't get it straight. I thought it was just a question of tamping up on them guys. But if it's Caminetti—well, that means—" He took a breath. "I ain't a knockover man, P.J. I don't even have a rod. I—"

"Don't tell me your troubles," Kelly said with dry malignancy. "Tell Caminetti. I don't know what he wants you for and I don't want to know."

For a moment the two men looked at each other across the lie which Kelly had told. The latter suddenly crushed his cigar in the ashtray and spat. "Don't tell me your troubles," he said again.

"Look," Lannigan began slowly. "I'm a two-time loser. I can't afford to go up again." There was urgency and fear in his voice and a kind of dumb appeal in his face. It gave Kelly a brief instant of pleasure.

"That's your problem," he said brutally. "You come in here thinking I wanted you for a nice easy job with some easy money in it. Don't tell me what your problems are."

"I can't afford to take the chance."

"No? You can't afford not to. Who runs your dock?"

"Moro."

"Moro sent you, didn't he? Where would Moro's loading racket be if I didn't want him to have it? Listen, I know how that dock's run. Moro don't even hire loaders—he just uses the longshoremen to do the work and collects their wages for the loading. You think I don't know? And what about the shylock down there, the one you give protection to? You think I don't know that if the boys don't borrow from him and kickback at the usual rate they lose their work? Moro's squeezing that dock for every nickel. It's a goddamn gold mine to him. You think he's going to take a chance on losing that to protect you, if I tell him you won't cooperate?"

"If I go up again—"

"There won't be any *if* about it *if* you don't get your ass in gear," Kelly said coldly. "Who got you paroled when you were up last time? Me. Well, I expect a little something for my efforts. You're scared of taking a third fall. Listen to me, Lannigan," he leaned across the desk, his eyes narrowed and ugly. "I can arrange that, too," he said. "I can *make* you a three-time loser. Now get the fuck out of here."

Lannigan got slowly to his feet. "I guess I got no choice," he said.

"You sure as hell don't," Kelly said derisively. He watched the man go toward the door and again a weak pleasure warmed him. When Lannigan reached the doorway Kelly called in a neutral, businesslike voice: "See Caminetti. He'll have something for you to do. I don't know what it is and I don't want to know."

With Lannigan gone, Kelly's day was finished, but he was reluctant to leave the office. He walked over to the window and looked into the street. The last of the cold daylight was gone, but it was not yet quite dark. People scurried along the sidewalk. Across the street in a loft he could see the girls clearing up their desks, dabbing their lips with lipstick, pulling their dresses to straighten their stockings. A bus jammed with its dark load lumbered away from the curb. Kelly felt lonely, standing at the window, watching the day break up, as if he were condemned to be a witness to a loved act of which he could no longer have a part.

He tried to shake the feeling away but it came back again, a dog with its tail between its legs, fearful, yet more fearful of leaving its master. Kelly saw Lannigan cross the street and go into the subway *that's the wrong side for Brooklyn* and realized abruptly that Lannigan too was a part of the swarm of life in the streets, that perhaps somewhere uptown there was an apartment, a wife, children perhaps, to whom he was hurrying now. The loneliness turned to bitterness. It did not seem fair of Lannigan; he began to hate the man and then realized that it was Husk he was thinking about.

No, it was not fair. Husk should have been there. Husk should have handled Lannigan, Husk or someone else should have made the arrangements *I got too many things to think about* instead of himself having to do it. But Husk couldn't help him; Husk would never do anything for him again. He bit down on the meaning as if he were grinding aching teeth together, and the self-pity blew away in a cold wind of bitterness as he admitted openly to himself for the first time what Lannigan meant. I can arrange my own killings, he told himself; I don't have to kid myself about how things are.

It was a poor crutch of a feeling. In a moment it was gone, leaving him depressed again. He did not want to think of Lannigan or any of it. He was too old now, too soft, too tired, perhaps, at the end of what seemed to him the longest day of his life, to be able to admit openly and freely that P.J. Kelly, standing like an abstract witness at the window of his office, maintained himself at the expense of fear and corruption and murder. Once he had been able to see himself in that light without blinking, but now the moment of insight and acceptance folded away and he came back to thinking as he had so often in the strike *it's not like the old days* that he only wanted to be left alone, to let things work themselves out in their old routines.

He put this feeling away too, thinking *it's finished now* that he had done everything that had to be done to break the strike. It would end now, tomorrow or the next day or by the beginning of the new week at the latest. He was absolutely certain in his own mind that he had won, and he achieved a moment of sorry triumph looking down at the street, gone into the dark now, before turning back to his desk.

He cleared the litter of papers away into drawers and emptied the ashtrays. Just before turning out the light, he looked regretfully at the box of cigars. Then he put them away carefully in the desk.

The street was dark and cold and the wind was strong. A thin dismal mist was coming in, sliming the pavement and the asphalt. P.J. Kelly stood in front of the building a moment, settling his hat firmly, buttoning his coat at the neck. The street was almost deserted as the last of the workers in the area plunged into the subway entrances. The bars were coming to life and beginning to shine cheerfully in neon, and the vegetable and meat markets were crowded with people buying things for supper.

It was an hour which Kelly remembered well from his childhood, but it had been years since he had walked through the ugly streets of the neighborhoods in the time just before supper. Instead of calling a cab or going around to the new offices of the union in the big modern building on the corner where his bodyguard waited, Kelly turned abruptly and started north.

There was no comfort in the street. The wind pulled at him and he was alone. Above the noise of the city he could hear a sound like dogs fighting in a vacant lot, but he could not see them. Two blocks up he almost collided with Brian Munson who was hurrying home to supper, who recognized him but did not speak since he neither knew nor wanted to know P.J. Kelly.

A few blocks north and his feet, as if they knew better than his brain where he was going, took him into one of the side streets. Kelly walked on, head down against the wind, trying not to think but unable to stop.

All the triumph which he had felt momentarily at the office was gone. He was thinking of his losses. It was of Husk he thought first of all, and as he thought of him he began to curse the strike with useless vehemence. His instinct had been to let it alone, to let it wear itself out like a natural process as the men became hungry and disheartened or merely bored with the waiting. His strongest wish had been to take no action at all.

He had been forced to act. That was the thing that he hated most because it pointed disturbingly to the failure of his own power. He had been forced against his will and, he saw now, forced not into one act but into a series of them, as if by making one move he had called mysterious forces into being, things stronger than himself. He had smashed the meeting. But then it had been necessary to go on—to the police, to Father Burke, to Caminetti, to Husk, to Lannigan—the consequences of his action seemed endless, spreading out in concentric circles like ripples of water after a stone is dropped in a pool.

He had wanted to break the strike and he was going to break it. That had been his will; it was being made perfect in action. But nevertheless, break it or not, the strike was forcing him to things that had not been his will at all, that had not been any part of his desire, that he had not even foreseen.

Well *They didn't get me this time* he was going to win, that was certain now, as he had been certain of it all along. *You win all but the last*. But Husk *Goddamn Annie, we might have had a kid* was gone. And Caminetti *I can't even fire the son of a bitch* could not be touched. He was too strong, too valuable even. "Christ damn him to hell," he said aloud, grinding his teeth in impotent rage. Even Lannigan—what would come of that? There was bound to be a stink. Kelly could see the dead man already, the abstract striker, and he could hear the voices of the others, talking about it. He had a sudden vision of it as pure as if he had already seen it happen, and thought, Al was right; I'm manufacturing Reds. He felt himself trapped in a net of circumstance from which he could not escape, helpless, willless, blind.

"Who're you?" a voice asked.

Kelly discovered that he was standing in front of four sandstone steps that led to the doorway of a tenement. From the hall came the smell of stale cooking and the fumes of kerosene stoves.

"What?" he asked stupidly. He looked along the street. It was unreal in the mist, and the houses were shapeless and strange looking. Across the street there was a grocery with the windows dark, and next to it a candy store. Kelly read the names, but they meant nothing to him. He looked along the street at the houses and business establishments, recognizing none of them, although he knew he must know the street as he knew all the others in the nieghborhood.

"What street is this?" he asked.

The boy was perhaps seven years old. He looked at Kelly solemnly, almost without curiosity, but did not reply.

"What street?" Kelly asked again, impatiently.

"Ours," the boy said. "We live here."

"What number is it?"

"Oh," the boy said, "I didn't know what you meant." And told him the number, the number of the old street in which Kelly had been born, where he had lived his boyhood.

Immediately he knew where he was, everything fell into place, the candy store and the grocery, the bar a little way up the block. The house in front of which he had stopped was his own house, the one in which he had been born. It was exactly like all the other houses, but he read the number in the stamped-out cheap tin numerals.

"Thanks, sonny," he said, got a quarter out of his pocket, and put it in the boy's hand.

Now that he knew where he was, the street held a different kind of strangeness, as if in not recognizing it he had given it an added quality. Funny, he thought, not recognizing the old block. Some of the names of stores had changed since he had last walked there, but that did not account for his mistake. It upset him again. He walked west toward the great apartment house where he now lived through the street which was no longer his even in memory. He felt terribly now the failure of his will in the strike, his loss of Husk. He walked along in the cold night, ridiculous, pathetic, ruthless, going over a rosary of the world's crimes against himself, alien and alone, knowing he was old, a survivor of a vanished world.

Friday 5:30 P.M.

Husk became aware of the seemingly disembodied head in front of him. Long, lank-haired, jowled, it gazed steadily at him, unblinking, with the quiet malignancy of a piece of statuary. Yet it was not a statue. Like a graven head, it was set atop a kind of pedestal, but bigger than a pedestal need be, a kind of table, square, white, and shining. Little pearls, like sweat or moisture condensed out of the air, trembled on the brow, in the folds of flesh under the eyes of the abstract head, fascinating Husk, so that it was some time before he noticed the others.

Like the first head they were arrangd on the tops of the white, antiseptic-looking tables, a whole row of them. Some, like the first, gave the impression of a kind of static rage; others seemed merely dead or sleeping. Whether their eyes were open or closed they resembled each other enough that Husk felt for a moment that it might all be done with mirrors, that there might in reality be only one head endlessly reflected in the sterile whiteness of the room.

A sustained hissing like a dream of serpents came from somewhere. The air became filmy and unclear and a man came through a door at the end of the room.

He was a big man in a white coat like a dinner jacket and there seemed to be something familiar about him, something that Husk should recognize. Like my father, he thought, at a formal dinner in summer; tonight he is dining on heads.

The figure moved to where the first of the heads was poised on the white table. Leaning, solicitous, it bent toward the ear but no sound came. It moved away from the head toward the next table, and the sustained hissing increased in volume. The head took on the appearance of mortal and immutable agony. The lips locked together, little rivulets sweated from under the head and along the nose. Husk closed his eyes. I'm still drunk, he thought.

"Are you all right, sir?"

He opened his eyes on two pools of gold in an expanse of snow. The attendant was standing in front of him, the buttons on his white jacket shining.

"Get me out," Husk said thickly. He blinked his eyes at the man, at the heads across from him which now seemed to be protruding from small private purgatories, white boxes in which their bodies suffered. It was intensely hot. Husk felt that his lungs and his belly were constricted, were burning, in some world apart from himself. His head and his body had become separate, existed on different planes. That his body did actually exist, he knew, aside from the pain, because he could feel it under his hands. His hands walked across it like an explorer in a new land, but it seemed to exist for itself and for the hands alone, not for himself.

"Get me out," he said again.

"Yes sir," the attendant said. He turned, grasping a handle; a door swung and Husk, clothed in steam as in a manifestation of grace, stepped onto the marbled floor.

"Jesus," he said.

"Yes sir. Would you like to go into the shower room?"

Weak, shaky, still only partly sober, Husk followed the attendant to the showers.

Leaving the turkish bath in St. Mark's Place, Husk walked aimlessly eastward toward the river. It was cold, windy, with a drizzle of rain. People in the street seemed shaken in the wind like empty clothes on a line. The sound of a ship's horn on the river brought him a memory of the bay at Seattle, of the long summers of his youth, but when he crossed the drive and stood against the fence, there was only a fireboat moving swiftly downstream. Rain pocked the surface of the water. Downriver a bridge, obscured in the murky weather, went soaring out over the water to end in air and nothingness.

It was not like the bay in Seattle. He was sober enough now to recognize his drunkenness. He had been drunk since the afternoon of the day before, since shortly after he had seen Kelly, and now he was tired. He turned away from the river, crossing the drive, and entered the city again. In the bad light the street looked like a cut-bank which has been bored with holes by cliff dwellers. Lights flashed from a mission: JESUS SAVES. Beyond the pawnshop, neon proclaimed: LOANS AT TEN PERCENT.

JESUS SAVES LOANS AT TEN PERCENTJESUSSAVES-LOANSATTENPERCENT. Kelly was due for a surprise, too, Husk thought with resentment; he thinks he can make things come around the way he wants them, but he is due for some surprises; he's caught in his own trap; he's manufacturing his opposition just as I said he would.

And what about me? he thought; I got a surprise too. Not a surprise, he assured himself; not a real surprise because there are no real surprises; all combinations come up, but without logic or order, senselessly, ludicrously, fantastically; if I was surprised, that too is part of the preposterous and monstrous quality of the world, that I was capable of surprise. JESUS SAVES LOANS AT TEN PERCENT the signs winked. PREPOSTEROUS RIDICULOUS they winked at him, lighting the street, comforting him.

Lucille met him at the apartment.

"Al!" she said in reproach and surprise, "I've been worried. I was here last night and you didn't come. Where've you been?"

"Where would I be? In the world."

"Are you drunk?"

"Alive," he said. "Merely alive. Alive, alive oh."

"You've got to get into bed. Let me help you."

"No. There's only one way you can help me. Get your ass out of here and leave me alone."

He saw the surprise and pain come into the good-natured, pretty, stupid face, then saw the disbelief. "I mean it," he said coldly. "I'm finished with you. Get out," seeing that this time he was believed.

"What happened?" she asked in the hurt child's voice which he hated. "What happened to you?"

"I got fired. I double-crossed Mr. P. Jesus Kelly and got fired. What?" he asked, seeing no change in her face. "You find that easier to believe than that I'm throwing you out?"

"Why do you, Al?" she asked in a low voice as if not really expecting an answer.

"What now, for God's sake?"

"Betray?" It was almost a whisper, as if she were unsure of the meaning of the word.

"Betray!" he said. "Is there such a word? But it doesn't surprise you, eh?"

When she did not answer he hit her backhand across the face as he would have struck an animal, seeing the shock in her face with pleasure. "Maybe *that* surprised you a little," he said and went into the bedroom without looking at her. When he came out a moment later she was gone.

While he undressed he let the water run in the tub. Then, when it was ready, he got the bottle of whiskey which he seldom opened and took it with him into the bathroom. With the liquor and the water in the tub warming him, he began to feel very good.

Rain at the window made him think of the world outside, the great open sewer of the street, swarming with manflesh, disembodied heads, dung and offal. Shifting himself in the tub his legs came into view, great mountains of meat rising from the watery plain. He could see the markings on them, like roads running nowhere, and curious blobs of pigment, patternless color. Under the flesh the blood and the lymph moved in their sluggish canals, bearing the life and the filth of himself into other parts of his body, and he felt a sudden excellent unity with the sewer which he imagined outside his window, a sudden sense of the fitness of the preposterous. He thought now of what had happened to him as a kind of capital joke and he began to achieve once more the feeling of having created himself anew, of beginning to move on a plane where new pressures altered all laws of being.

When the phone rang he was certain that it was Lucille calling him, but it did not disturb his feeling. He got out of the tub to answer it, lifting the receiver and saying: "You are wrong; no one lives at this address," and hanging up without waiting for a reply.

In the tub once more he began to be genuinely happy, happy in the way that he had only been happy once, a long time ago. He began to doze, sitting comfortably in the tub, relaxed by the whiskey and comforted by the warmth of the water.

Friday 8:30 P.M.

Mary Carmody sat on the steps of the tenement. It was night, dark and cold, with a drizzle of rain falling, and there was no one in the street. She sat back against the tenement door, almost in the hallway, in order to be out of the weather, watching Harounian who, behind the counter of his store, was moving boxes and cans on the shelves. It was dull with nothing to watch but Harounian, and she was beginning to be cold, but she did not want to go up to her mother's apartment.

When they had brought Blackie back from the hospital, the apartment had become unbearable not because of anything that was demanded of her, but because she still had a child's feeling of distaste for the sick and crippled. Lying in bed, pale, silent, his legs in the heavy casts, Blackie appeared strange to her, leprous with his new infirmity.

Her mother too had changed. Formerly the apartment had been hard to bear because of the friction between Blackie and her mother, the constant battle of attrition which had gone on between them. Now, her mother, lavishing on Blackie the same intense and almost destructive love which she had used to fight him, had become a virago of comfort and tenderness, and in the transition Mary had discovered herself clumsy, loud, fumbling and totally unsuitable for tenanting the small apartment in which her brother was beginning his sullen convalescence. After the supper dishes were done she had come downstairs to see Hope, but Hope had gone out somewhere. Mary pulled her legs back against her buttocks and wrapped the slack of her dress around them, watching Harounian make mysterious entries in a small book.

The sound of muted laughter came from the darkness down the street; and she heard Hope's voice before she saw Hope with a handful of boys and girls. She recognized the laughter. It was of a special kind that meant something of which she was not yet quite sure. It gave her a queer unsettled feeling in the pit of her stomach, and she felt the swift jump of her heart. Then she saw Lonnie and the feeling was stronger and with it there was something—not quite curiosity, not quite fear—which was part of the special atmosphere, the first complex of feelings, which he had created around her.

"Hello, Mary," Hope said casually. "With you in a minute."

"Hi," Mary said, calling the girls by name, avoiding Lonnie's eyes. She watched them file past her down the hall, heard the door open and again caught the hushed, secret, terrible laughter.

A light went on in the front room of Hope's apartment. For a moment Mary had a glimpse of the room, the bodies of the boys and girls moving as in some ballet with which she was half-familiar. Then the curtains came down to the bottom and the window went shut and there were only the voices, provocations, whisperings and stirrings, the frightening sounds of adolescent love. She tried to concentrate on Mr. Harounian who was now engaged in transferring eggs from one basket to another, bringing one now and again close to his ear, as if he were listening for some expected or dreaded sound like the ticking of a bomb, a dazed meditative look on his dark face. Joe Hunter came down the street, peering at her as he came up the steps, and said hello. She tried to give him the practiced look which she had used on him before, but now it would not come off and she said hello in the meagre girl's voice which she no longer used, thinking that he looked worn and unhappy and almost sick, not at all like the person who had come up to the apartment with Blackie less than a week before. While she was thinking of him the light in the window beside her went out, and with the darkness the whisperings and the laughter seemed to take on a new quality, to become wild and mysterious with maturity. Even less, now, did she want to go up to her mother's apartment.

"Mary," Hope called. "Come here, huh?"

She went along the hall to the doorway.

"You wanna come in on the party?" Hope asked in a low voice.

"Oh—I dunno," she said uncertainly, and again the feeling, curiosity or fear or the two together, crawled through her body.

"Aw come on," Hope said. "It's fun."

"I don't know. Your mother—"

"Ma's out."

"Yeah, but mine isn't," Mary said, making a grab at practicality.

"With Blackie like that, she won't be comin' down. What's the matter? You ain't afraid?"

"Nah," she said immediately, knowing that she was.

"Come on, then. What's stoppin' ya?" To Mary she seemed feverish, excited.

"Well, I don't know." She felt stupid and useless, standing at the door, arguing while the voices whispered from the dark apartment.

"Listen, Lonnie likes you. He said so. He'd like for you to come."

"Does he?" The other feeling—not fear—was stronger now. She crossed the sill into the kitchen and Hope closed the door behind her. The voices were louder now, more meaningful.

"Take off your coat," Hope said, and taking it from her put it with the others on the table. As her eyes became used to the dark, Mary could see the outlines of chairs, the dark oblong of the door into the next room. Suddenly she was desperate to get out and turned toward the door.

"You scared?" She heard Hope's whisper, and this time it was not purely a question but was sharpened with a hint of derision.

"I'm not scared," she said, more loudly than she had intended, thinking of Hope: she's one of them too, they won't let me alone. Again Mary heard Hope's urgent whisper:

"Lonnie's in there. He's nice—you don't have to be scared. You go on right in." Then coyly: "Don't forget he's my boyfriend. I wouldn't let you, if you wasn't my friend too."

She forced her feet to take her through the dark doorway. She could see nothing in the other room as she stepped into it, but beyond, in the next room of the railroad apartment, she saw a moving whiteness which she knew instinctively was nakedness and she stopped in outraged impropriety.

"Mary!" She heard the whisper from the dark and Lonnie was beside her. "I'm sure glad you came," he said in the same strained whisper. He led her to the edge of the bed and she sat down awkwardly. He put his arm around her. "I been watchin' you on the street," he said.

"Yeah?" Her hoarse whisper matched his own. A warmth began to go through her and she tried to push all other feelings away to make room for it, but he leaned forward, crushing his mouth clumsily against hers, forcing her back on the bed. She lay there, feeling the warmth go away as his hurried hands moved under her dress, its place taken by a kind of forced determination to go through with it.

Later, lying on the bed in the dark room, she heard Hope congratulate her and thought that the grown-ups had tricked her again by making her believe that there was some special difference between herself and them. She thought with bitter pride: Now I'm grown up. Now I'm like all the rest of them.

Friday 9 P.M.

I went around to Blackie's place after I was finished with Bill.

I had left the funeral parlor with the box in the back of the hearse and drove over to the West Side freight yards. In the darkness everything seemed unstable, in motion. The cars crawled on the tracks, shunted here and there in aimless patterns. Jitneys moved along the loading platforms and car-knockers and loaders appeared and disappeared, moving through the lights and shadows like fish in the shallows.

We took him to one of the warehouses. Huge, cavernous, shadowy, the place seemed to hold the coming winter inside it. Then I remembered: it would be a refrigerated place of course, where we would leave him.

"You want to give me a hand, buddy?" the hearse driver asked.

I got hold of the box and we put it on a high dolly which they carried in the car. Then we rolled him up the ramp and into the big shed.

"What is it?" A warehouseman, an old guy, was standing beside me. He looked at the box and said: "Oh, a stiff. You'll have to bring him down this way."

We followed him down the darkness of a corridor and into another section where it was even colder. Long rough boxes like the one we had brought lined the walls, piled on top of each other. There were a lot of bodies on their way out of town that night.

"Hell of a crop of them," the warehouseman said as if reading my thoughts. "It's always worse toward the end of the week, seems like. Where's it going?" He nodded at the box we had brought in.

"West."

"Sure, west. They all go west, you might say. When you ship a body out of New York, about the only place it can go is west."

"Ohio."

He began filling out a tag.

"When will he go?" I asked.

"When? Christ, I don't know, pal. They move them pretty fast, but I don't know when it'll be. You could go ask the head clerk, maybe he could tell you."

"I guess it's not that importanat. I thought I might wait around if you knew when he'd be going."

"Nah, I can't tell you. Might not be until tomorrow morning."

"I guess there isn't much point of waiting, then."

"No, there ain't much point to it. He won't get lonesome. Look at all the company he's got." He gestured at the boxes along the walls.

"What a sense of humor," the hearse driver said.

"Sorry," the warehouseman said in an unperturbed voice. "I guess it's because I'm around them all the time."

"I'm around them all the time too," the hearse driver said.

"Yeah, but to me they're just so much freight. Just another commodity. So much a pound like any other commodity." He scratched away at the forms he was filling out. "Friend of yours?" he asked me.

"Yeah."

"Well, here it is. Everything right?" He showed me the forms all filled out, correct address and everything.

"Yes, I guess so." Bill had now been translated into a few sheets of statistics. I turned away with the hearse driver. The old warehouseman came after us.

"People usually give me a little something for seeing that he's handled right," he said. "See that he gets put on board O.K."

I gave him the coin to see that Bill was ferried over.

"If it's on my way," the driver said, "I'll give you a lift."

I told him the address of Blackie's place. During the day I had seen Riverboat Conn who had told me of the beating.

"I'll let you off at the corner of Ninth Avenue," the driver said. "Some people, they're funny about having a hearse stop in front of their place. Figure it's unlucky or something." He sounded a little resentful. "It's perfectly natural," he said.

"Sure." I didn't know whether he meant that the feeling of other people or his own occupation was natural.

"Say," he said, "was that guy a Red?"

"Yes."

"I thought so. The boss said something that it was the Communists that was paying for him."

I didn't say anything. Two minutes later he stopped at the corner of Ninth.

"Funny," he said. "The first one I ever met, and he had to be dead."

Blackie's sister was on the steps of the apartment when I got there. She looked bored and sleepy and since she was sitting there in the cold rather than being upstairs, I thought that perhaps the apartment had become even harder to live in than before. I said hello and went on up and Mrs. Carmody met me at the door.

I was surprised by her appearance. I don't know what I had expected. I supposed I had imagined that she would be pretty well knocked to pieces, first by the continuation of the fight with Blackie, and secondly because of what had happened to him. But instead there was a serenity about her that was pleasant to feel. She even looked less ill and tired than she had when I had been there before.

"It was nice of you to come," she said. "Francis will be needing company now for a while."

I mumbled that I had been sorry to hear what had happened. She did not appear to be listening to what I said. When I was finished there was a moment of silence and then, as I started back through the apartment, she said softly, almost to herself: "He'll never walk good again, the doctors say."

It stopped me like a blow. Blackie had always been full of excess energy. I wondered how he would take it. Then the other thing hit me—that she didn't seem to regret that he was going to be a cripple.

"Maybe it won't be so bad," I said. "Doctors don't always know."

"At first I blamed myself," she said. "I made him take that job with Mr. Kelly. Then, when it happened, I thought that some of the strikers had done it and that it was my fault because I made him. I didn't know he was going to be in the strike. But it wasn't the strikers that did it. It was some men who thought he was—who thought he was one of your people."

She paused and I waited for her to continue. "It was an act of God," she said.

"Well—"

"I know you don't believe, but it seems like that to me. I was always worried about Francis. He was too much like one of my brothers. But now—now—"

Again she broke off, the serenity still in her face, and I thought yes, now you think he can't go out in the streets and try to take a corner or a dock away from Kelly's hoodlums, you think he's safe. Her calm seemed frightening now, unnatural, almost crazy.

"I'm sure Blackie will make a go of it," I said with false assurance.

"He'll have to get another job, something easy."

"Have you talked about it?" I was thinking that, bad legs or not, Blackie might think he could even things up with a gun once he began to get around.

"No."

"I'll talk to him." I had no reason to be confident that I could convince him.

"I'm not going to live much longer, Joe."

"That's no way to talk," I began. "You—"

"I have cancer. I suppose Francis told you. It was the thing that he was thinking about so much."

"Did you tell him you knew?"

"Yes. This afternoon. When Francis is well, I'll go to the hospital."

"You'd better go immediately."

"There's plenty of time," she said, and I knew then the reason for the serenity. With Blackie the way he was, she felt that she had settled all her earthly affairs, and there was always plenty of time to die. I went back through the apartment.

"Hello," Blackie said. "I didn't think you'd come."

He was lying on the sofa which had been turned so that, propped up on pillows, he could see a strip of the sidewalk on the other side of the street. There was nothing to see now but a storekeeper who was transferring eggs from one basket into another. Lying there Blackie looked pale and thin.

"Why the hell wouldn't I come?"

"Well, that thing the other night—"

"If I'd gone through that window, it wouldn't have been good. I owe you one for that. That's the second time."

"I figured that washed out the first."

"I came as soon as I heard."

"I just got back from the hospital this afternoon. A quick job," he said bitterly. "They let you out quick when they find you don't have any money."

I suppose he was thinking about his mother.

"Not all of them," I said. "There are some that don't."

"Charity places," he said, but without the old bitterness.

I heard the sound of slow footsteps come toward the room and it was Manta. He had an arm in a sling and there was a patch of adhesive on his face, but otherwise he was as impassive looking as ever.

"What happened to you?" I asked.

"He was there," Blackie said. "I guess it's a pretty good thing for me that he was."

"You got it busted by those goons?"

"Yes," Manta said. He gave me a queer challenging kind of look, half defensive, the first expression of any kind which I had seen him show.

"You can't keep out of everything," I said. "You can retire from the world, but sometimes the world doesn't know it." I got a certain amount of satisfaction out of being able to say it to him.

"Sometimes," Blackie said, "you don't want to retire, but the world retires you anyway."

"You're not thinking of crapping out?"

"What the hell can I do? Jesus, do you know what they did to me, Joe? I'll be a gimp. A cripple."

"Maybe you'll limp a little. That won't be so bad."

"Christ, it's funny," he said. "You know who got me? Some men on my own side! It was all a damn mistake. That's a good joke, huh?"

"I don't see that it's so funny." I was thinking of Bill Everson. I didn't want to believe that he had been killed by accident, by mistake, perhaps for Blackie. "What are you going to do?" I asked.

"I don't know. My old lady—Mom—she knows about the cancer." His face twisted and he looked out into the dark street. "I'll be here, two, three months maybe before I can walk. By then—hell, I can't do nothing before it'll be too late."

"Get her to a hospital right away."

"Yeah," he said in a voice without any hope.

"I can help you there, maybe, but what about you?"

"Me?" He gave a short laugh.

"The world doesn't end tomorrow. You've got to think of youself."

"That's what I keep telling him too," Mrs. Carmody said. She had come into the room on slippered feet and now she sat down beside Manta. "The world is for the young," she said.

"The world is for itself," said Manta.

"It'll be hard, Blackie," I said. "It'll be a fight, but hell, there's lots of things you can do."

He turned away from the window and faced me. "Oh, I'll get something," he said. "I'll keep scuffling." Something of interest came back into his voice. "I used to draw pretty good when I was a kid. Maybe I could learn some mechanical drawing while I'm lyin' here. I could go to one of them schools where they turn them out quick."

"Sure," I said, thinking of all the others who had come out of the army with three or four years out of their lives and who were thinking of the same kinds of shortcuts.

"That would be just fine, Francis," Mrs. Carmody said comfortably. Manta looked at the floor without speaking. "You were the one I worried about," Mrs. Carmody went on, still with the composure of one who is talking about some event long gone in the dead past. "Mary is more easygoing."

"She ought to stay home more," Blackie fretted.

"Mary is a good girl. She'll be all right."

"Look," I said, getting up to go, "I'll drop in on you every day or so. Maybe I'll run across something that might turn out to be a good job." I didn't have God's own notion what that would be.

"Sure," Blackie said. "Maybe when I get back on my feet I can give you a hand. I owe those goons something."

"Fine. Take it easy and don't worry." Nothing like a good bromide.

We said good-bye and I went back out through the apartment. Manta followed me. Mary Carmody was gone from the steps of the building now. It was cold, and raining slightly. Across the street a couple of dogs were fighting over a scrap of garbage.

"Do you remember the story I told you the other night?" Manta asked.

"About the wounded man in the car?"

"Yes. Remember what I said it meant? I told you wrong."

"I know you did. Why?"

"I didn't think you'd understand. It meant that when you give up you can be happy. I didn't think you'd understand that."

"Do you think Blackie will?" I asked.

"I don't know. He'll have to now, or die."

"No he won't. He isn't licked. Why, even you haven't stepped aside all the way. You got that the other night when you couldn't turn away and leave him." I put my hand on the arm in the sling. The cast was as hard and cold as a chunk of rock. "Blackie isn't licked yet," I said.

"You people," Manta said wearily. "People like you never admit you're licked. You're crazy. You go on fighting as if you were in a ring of some kind. What you don't know is that there's nobody watching, nobody at all, and you can admit you're licked without being ashamed."

"People can't stop struggling. That's what life is."

"Maybe people can't, but I can. You can. Blackie can. If you've got food and a place to sleep, bad as it may be, that's all you need. Maybe people can't stop, taken as a whole, but a man can."

"I don't think Blackie can. To eat isn't enough to make you a man. Blackie's like that." I was afraid to make the claim for myself, standing there in the wind, in the iron city which I had come to hate.

"Nobody's watching," Manta said with wintry kindness. "Nobody at all. Everybody's gone home."

Friday 10:30 P.M.

Crip heard the sound beginning a hundred yards away and braced himself, cursing. The clashing of metal became louder, like rolling thunder but harsher, or like an avalanche, as the cars rammed each other. Then the sound was under and around him, throwing him from one end to the other of the narrow compartment in the refrigerator car. The car began to move slowly. A moment later the sound was repeated, coming this time from the other direction, and the car came to a thundering halt, throwing him again. He cursed in senseless fury. For an hour the car he was in had been shunted about the freight yard and each time it moved he had hoped that it would be heading out on the main line. If it had not been shunted around so much he would not have minded. He did not mind waiting, but he hated the aimless moving, the feeling of not knowing what was going on, and it aggravated the terrible feeling that his will was no longer the slightest determinant of his fate.

He had got this feeling, in its essence, in the instant of gun flash when he realized that he had shot the wrong man. All of the sense of outraged belief and feeling which came from his knowledge of the world, all the sense of being tricked by life, came to focus in the sound of rushing water, the smell of gun smoke, tearing away from him the one competence he had felt: the ability to do his job, which, in a wider sense, meant to him the ability to keep out of the processes and hypocrisies of the world.

He had got away from the scene of the shooting easily enough. There had been no pursuit, but even then he knew that he was going to have to run. If he had shot the right man, it would have been all right. He could expect that the police would be interested in a routine way, since the dead man—Crip did not know this, but he surmised it—would be some gangster whom they would be glad to see dead. But now it would be all different. There would be a rumble about it. Even the Big Fellow, whoever he was—and when he thought of him, Crip felt the same impotent rage which he had felt in reading the history books, a sense of being deceived—even the Big Fellow would condemn him.

All of the night after the killing, helplessness and rage worked on him as he lay in the bed in the new room. In the morning he had gone around to the meeting place he had arranged with Jake. Even while he was going there he knew that Jake would not turn up. It was senseless to suppose that he would be paid for a job which he had not done. Nevertheless he went there, knowing that it was dangerous, out of an obscure demand for justice, the opposite and the source of his rage and hatred of the world. It seemed to him that since a man had been killed, he should be paid for it, otherwise his action had no meaning at all.

Jake was not at the appointed place. Crip waited for a long time, not even hoping, but unable to leave. When he was satisfied himself that the man was not coming—satisfied but not convinced, because he was convinced even before he had left his room—he knew that he could not even go back to the cheap rooming house again. He would have to run. Even in that, which was raw necessity, there was no area of choice—all he could do was get off the streets until nightfall. His bad leg now was like a visible mark of his guilt.

When night came he went to the freight yards, to the reefer in which he now waited, a small parcel of consciousness hunted around in the darkness. There was ice in the reefer. Although it was very cold, he had chosen the car because the ice indicated that the car would be moving soon. I got to get to Jersey, he thought; at least to Jersey.

Again the racketing of metal swept toward him and the car moved. This time it covered a fair distance and when it stopped he could hear voices. A line of cars was drawn up alongside a loading platform. He could hear the sound of jitneys and hand trucks and for a moment was content, thinking that the car would be soon rolling west.

"What in the name of Christ have you got there?" he heard someone say.

"A stiff. Headed for Ohio."

"Better Ohio than hell I suppose," the first voice said. "In here?"

"Maybe in Jersey they'll take him out and put him on a hot shot. Baggage car, maybe. But he's supposed to go on here."

"Easy with that," a third voice said.

"What's the matter, Pop?"

"A man gave me a dollar to see he was handled easy."

"I don't hear him complaining."

"You know what that is?" the new voice asked.

"Who is he, Pop? The Unknown Soldier?"

"A Red," Pop said. "Hearse driver told me. Killed in the strike."

"I don't care what he is," the first voice said. "Get him in the car."

"What do you suppose those guys want, anyway?"

Crip heard the voice over the sound of something heavy being shifted, and leaned forward, feeling strange because he was going to be riding the same car as a corpse, hearing, "Them damn Reds," then more sound of movement, and finally the only words that in his whole lifetime had any meaning: "The bastards want to change everything."

The rumble of couplings rolled down the string of cars and they went away in the darkness.

Friday 11:30 P.M.

Barney lived over to the west, toward the river. It was late when I finished my chores and started for his place. The streets were deserted. All the gashounds who had been used to keeping the night alive were departed, gone into winter quarters, perhaps, in the flophouses downtown. It was as lonely as a landscape of the moon, and seemed as empty, but I had the feeling, which I had not lost after it had first come to me the night I left Kay, that I was being followed. Crossing the avenue I waited for a moment under the streetlamp. If I were going to be jumped I wanted it to be in the light. No one came across the avenue after me. The wind howled in the street and a loose sign, swinging, wailed like a banshee, throwing shadows across a small lot where a tenement house had burned down.

I went on but the footsteps seemed to come after me. I knew I would not be able to hear them with the wind, but the feeling persisted. Then a figure stepped out of the darkness beside me. It was startling enough so that even without my bad nerves I might have swung at him in reflex. My arm was going back when he said, "Matches, buddy?"

"Sure," I said rather shakily, cursing my jumpiness, and held them out to him. He lit one, cupping it against the wind and I saw the hard, stubbled face. He looked a little drunk. He held the match for a moment longer than he needed to, as if wanting to look at me, and then said in the kind of false-friendly voice that was a threat:

"You can stake me to a flop."

"No," I said, taking the matches.

"Listen," he said. "All I want is a buck. Fifty cents even." He took a step toward me and I got a whiff of his breath.

I walked around him and went on, hearing him swear behind me. Jesus, I thought, if you're going to start feeling that every bum you see is one of Kelly's goons out to dump you, you'd better quit.

Barney's apartment was in the one elevator building in the block. It was a big house, built badly and hurriedly, and now it was falling apart. Under the bells the kids and the superintendent were having a war of words, the kids writing them, the landlord rubbing them out. Now it was all smudged and dirty. I pushed the bell and waited at the door and pretty soon the lock began clicking. I went in. The elevator groaned and whimpered in the shaft. I got out at the fifth floor and went down the hall.

Two comrades were just coming out of the apartment and we said hello and good-bye and I followed Barney into the living room.

"You want a beer?" he asked, and went back to the kitchen without waiting for an answer. He brought back the open bottles without glasses and sat down.

"Big day?"

"Nothing much." I told him about the assignments I had been given and what luck I had had. "I took Bill down there," I said. I wondered if his train had gone out yet. For a moment I had a vision of it—the car—a refrigerator car, I supposed—and the train rolling westward. I could see all the trains running out to the west, corpses on all of them, great metal conduits filled with dead bodies all streaming to the west the way the sun sucks up moisture in long filaments of light on a midsummer evening. I was the one who was supposed to go west, I thought, not Bill.

"Yeah," Barney said. "I guess it was a big enough day at that."

"Well, it's done. We can't change what's happened."

"In a way we can. If it doesn't turn out to have been for nothing."

"Yes. What about Keyes?"

"That's what I don't know. He was supposed to show, but he hasn't. It's getting pretty late and I'm worried. A hell of a lot depends on him and what he can get together out of the committee."

"Can he get in touch with you here?"

"Fred and Jim are sleeping at the section tonight. If he comes in or calls they'll get in touch with me. I'm afraid he won't turn up tonight."

"What about tomorrow? What do we do?"

"More of the same," he said tiredly. "Leaflets on the front again—a lot more men made the shape-up this morning and that means that a lot of them think the strike is just about over. A couple of piers have started working. So—more leaflets, although propaganda isn't much good now, all that's needed has been done. We should be going on to organization. That means we've got to shoot for another meeting, and without the committee to back it, it'll be hard. The boys will figure that if the committee won't stick its neck out, then they've got a good reason to be scared themselves."

"I guess they'd be right."

"Oh, they'd be *right*. There were a couple of pretty bad dumpings today. Pete and Tony. Tony got a hook in his head."

"Bad?"

"Bad enough. I got a feeling somebody was laying for me too. I got a notion somebody tailed me home."

"I've been having that too."

"I don't think it was just a feeling, so keep your eyes skinned."

"O.K. What's next on the docket?"

"Oh, hell, come around to the section tomorrow. If Keyes comes, it'll be one thing. If not it'll be another."

"All right." I got up to go.

"You want to stay here, Joe? You can sleep on the couch."

"I think I'll go back to Bill's place. I guess I should tell the guy he was sharing his place with, in case he doesn't know."

"You're welcome to stay."

I shook my head and he got up and followed me down the hall. His wife was in the kitchen as we went by, making some coffee.

"You've got a racket," I told Barney.

"Sure," he said smiling. "Coffee tempt you?" I said no and went on out.

The elevator was there waiting for me and I got in and pressed the down button. It let out a long moan as the door clanged shut and began the creaking descent. From far below in the shaft I could hear something else, a kind of muttering and grunting sound. The lights went off.

I had a sudden manic fear of being trapped, real almost as that time in the tank, and began a frantic search for my matches. I couldn't find them. I remembered the panel of buttons and began fumbling over it, searching for the light switch. A strip of light went past. The second floor. And then, even before the elevator had got there I knew that it was going past the first floor and down to the basement. Somebody must have rung for it before I got on. But who? Who would be moving around in the basement at that time of night?

The elevator ground past the strip of light that was the first floor. It was as slow and inexorable as judgment. I scrabbled for the panel buttons, panicky now, certain that someone was waiting for me down there in the dark, feeling constriction like an iron band at my throat.

The elevator banged to a stop and I heard the iron grating of the door as it went back. I got hold of it, pushing it to make it go faster, but it would move only with the slowness of nightmare. When it was wide enough I squeezed through and jumped into the dark.

Something struck me on the head and I put up my arms. An overhead pipe. I moved and a thin sticky film, lighter than dust, closed around my face. I stood against the wall brushing the cobwebs off, waiting.

Something was there. I heard a scratching sound and then the muted clash of metal and began to move, almost running, going as rapidly as I could in the dark. Something hit my knees, tripping me, and I got up and began to run again, ran into something and felt on my left hand the texture of cloth.

I swung as hard as I could but there was nothing there. I reached out again in the dark but he was gone. Once more I turned, running, and there was again a great hammering and banging of metal as I went along the wall, touching it with my right hand, going very rapidly.

Then, suddenly, I didn't want to run anymore. I hit another garbage can, sending it roaring along the passage, and a great anger shook me in its fits. I couldn't stand it, to run like an animal in the dark. I put my back against the wall, feeling an absolute defiance that was beyond any hope, shouting at them to come after me.

Nothing. Then the same stealthy scratching sound. Something brushed my foot and I kicked with all my might and heard the stark inhuman scream of what could only be a cat. Shaking a little I found my matches.

The cat was three feet away, its back arched, spitting. There was no one in the basement except myself. Garbage cans lay where I had knocked them. The cloth was a curtain over the door of another room. There was not even a corridor, although it had seemed that I had run miles along one, stumbling and falling; only a small square room with the garbage cans and the cat and myself. It was only myself I had been fighting with all the time.

I found the right button and the elevator took me up to the fifth floor again. I went to Barney's apartment, waited a moment while I rubbed my face and hands with my handkerchief to take off the smudges of dirt, then knocked. Barney's wife opened the door.

"Hello, Joe," she said. "I knew you'd want that coffee."

Barney said, "The couch is still sleepable. Change your mind?"

"I guess that's what you would call it," I told him. I put my shaking hands in my pockets and went over to the kitchen table and sat down.

Friday Midnight

Somewhere in the apartment house a clock rang the midnight hour, fragile, glassblown chimes, sounding faint and far off as if borne over water. Barney Last turned restlessly but quietly so as not to waken his wife and reached for the cigarettes on the night table beside the bed.

Shouldn't have drunk the coffee, his mind said. But he knew that it was not the coffee which was keeping him awake; it was the thought that Keyes might still turn up. He tried to think of what that would mean, going over again a provisional program of action which the section committee had agreed on, wondering how much of it Keyes and the other members of the committee would be wanting to change. From the old habit of considering other alternatives he shifted to thinking of what must be done if Keyes did not turn up, if the committee were paralyzed by fear into taking no action at all. His mind went on like a machine endlessly turning over the possibilities for a long time while his cigarette smoldered in the ashtray.

Taking a last long drag, Joe Hunter sat up on the couch and looked out onto the darkness of the city. The rain had stopped and the wind had died down, but there was dry cold in the air. Moonlight lifted the taller buildings out of the sea of shadow and held them gaunt and insubstantial against the sky. In the moonlight only the Empire State Building to the north and east looked absolutely solid and stable. Then a low cloud went over it and the tall tower seemed to sway, graceful and flower-like. The apparent unreality of the city gave him a stronger sense of his own existence. He turned his eyes away from the buildings and down into the well of blackness that was the street. The cellar of the world, he thought, but I was the trouble with myself.

He stubbed out his cigarette as Barney Last turned again, freeing his legs of the blankets and P.J. Kelly got out of bed on naked feet and padded to the bathroom for a drink thinking *I've got to cut down* that the cigars he had been smoking the last couple of days were making him feel bad, seeing in the bathroom mirror his night face, uncertain and almost weak without the glasses.

The face made Husk vaguely uneasy. Pretty, good-humored, stupid, it invited the world into its confidence, trusting as a dog, willing, even, to be hurt if that were necessary, but begging from the world that modicum of awareness which makes loneliness bearable.

It was a lost face, perhaps that was what made Husk uneasy about it as he took the picture of Lucille and tore it once across and then once again and dumped the pieces into the wastepaper basket. He was going through a litter of papers, bills, letters which had accumulated with time. One by one he shook them out of their envelopes, glanced at them and tossed them away. When he had finished, he carried the wastebasket into the kitchen and then went back to his bedroom. All his bags were packed. He stood at the window, looking into the darkness, wondering where he could go. Black lines of streets, like lines on a map, crisscrossed below him, but there was no point on that map that would do.

The street was very dark. Everyone in it seemed to be sleeping. He could not even see the sign HAROUNIAN MEATS AND GROCERIES which was his horizon marker. Yet in the still night Blackie could hear the sound of someone walking in the street, swift resolute footsteps. He had a sudden crazy notion, like the feeling he had had on the night when he gave in to his mother's wish, that they were his own footsteps that he was hearing. The idea passed without leaving him bitter, even when it brought its corollary, the knowledge that his footsteps would never sound like that again, quick with health and spirit. I've got to work something out, he told himself, some kind of job. He thought of his mother now with tenderness and grief, as if she were dead, and of himself with a kind of sad wisdom which had been born of the last few days. No use kidding myself, he thought, the world is always bigger than you. Sooner than you, later than you, the thought went on completing itself nonsensically in his head. We all got to die, he thought, feeling a sad and useless responsibility for the street, for the footsteps that were just going out of his hearing as they were going out of the hearing of his mother, who lay on her back, sleepless, feeling the pain inside her but feeling it almost with indifference, thinking: yes, it was a fine life that I had and now all the trouble is past.

She turned on her side softly, so as not to waken her son, and woke Mary Carmody out of a dream wherein something was being stolen from her. The girl lay awake trying to think what it was and then put her hand on her body, thinking of Hope's apartment. And that's being grown up, she thought; can that be all there is? thinking of older people with a child's contempt: that's what they were pretending was so important; thinking sadly: I'm grown up now too. Still, she could not dispose of it so easily. She began to think of Hope's apartment again, and of Lonnie, and the feeling—not quite fear, not quite curiosity, more curiosity than fear—came back and she drifted once more into sleep and into a deliciously terrifying dream of a man who was firing a pistol at her, or was it at a picture of her? or was it herself reflected in a mirror?

The picture stared back out of the frame. It was finished now, or at least Kay thought that it was finished. There was something about it that was unsatisfactory, beyond the usual dissatisfaction of never being able to do exactly what she wanted to do with a picture. Was it the hair? Perhaps. Or the eyes? Joe had not liked the picture. He doesn't really see me as I am, she thought, or himself either. He sees the world but not himself, or himself and not the world; when he sees me, I am all out of focus. She thought of Hunter now with a greater objectivity than when he had been there. Always when talking with him she was aware—or rather was aware later, after the talk had ceased or when they were apart—of things unsaid, forgotten, undared or, as they often seemed, unnecessary. Now she thought: It won't work out; he won't change and I won't. That was what she felt most strongly at the moment, away from him, feeling it stronger than she ever had before: that she would not change. She was aware of making the statement stronger to herself than seemed to be necessary, and had a momentary uneasy fear of what might happen to that resolution when she saw him again. Tiredly she emptied the ashtrays into the shallow fireplace and got ready for bed. At the last she said as a kind of prayer: I'm going to be a painter; I have my own life here. Then she wound the clock and reset the alarm; it rang one short reluctant burst as the hand passed the hour.

The one o'clock chime pushed a splinter of sound through the cold air and simultaneously the phone rang. Barney Last put out his hand for the light and stumbled into the living room. Hunter held the phone out to him.

"Fred," he said.

Last said "Barney" into the mouthpiece and listened. Then he put down the phone and turned to Hunter.

"Better get dressed," he said. "They've heard from Keyes' wife. It sounds like something might have happened to him."

Outside the moon shed its consistent light on the Jersey coast.

PART IV
Saturday

The car came down the street going very fast and turned with a whine of rubber into the approaches of the tunnel. It straightened out, picking up speed, and plunged into the opening. Lights flashed on the white line, on the curving tiled walls, and then came into focus on the back of a truck. The driver swore.

"Take it easy, Fred," one of the men in the back advised him. "We've got all night." The driver said nothing.

"You think we have?" Hunter said, as if he were talking to himself. "I won't mind that, if we find him."

Barney Last shrugged his shoulders, turned as if he were going to speak and then shrugged again. He ran a hand over his high round balding forehead. He looked very tired.

Hunter's coarse blond hair was touched by the dashboard light as he turned toward Last. "What do we try next?" he asked.

"I don't know, Joe," Barney Last said. "When we get over to the other side we can try phoning the section. They might have some dope." He sounded as if he didn't believe that they would.

"What could they have found out?"

"There're a couple of other teams working on it too. They might turn up something."

"They don't know where to start," Joe Hunter said.

"Well, neither do we."

Fred swore again and turned out to cut around the truck. In front of it he turned into a pocket behind other cars.

"Take it easy," Last said again.

"Take it easy, hell," the driver said. "I got an idea somebody is interested in us."

Last turned to look through the rear window. The curving wall of the tunnel winked away in a succession of lights behind them, empty.

"You're getting nervous in your old age, Fred," Barney Last said.

"What would anyone be interested in us for?"

"What would anyone be interested in this guy Keyes for?" Fred answered, turning his head slightly. "What was anyone interested in Bill Everson for?"

"They hit him by mistake," Barney Last said, hunching himself forward in the rear seat so that he wouldn't have to speak so loudly to be heard over the humming motor noises.

"I don't want that kind of mistake to happen to me," Fred said. With his head half turned the light of the dash silhouetted his square face. "I don't think it was a mistake. Does Hunter think it was a mistake?"

"A different kind of a mistake," Joe Hunter said, so quietly that Fred did not hear him.

He was sitting far back in the corner of the rear seat. In the shadow his eyes looked black and enormous. "Mistake or not," he said, "it doesn't cut any ice with us. We've still got to find Keyes. Barney's right, Fred. It's too early to have to worry about trouble. What we've got to figure out is where Keyes might be."

"You might try a waterfront alley," Fred said bitterly. "Did you ever think of trying the morgue?" He believed that if you said the worst you were thinking it would not happen.

"We'll try calling the section first," Last said tiredly, leaning forward with his arms on the front seat. "After that we'll see. We've got to hope for the best anyway. There's no use to try the morgue. It wouldn't help a damn bit to get the cops into this, not now anyway."

"Fred was joking," Joe Hunter said.

"Well, I wasn't," Last replied. He looked at Hunter, slumped in his corner, at the white strained face. He wondered what Hunter was thinking. "You look pooped out, Joe," he said kindly. "When we get finished with this business you better take a week off with that girl of yours. Hell, man, you didn't even get a day off after they let you out of the army. I'm sorry we had to rope you in like that right away."

"Nobody roped me in," Hunter said. "I roped myself in. We didn't get any sleep last night, that's all. I'm sleepy." He was thinking of Bill Everson who was dead.

"Barney must be going fruit," Fred said. "You better take him up on that pretty fast, Hunter. He never gave anything away yet, the bastard. When I get through running around on wild-goose chases with you guys, I'm going to ship out on a South American run and have myself a long vacation."

"Joe's been talking of going West when the strike's over," Barney Last said. "Where do you figure on going, Joe?"

"I'm not going anywhere," Hunter said. Last looked at his face without speaking.

In front of them the curve of lights fell away into the darkness of the tunnel mouth and they came out into the great empty shadowy plain of the approaches. They picked up speed, turning out of the deserted confluence of streets northward along the waterfront. To their right, massive buildings lifted into the dark sky. The driver put his hand to the rearview mirror, straightened it, and sat back against the seat with his head lifted.

"You're crazy," Barney said, looking through the rear window again.

"I guess I'm getting old," Fred grumbled. He dropped his hand and concentrated on driving. "Just the same," he said, "I'm going to cut over up here a ways."

He swung the car into a narrower street, followed it for a block and swung northward again. At the next corner he turned right once more. When he had worked his way over to Sixth Avenue he tramped on the gas and raced uptown. At Houston he turned left again and pulled up in front of the neon of a corner drugstore.

"You want me to call?" he asked.

"I'll call," Hunter said. He was at the side nearest the curb. He pushed the door open and jumped out.

"Tell Tony we'll try to call in every half hour or so," Last told him. "Ask if they've heard anything from Brooklyn."

"O.K.," Hunter said. He ran across the sidewalk toward the lighted door, reaching in his pocket for a nickel,

Fred watched the lights of the approaching car. It was coming slowly along the wide street as if the driver were searching for something. Fred could feel his shirt growing suddenly too small for him as his breathing deepened. He opened the door quickly and got out, standing on the sidewalk out of the lights, looking over the top of the automobile.

"What is it?" Barney asked.

Fred did not answer for a long moment while the long car went by. He heard the laughter of a girl, a quick flash of sound, and then the car was past, rolling slowly and almost noiselessly along the street. He let out a long sighing breath and unbuttoned one of the buttons on his blue work shirt.

"Nothing," he said laughing. "I guess I've got the jitters. You got a cigarette?"

Last handed the pack to him through the open window and the driver shook out a cigarette and lit it, snapping the match on his thumbnail. He handed the pack to Last, took a deep drag on the cigarette and held it. Then, as if he had come to a decision, he opened the rear door.

"Get up," he said.

"What the hell's the matter now?"

"Get up."

Last lifted himself, bending the upper half of his body forward across the driver's seat, resting his hand on the wheel. Fred lifted the rear cushion and ran his hand into the darkness.

"What are you looking for?"

"This," Fred said. He dropped a tire iron onto the front seat and fumbled again. There was a clash of metal as he dropped the other irons near Last's feet. "I just feel more comfortable if I got something to hold onto," he said grinning. He got behind the wheel again.

"I thought it was just part of your usual bitching," Last said. "You really see anything back there?"

"I don't know." He took another deep drag on his cigarette. "Just a feeling maybe."

"Joe's pretty jumpy tonight too."

"He's always jumpy. What the hell's the matter with him? What's this about his going West? Is he going to retire or something?"

"I don't know," Last said, turning toward him. "He had some crazy notion—I don't know just what it was. I guess when he got back he thought everything would be easy and it turned out to be hard. He was too cocky. He expected too much maybe. He's O.K. now."

"What the hell's keeping him anyway?" the driver asked irritably. "He's had time to call the West Coast." He shot his cigarette through the open window onto the sidewalk just as Joe Hunter came out of the drugstore. He got into the backseat and closed the door.

"Nothing," he said. "I talked to Tony. The Brooklyn outfit doesn't know anything. Tony said that he had heard that Keyes had a friend in Jersey that he used to go to see sometimes. That must be Daniels. Tony didn't even know his name or where he lived, but it must be Daniels." He spoke very quietly as if he were thinking out loud.

"Daniels!" Fred snorted. "That goddamned gas-hound."

"Yeah," Hunter said, as if he had not heard him. "Tony said that he was getting some of the Jersey guys to have a look around the waterfront bars, but I told him there wasn't much point to it. Keyes doesn't drink to amount to anything."

"How the hell do you know?" Fred asked. "You don't know the guy, do you?"

"It doesn't sound as if he did anyway, from what we've learned about him," Hunter said. "The people who knew him didn't say anything about his hitting the bottle."

"For Christ's sake!" Fred said, kicking the starter. They rolled down the street and turned uptown again. "Where to?" he asked over his shoulder.

"Just keep on," Barney said patiently. "We'll work something out."

The car followed the quiet avenue. Fred put his hand up as if to adjust the mirror and then checked himself. He was beginning to be jittery again. He felt that they had been driving for hours.

"Godalmighty," he said, "what an assignment—hunting for a guy and we don't hardly even know what he looks like."

"There's no reason to expect that anything has happened to Keyes," Barney said. He looked at Hunter but the other did not answer.

"Just the same," the driver said, squinting into the rearview mirror.

We were hunting for a man, but where do you find a man?

For almost twenty-four hours, from the time Barney had got the call from Fred at the section, we had been hunting. Keyes had been missing longer than that. It was his wife who had called the section, afraid that something had happened to him. We had gone out there, to Keyes' home in Jersey City, first. Since then it seemed that we had been almost everywhere—the towns on the Jersey coast, Brooklyn, Long Island, Queens, the Bronx, Manhattan, Staten Island. You would think it would be easy to find a man, because a man is usually not much more than a kind of filament that binds his job, his home, the bar, the church, the movies, and the corner store into the inevitable nexus of living. Long Island to Jersey, Staten Island to the Bronx, the four corners of the world, and there were traces of Keyes in all of them, but nothing to help us, nothing to tell us where he was at that moment.

It had been only two days from the time of the smashed-up meeting when we started hunting. It had seemed longer than that, as if time had become elastic to allow for the enactment of many events. About forty-eight hours, then, since I had seen Keyes for a few minutes, a fantastic figure moving through that crazy meeting which seemed to me to have already gone over the boundary into dream at the time when he got up to speak; as if the meeting upon which we had hoped to build so much, and which had been as logically organized as we could make it, a construct of our consciousness, as if that meeting had suddenly turned inside out on us, so that instead of getting from it the fruits of consciousness it became a wild dance of instinct and emotion, every speaker adding to it the unhappy fantasies of his own tormented being until the meeting took on a will of its own. Keyes had seemed to me then willful, blind, anarchic.

Even in the two days that followed, when we had reports of Keyes' activities, a word from someone here or there who had seen him, or seen someone who had seen him, he seemed to me to keep this same irrational character. The vagueness of the reports of what he was doing, his appearances here or there, in Manhattan or Brooklyn or Jersey, on this dock or in that bar or with one man or another, seemed to me to have no pattern. It was like getting infrequent and partial reports of some mad explorer, moving toward the headwaters of an impossible Amazon, reports which had been passed by word of mouth from one native tribe to another, to arrive at last, garbled almost beyond any understanding—and certainly almost beyond belief—to be spilled into the ears of some lazy and drunken reporter who adds to it the romancings of a sublimated poet before sending it on to his paper. When you read the report you can look at the map and say: here. But you will know that at the time you are looking at the exotic place name, a black dot on the green or brown or yellow of the map, the explorer has already gone on somewhere else, or is dead, or has given up his mission (whatever it was) or has begun the long return to civilization. And even if you can accept him, believe that he is actually following a line from point A to point B, it will probably be impossible to feel your way to the difference between the flat and easy green of the map and the living green of the jungle and the poisoned rivers.

So we were looking for a man who was, at least to me, a little unreal. And where do you find a man?

Unreality can become real. The partial and incomplete glimpses we had of Keyes made him, for me anyway, a distorted picture. Nevertheless, the news we had of him was authentic; he had been seen; he was working. We even had the one phone call from him where he had promised to come in to a conference with Barney. During the twenty-four hours of the hunt we had talked to dozens of people who had seen him and talked to him. He was real enough, as a piece of external reality, moving like a particle in the theories of old-fashioned physics, having momentum, occupying space and time, colliding with other particles. It was his reality as a man which I could not feel. Where do you look for a man?

The hunt would begin in childhood, in the enchanted forest, in Port Random, Long Island.

It was not a successful town, the town where Keyes had been born and where his parents still lived, the town to which he went back periodically, the way a child might go back to a place again and again, looking for something that has been lost, the way a person might go back to a place sometimes, a town maybe, looking for a meaning that has escaped him. Or perhaps he went there to fish or because he liked the sound of water against the piers.

Not a big town, not a successful one, Port Random. Not much character to the land there, land that only lately had been lifted enough out of the mud flats to be land at all; no bluffs overlooking the sea; no chalk cliffs or sea rocks, only the narrow creeks, mud bottomed but sometimes surprisingly deep, not so much creeks as tentative approaches of the sea, going crookedly through tidal meadows choked and drowsing under the coarse grass.

That was the town. Small, sprawling, going down to the water where the piers went out, some of them crazed and ramshackle, their pilings bent by a trick of light in the still water which was never quite still, but which kept up the moronic slop-slopping of the sea, uneasy and sleep-making at once.

Since the town bore the character of something changeless, built for all time, it was not hard to imagine Keyes as a child there, going along the undisciplined streets to the piers, listening to the talk of fishing men and the talk of the old men who had been seamen.

It was possible to imagine him in school there, the small school where everyone knew one another, a small boy, small for his age most likely, because he had not been a big man at maturity. That would mean fights, of course, a great many of them, for that is the natural heritage of a boy who is smaller than he should be at a given age. After a while the fights would stop, just at the age where the boy is already turning into a man, for the reason that boys can fight more easily and forget more easily than a man can. There must have been a lot of fights, because Keyes was known to some of the men we saw as a handy man with his fists, but the fights seemed not to have left any scars. He was not an embittered man, nor like the small man who, because he has fought so often and been defeated so often and no longer cares except to make the world aware of his own presence, is the constant challenger of bigger men.

School days. Naturally he falls in love with his teacher when he is in the fourth grade. Later he falls in love with a teacher when he is in high school. Nothing there. The high school teacher has married and still lives in the town; she is a pleasant, unremarkable-looking woman.

Then there were the girls, of course, but that was hard to know about. The loves of youth, so clumsy and poignant and unredeemed, can never be kept or catalogued. They exist in a black and golden, a bitter, honeyed weather which is their own emanation, and they vanish with it. Nothing in the world is more lost than early love, nothing is more impossible to go back to than the loves of the time when you and the world were growing up together. It is easier to find the pony or the rifle, the bicycle or the boat. In the case of Keyes, it was a boat.

A small one, no more than a skiff with patched-on mast and a clumsy sail. Keyes' father had been a Brooklyn teamster until an accident had left him partially crippled. After that he had worked in Port Random, going out on the fishing boats sometimes, doing work of one kind or another in season. There hadn't been enough money for a real boat.

The name of the boat had been *The Independence*, which might have been a clue, or it might merely have been the result of a history course. It had probably served Keyes, during his three years in high school, the same function as an automobile, the vehicle of love, but there would have been nothing to show any of that, nothing to indicate how he had undergone the rites of passage lying in the skiff on the ocean's rocking floor.

And so, the childhood of Jim Keyes.

"Ay-yah, he was a cocky one." "Jim never took nothing off nobody." "Good hard worker." Chuckling at a long forgotten joke: "He had a mighty good sense of humor."

All statements of categories, the imprecise labelings that are always used.

Perhaps something in the father, who was intelligent, kindly, non-intellectual, a worker born of the proletariat with only a rudimentary class consciousness. Something of the mother, who was warm, sensitive, and practical: the pictures on the walls were not the run-of-the-mill calendar kind of picture: but the coffee she gave us was the breakfast coffee warmed again for lunch.

Finally, there was only the fact that the boat had been named *The Independence*, and, from his father: "Jim was always kind of restless, he had so much curiosity. He wanted to know why things happened. I bet he read almost all them Julius Haldeman books."

So he was looking for the world. We went away from Port Random as Keyes must have done, with the sound of water clapping sleepily at our ears.

It was not like the sound of lake water in Michigan. Seeing that time against the time of Keyes, his boyhood seemed wrapped in richness and light while my own was empty and barren. Not bad or wrong, but simply barren. Yet it had been full enough. It had been in many ways like Keyes' own boyhood; there was a similarity in the pattern. I had had no parents, it is true, but since they had died when I was very young, the aunt and uncle had done just as well. No, it had not been the conventionally bitter childhood, it had been the conventionally full childhood, yet now it seemed empty by comparison with that of Keyes.

It was almost impossible to find Keyes, the man, in Keyes' childhood. There were only the clues of the boat's name, the Haldeman-Julius Little Blue Books, the fights, the boy who took nothing off nobody. That to the beginning of his young manhood.

At the beginning of my young manhood, there was the cold sea floor of the square in Detroit where I was born out of the contradiction between my head and a policeman's club. I could see where I began, all right, if I could not see where Keyes did.

Perhaps that was it, being born too quickly, passing the initiation into manhood before I was ready, that made my own childhood empty while Keyes' now seemed to me so rich and exciting. All that had gone out of my head there. I had had nothing to go back to because I was begun right there out of my hate. Keyes had always gone back again, not for sentimental reasons, it seemed to me now, but out of some instinct for the place that was one of the sources of his power. His pattern had been an ancient symbol of power, the spiral, taking him from Port Random to the Brooklyn docks, back again, then farther out and back once more, journey and return, passing the source of power each time at a different altitude, returning each time with new tests, new requirements, a continuing dialectic.

Yes. But what did that explain? What had Keyes found there that he came back to again and again, not as the eternal child, but as a mature man, a man a little cynical of the announced values of Port Random, a little impatient of the constricted life of the little lost town? What was the source of the power?

I, anyway, had the hate. That was my power source in the years between the nightstick and the war. Then it wore away, died out or was lost. Somewhere in the war perhaps. In the tank? In the tank, which was like New York with the lid screwed on and everyone screaming, the cellar of the world?

Wore away, died out, was lost. That was the way it happened, so that when I came back and got into the strike I had nothing to go on. I had not thought I needed anything to take part in the strike, that it could be done simply, like a reflex. It couldn't be done that way. I was cocky enough, but I found out it couldn't be done that way, and that was why, in the first days, I had always felt held back, felt like a man on a treadmill. That was why I began dreaming of my town again, the town lying in the sunlight, the sound of the fountain in the square, piers leaning on the still water—but that was Keyes' town. I saw now the similarity between them.

When the hate went away I had nothing to run on. That was when my town became most important. The town and Kay. Why was that? I associated the two together. Why? Because Kay was love, perhaps that was it, and passionate love is always a turning away from the world. But the town was the world too, wasn't it?

What was it Keyes had found that made it important to come back to Port Random? It seemed to me that it could be only one thing. Not simply the easy life of the instincts, because that cannot be returned to, but a life, a piece of life, that did not contradict them. That was what Keyes had had in his boyhood, that was his source of power. He went back to it, not completely in fact or in memory, but using the stuff of the town, its streets and houses, as the words of a poem are used, to stir up the great emotional images of a world behind the words. Keyes must have seen his boyhood, the town, as an image of freedom. It was not a freedom that he could return to, because he was no longer a boy and he was not making the neurotic's backward journey. Nevertheless it was, in small, in a distorted and cramped but nevertheless real and good way, a world of freedom. What he must have been thinking was how the world beyond Hoboken might be made to contain some of the ease and love and certainty and freedom of which Port Random and his childhood were a miniature crude foreshadowing.

Did my town mean something like that? It seemed to mean only Kay, love, seaborne Venus. Sound of lake water, clapping of waves at a pier. Keyes was sea born. Shining he rose from the sea of Port Random.

"Goddamn rain beginning," Fred grumbled.

Jim Keyes was growing real and fabulous.

The car swung out of the quiet one-way street and onto Seventh Avenue.

It had begun to rain and the street was a wash of black, as dark as an oily river, stippled with points of light where the rain bounced on the pavement. Looking through the streaming windows of the car it seemed to Joe Hunter that the neon of the bars and drugstores was beginning to run like wet paint. He saw the lighted signs melting and running together down the street like a line of fire. People were huddling under awnings and in doorways, and for a moment he felt the reflex of pleasure at being in a dry place. The feeling went away and left him with another: that he was boxed in a little form from which he could not escape. For a moment he had a wild longing to be one of the people on the street in the rain, but he shook off the feeling, thinking that he had put that idea away from him.

He was thinking of Keyes but not about the usefulness of Keyes, about the work which Keyes had started and that seemed to Hunter so necessary. He was not even thinking of Keyes' wife or son, both of whom he had seen in the last few hours and who were crazy with anxiety at Keyes' absence. For Hunter, Jim Keyes had come to possess an absolute value which Hunter himself could not define.

"If we find him we'll win." he said involuntarily.

"Sure," Barney Last said. "And if we don't—well, it'll be tough. Daniels is dead weight already—you saw that when we were out there. He'll stay gassed up until the strike's over and then sneak back to work hoping that no one sees him. Why do you suppose Keyes worked with him anyway?"

"Daniels has some pull on his own dock," Hunter answered. "I suppose that's the main reason. He had to work with somebody, didn't he? Jesus, we didn't give him much of a chance to work with us. That section out in Brooklyn just lost track of him when he moved over to Jersey, and then they lost him over there when the war came.

"Keyes didn't have to stay lost."

"What the hell could he do when he came back? There was no organization on the job. He did turn up once at the section over there and they sent him around to some housewives' branch or something. When the strike came, we didn't have anybody over in his local, so the poor bastard had to work alone."

"Yeah, I guess so," Last said. "God, it's crazy. We work our nuts off in one direction trying to set up a committee that will have some authority and then, bang, get this. If we don't find him, it's up the spout probably. Daniels will fold and this other guy, the one in Brooklyn maybe. Christ—"

"I won't give a damn about that if we find Keyes."

"Stop letting it ride you."

"Is this the street?" Fred asked, half turning to speak to them.

They were moving slowly past the post office on Ninth Avenue.

"This's it, Fred," Joe Hunter replied. "It's about halfway down the block."

"I hope to hell we get some action on this pretty soon," Fred said. "I begin to think I'm on a merry-go-round." He pulled the car into the street and cruised along near the curb. "Say when, Joe."

"Right about here," Hunter answered. The car pulled up at the curb and for a moment he waited. "Nothing may come of it," he said. "I saw this fellow, Munson, a few days ago. He said something about Keyes then, but I didn't even know who he was talking about—"

"What's another blind alley to us?" Fred growled. "We've been in one all night."

"All you can do is try," Barney Last said. "Sooner or later we may run across someone who knows where he's at."

Hunter opened the door and rain whipped in at them. He jumped out onto the sidewalk, raced across toward the doorway of one of the houses. It was dark in the hallway and he peered at the names on the letter boxes. It was impossible to read them. He scratched a match and looked at the scraps of soiled paper. Some of the boxes had no identification at all. The match went out in the wind and he lit another. He read the name: MUNSON. It was the right house.

There was no bell and he started up to the third floor. It was a rear-room box apartment, he remembered. The house was quiet and the hallway was dark on the second floor. He almost tripped over a boy and girl sitting on the stairs.

At the Munson apartment there was no sign of light under the door nor any sound of movement or voices inside. He wondered if it were too late, if they might have gone to bed, but it was not quite ten o'clock yet. They're out, he thought with a sudden sinking of heart that told him how much he had been counting on Munson having some information. He rapped softly on the door.

There was no sound at all from within. He knocked again, louder this time, and heard steps in the next apartment. Still there was no sound from Munson's place. He knocked again. There was a whisper of slippered feet and then a guarded voice.

"Who's there?" It was a woman.

"It's—" Hunter hesitated, not knowing quite how to reply. "Is Mr. Munson there?" he called.

"What do you want?" The voice was low, as if whoever was speaking were afraid of waking someone.

"Mrs. Munson?" Joe remembered her as a thin indecisive woman who had let him in the day he had come around to see her husband.

"What do you want?" He sensed a kind of panic in her voice, as if she were afraid of something, afraid to find out who might be out in the hall wanting to come in. There was the suspicion and the anger in her tone that he remembered from other places and other times.

"It's me, Joe Hunter," he said. "I'd like to see Mr. Munson if I could. You remember I was around here to see him a few days ago."

There was silence on the other side of the door for a moment. She's getting ready to ask me what I want again, he thought. He was standing with his head bent toward the doorjamb. "I'd just take a minute of his time," he said, trying to make his voice soft and winning. He felt as if he were talking to a child.

"He's not in," the woman said in a low voice. He could feel her on the other side of the door, standing just as he was, her head bent toward the opening edge of the door.

"It's very important. It's about Jim Keyes. We can't find him. I thought maybe Mr. Munson might know something about him." He was struggling to keep his voice quiet and controlled.

"He's not in," the woman said again. "Go away."

"Can you tell me where he is?"

Silence.

"Do you know when he'll be back?" He was sweating now, and his fingernails were biting into the palms of his hands, but he didn't notice. He held his breath waiting for her answer.

"Go away," she breathed from the other side of the thin door. "Go away."

He turned away and started down the stairs. He was trembling with anger and the sweat was cold on his forehead. He had forgotten about the lovers on the stairs and almost tripped over them. He was in the lower hallways when he heard his name being called from above.

"What is it?" he answered, returning to the foot of the first flight of stairs.

"Hunter?"

"Yes."

"Come on up again."

He went wearily up the steps, remembering the pair on the second landing this time as they remembered him, standing back against the wall to let him pass, their faces indistinct in the shadows. Munson was waiting for him at the top of the stairs. He was in his bare feet and wore no shirt. He held his trousers up with one hand, clutching them at the top in front. He put out his hand to Hunter and welcomed him into the apartment.

"I'm sorry," he said. "I guess Effie figured you didn't have anything much to see me about. I was asleep."

His wife had switched on the lights and was standing in the doorway of the kitchen. She gave Hunter a look of dumb resentment and went back into the apartment.

"We can sit here if you don't mind," Munson said, going into the kitchen. "I can rassle up a bottle of beer for us maybe."

"Sorry I woke you up," Hunter said. Then: "I don't have too much time."

"It ain't late anyway. Don't know why I went to bed so early. Nothin' to do, I guess. Gettin' lazy, now that the strike is runnin' on so long."

Hunter got the feeling that Munson was talking in order to postpone something, as if afraid that Hunter had some request to make of him which he would not want to fulfill. He punched open the cans of beer and shoved one of them at the visitor and then went to a cupboard for a glass.

"I came to ask you about Jim Keyes," Hunter said abruptly.

"Has he been blacklisted?" Munson asked immediately.

"I wish that was all."

"What about Keyes?"

"I'm trying to find him. I remembered that you said something about him to me the other day when I was around here talking to you. I didn't know anything about Keyes then. I didn't know much about anything, I guess. I was too dumb to listen to what you were saying.

Well, I know about Keyes now. But he's missing. He hasn't been home for a day and his wife is worried sick. If he doesn't show up soon the committee will fall apart. They're already scared about Keyes."

"I know," Munson said, nodding slowly.

"You mean you knew about Keyes being missing?"

"No. A delegate was up to see me today, that's all."

Hunter looked at him carefully, considering what he had said. Munson had been worried when he had seen him before. He had been afraid, eager to do something to assist the strike, but afraid.

"He told you to go back to work," Hunter said, turning his eyes away from the older man. "Or you'd be out. That right?"

The other nodded, pushing his beer around the table in a slow circle. He turned toward Hunter a steady level glance and his eyes were proud. He started to add something to what he had said but checked himself. Hunter did not want to look at him, did not want to ask what he had said to the delegate in reply.

"I just thought you might know where Keyes might be found," Hunter said hurriedly. "We thought he might be staying at a friend's place somewhere. He's been moving around a lot ever since he began to get the committee working. I guess he was worried that Kelly might send some goons after him. You don't have any idea where he might be?"

Munson slowly shook his head. "I didn't hardly know him," he said. "When I did, that was a long time ago. Keyes used to live over here—on Twenty-second street. Then he moved over to Brooklyn, around Red Hook, and then after that over to Jersey. It was like he couldn't stay anyplace a long time. I don't know what was eatin' him. Falls he used to go to Pennsylvania, huntin'. He asked me to go huntin' with him once. I never went. Couldn't afford it. He used to go out with a guy named Gates, little guy, he's a teamster now. I don't think he ever got a deer, but I guess he didn't care if he never. He just liked to go out there, I guess. It was just to get away from the job and the city. I don't blame him. I was always sorry I never went out that time." His voice trailed off into a dream of the Pennsylvania woods.

"All right," Hunter said. He was impatient and trying not to show it. "You don't know anywhere he might have gone?"

Munson shook his head. "He used to come over to see a woman here, sometimes," he said. "Mrs. Karpovich, she's Irish but she married a Yugoslav. She used to be in school with Keyes, out on Long Island somewhere. Keyes, he had a crush on her, but he was pretty young then. Seemed like Keyes always liked her, and he used to go see her sometimes."

"We've got to try everything," Hunter said tiredly. "You know where she lives?"

"Just up a ways, on Twenty-fifth. Right near Ninth. Three-ninety something—it's got a little tree in front there, you can't miss it. Only tree in the block. And there was a guy in Harlem, a Negro guy—" He paused. "Keyes was a funny guy," he said. "He wasn't after the woman, see? He just used to stop in sometimes. It was like he never forgot nothing—" He let the sentence trail off again.

"All right," Hunter said. "We'll try there. You know where this Negro guy lives?"

"No."

"Maybe the woman will, then. We've got to try everything." Hunter got up, leaving the half-empty glass of beer.

"My kid," Munson said. "My son," he paused over the unfamiliar term. "He was with that mob, you know?"

Hunter nodded indifferently. "You can't help that," he said. He paused partway to the door and waited.

"Yeah," Munson said. He paused, then said abruptly, "He was wrong. I fired him out, see? Then I went around, I was going to see this guy Last."

"I'm sorry about your son," Hunter said. "We can use you, though, in the Party."

"I didn't go in," Munson said. "I didn't see Last nor nobody." When Hunter did not answer, he went on. "He's just a kid. He came back from the army and he was sore. He figured he had somethin' comin'. I'll take him back, but he's got to see he's wrong. He's got to see he's wrong, first. Maybe I'll come around and see you then."

"You don't have to score a point over him," Hunter said. "Not if he's just a kid and didn't know any better. Come down to the section. We can use you."

"Yeah? Yeah, I guess so. I guess I wouldn't be much good, though."

He waited for the other to say something, but Hunter said nothing at all, pausing between the table and the door, looking back.

"You think the strike is lost?" Munson asked, blurting it out as if he were ashamed of the question.

"Lost?" Hunter asked as if Munson's question had no meaning for him. He looked directly at Munson. "No, I don't think so," he said. "It's important to find Keyes, that's all."

"Maybe it's not lost. Me—I don't know. We been beat so often," Munson said, looking at Hunter in dead seriousness. "Since I don't know when. Even when it doesn't look as if there's nothin' goin' on, we're still bein' beat by something or other. It's always depression, or war, or hard times or high prices—Jesus you never got a time when you can sit down and just not worry. You read the papers?" He rushed on without waiting for an answer. "They'll drive you crazy, I swear. It's a different world," he said angrily. "You read them and you don't know where you stand, you can see that you're not the same kind of person you thought you were, everything's changed, the goddamned lying sons of bitches."

"Take it easy," Hunter said. "There's nothing new about that. It's gone on for a long time now. You're just seeing them differently, that's all."

Munson pushed his beer away from in front of him and put his arms on the table. "They just won't let you alone," he said bitterly. "Somebody always wants your blood. Look at this," he said, sweeping his arm around the room. "This's all I got." He shrugged his shoulders in defeat as if it were not what he had meant to say at all.

Hunter came to him and put an arm on his shoulders. "You aren't the only one," he said. "There isn't anything I can tell you. You did all you could. Come down and see us tomorrow if you want to. Nothing is easy."

He went out the door and down the stairs without waiting for Munson to speak. The lovers on the second-floor stairs drew away for him to pass. Outside it had almost stopped raining.

"Munson is suffering from an acute case of working-class alienation," he said, opening the rear door of the car. "It hurts when it doesn't hit until a man is past forty—like the measles. You made a recruit today, Barney." He seemed to have lost his fatigue and depression.

Neither of the men spoke to him. Both were looking back up the street toward Ninth Avenue. Lights flashed at the corner and a car turned in toward them.

"There the son of a bitch is again," Fred said. He kicked the accelerator and the car roared. "I'll give him a run for his money anyway," he said, whipping the car away from the curb.

The night was transforming itself into blind circles of speed. Hunting and being hunted we rounded the island.

Where do you find a man? You may find him in his friends.

They stood at the four corners of Keyes' world. Some of them we saw, and some of them we did not, so that putting him together out of their reactions to him was like putting together a jigsaw puzzle with some of the pieces missing.

It was a historical process because friendship itself is history, the separation of the boy from the warm ahistorical world of childhood, the creation of the formed ego which needs the world now in a new way to complete itself, and finds the world first of all through other people. Friendship, love, solidarity, these are the chinks where man looks into sunlight from the dungeon of the world, and in themselves they presuppose another world, a world as it could be. Find him in his friends.

That meant first of all the old-country Irishman, eaten by age now and badly gone with the drink, who had been Keyes' first workmate when he had gone down to the Brooklyn docks. A raddled and over-powering imagination like an engine with the governor missing, an engine declutched from the world which had become with time mythic and unreal, Paddy had already translated Keyes into a shadow figure. He could not remember when he had last seen Keyes. It might have been a month or two. It could have been a year perhaps. The real Keyes and the real events of his life were mixed by Paddy with bits of personal biography, stories, snatches of poems, bawdry. "He thought of the work as the rent of his body," he said. "Aye, Jimmy, he was the world's long wound."

And then cross the bay to Staten Island and the one-man commune of Sven Pederson, the hut which he had put together with his own hands, the boat which he had salvaged for fishing, the carefuly preserved copies of the *Industrial Worker*, and the equally carefully preserved reverence for Mother Anarchy. Here were the books too, not Haldeman-Julius now but the *Communist Manifesto*, the first volume of Marx's *Capital* and, in places of honor, Bakunin, Sorel on violence, Nietzsche.

Sven was history, the history of a false theory and a correct feeling, the history of the IWW from its early heroic days to its degeneration. He was the living chronicle of the great struggles, of Paterson and the free-speech fights, of the factory East and the agricultural West. "Jim was a good head. Too good, maybe. He wanted a plan for everything."

There were the two poles of him, Paddy and Sven, so that he was at once the world's long wound, whatever that meant, and a man with a plan, whatever it was. Distortions of art, distortions of science, where was Keyes, lost on the equator of that divided world?

There was a connective tissue of a kind. There were the other men, dozens of them, with whom he had worked, associated in unions, disputed with. Most of them were men like Munson, less developed, perhaps, less hard-pressed. Some of them were drawn along invisible lines of force toward that pole represented by Paddy, open-handed, easy, explosive, unreliable; others made a rough constellation around the magnetic north of Sven, and these were dogged, sometimes hard, taciturn, thoughtful, or even scheming.

That was the connective tissue. Then there was his wife and child. The Jersey tenements were not much different from the New York ones. On the bottom floor, melancholia; at the top, epileptic seizures; in the basement apartments they are already buried, while up on the roof they are throwing one another into the street. Nothing about the apartment to suggest a special character for Keyes. There were a few things he had made—he had worked as a carpenter at one time—some bookcases and cupboards. What there was about his wife that was special, if anything, it was impossible to tell because she was almost destroyed by fear and anxiety at his absence. She was a woman who had grown up in the Brooklyn waterfront area, and there was no use trying to convince her that Keyes' disappearance could have an easy explanation.

So it came back to a puzzle again: the man who was the world's long wound, the man with the plan.

I had had plans too, the plan of the meeting, the plan of going out to my town, the plan for Kay. They had filled me with joy at the time, had seemed profoundly liberating. That could not be because the idea of plan was a new thing. Why had the plan for the meeting seemed so indescribably important? I could see the answer to that now. It was because, after I had discovered that my hate had worn out and I had nothing to run on, the plan had seemed all that was needed. It could generate the power which the hate had generated before. The plans promised everything—victory in the strike, my trip West, Kay, everything.

All that fine and fragile ordering in the mind had come apart in my hands. Everything backfired. It had thrown me so hard that all I had been able to think about was getting away. The town became simply a refuge—as Barney had hinted—and in that hurry to escape I stood to lose everything, including Kay. Including even myself, the way I wanted myself to be.

Absolute freedom, that was what the plan had seemed. It stood in the place of my hatred which had driven me and determined me up to the time it was worn out and lost. Both of them went bad on me, hatred and will, determinism and freedom.

Hatred, the fit of conscience; intellect, the plan. Each was defeated in turn. The world fell apart for me. After the meeting I was lost in the cellar of the world. There was no way to put them together.

There seemed no way to put them together in Keyes either. He too was hatred, conscience—"the world's long wound." He was also the man with a plan. But with him these opposites met, interpenetrated, held him in the equilibrium of movement.

That was the importance of Paddy and Sven. They were in a way the symbols of the two halves of Keyes' world, but they were not two separate halves. They met in him. Marriage of Staten Island and Brooklyn.

"There the bastards are again," Fred said.

Marriage of heaven and hell.

Moving lights gleamed in the black tunnel of the avenue. Turning on the backseat Joe Hunter saw them through the rear window as a running radiance, half washed out by the continuing rain. There seemed to be nothing behind the lights. They were like ghost lights moving in a swamp, foxfire, or as if the street were a running ribbon of black, an assembly-line belt moving at high speed with the lights fastened to it. Hunter felt that he was on an assembly line only a little way ahead and that the distance between himself and the moving lights was fixed and unchangeable. The car behind swerved slightly and moved closer and Hunter remembered that behind the blur there was an automobile. Moving his feet on the floor of the car, he felt the tire iron, reached down for it and put it in his lap.

"They can't try anything here," Barney Last said, turning from the rear window. "You won't need that thing."

Hunter did not reply. He could not have said how he felt, except that, clutching the iron in his hand, he had a profound and unfocused desire to strike something with it. He glanced back at the lights indifferently as if he had forgotten their significance. In the front seat Fred was sitting relaxed against the door, his hands resting easily at the bottom of the wheel. The dash light caught the side of his square face and the rhythmical movements of his jaw chewing gum.

"We'd better get over into the traffic, then," Hunter said. "It's lonesome out here on the lone prairie."

"I'll cut over at the park," Fred said. "Maybe we can shake them uptown. What's next on the ticket anyway? Munson know anything about Keyes?"

"He mentioned a woman Keyes used to see sometimes. She lives in the west Twenties."

"We'll have to get rid of those girls behind us before we can get over there, anyway," Last said. "Some of those streets will be damn near deserted already."

"Unless you want to skip it," the driver said over his shoulder.

"We can't quit," Hunter muttered. Neither of the men heard him speak. There was no need to say it, since it was what all three of them felt.

Ahead a traffic light glowed in a sudden splash of dirty red, and Fred, swearing, swung into the middle of the avenue, avoiding a car that nosed slowly out of the side street, and increased his speed. Barney

Last turned to see the car behind go through the light without slowing. It hung in position behind them like a trailer on a very long hitch and then was lost when they turned east in a quick squeal of rubber.

There was traffic as they crossed the top of the park, and the driver cut his speed, shuttling the car in and out among the slower automobiles.

"He still with us?" he asked, turning his face slightly to the side.

"I suppose so," Barney Last answered. Lights bobbed behind them now, like buoys on a narrow channel. "I can't see the bastard," he said.

They turned south on Broadway, losing speed, cut over again and turned south on Sixth Avenue. At Forty-second they were caught by a light and turned crosstown, crawling along in a herd of traffic. At Broadway they turned north again.

"I guess we lost him," Last said, finally. He settled back against the cushion and lit a cigarette. "What you want to do, Fred?"

"I'm going to cruise up here and then pull into one of the side streets," the driver answered. "If we just go mushing around here, they may spot us again."

"You can't park there."

"For a few minutes I can. Then we'll run down the East Side and cross over to this dame's place."

"How did they pick us up anyway?" Hunter asked.

"I told you the girls were on our tail when we come over from Jersey," Fred said with satisfaction. "You guys thought it was my delicate nerves."

"They came past while you were up there talking with Munson," Last answered Hunter. "I suppose they had been running back and forth along the streets there. They passed us and then came back for a second look. I guess they were just making up their minds when you came down from Munson's place. We were figuring on making a run for it and shaking them and then coming back to pick you up."

"How many are there?"

"A whole goddamn platoon," Fred answered. He rapped on the horn and swung the car to the left. "They're stickin' out through the windows. They're hangin' on the goddamn bumpers. One of you jokers give me a cigarette." He pulled the car over to the curb. They were on a crosstown street, almost at Eighth Avenue. "I got a goddamn five-minute break comin'," Fred said, rolling down the window and spitting his gum onto the sidewalk. His hard square face gleamed redly as he took a long drag on the cigarette.

They drove through the green island of Central Park, the car whispering along slowly on the deserted drive. Their headlights picked out the leaves, a wet shine of decayed green. It was very quiet after the traffic of midtown, and they could barely hear the muffled growl of the city and an occasional horn-blast, far and faint with distance.

"I don't like this," Fred said uneasily. "You're nuts, Barney. If they jump us here we don't have a prayer."

"Relax, lad. They won't jump us. We lost them and now all we have to do is stay lost for a while. They're probably down on the West Side now, cruising around. Give them a little time to see we aren't there, and when they take off we'll go down and see this woman Munson told Joe about."

"I think you're nuts. Who ever heard of runnin' out into the open when somebody's taggin' you?"

"That's why they won't look here," Last said comfortably.

Hunter sat slouched in his corner without speaking. He had rolled down his window and was smelling the green wet smell of the park. It almost seemed to him that he could detect, faintly, the smell of burning leaves, but there would be no leaf fires at that time of night, and the leaves lay in sodden drifts across the drive, under the lamps. Black cliffs rising into the dark sky to the south were the expensive hotels. They were hung with ladders of light and were crowned with the aureole of luminous mist. To Hunter they looked as if they were floating up into the night that was over the city, as if they were enormous chunks of black ice, rotted loose from the bottom of some great ice island, rising slowly from the depths of a cold midnight sea hung with chains of freezing phosphorescent light. Other images glowed and darkened in his memory: the sound of water on a lake shore, the appearance of a large square as dark and chill as the bottom of the sea. Rain touched his face and he inhaled the autumn smell of the leaves. He relaxed against the cushions, yawning, shivered, hearing a distant horn, and rolled up the window.

"Let's get out of here," he said. "We shouldn't be up here taking it easy when Keyes is somewhere in the mill back there." He jerked his head toward the dark towers of the city.

"Chance it," Barney said. Fred snapped his cigarette into the darkness and grunted.

"This the street?" Fred asked, turning into Twenty-fifth.

"That's what Munson said. Three-ninety something. It's got a tree in front of it."

They nosed slowly into the dark street. Last and Hunter rolled down their windows and peered at the house front.

"That looks like it," Hunter said, pointing to a house on the north side of the street. "Pull in there."

The car pulled in to the curb and was almost stopped when they heard the roar of a motor behind them. A car had turned into the street with its lights off and had followed them. Now the lights flashed on the street, the car whipped past them and stopped, with a squeal of brakes, blocking the street ahead.

"Now," Hunter said, feeling for the tire iron.

"Hold it, for Christ's sake," Fred answered in a high strained voice. He slammed into first gear and gunned the motor.

"You can't get around."

"Maybe." The car leaped forward, catching the men in the light. They were spilling out of the car ahead. Metal gleamed in their hands. Hunter felt himself thrown violently against Last as the car leaped the curb onto the sidewalk. He could see Fred fighting with the wheel and there was a ripping smash of metal and glass as they roared past the car ahead and turned in a drunken racing lurch back into the street.

We cruised the night. Once the car that had been following us almost got us, but Fred took us out of there and away. The search kept on. We checked in periodically with the section. No one had turned up any information that was more exact than our own. Already the various people in the search were beginning to find that their efforts were overlapping, that we had begun to exhaust all the possibilities.

You find a man in the world, in his actions.

A part of Keyes was in Port Random, in the free world of childhood which is free because it does not know that it is in any way determined. It is an illusory kind of freedom, but nevertheless it remains, for the man who can look back at it dispassionately and without regret, an image of something like what the world might be. Going out of boyhood you discover history, necessity, and you try to oppose it with a plan. But that plan will have no meaning except in the concrete world. If Keyes had married the opposites, then he would be found in the world. A part of him, anyway, was there.

Item: That he had been the secretary of an Unemployed Council in the Bronx during the Depression.

Item: That he had been for a time an unpaid organizer of a small union in the early days of the CIO.

Item: Job actions on the docks in Brooklyn and Jersey before the war.

Item: That he was known to more than the men in his own local as an honest man and a militant.

Item: That he had been elected head of the committee.

Item: That he was important enough for Kelly to send his goons after him.

There were contradictory elements too. Why had Keyes been so slow to come forward? Why hadn't he been in touch with us from the beginning? Part of that was answered by one of the Jersey sections of the Party. Keyes had only recently come out of the army. The organization was shot to nothing on the docks in Jersey, and there was little more in New York. The organizer over there had been a fool and a bureaucrat, too busy building up little worlds inside his own head to find any place in the actual world for Keyes to function. He had been forced to go almost on his own. Then, with the committee only half formed and the meeting smashed, he had to begin to pull the committee together again.

There was something else about Keyes that I began to see as we found out more about him. He was not yet fully formed. He stood somewhere between Munson, or better yet the average dockworker, and someone like Barney, who was complete. And that was his importance too. He was the bridge and an index to the strike and to the maturity of the rank and file.

All that was easy enough. The thing that made him puzzling to me was how he had become the Necessary Man, the combination of the long wound and the plan, how he had put the two together so that they had not fallen apart as they had for me. Then I began to see that it was not Keyes for whom I was searching a meaning, but for myself.

What was it then? Both instinct, which was my hatred, and consciousness—the plan—had failed. But Keyes had put them both together. What did that mean?

It meant, first, that my simple instinctive revolt was not enough. That hatred can power you only so long before it runs down. It must exist, of course, but it cannot exist by itself. Sven had been an example of what it did to you. You formed your own one-man commune on a Staten Island somewhere. Perhaps that was what I was trying to make out of the town that I continually dreamed about. Nevertheless, the beginning of wisdom for me had been that encounter with myself in the cellar of Barney's apartment house. There, I had been my own enemy. The reaction had been in terms of hatred, of defiance. Yes, but there was no one there, no one to hate. The defiance had been against the whole world, which was a cellar and a man with a club who wanted to beat my brains out—like Kelly at the meeting. It was impersonal. Even when, in the hunt, we had almost been caught by his goons, and I had picked up the tire iron, I hadn't been hating a conscious individual but only the whole business of running, fighting in the dark. The instincts had become more generalized in their demands; the hatred less personal. Was that enough?

I looked at it another way: the failure of the plan which was also the failure with Kay. I could see now that a plan in itself meant nothing.

The world is always more varied than your plan; more complex; it involves you more than you involve it. You are determined by the world, and your plan is determined by it. If you understand that, you have a kind of freedom. It is not the freedom to do what you want; only the freedom to do what is necessary. If you know what is necessary, you can will in agreement with it. If you know how the world is moving, it tells you where to put the lever where it will pry the hardest. That is about all. Seeing my desire for my sunlit town as blind, driven, I could now see it in a different light. I still didn't know what it meant.

And Kay? That was the biggest blunder of all. It was easy to see now how selfish I had been. I had made up a plan in my head, in every way beneficial to me, and had assumed her as a kind of object to be coerced by it. But she was tougher than that, just as P.J. Kelly and the world were tougher than our plan. She was a part of the moving world. More, she had a value and a dignity of her own which I had no right even to wish to coerce. To stay in New York and go on with her had seemed to me like getting caught in a machine. The machine was the world, of course, the machine I was already caught in, the one which, with my energy gone and the plan knocked out of my head, terrified me.

Then the strike. I had seen it once as a conflict of wills, which balanced each other and canceled each other out, so that the strike was growing up in the tolerance between the oppositions, growing up on its own, and assuming more of a pattern of a wish than a will. Now I could see that although what we had willed had been canceled out by the will of Kelly who had broken up the meeting, nevertheless the strike was not taking the pattern of his will either. That was because his will was contrary to the real growth and direction which the strike hinted at. He was going to win. That was inevitable. Just the same, our actions gave some direction; even more important, *his own* actions were creating their opposites. He could kill Everson, maybe Keyes, but in doing so he was creating his own opposition. No, the contradiction was not going to be solved in the strike; the contrary force, the one we represented, was going to be stronger, not just in spite of, but partly because of Mr. Kelly.

The strike was what no one had willed. Therefore it was not Kelly's victory. In that light even the death of Bill Everson became something else. Once, it had been impossible for me to admit that it could have been an accident because that seemed to me to rob his life of all its meaning and worth. Now I saw it differently. Yes, perhaps he *was* shot instead of Blackie. But it did not leave his life without meaning. Bill was the kind of guy who *might* have been shot by Kelly's men, because he was dangerous. That was no real accident. All his life pointed toward an earned death at the hands of Kelly and Kelly's masters. Yes. It could be that way with Keyes too. Both were Necessary Man, the way Barney was, or even Fred, who was moved in the same way that I had been moved before the long hunt and my discovery. He was not yet complete, as I had not been.

So, finally, I had found Keyes. Not in the flesh, but nevertheless in reality, just as I had found myself. Even my town came into a kind of focus. It was not something to run away to: that would have negated it; it would not have meant freedom any longer. Would I ever see it? Maybe. It was something to keep, like a talisman, like Keyes' childhood in Port Random, a circumscribed image of the full and golden life that I wanted for the world. Keep it as a talisman. Any place was a place to start from, even New York, even the tank with the lid welded on and everything burning. It did not really matter—you are never free of necessity, even in the town that you remember as if it were the coinage of gilded and fabulous years.

Kay. By accepting the world as I now saw it, the world neither to be coerced by intellect alone nor won by blind instinct, I could see her more clearly. It might be that nothing would ever work out for us, because there is so much that no one can control, but at least when I went back to her, if I did, it would be without the demands of one who wants to put all the world outside the fine—yes, but selfish too—circle of love.

Where do you find a man? Well, I had found Keyes. I felt I knew him thoroughly now. He would have been good to have for a brother.

We bored on through the night, stopping at all ports. It was morning when we pulled up in front of the section again.

"I'm going in and see what they know," Barney said. In the steel cold light of dawn he looked beat and sick.

"He won't find nothin'," Fred said viciously. I suppose at that time he felt like dynamiting the Empire State Building. "Want a cigarette, Joe?"

We had the cigarette and waited. After a while Barney came out.

"Well, they found him," he said.

"Where?" Fred asked. "In the river?"

"I never figured anything like that," Barney said. "I guess I couldn't afford to. They've got him in the morgue."

For a while none of us said anything. Fred threw his cigarette into the gutter as if the taste had suddenly become unbearable.

"Ah, Jesus," he said like a prayer.

"Two good men," Barney said after a while.

"Well," Fred said. "I guess that finishes it. Keyes was the link."

"Yes. We couldn't find the keys this time," Barney said. He said it in a solemn voice, not even thinking of the pun.

"Well, then, we're finished."

"No," I said. "We can't let it go at that. It just makes it harder. We've got to begin again."

"Begin?"

"Building the committee again."

"Joe's right," Barney said. "Even if we're beat, we have to make a decent retreat. Something has been won. We can't lose it. The killing of Keyes—that is going to mean a lot to the boys. Keyes is going to be as strong now as he ever was."

"O.K.," Fred said. "You want a lift home? I'll be around to the section whenever you say. What about you, Joe?"

"I'll get out here, I guess."

"All right," Barney said. "We may as well go home. They've got Keyes down there—" His voice broke a little. "Be back here at nine. We've got a million things to organize."

They got in the car and drove off.

Finally, it wasn't unexpected, not after the first ten or twelve hours of the hunt. But, going down the street, sorry as I felt, I did not feel alone. Bill and Keyes were still around; they would be part of the hatred now. Of the plan too. You lose all battles but the last, Bill had said. Yes, it was to be expected.

Walking through the park in the early morning, the sun just coming up out of Long Island, beyond Port Jefferson, bound for Ohio, I felt the change in the weather. The false summer and the false winter of the last few days were both over. We had entered into the grave, melancholy, freighted weather of autumn, the time when far voices sound near.

I walked through Washington Square, toward Kay's place, in the clean impersonal light.

About the Author

Thomas McGrath was born on a North Dakota farm in 1916. He attended the University of North Dakota, Louisiana State University, New College, and was a Rhodes Scholar at Oxford University. During World War II, he served in the Air Force in the Aleutian Islands. He has taught at colleges and universities from Maine to California, and has held the Amy Lowell Traveling Poetry Scholarship, received a Guggenheim Fellowship, a Bush Fellowship, and a National Endowment for the Arts Fellowship.

Among his many books of poems are *Movie at the End of the World: Collected Poems* (volume one), *Passages Toward the Dark* (collected poems, volume two), *Echoes Inside the Labyrinth*, and the two volumes of *Letter to an Imaginary Friend*. He has also published a novel (*The Gates of Ivory, The Gates of Horn*), and two children's books.